VOLUME ONE

The
GUARDIAN

Gables of Legacy

VOLUME ONE

The GUARDIAN

a novel

ANITA STANSFIELD

Covenant Communications, Inc.

Cover image map © Photodisc, Inc./Getty Images

Cover design copyrighted 2002 by Covenant Communications, Inc.

Published by Covenant Communications, Inc.
American Fork, Utah

Printed in the United States of America
First Printing: August 2002

09 08 07 06 05 04 03 02   10 9 8 7 6 5 4 3 2 1

ISBN 1-59156-059-4

To my son, Jake . . .
For the gift of laughter you've given me.
For your strong spirit and your "warrior heart."
The world is within your reach,
and it's a far better place for having you in it.

Chapter One

Tamra Banks emerged into consciousness and groaned. Her recent memories were a blur of blinding headaches and extreme fluctuations between shivering and sweating. Pushing a hand through her long, wavy, red hair, she found it grimy and matted. She wondered how long she'd been ill. How many days had she lost? She vaguely recalled being taken from the grass hut where she'd been living, while comforting voices assured her that she would be all right. Attempting to focus on her surroundings, Tamra groaned again, reminded that the headache still plagued her—a headache unlike any she'd ever experienced in her twenty-two years. She opted to keep her eyes closed, praying that this inability to see anything beyond shadows was only temporary. She'd been in the Philippines for more than a year, and had managed to avoid any illness—and now she couldn't keep herself from wondering if she would ever make it out of this country alive.

Feeling a soft hand squeeze her fingers, Tamra returned the gesture and forced her voice enough to ask, "Where am I?"

"You're in the hospital, sweetie," a feminine voice said in mildly accented English. "And so you don't have to ask, it's a good hospital. It's clean, and most of the doctors are American trained."

"Where's . . . Sister Sakaguchi?" she asked, her next thought going to her companion.

"She's resting," the voice replied. "We're looking out for her as well."

"Am I . . . " Tamra began, but couldn't form words through the fog in her brain.

"You're going to be fine, if that's what you're wondering. They've got you hooked to an IV, and they're taking very good care of you."

"What's . . . wrong with me?" Tamra asked.

"It's one of those dreadful illnesses the mosquitoes carry around here. I can never remember the name. But it will pass, and you'll be up and about in no time, spreading the Good News."

Tamra tightened her fingers around the hand in hers, knowing now that she was speaking with someone who shared her faith. Once again she attempted to open her eyes but failed. "Are you here to . . . " she began and faltered.

"I'm Sister Hamilton," she said. "My husband and I are here serving a mission, just as you are. The president asked us to watch out for you until you get back on your feet."

Tamra felt a bit panicked. Would the mission president have assigned a couple to look out for her if this weren't serious? While she was contemplating how she might ask, Sister Hamilton added, "Sister Sakaguchi isn't feeling well, either. Although we believe she's just got the flu, we're looking out for her as well. Opposition does come in torrents sometimes, doesn't it?"

"Is your husband . . . "

"He just went to make a phone call. He can be a bit of a tease, but I'm certain you'll like him. After all, I do." She laughed again. "We have seven children; three daughters are from my first marriage. Those three are all married now, two of them are living in the States. Michael and I have two sons and a daughter. Jess just returned from a mission in Salt Lake City, of all places. We've not seen him yet, since we've been out here. James served a mission in Spain. He got married just before we came here, and they had a baby girl about five months ago. Evelyn is her name, but we've not seen her yet at all." She laughed softly and said, "Listen to me running on. You probably should be resting."

"No," Tamra insisted, tightening her hold on this woman's hand. "Keep talking. How many grandchildren?"

"Fourteen," she said with pride in her voice. "Three that we haven't seen yet, but we do get pictures."

Tamra wanted to tell this woman how grateful she was for the sacrifice her children and grandchildren were making to be without her—so that she could be here now. Sister Hamilton could never understand how this illness had brought back familiar insecurities that she had believed to be long buried. She tightened her fingers once again, just to make certain they were still holding hands. Sister Hamilton rambled on about her children and grandchildren, their names and ages, hobbies and occupations. Tamra simply listened with her eyes closed, enjoying the sound of her voice and the quaint picture she painted of her life.

When she paused for a moment, Tamra said, "You told me there were seven children, but you only mentioned five."

"Oh, well . . . Emma's our youngest. She's actually not graduated from high school yet, but she's living with her sister in the States. She had some strong feelings about getting part of her education there, and it worked out nicely since her sister is living there. We miss her, but she's doing well."

Tamra wondered where they might be from, if their daughters were living in the States. But she had to stick to one question at a time. "That's six," Tamra said.

Sister Hamilton's voice softened reverently as she said, "Little Tyson died soon after he was born, but he's being well cared for by his great-great-grandmother until we can be with him again."

Tamra felt a rush of goose bumps that she knew had nothing to do with her illness. When the feeling subsided and nothing more was said, she went on to her next question. "Your accent is . . . "

She heard Sister Hamilton laugh softly. "Actually, I'm American born and bred, but I've lived in Australia for so many years that the accent's rubbed off on me. My husband is Australian."

"Australia?" Tamra gasped, and that shivery sensation encompassed her again. She pressed a hand to her forehead, as if that might lessen the pain enough to allow her to open her eyes. She desperately wanted to see this woman, but she could see nothing beyond a shadowy image and surrendered once again to the headache.

"What is it, dear?" Sister Hamilton sounded concerned. "Is there something about Australia that—"

She was interrupted by a man who entered the room and quietly reported something to her. Tamra couldn't make out what they were saying, but she caught a distinct Australian accent that made Sister Hamilton's seem mild by comparison. They spoke in hushed tones for a minute, then Sister Hamilton raised her voice to say, "Michael, this is Sister Banks. And this is my husband, Elder Hamilton."

Tamra felt a rugged hand move gently over her lower arm. "It's a pleasure to meet you, dear," he said. "When you get out of here, I'm going to cook whatever you want—provided we can get the ingredients. You name it."

"He's an excellent cook," Sister Hamilton said.

"Then I have something to look forward to," Tamra said. She wanted to ask more about their being from Australia, but a nurse came in to give her something to ease the pain. She was certainly eager to take it, but she quickly fell asleep as a result, her final thought being the hope that Elder and Sister Hamilton would still be there when she woke up.

Tamra drifted in and out of sleep throughout the night, with only medical personnel checking on her. When she woke to daylight, she found that she could actually open her eyes and focus on her surroundings. The headache was still there, but it had lost its blinding intensity. She ignored the pain enough to turn her head and take in the full spectrum of the room, and was surprised to see one of the young elders whom she recognized as being in her zone. He was talking quietly with a man who didn't look old enough to be a senior missionary, but his attire was more missionary than medical; and although she could see him in profile, he was turned so that she couldn't see a name tag. He was lean and handsome, with gray mildly interspersed through his medium brown, short-cropped hair. The only other hint of his age was the lines in his face that suggested to Tamra a life spent working in the sun.

Tamra shifted in her bed. Both men turned toward her and the familiar black name tags came into view. "Hey, you're coming around," the older of them said with that Australian accent she recognized from the day before. "How are you feeling?" He pressed a fatherly hand to her brow, as if to check for fever.

"A little better, I think," she said.

"Works every time," the young elder said in American English.

"We gave you a priesthood blessing a while ago," Elder Hamilton explained. "In case you're wondering, the Lord told you that you were going to finish a successful mission and live a long life."

Tamra smiled and closed her eyes, inhaling deeply. She knew everything was going to be all right.

Sister Hamilton appeared a few minutes later with something for Tamra to eat. Her appearance matched well with the voice she had heard the day before. She too didn't look old enough to be retired. Her ash-blonde hair was pulled back in a loose ponytail, and she wore only a hint of makeup. Like her husband, she appeared to be in good health, and only the faint lines in her face revealed the years of life she'd lived.

Through the next few days, Tamra continually improved. Sister Sakaguchi was up and around and often sitting close by, reading to her or visiting in Cebuanu, the only language they shared. Elder and Sister Hamilton checked on them frequently, never speaking in English when Sister Sakaguchi was present. Tamra longed to ask them about Australia, but the right moment never presented itself.

On the morning Tamra was supposed to be released from the hospital, she sat on the edge of her bed while Sister Hamilton helped her communicate with the nurse about what she needed to do to prevent a relapse. Sister Sakaguchi had gone to a zone conference with another pair of sisters, and Sister Hamilton would be staying with Tamra until she returned and met them at home.

After the nurse left, Sister Hamilton sat down and announced, "Now we just have to wait for the doctor to release you." She then leaned forward and said earnestly, "I got the feeling the other day that you had some interest in Australia, but we got interrupted." Tamra loved hearing her speak in English. She had grown to love the language of the people here, but hearing English spoken always made her feel somehow more secure.

Tamra felt something warm from the inside out that compelled her to admit, "I think you're the answer to my prayers . . . I mean, you have been from the start—taking care of me, and all. And I want you to write and tell your children how grateful I am that you were here for me, or give me their addresses and I will."

Sister Hamilton smiled and said, "I'll tell them. I'm sure you stay plenty busy writing to your own family."

Tamra felt hot tears rush into her eyes before she had a chance to urge them back. She looked away just as Sister Hamilton reached for her hand. "What is it, dear?"

"When I made the decision to go on a mission, my mother told me that if I went, I could no longer consider myself a part of the family.

She was angry when I joined the Church, but when I told her I would serve a mission, she was furious. She had always wanted me to help run the business she had spent her life building, but I just . . . couldn't."

Tamra watched the compassion rise into this sweet sister's eyes, but Sister Hamilton said nothing beyond, "What kind of business was it?"

"She owns a bar in downtown Minneapolis. I told her I respected her and her life, but it wasn't for me, and I knew in my heart I needed to serve a mission. She told me to never come back."

"I'm so sorry," she said, and Tamra knew she meant it. "And what of your father?"

"He left my mother when I was very young. I've only seen him twice for a few minutes. My mother's been married several other times."

"Do you have siblings?"

"Lots of step-siblings, but none that I know well. Only one blood brother, and he works with my mother. He pretty much took a stand beside her, if only to keep his job."

"Do you have any other family . . . at all?" she asked, astonishment in her voice.

"I have one aunt—my mother's sister. She lived near the elementary school I attended, and I visited her nearly every day after school. We were very close. She lived a rough life, much like my mother, but she still had a way of understanding me that my mother never had."

"And where is she now?" Sister Hamilton asked.

"Australia," Tamra said, hearing her own voice crack. The older woman smiled and motioned for her to go on. "When I was fifteen, she married an Australian and moved to Sydney. We've kept in touch through letters, and before my mission she told me I would always have a home with her, no matter what. I've gotten permission, when I leave here, to fly to Australia instead of the States—if that's what I want. And that's the problem. I've stewed and stewed over it. If I went back to the States, I'd have to work a long time to save airfare to Australia. But if I go to Australia and I don't like it, or it doesn't work out . . . I'd be so far from home. And what would I do? On the other hand, if I go back to the States, where would I go? I don't really have a home. Either way, I know I can find work and take care of myself, but . . . I sold everything I had before I came. I have nothing to go back to. There is, however, a sweet family in my ward that has supported me here, and I keep in touch with them. They've told me I could stay there when I return until I can find a place of my own, but . . . Oh," she groaned, "I don't know. I've prayed that I could come to a decision. I don't have much time left. But I . . . just felt like I didn't have enough information. Am I making any sense?"

"Absolutely," Sister Hamilton said. "I certainly can't make such a decision for you, but I can tell you that the years I've spent in Australia have been good. I love my homeland, and in my heart I will always be an American. But I've never regretted going to Australia. I've known from the moment I agreed to marry Michael, that was where I needed to be. I can tell you this, my dear, if you decide to go to Australia, we would always be there for you. We live on a station in southern Queensland, and—"

"A station?" Tamra asked, uncertain what she meant.

Sister Hamilton laughed softly. "A ranch, actually. We raise and train horses. And we oversee a home for wayward boys. Both have been family businesses for well over a century. We have lots of space, and there's always something to do." While Tamra was attempting to decipher what she meant exactly, Sister Hamilton clarified, "If you ever need a place to go . . . to stay for as long as you need . . . or a job . . . you can always know we're on the same continent, and not so terribly far from Sydney. We've always lived by the adage that anyone who is trustworthy and willing to work is welcome to stay as long as they like." She laughed softly and added, "It's kind of a family tradition to take in lost souls; it goes way back."

Tamra wanted to question her more on that, but Elder Hamilton came in with the doctor and their conversation was brought to a halt. Later, after the Hamiltons had helped Tamra settle into the grass hut on stilts that had temporarily become home, Sister Hamilton said to her husband, "Sister Banks is considering going to Australia to stay with an aunt. I told her if she ever gets out our way, to come and stay."

"Oh, that would be great," Elder Hamilton said. "We'd put you to work."

"That sounds nice, actually," Tamra admitted. "But I'm not sure I know how to do much of anything on a ranch . . . oh, excuse me . . . station."

Elder Hamilton chuckled. "Oh, there's plenty to do that doesn't take much skill; you can work up to other things. If you're trustworthy and willing to work, we'll keep you indefinitely." Tamra saw his wife smile at him, and she recalled her saying that very thing earlier. "Do you know anything about horses?" he asked.

"A little," she said. "I grew up in the city, but I had a friend who lived on the outskirts. Her family had horses, and I spent a lot of time there, especially during the summers. I love horses, actually."

"Well," he said with a smile, "you're definitely going to have to come and spend some time with us. Whether or not you stay will have to be up to you."

Tamra took a deep breath and admitted, "Thank you. It certainly gives me something to think about."

Tamra excused herself to take some medication. As she returned quietly back to the room, she was surprised to hear Sister Hamilton say, "There's something about that girl."

"You noticed that too," her husband replied. "I have a feeling she's going to do great things with her life."

"Yes, I believe so. I just hope we won't lose touch. I don't like the idea of never seeing her again."

Tamra wasn't sure why she felt such a rush of emotion, but she forced back her tears and entered the room again, more loudly, to alert them of her presence. She could never tell them how their candid confidence in her was somehow compensating for the lingering residue of an ugly childhood.

Before Sister Sakaguchi returned from the meeting, Sister Hamilton had given Tamra their home phone number. She and her husband both stressed repeatedly that if she ever needed anything—ever—to simply call. Tamra couldn't deny feeling an added sense of security in her life that she'd not felt since she'd made the decision to go on a mission. She'd done it knowing in her heart that it was right. She'd never doubted her decision, and she'd always believed that God would see her cared for as long as she did her best and trusted in Him. But there had always been an underlying sense of uncertainty in not having any family support at home, and not knowing where she would go when her mission was done.

A few days later, Elder Hamilton came and cooked for them, with his wife helping a little here and there. It was positively the best meal Tamra had eaten since she'd come to this country. Their visit only deepened her warmth toward these people, and again she thanked her Father in Heaven for sending them to the same mission.

Through the following weeks, Tamra felt her health return. The fulfillment she found in her mission made the prospect of having it end all the more difficult. Elder and Sister Hamilton checked in on her once in a while, and their paths crossed at an occasional district or zone meeting. Each time she saw them, she felt something rich and warm inside herself that tempted her to believe these people would play a part in her future—whether she decided to accept their offer or not.

When Tamra arrived at one such meeting, knowing it would be the last of her mission, she looked forward to seeing the Hamiltons, if only to tell them that she'd made a firm decision to go to Australia and stay with her aunt. She wasn't certain what might take place beyond that, but she knew in her heart that, for now, it was where she needed to be. Flight arrangements had been made, and her aunt had written to eagerly express anticipation for her arrival. But Tamra was disappointed to learn that the Hamiltons had been called home early, due to a family emergency. Her heart sank as she wondered what might have been so drastic as to cause them to leave early. She prayed that all would be well with them and their loved ones, and she thanked God, once again, for sending them—if only briefly—into her life. Just knowing they were there to give her a backup plan shed a measure of light on her future.

* * *

Tamra's heart was pounding with excitement as she stepped off the plane into the Sydney airport. Rhea was there to meet her, and their tight embrace made Tamra feel even more secure about her decision to come. It felt good to simply have contact with a blood relative.

"So, how was the flight?" Rhea asked while they walked side-by-side. Tamra noticed how her voice had taken on a subtle accent from her years spent in this country—much like Sister Hamilton.

"Long . . . but good," Tamra answered. "It's so good to see you."

"And you," Rhea smiled through her pink lipstick. Tamra's aunt wore her bleached hair ratted and poofed around her head. She wore high heels the color of her lipstick, which was the same flamboyant pink as her sweater—and her dangling earrings. She wore brightly flowered capri pants over a figure that was far too thin, in Tamra's opinion. She was built much like Tamra's mother, with a thinness that became unattractive with all the smoking and drinking they did, although Rhea handled her liquor much better than Tamra's mother ever had. The aroma of cigarette smoke hovering around Rhea suddenly left Tamra somewhat apprehensive about what she'd gotten herself into. But Rhea chatted comfortably about everything they were seeing as they drove away from the airport, and she speculated on all the fun they would have together. Her apparent happiness at having Tamra there made up for a great deal.

* * *

Tamra quickly acquainted herself with the differences between Australia and the States, and found she truly liked this country and its people. But she still found the transition somewhat difficult. Luckily, Tamra's aunt was there to make her feel right at home. With no children of her own, Aunt Rhea welcomed her fully, and Rhea's husband, Art, was equally open and affable. Their eager acceptance more than compensated for the challenges of living with them, but after being a missionary it was difficult to get used to living in a home with cigarette smoke in the air and liquor bottles in the fridge. And they often watched things on television that she simply didn't want to be exposed to. Tamra had grown up surrounded by such things, but that didn't make it any more pleasant to live with. For all of Rhea's love and approval, the atmosphere of her home brought back Tamra's child-hood memories all too clearly; memories that stirred a deep uneasiness. Still, the lack of contention in Rhea's home made the situation far better than living with her mother ever had been. But she also felt a lack of respect and appreciation between Art and Rhea. These were qualities Tamra instinctively believed were meant to be part of a good marriage relationship. But at least her aunt and uncle shared some degree of commitment—something Tamra had never witnessed in any of her mother's relationships. So she did her best to look at the positive aspects of the situation and ignore the rest. She knew that being in Rhea's home was right for her—at least for now.

Joining the Church had made a huge difference in Tamra's life. The sense of belonging she had gained was only the icing on the cake. Her testimony of Christ and the presence of the Spirit in her life had more than compensated for all she had lost. But still, she longed to find a life for herself where she could be loved by people who lived her beliefs. She simply had to believe that one day the right doors would open to bring such a life. It was her deepest dream.

In the meantime, living with Rhea did have its bright points. On the positive side, the room she was given to use as her own was lovely and comfortable, and there she could find complete peace and serenity. Art and Rhea refused any offer to pay rent. But once Tamra started bringing in regular paychecks from working as a receptionist in a legal office, she insisted on helping buy groceries and contributing money for extra expenses.

Tamra and Rhea became as close as they had been in Tamra's childhood. She felt comfortable around her as long as the television was off. Rhea rarely smoked when they were visiting, and she usually kept her colorful language to a minimum. They shopped and went sight-seeing together when they weren't working, while Art golfed and went to sporting events with his *mates,* as he called his friends.

When Tamra became more established financially, with money accumulating in the bank, she began to wonder if she should get her own place and avoid the negative aspects of living with Art and Rhea. She prayed and searched her feelings, but still felt that she needed to be there—at least for the time being. She was able to buy herself a car and had it quickly paid for, which added to her independence and sense of security.

Tamra found many opportunities for dating. While she wasn't necessarily feeling ready to get married, she figured when she found the right guy her perspective would probably change. Most of the men she dated were members that she met through the Church, although she dated a few men who were not members that she had met through her job. Some dates she found enjoyable, others were a disaster. And there were very few men that she went out with more than once. Simply put, she found no one that sparked even the slightest bit of attraction, and when conversation became stale after one or two dates, she couldn't imagine what they might talk about for a lifetime. After losing count of the dates she'd gone on, she became relatively indifferent toward men. If an offer for a date came along and she was feeling in need of some distraction or a night out, she accepted. If not, she declined, gradually finding her mind far more preoccupied with other interests.

Tamra enjoyed being only a few miles from the Sydney Temple, and she attended regularly. As Rhea became more busy at the bookstore where she worked, Tamra found a need to fill her life with something beyond her job and an occasional date. She didn't have to search her feelings very hard to pull up her long-time desire to do genealogy work for her family. Being the only member, she knew there was a great deal of work to do. As soon as she got the idea, she felt so compelled by it that she was convinced that her ancestors were pushing her from the other side of the veil. She purchased a laptop computer which she mostly used in her room, but she knew she could carry it with her if necessary. After collecting some books and software and hooking up to the Internet, she dove into a project that completely consumed her, gradually replacing any desire to date at all. It crossed her mind more than once that perhaps she had more subconscious residue from her abusive childhood than she wanted to believe. Perhaps that was the reason she'd not felt attracted to any of the men she'd met. And perhaps that was why she gradually became more and more content to spend time uncovering her ancestors and doing their temple work.

Months slipped by while she explored the lives of her progenitors on both sides of her family, going back for several generations. Each week she went to the temple at least once to do the work for many of the women who had come and gone from this world long before her birth. She uncovered so many names that she certainly couldn't do all of them, but there were some in particular that she felt especially close to, as if they were somehow luring her to do their work and they would not allow her to rest until it was done. At times these sensations were so powerful that Tamra was left completely in awe of how very thin the veil could be when the Lord's work was taking place. Her testimony of the gospel deepened readily, as did her conviction concerning the spirit of Elijah. Her heart had certainly been turned to those who had left this world without the blessings of the gospel.

Consumed as she was with the work, she once tried to explain to Rhea the sensations she often experienced that she knew were spiritual connections to relatives on the other side of the veil. But Rhea went off on a tangent about psychics and reincarnation that made it evident Tamra would do well to keep such experiences to herself.

Eighteen months had come and gone since Tamra had left the Philippines, and she marveled at how quickly time had passed. She felt a deep fulfillment in looking at the growing list of names on the wall of her room, each individual now an endowed member of the Church on the other side of the veil, if they had chosen to accept the work. Certain names had been highlighted in pink; they were the ones she felt she had come to know personally through the work she had done on their behalf. She felt as if she could continue forever, then suddenly she reached dead ends in every direction. It was as if she had simply done all she could for her family, and every possible avenue she took to go back further in time simply ended in a road block.

A deep restlessness began to fill her. Where she had once felt that she needed to be in Rhea's home, she began to feel that being there was all wrong. But when she prayed about moving on, she felt only a stupor of thought. Even though she felt no interest in getting back into the dating game, she had to admit to feeling restless and lonely. The idea of getting married and having children appealed to her greatly, but the prospect of what she might have to go through to find a good husband held her back. And that's when she met Jason.

She first saw Jason Briggs when he walked into the chapel where she attended sacrament meeting. He was six-foot-three with thinning blond hair, and a refined, studious manner. She couldn't deny that he was attractive. In fact, with the way he dressed and carried himself, she could well imagine him modeling men's fashions in *GQ Magazine*, and at the same time being head of his class at Harvard or Yale. In truth, she discovered through the grapevine that he had been born and raised in Sydney, and had come from an impoverished background. He'd earned scholarships that had eventually enabled him to become an accountant. He was in his late twenties and had only joined the Church a couple of years earlier. He had recently purchased a home in the area, and had therefore moved into the ward. By the amount of information that came to her from other members of the ward, she began to wonder if there were some kind of plot to link the two of them together. And then they were both called to serve on the activities committee.

At their first committee meeting, they both arrived a few minutes early. He eagerly extended a hand and shook hers firmly as he said, "You must be Sister Banks."

"Yes," she smiled, "and you must be Brother Briggs."

He chuckled and added, "I must confess . . . I actually know a great deal about you—assuming, of course, that I've been told the truth."

"Well," she quipped, "if what you heard is good, please assume that it's true." He laughed gently and she continued, "But as long as we're confessing, I've heard a great deal about you as well."

"I sense a conspiracy here," he said just before someone else entered the room and their conversation was diverted. But after the meeting was over, they ended up talking in the parking lot for nearly an hour. They both determined that everything they had heard about each other was, indeed, true. And she quickly felt at ease with this man who was intelligent, perceptive, and had a great sense of humor. Before they finally parted he admitted, "In spite of not wanting the matchmakers of this ward to believe they've succeeded, I would very much like to take you out. How about dinner? Tomorrow, maybe?"

"Actually, I would like that," she said, and through the following day she found herself anticipating her date with Jason very much. They talked and laughed and shared their conversion stories. He left her on the porch after he kissed her hand and she told him she'd had a great time. But lying in bed that night, she had to wonder if something was wrong with her. While she certainly found Jason attractive, she wasn't necessarily attracted to him. She finally fell asleep once she'd pushed her concerns aside, telling herself that such analysis was ridiculous when she hardly knew the man.

Within a few weeks, she was seeing Jason quite regularly, and they always sat together at church. She thoroughly enjoyed his company and became completely comfortable with him. But while she'd almost hoped that finding a good man would stir her thoughts toward settling down, her feelings of restlessness didn't relent. She knew that Jason's feelings for her were growing into something she simply didn't share. While she was hoping they could maintain their comfortable friendship, she knew he was frustrated by her lack of romantic interest, which she made no effort to hide. If nothing else, she appreciated the way they were able to communicate openly. But that didn't alleviate her own frustrations as she almost wished she could feel something for Jason that she simply didn't feel. She began to wonder if the problem was just her, and perhaps she should adjust her expectations and appreciate the fact that she'd found a good man.

Confused and discouraged, Tamra took to wandering the streets of the city, contemplating the experiences of her past, and praying for the paths to open up before her that would take her to her future. She sat for long hours in the celestial room of the temple, feeling instinctively unsettled, but receiving no answers. And then Art died. Tamra came home from work one afternoon to learn that he'd suffered a stroke while at work and had died almost immediately. With no comprehension of the plan of salvation, Rhea was completely shaken. Tamra's entire focus turned to helping her aunt go on living, while Jason remained supportive and compassionate. Rhea grew to care immensely for Jason, and the feeling was mutual. But her stubbornness in accepting any measure of peace often frustrated Tamra, when every effort to explain what she knew from a gospel perspective only fell on deaf ears. It was as if Rhea was determined to believe that death was the end, and nothing would convince her otherwise.

Tamra suspected there were issues from Rhea's childhood that had contributed to such feelings—the same issues her mother had struggled with. But the day came when Tamra had to accept that the only thing she could do for Rhea was love and sustain her until she could adjust to being without Art. As the weeks passed, Rhea showed gradual improvement. If nothing else, Tamra came to understand why she had needed to stay with her in spite of the restlessness she'd been feeling.

Five months after Art's death, Tamra could see that Rhea was managing well enough. They had gotten through the holidays in spite of Rhea's grief, and she had begun spending more time with friends, getting out and doing things, and living much as she'd lived before— even though the sadness in her eyes never disappeared. As Tamra began to feel that Rhea could manage without her, that restlessness returned with added intensity. Her relationship with Jason had settled into something bland and insipid, making her feel completely indifferent toward him. In fact, she began to wonder if she'd completely lost her ability to feel anything at all, until familiar sensations began stirring inside her, as if she was being lured to find some long, lost relative beyond the veil that she had somehow missed somewhere. She found a fresh zest for life as she once again searched every avenue she had already searched multiple times. But she still came up empty, and her sense of urgency only intensified. At certain moments she could almost literally feel the presence of a woman, long passed from this earth, speaking to her feelings, begging her to do work for her that she could not do for herself. Frustrated beyond her ability to bear, Tamra sat in the temple praying with all her heart and soul that she would be guided to do what she needed to do on behalf of whoever was prompting her. After more than an hour in the celestial room, it occurred to her that she could not accomplish this quest by staying where she was in her life. A new peace and excitement filled her at the prospect of making some changes. But what? Should she quit her job? Break it off with Jason? Get a place of her own? Move elsewhere?

A few days later, still searching for the specifics of how to carry out some necessary changes, Tamra thumbed through her scriptures sporadically. While she was hoping to miraculously come upon a particular verse that might guide her to an idea, her heart quickened as she found a little piece of paper with a name and phone number written on it, tucked into the pages of Second Nephi. Instantly, everything changed. She knew where she was going, and she knew beyond any doubt that it was right—even if she didn't know why.

* * *

Tamra uttered a quick prayer, took a deep breath, and dialed the phone number that Sister Hamilton had given her well over two years ago. She wondered if they would still live in the same place, or if they would even remember her. A woman's voice answered that didn't sound at all familiar. Tamra cleared her throat and said, "Hello, I'm looking for a Mr. and Mrs. Hamilton. Are they—"

"They're out of the country at the moment. Might I take a message?"

Tamra was taken so off guard that it took her a moment to gather her words. "I . . . uh . . . my name is Tamra Banks. I met them in the

Philippines a couple of years ago, and . . . "

"Oh, did you serve a mission there as well?" the woman asked eagerly.

"Yes," Tamra said, immediately feeling more relaxed. "They knew I might end up in Australia, and invited me to come stay with them. I don't know if that's a possibility after so much time has passed, but . . . I felt I had to call."

"Well," the woman said, "they're in South Africa at the moment, serving another mission, in fact."

"That's wonderful," Tamra said, amazed at the devotion these people had to spread the gospel. But she couldn't help feeling disappointed to know they were not around. She'd felt so strongly about this decision, and it took her a moment to be able to respond. "Okay . . . well . . . I guess I'll just check back when—"

"Now, wait a minute, love," the woman said. "If you're needing a place to stay, Michael and Emily don't have to be around to make that happen."

Michael and Emily, Tamra repeated in her mind. She vaguely recalled Sister Hamilton calling her husband Michael, but she realized now that she'd never known the woman's first name. Keenly aware of the awkwardness of the situation, Tamra hardly knew what to say. She could never explain to a complete stranger this bizarre urgency she felt to make drastic changes in her life, but she believed in her heart that staying with the Hamiltons was the right thing to do—or at least she had. In spite of her impatience, she had to say, "Perhaps I should just write to them, and see if—"

"That won't do much good now," the woman on the other end of the phone said. "They'll be on their way home before a letter would ever get to them; and even if it did, they'd not have time to respond. They're set to be back in a couple of weeks. In the meantime, if you need a place to stay, just come. Missionaries are always welcome."

"Well . . . I'm not a missionary anymore," Tamra said. "And I certainly don't want to impose or—"

"Every member a missionary," the woman said with a little laugh. "You're not imposing, dear, and I can assure you that the Hamiltons have left me in charge in their absence. I'm Sadie, by the way. I'm seeing that the house is cared for while they're gone. But I could use some help, if you must know. I've been having some trouble with this arthritis of mine off and on, and I just keep getting steadily more behind on the extras. Not to mention I could *really* use some help with . . . Oh, I don't need to go into details now, but you just might be the answer to my prayers. So, if you have a way to get here, I'll just plan on seeing you soon."

Tamra quickly absorbed everything she'd just been told. She searched her feelings just as quickly and found the awkwardness was outweighed by an undeniable peace. She finally forced her voice past her own nervousness enough to admit, "I'd love to. Thank you. I'll be there in a few days."

Sadie gave her directions, and Tamra immediately started packing while Rhea sat on the bed and visited. "I'm surely going to miss you," she said. "But I understand that needing-to-move-on feeling. You've been good to stay as long as you have and put up with all my blubbering."

"Staying has not been a burden, Rhea," Tamra said. "And I could never repay all the love and generosity you've given me that has made up for so much. But, yes . . . I need to go. I just feel it."

"You'll write, of course," Rhea said.

"Of course," Tamra agreed and they shared a firm embrace before she forced herself back to her packing, nervously glancing at the clock.

"You haven't told Jason yet, have you," Rhea said, as if she could read her mind.

"No. He's picking me up in an hour. I'm not sure what to say, or—"

"You just have to tell him the truth—straight out. It's much kinder to be honest than to lead him on."

"Yes, I know you're right," Tamra said and hurried to finish as much packing as possible, if only to keep herself busy.

* * *

She was sitting across from Jason at a table in a fine restaurant, halfway through their meal, before she mustered the courage to open the subject. She was prodded along by Jason saying, "Something's wrong; I can tell. What is it?"

"Well," she sighed, "there's something I have to tell you . . . and it's not easy."

"I'm listening," he said when she hesitated.

She cleared her throat and forged ahead. "I've told you how I've been feeling restless and unsettled, and about these feelings I have that I'm supposed to be doing something I'm not doing."

"For someone on the other side of the veil," he said easily. If nothing else, she appreciated the openness between them that meant having to explain less now.

"That's right," she said, grateful for the beliefs they shared that made such a concept not sound completely crazy. "The thing is . . . I went to the temple, and I've fasted and prayed, and I just know that . . . I need to leave."

Following a moment of stunned silence, he echoed in disbelief, "Leave?"

Tamra quickly explained the situation with the Hamiltons and the feelings that had led her to call them. She firmly stated that she knew in her heart it was the right thing to do, even if it didn't completely make sense.

"And your job?"

"I talked to my boss a while back about going and . . . he doesn't want me to, but he's okay with it. Frankly, I'm packed. I'll be leaving in the morning." When he seemed too shocked to respond, she took his hand across the table and said gently, "I care for you very much, Jason. You're a good man, and I appreciate our friendship. But it could never be more than that to me. And I know I need to do this. I'm sorry for any hurt I may have caused you, but . . . I have to say that this restlessness inside of me has turned to . . . How do I explain it? Urgency? I just have to go, and I can't wait another day."

Jason said little while they barely picked at the remainder of their meal. As soon as they were done, he paid the bill promptly, and they left. When they reached home, he embraced her tightly on Rhea's porch and made her promise to write to him. But after he'd left, she had to admit that she almost felt a little disappointed. All these weeks she had believed that his feelings for her went deep, and yet he'd just said good-bye with practically no emotion whatsoever. She told herself it would have been much worse if he'd been blubbering all over the place and begging her to stay. Still, she had to admit that she probably didn't know him as well as she'd thought. Or perhaps she knew him too well, and that was the very reason she knew he could never be the man to make her happy.

* * *

Tamra was ready to go by dawn the following morning. Saying good-bye to Rhea was difficult, but she knew her aunt would be fine, and her anticipation of embarking on a new season of her life more than compensated for any sadness. She promised to keep in touch, and set out feeling a lack of restlessness for the first time in many months. And surprisingly enough, putting distance between her and Jason actually felt good.

Her drive to Queensland was long and tiring—and hot. She still hadn't gotten used to the seasonal differences living on the bottom half of the world. It seemed strange that the holidays were barely over, and it was the middle of summer. But Tamra was grateful for the air-conditioning in her car, and each night when she stopped to get a room and rest up, she felt that much closer to a destination that she almost believed was destiny. The feelings that drove her were beyond her ability to put into words, but she'd come to rely on such feelings to get her through when nothing else made sense. She had followed such instincts deep in her heart when she joined the Church, in spite of how it had angered her mother. And her heart had also compelled her to serve a mission and sacrifice her connection to her family. Such inexplicable feelings had led her to a number of people long dead who had been urging her to see that their temple work was done. After so many confirmations of the importance of following her heart, how could she deny what she felt now? The apparent absurdity of such illogical circumstances seemed petty in contrast to what she felt in her heart she had to do. Even if she didn't know why.

Tamra felt a growing excitement as she began to pass landmarks that Sadie had described over the phone. Once off the main highway, the endless miles of dirt road were well groomed and Tamra found a silly fascination with driving as fast as she could manage without feeling unsafe. She liked the cloud of dust in her rearview mirror that seemed to separate the future from the past. She caught her breath when the dirt road merged into pavement and the endless miles of open land became suddenly greener, showing the evidence of being cared for by human hands. Clusters of trees hid her view of the home that she knew must be just up the road. She stopped the car briefly when a large iron archway appeared before her. She suspected the house was very old, but it seemed well kept. And something quivered inside her when she read: *Byrnehouse-Davies*. Having never heard the name, she might have wondered if she was in the wrong place, except that the directions she'd followed had been so precise.

Driving further, the trees receded behind her, and a large building appeared in front of her. It had a look that was a combination of a hotel and a school, with a high roof and several gables jutting outward from the upper story. Tamra heard herself gasp and stopped the car again. She knew she had never seen this place before, and yet . . . Could it be? Yes, she decided with certainty. It felt somehow familiar. But how? If she believed in reincarnation, she might have mused over the idea that she had seen this place in another life. But she knew better. There was only one logical explanation—if spiritual matters could be called logical. This place was familiar to the woman on the other side of the veil who had seemed to be calling to her. Tamra felt a brief rush of unfathomable joy surge through her. She knew this was where she needed to be; she knew it with all her heart and soul.

Chapter Two

Tamra drove the car around the bend, through more trees, and realized that the gabled building was connected to a large, beautiful home. "Incredible," she murmured, viewing the structure with awe. The driveway circled around the house and stopped between a lawn that sloped up toward the house, as well as an enormous conglomeration of stables, corrals, and even a racetrack. The wide spans of meadows merged into a distant mountain range—a vista that took her breath away. But still she felt more compelled to turn the other direction and admire the house. She wondered how old it was. The architecture appeared Victorian, although it seemed to be in perfect condition. Recalling her experiences in getting to know Elder and Sister Hamilton, she found it difficult to believe these sweet humble people came from such an affluent background. She contemplated the possibility that they simply lived and worked here, rather than actually owning it. And yet they had specifically told her she could work for them. And Sadie had said she was seeing that the house was cared for while they were gone. "Incredible," she said again as she got out of the car.

Realizing she'd driven around to the side of the house, she walked back around to the front and up the steps of the porch. She rang the bell and briefly turned to survey her surroundings, once again feeling a tangible warmth encircle her. A slightly thick, rumpled woman, who Tamra guessed was in her late fifties, answered the door. Her gray hair was cut short and was full of tight curls that clung close to her head. She wore thick-rimmed glasses that framed her smiling eyes.

"Hello," she said with an inviting grin.

"Sadie?" Tamra asked, and the woman laughed.

"You must be Sister Banks," she said, motioning her into the hall. Tamra stepped inside and admired the large staircase that rose from a polished entry floor.

As Sadie closed the door, a tiny girl with reddish-blonde hair came running up the hall to see what might be happening. She looked up at Sadie and said, "Come see my bwocks, Sadie."

"Just a minute now, love. I'll be right there," Sadie said to the child, then to Tamra, "Evelyn is two. We're taking care of each other for the time being."

"Mama," Evelyn said and Tamra looked down to see the child tugging on her skirt. "Mama. Mama. Mama. Come see my bwocks."

Tamra laughed softly, then looked questioningly at Sadie. She explained quickly, "I'm told she calls many women mama. I think it's her way of saying that you're a lady. And she calls some men 'Daddy.' She's a silly girl." Sadie added in a high-pitched voice, "Aren't you a silly girl?"

Evelyn giggled and ran back the way she'd come, disappearing into a door off the hall.

"You must be exhausted from your long drive," Sadie said, moving down the same hall. Tamra followed and watched Sadie stick her head into the room where Evelyn had gone. It was furnished with a table and four chairs, a sideboard and two small sofas; some of the furniture looked like it might have been there since the home was built. And toys were scattered everywhere. Sadie said to the child sitting in the midst of them, "Sadie's going outside for a minute. You stay right there."

They continued down the hall, past a large dining room and bright kitchen that she barely got a peek at. The house was far from gaudy or excessive, but its size and elegance left her a little overwhelmed.

"I'll help you get your things," Sadie said, "so you can freshen up and settle in. And I can show you around a little. I'm working on some soup and bread sticks for supper; we can eat around six, which should give you a couple of hours. Unless you're hungry now. I can—"

"No, I'm fine, thank you," Tamra said. "And I can get my things if you need to—"

"Nonsense," Sadie insisted, going out a door that exited to the side of the house, close to where Tamra had left the car.

While Sadie rambled on about the horse business and the many employees coming and going, she helped Tamra carry the important bags into the house. The rest could wait until she was settled in. Sadie's ongoing, one-sided conversation prevented any uncomfortable silence while Tamra gazed at her new surroundings, totally enthralled.

As Tamra followed Sadie up the back stairs, Sadie told her the house had been built in the 1880s as an exact replica of a house that had burned to the ground in the same place. She told Tamra that the house, as well as the businesses, had been in the family since that time. Tamra recalled the horse business, but she had to ask, "What business is there besides the horses?"

"The boys' home, of course," Sadie said. "It's connected to the house. I'm sure you saw it when you came in. It's hard to miss those gables."

"Of course," Tamra said, distracted by her memory of the gables and the feelings that had been stirred by just looking at them. She vaguely recalled Sister Hamilton mentioning something about caring for wayward boys. "Do they have some significance?" she asked. "The gables?"

"They're just gables, as far as I know," Sadie said, leading Tamra along an upstairs hall and into a beautiful room. The decor was simple and elegant, and most of the furnishings appeared to be authentic to the house, just as they had been downstairs. Barring its simplicity, the room reminded her of something she might have seen at a bed-and-breakfast. She found it difficult to believe she would be staying in such a fine room, even when Sadie said, "I hope you'll be comfortable. There's a bathroom through that door. Of course, if you need anything, all you have to do is ask. It's a relatively large house, but once you get the feel of it, you'll know where to find me. I'm usually where Evelyn is. I'm going to run down to check on her. You go ahead and make yourself at home. You can find me in the kitchen or nearby for the next little while."

"Thank you," Tamra said, "for everything."

"It's a pleasure, dearie," Sadie said and bustled out of the room.

Tamra moved slowly about the room and its adjoining bathroom, feeling close to tears for reasons she couldn't quite decipher. She thought of the love and acceptance Rhea had given her these past couple of years. But the atmosphere of her home had been less than favorable. Yet here she had been taken in by this good woman who had nothing but Tamra's word to make her believe that she had any right whatsoever to be here. She looked out the window to see a perfect view of the yard below and the mountains in the distance. With a prayer of gratitude in her heart, she unpacked just enough to have access to what she needed, then she freshened up a bit and retraced her steps downstairs to the kitchen. She found Sadie there, chopping some vegetables at a large table, while Evelyn sat in a booster chair at one end, scribbling with crayons in a coloring book.

Evelyn noticed her first. "Wook, Mama," she said to Tamra. "I cuwah."

"It's beautiful," Tamra said to the child, who beamed in response.

"So, how do you like the room?" Sadie asked.

"It's incredible," Tamra said. "I can't thank you enough for your kindness, for making me so welcome."

"It's not a problem," Sadie said. "In fact, it will be nice to have some female company. The hired hands are in and out some, but they're just a bunch of ornery blokes." She chuckled as if she'd told herself a joke. "I did get the feeling," she added, "that you really needed a place to stay."

"Well," Tamra clarified, "I've been living with my aunt since my mission, and she's always made me feel welcome. I could have stayed there indefinitely, but I just . . . knew in my heart that it was time to move on. I've been feeling terribly restless, but not quite certain where to go or what to do. I'm certain I could have gotten a place of my own, but . . . I must admit that I prayed about what to do, and I just felt like I needed to come here. Even if I don't end up staying long, I just . . . " She sighed, not knowing how to put into words what she felt.

"Funny how the good Lord guides us, isn't it?" Sadie said. "I lived in a nearby town for many years. My husband and I joined the Church when our children were young. Michael Hamilton was the branch president when my husband passed away. He and Emily helped me through the toughest years of my life. Once the kids were grown I felt so out of sorts with my life, like I was supposed to be someplace else . . . doing something else. So, maybe I know how you feel, dearie."

"Maybe you do," Tamra agreed. She motioned toward Sadie's work at the cutting board and asked, "May I help?"

"Oh, I'm fine. I enjoy this sort of thing. But the company's nice. Maybe you could help wash up the dishes after supper. That's always a tedious chore."

"I'd be happy to."

Evelyn interrupted with her two-year-old language to explain something to Tamra that she barely understood, then she returned her concentration to her coloring book. Tamra sat beside her and picked up a crayon and started coloring with her, which seemed to please Evelyn. "So," Tamra said to Sadie, "what did you do when you felt you needed a change?"

"I came here," she said. "They needed someone to help around the house, and I needed a place to go. From the very first day I came here, I've felt as if I were home. My kids come to visit when they can, but they're spread out all over the country. The Hamiltons have become my second family. Of course, with everyone off serving missions and going to school, it's become pretty quiet, but it's still home. And I'm certainly looking forward to having Michael and Emily back." She started into a new dialogue about her children and what they were doing, and Tamra decided that she truly liked this woman.

Sadie stopped mid-sentence when a man entered the kitchen, looking as if he'd just woken up. Tamra caught a quick glimpse of him as he walked past, and knew that he was unaware of her sitting close to Evelyn. His dark, slightly wavy hair was slightly longer than average for a man, worn back off his face and hanging to the bottom of his neck. His hair looked as unkempt as his khaki pants and white polo shirt that looked as if they'd been slept in. His feet were bare. His face had the dark shadow of a few days' growth.

"You got anything for a sandwich?" he asked Sadie, his voice sounding vaguely familiar to Tamra.

"Of course," she said, responding warmly to his gruff request. "There are cold cuts and two kinds of cheese in the fridge, and lettuce in the orange bowl. You know where the bread is."

"What?" he said in a voice that made Tamra think he was trying to tease Sadie. But there was too much of an edge in his tone. "You're not going to fix it for me?"

"You're a big boy," Sadie said. "I'm certain you can handle making a sandwich."

As this man pulled open the refrigerator, he caught sight of Tamra and did a double take, obviously startled to find a stranger there. Tamra barely managed to keep from gasping when their eyes met. She had not seen Michael and Emily Hamilton for well over two years, but she had no doubt this was their son, simply by the strong resemblance—especially to Michael. She felt certain the familiarity of his voice was because he sounded like his father. His eyes were neither distinctly green nor blue, but they held a piercing intensity that provoked an involuntary quiver in her stomach.

"Who are you?" he growled, bringing her out of a brief trance.

"This is Tamra Banks," Sadie provided, much to Tamra's relief. She could make no sense of why she felt flustered and uncertain, but she was relieved to not have to explain. "She was on a mission in the Philippines with your parents."

"How quaint," he said, pushing his head into the fridge. His tone was icy, his entire aura suggested a harsh bitterness that tempted Tamra to disbelieve his relationship to the Hamiltons. If not for the resemblance she would have trouble being convinced.

"Tamra," Sadie said, "this is Jess Hamilton—Michael and Emily's oldest son."

"Only son, you mean," Jess said from inside the fridge. His words sent a sharp chill down Tamra's back. She tried to think what Sister Hamilton had once said concerning her family, but she couldn't recall. She wondered if something had changed, but she was in no position to ask.

Sadie's frown made it evident she had picked up on the same edge Tamra had sensed in Jess's voice. With a positive lilt, she changed the subject by saying, "Tamra is going to stay with us for a while. Your parents invited her to come if she ever—"

"Oh, another one," he growled, haphazardly putting a sandwich together. Tossing a brief, skeptical glance toward Tamra, he added, "It's some unspoken family legacy, you know, Ms. Banks. We take in lost souls." He said it with deep resentment, and Tamra felt the stirring of a memory. Funny that she could clearly recall Emily Hamilton once saying to her: *It's kind of a family tradition to take in lost souls; it goes way back.*

Jess Hamilton put his sandwich on a plate, grabbed a can of soda from the fridge, and left the kitchen, saying, "And then some of us lost souls were just born here."

For a long moment Tamra sat frozen, wondering what to make of the exchange. Sadie seemed equally affected, as if she had trouble gathering her thoughts. Sensing that she was even more troubled than she was letting on, Tamra crossed the room and began cleaning up the mess the younger Mr. Hamilton had left from making his sandwich.

"Oh, you don't have to do that," Sadie said. "He wasn't raised to be so inconsiderate."

Tamra started putting things away in the fridge, saying quietly, "I'm glad to help. That's why I'm here, remember?"

"Well, I'm certainly glad you are." Sadie sighed, turning toward the soup she was preparing at the stove. "I must confess I've been a little uneasy with Jess here." She looked alarmed and added quickly, "I don't mean that I think he would harm me or anything. It's just that . . . it's nice to have someone to help buffer his sour mood."

"How long has he been this way?" Tamra asked, hoping in a roundabout way to get some information concerning the problem—whatever it may be.

"Oh, he just arrived yesterday; completely unexpected. He's been going to school in the States, and hasn't been home for more than a year. Then all of a sudden he shows up without a word of explanation. As far as I understand, he should be in the middle of a term. He must have left with who knows what undone back there. He's barely come out of his room to grab something to eat here and there, and he's . . . " Sadie's voice broke as she finished. "He's just not the boy he used to be, and I wonder if he ever will be again."

Tamra wanted to ask what had happened to bring about such change in this man who was practically a stranger, but Sadie hurried from the room, barely saying through her emotion, "Excuse me. Make yourself at home."

Tamra stood in the kitchen for several minutes, surrounded by the dark cloud that had been left in the wake of those who had exited the room. She was grateful for the conviction she'd felt only an hour ago that this was where she needed to be; otherwise she'd be packing her bags that were barely unpacked. She felt as if she'd unwittingly stumbled into the middle of a situation that had nothing to do with her, and was therefore none of her business. And yet she believed she was supposed to be here. *Why?*

She recalled the advice her bishop had given her when she'd been upset about her mother cutting her off. *Don't waste time with asking why, just ask what you can do—and eventually the why presents itself.*

Tamra's attention was drawn to little Evelyn, who was diligently creating little spots of color all over the page in front of her. Tamra sat down and picked up a crayon to color an elephant on the opposite page, chatting with Evelyn and attempting to understand her baby talk. Tamra wondered who she belonged to, and why Sadie was caring for her. She hadn't introduced her as a grandchild. Was she the child of some station employees or friends that Sadie watched while they worked? Perhaps, but Tamra had gotten the impression that this was Evelyn's home.

Sadie returned to the kitchen a few minutes later, once again composed and cheerful. But Tamra could see the cloud of concern in her eyes. Was her concern wholly for Jess Hamilton? Or was there something else? She began chatting comfortably about herself, also listening to Tamra's responses to questions about her own life. Her tender compassion on behalf of Tamra's family situation came as a soothing relief. Occasionally it was simply nice to hear others acknowledge that being without strong family ties was difficult.

Their conversation was frequently interrupted by little Evelyn. At times she simply wanted to be a part of the discussion and began chattering in a language that Sadie seemed to pick up on more easily than Tamra. She played off and on in the room just off the kitchen where Tamra had seen her toys earlier. But every few minutes she needed help with one thing or another. Sadie handled every interruption with love and tenderness, frequently hugging the child and saying, "Sadie loves you, baby girl."

When Sadie announced that supper was ready, they sat together to eat, with Evelyn sitting on her booster seat at one side of the table. Sadie asked Tamra if she would offer a blessing. The amen was barely spoken when Jess Hamilton reappeared, looking every bit as rumpled as he had earlier.

"Hello, my boy," Sadie said.

"Did I see some cookies in here somewhere?" he asked tersely.

"Cookies?" Sadie repeated, sounding confused.

"Biscuits," Jess said, his voice irritated. "You've lived in this house long enough to know what I mean."

Tamra listened with some measure of amusement. She knew that what Americans called cookies, Australians called biscuits. Emily Hamilton's American influence in this home was evident.

"Why don't you sit and have some soup and bread sticks with us?" Sadie asked.

"It's not been that long since I ate a sandwich," he said, opening and closing cupboard doors.

"Yes, but you didn't eat anything before that all day, and a little bowl of soup would settle a lot better than biscuits . . . cookies . . . whatever. Come eat some soup, and then I'll find the cookies for you."

Jess gave a humorless chuckle as he turned toward her and put his hands on his hips. "You're regressing, Sadie. I'm not a child who needs to eat my supper before I can have dessert."

Sadie looked at him firmly and stated, "If you're going to act like a child, I'll treat you like one."

Tamra barely kept herself from sniggering. She sensed a harsh retort on the tip of Jess's tongue, but his eyes shifted to Tamra and she felt sure that the presence of a stranger curbed his anger. He stared at her as if he expected her to be intimidated, which prompted her to stare right back. Once again she felt a subtle quivering in her stomach, which made her heart quicken. The sensation increased when she realized that within the few minutes she had spent in the same room with this man, he had provoked more emotion in her than she'd felt for Jason through a matter of months. While she was toying with the idea that perhaps she didn't have some deep emotional illness that kept from being attracted to the opposite sex, she saw Jess's brow furrow, as if their silent exchange had provoked deep thought for him as well. Something almost soft filled his countenance for only the tiniest second before the hardness returned to his eyes. Just when she thought he would hurl some harsh words at her, he said with subtle sarcasm, "Thank you, Sadie. I would love a bowl of soup."

He sat down across from Tamra, and Sadie dished up a bowl for him from the pot on the stove. She set it in front of him before she sat down and passed him the basket of warm bread sticks. He shot a glance of disdain toward little Evelyn, who had become unusually quiet in his presence. Before he made any effort to eat, he said, "So tell me, Ms. Banks, do you ever eat dessert before supper?"

"Never, Mr. Hamilton," she said and took a spoonful of soup.

His brow tightened and his scowl deepened as he said, "You're American." When she made no response, he added, "I have an aversion to American women."

Sadie's shock over the statement was evident. Tamra responded with an even voice, "Would your prejudice include your mother?"

He looked startled, as if he'd honestly forgotten that his mother was American. He quickly said, "There are certain exceptions."

"Oh," Tamra said, "then you're selectively prejudiced."

She found his asking for *cookies* doubly amusing, given the present conversation, but she decided against mentioning it. She sensed his anger rising, and knowing it wasn't far beneath the surface, she doubted it would take much to urge it into the open. He curtly said, "I have an aversion to American women who come into my home and make themselves a part of the family, only to move on when we no longer suit them."

Tamra held his gaze while Sadie said, "If I'm not mistaken, young man, you're the one who brought the last American woman into this home, and you were only too pleased with the way she made herself a part of the family."

For a brief moment, Tamra saw his bitterness disappear. A raw, unmasked pain appeared in his eyes just before he squeezed them shut and looked down abruptly. Without looking back up, he said in a hard voice, "Yes, well . . . she left me, Sadie."

Sadie gasped softly and put a hand over his arm. "I'm so sorry, Jess. What happened?"

"She just . . . left me. She met someone else and decided she'd had enough of me, so she's marrying him instead."

"Well, that certainly explains why you came home," Sadie said gently. "Is there anything I can do to—"

Jess rose abruptly from the table and left the room, leaving his bowl of soup untouched.

"Daddy go bye-bye," Evelyn said. It took Tamra a moment to recall that the child referred to most men that way.

In spite of her curiosity over Jess, Tamra was relieved when Sadie started some light, casual conversation. At a lull Tamra attempted to ease her curiosity. "So, how long have you been with the Hamiltons? Were you really here when Jess was a child?"

"Only on occasion," she said. "I came out and helped here and there when circumstances called for an extra hand. So, I've been close to the family for many years. I didn't come to stay until . . . well, let's see . . . I guess it was about the time Jess left for his mission."

They finished their meal amidst Evelyn's antics, then Tamra helped with the dishes. When the kitchen was clean, Sadie and Evelyn took Tamra on a brief tour of the house and yard. Tamra loved the entire aura of this place. She could see personal touches of different generations, and it was easy to imagine the lives that had been lived on this land, and amid these walls, woven into a delicate tapestry that gave this home and the grounds surrounding it an almost spiritual quality. She especially loved the seemingly countless framed photographs that filled the wall of a long hallway. She wanted to admire them further and learn more about the people in the pictures.

Tamra longed to explore the stables, but Sadie didn't suggest it, and she didn't want to be too presumptuous. The stable yards were quiet and Sadie commented that most of the hired hands were off duty by now and they had either gone home or retired to the bunkhouse. However, Sadie did take her to a smaller home not far from the main house. She called it "the old house." After she knocked lightly at the door, a man in his early thirties answered. His rough appearance was softened by a warm smile when he saw Sadie.

"Murphy," she said, "I'd like you to meet Tamra Banks. She's going to be staying at the house and helping me out for a while. She got to know Michael and Emily in the Philippines."

"It's nice to meet ya," Murphy said, giving her a hearty handshake.

"And you," Tamra said.

"Murphy is the stable master," Sadie explained. "His family has worked here for many generations."

Tamra felt a subtle onslaught of goose bumps. "What a wonderful heritage," she said.

"It is indeed," he agreed, motioning them inside. "Come in a for a minute. Mum's in the kitchen."

He led the way into a little kitchen where a woman about Sadie's age was stirring something at the stove. She offered a kind smile as Sadie repeated the introduction, then added, "This is Murphy's mother, Susan."

"Hello, Susan," Tamra said, stepping forward to take the woman's outstretched hand. Only then did she notice that the woman was leaning against a walker. She obviously had some kind of disability, and Tamra wondered what it might be. They visited for a few minutes until Evelyn was getting into so much mischief that Sadie insisted they must go. Tamra genuinely liked Murphy and his mother, and looked forward to getting to know them better.

Walking back toward the main house, Tamra asked, "So is Murphy not married, then?"

"No, he's a good man, but he's kind of a loner. But then, this life out here tends to attract that kind of man. Of course, he grew up here and he seems content to stay. Murphy is actually his surname, but I think that's kind of a tradition or something; his father went by the same. Susan developed some illness about . . . well, it was before I came here, I guess. She has trouble getting around, and Murphy takes good care of her. They're fine people."

"I can see that," Tamra said, loving it here more every minute. She stole another glance at the stables before they went into the side door of the house. She couldn't wait to explore them, even if she didn't fully understand why. She liked horses well enough, but she felt drawn to the stables for reasons that had nothing to do with wanting to see the horses.

When Sadie left to put Evelyn to bed, Tamra settled into her room, unpacking more fully and acquainting herself with her surroundings. Following a long, hot bath, she sat at the antique dressing table and brushed out her hair. Looking at herself in the mirror, the subtle spiritual quality she'd felt in the house became more defined. Something warm and familiar enveloped her, and once again, she felt relatively certain that someone in particular was luring her from across the veil to find some work undone that she needed to do on their behalf. Tamra recorded her feelings in her journal, studied the Book of Mormon by habit, and knelt to say her prayer.

As Tamra crawled into the big bed, she let out a childish giggle and contemplated how good it felt to be here in this home, surrounded by so much beauty and history. She willed herself to relax and was surprised at the way her thoughts strayed to Jess Hamilton. Recalling a clear image of him standing in the kitchen, her heart quickened and she was enveloped with a sensation not unlike that which she'd felt sitting in front of the mirror only a while ago. Well accustomed to paying attention to such feelings, Tamra had to ask herself what it could mean. Was it possible that she could really be feeling some attraction to this rude, unkempt man with a look of repressed torment in his eyes? The very idea seemed completely absurd, and at the same time intriguing. She wondered about the source of his heartache. Was it simply the loss of a woman in his life? Or was there more?

"Jess," she whispered into the darkness, just to test the feel of his name on her lips. It floated back to her in a silent whisper and ushered her quickly to sleep. She woke up later on that night, unable to go back to sleep for quite some time as her mind reviewed the feelings that had led her to this place—feelings that seemed to be steadily deepening every hour since she'd arrived. When she finally fell back to sleep, she dreamt that she was embracing a woman in white. Then the woman disappeared into a huge house, a literal labyrinth of hallways and staircases, and Tamra was unable to find her. She woke feeling unsettled but determined to find the answers.

At breakfast Tamra said to Sadie, "Well, what do you want me to do? I came here to work, and at the very least I must earn my room and board. So put me to work."

Sadie seemed a bit flustered, as if she might prefer just having Tamra be a guest. But she did come up with some extra jobs around the house that she'd been unable to get to. Between her occasional arthritis and watching little Evelyn, she kept to the basics. Tamra still wondered about Evelyn but felt hesitant to ask in the child's presence.

Tamra watched Evelyn while Sadie made a quick trip into town. She felt comfortable with the child, and was pleased that Evelyn seemed to feel the same. They looked at story books and built with blocks, and fed dollies with little plastic baby bottles. Tamra watched as Evelyn patted her little babies and laid them down to sleep, covering them with a little blanket, using all the gentle care of a mother. She marveled at the apparent maternal instincts of a child so young, and often laughed at Evelyn's humorous chatter and her need to break into dance occasionally for no apparent reason.

Once Sadie returned, Tamra set to work scrubbing long-unused items that hung in the kitchen, washing the walls in the hallways, and polishing the wood stair rail that curved gracefully to the second floor.

She shared lunch with Sadie and Evelyn, and didn't see any sign of Jess Hamilton. That evening at supper, Tamra asked Sadie, "I was wondering . . . would you happen to know where the family genealogical records might be kept?" Realizing that sounded terribly bold, she added quickly, "I have rather a passion for genealogy, and . . . I just can't help being curious about the family's history. Do you think Michael and Emily would mind if I just had a peek at them?"

"I think they'd be thrilled to share them, were they here," Sadie said. "I believe they would be in the library."

As soon as Tamra had finished loading the dishwasher, Sadie took her to the library. She barely opened the door and they could hear Evelyn crying in the next room. Sadie hurried away, saying, "I've got to see what Evelyn is up to. You make yourself at home. I think they're in there somewhere."

Tamra stepped into the room and flipped a light switch. The room itself took her breath away. There were leather sofas, a long table, and walls lined with shelves and shelves of books. A quick glance revealed that one side of the room housed books that were terribly old, and the other side was a more contemporary display, with old gradually merging into new in between. Tamra moved to where the books looked the oldest, and while she was fascinated with them, they were just books. It was something more personal she wanted to find. She scanned shelves for several minutes and decided she would like to read every book in this room, but she could see nothing that resembled personal histories or family records.

"Did you need something?" Jess Hamilton snapped from the open doorway.

Tamra started and gasped before she realized it was him. Just seeing him provoked a sensation much like she'd encountered just thinking of him the night before; a sensation that she found unnerving, at the very least.

"Yes, actually," she said, forcing her eyes away from him. "I'm kind of a genealogy buff, and I was just . . . wondering if there were any family records that I could—"

"If you're looking for dark family secrets . . . " He walked toward her, his hands deep in the pockets of his jeans, his feet bare. " . . . you'll probably find them."

"Actually," she said, "I was just looking for some pedigree charts or something."

He stood directly in front of her with a searching gaze that seemed to suggest suspicion more than curiosity. Tamra, being five-foot-ten and wearing her clogs, faced this man eye to eye, which she figured made him about six foot even. While she was searching for a way to apologize and excuse herself, he motioned idly to his left and said, "They're in the drawers."

Tamra turned that direction and realized the shelves all began from about three feet above the floor. Below that there were long, narrow drawers—several of them—with ornate handles. "The drawers," she murmured, as if she'd just found buried treasure. "Thank you," she said more loudly, recalling that she wasn't alone.

"Glad I could help," he said with a definite ring of sarcasm.

Tamra was vaguely aware of Jess sitting on one of the sofas and putting his feet up on a coffee table. She pulled open a drawer and found it to be quite shallow, with two binders laid side by side. On the covers was a reference of time, not so many years ago. She only lifted one cover enough to realize they were photo albums, and the pictures were all in color. She opened several more drawers to find similar books. She'd almost begun to believe she wouldn't find what she was looking for, when she opened a drawer to see a long, old-fashioned *Book of Remembrance*. She pulled it out reverently and sat on the floor.

Oblivious to Jess's presence, she was startled to hear him say, "My father has always been into that family history stuff. I think he's got everything—every journal, every record—all on the computer, backed up on several floppies."

"Very impressive," she said, appreciating the amount of work that would have gone into such a project. "But," she had to admit, "there's something so wonderful about these old books. Just the smell and the feel of the paper—it's incredible."

She opened the book to first see a picture of the Sydney Temple. The next page had a copy of Michael and Emily's marriage certificate. And on the next she found a pedigree chart. "Jackpot," she muttered under her breath. Starting at the left side, she was surprised to see the name *Jess Michael Hamilton IV*. Moving over to the names that branched off, she saw *Emily Ladd Hall Hamilton,* and *Jess Michael*

Hamilton III. The beginning name on the pedigree was obviously the man sitting in the room with her, but she knew that he had older siblings. Deciding to take advantage of the resources available at the moment, she just came out and asked, "Why is your name at the top of the list on the pedigree? Don't you have older siblings?"

She turned to see his startled expression just before he said, "Half siblings." He returned his head to its comfortable position against the back of the sofa. "It never seemed that way growing up. We were always just one family, but genealogically, I'm the oldest child of my father. My mother was married before and widowed. But if you're following the Hamilton line, that's the way it goes. I'm sure there are records there that follow my mother's line, through my half sisters."

"I see," she said and turned her attention back to the page in front of her, doing as he'd suggested—following the Hamilton line. Jess Michael Hamilton III was the son of LeNay Parkins and Jess Michael Hamilton II. He was the son of Michael William Hamilton and Emma Byrnehouse-Davies. And she was the daughter of Jesse Benjamin and Alexandra Byrnehouse-Davies.

Tamra felt her eyes become fixed to that last name. *Alexandra Byrnehouse-Davies.* That subtle feeling she'd felt come and go over the past several weeks suddenly became anything but subtle. She gasped and pressed a hand over her quickened heart. "She's the one," she murmured.

"Are you okay?" she heard Jess ask, and looked up to see him kneeling on the floor beside her.

"I'm fine, why?" she asked.

"Because for a second there, you sounded like you were going to stop breathing or something."

Tamra looked away in an attempt to hide her embarrassment. "I'm sorry. I just . . . "

"What?" he demanded in a tone that did *not* encourage her to share what she'd just felt.

"Nothing," she said, but his hard eyes made it evident he was not going to dismiss the situation so easily. "I just . . . felt suddenly . . . intrigued with . . . your ancestors." *One in particular,* she added silently.

He gave her a disbelieving glare and she looked at the page in front of her, attempting to find some point of conversation that might distract him. "I see you share your name with many great men."

"How do you know they're great?" he asked.

Once again faced with a question she couldn't answer on any logical level, she turned to look at him and simply said, "I just know." She glanced back at the pedigree and said, "So, did this passing the name down ever get confusing?"

"My grandfather died when my father was a child. As far as I know the Jess and the Michael alternated generations in order to avoid confusion, but it was never an issue with me."

Tamra attempted to focus on the book she was looking at, but she felt completely distracted by Jess's nearness. When she caught a subtle hint of aftershave, she realized that he'd shaved since the last time she'd seen him. She wondered why he was hovering so close and glanced up to see him watching her. Her temptation to turn away was quickly overpowered by an inexplicable need to search his eyes, as he seemed to be searching hers. Her heart quickened in response to his silent implications, and she had to convince herself that they were practically strangers. When she found herself wondering what it might be like to have him kiss her, she snapped her head the other direction and tried to force her thoughts elsewhere. Had she lost her mind? Through months of dating Jason she had longed to feel some kind of attraction to him and had politely endured an occasional kiss. And here she sat, so thoroughly drawn to Jess Hamilton that she could almost believe she had known him in another life. She found the distraction she was seeking as she thought of how Aunt Rhea would have responded to such an idea. She would have carried on with speculations of reincarnation that would be entertaining simply because of their ridiculousness. But Tamra knew better. She had a deep testimony of spiritual connections that somehow bridged this life to that beyond the veil. Was it possible that she could have actually known this man in another place and time? Or was she simply trying to rationalize this intense attraction she was feeling? Stealing another quick glance at him, she had to admit that what she felt was more spiritual than physical. But still, it seemed so absurd.

Tamra gasped when Jess reached out and lightly took hold of the ponytail that hung forward over her shoulder. She watched him gently finger her reddish-gold curls, as if they were fine and rare. She met his eyes to silently question his motives. As if he had understood the question clearly, he said in a husky voice, "You have beautiful hair, Ms. Banks. Irresistible, in fact." She drew a sharp breath as he bent forward and lightly pressed her hair to his face, inhaling deeply. "And it smells good, too," he said before he let it go with obvious reluctance, as if he'd just realized that his behavior might not be appropriate.

Following another searching glance, Jess moved back to the sofa and plopped himself down, reclaiming his comfortable position, as if nothing out of the ordinary had occurred. She couldn't help thinking if he wanted to rest, there were other places in the house more comfortable—and private. Combined with his behavior toward her, she had to wonder if he actually wanted her company, but she doubted he would ever admit to it.

Tamra forced her attention back to the woman's name in front of her. *Alexandra Byrnehouse-Davies.* She would be Jess's great-great-grand-mother. And for some odd reason, the woman had lured Tamra to this place. Her natural assumption was the need to do this woman's temple work; it was the reason she'd felt such things for other people in the past.

If only for the sake of conversation that might break the tension hovering in the room, she said to Jess, "Have you ever considered doing the temple work for these people?"

"No need," he said almost flippantly. She felt briefly angry until he clarified, "Do you honestly think *my* parents would go out into the world to preach the gospel without first knowing that every dead relative had been saved? I'm sure it's all right there in front of you if you search long enough."

Tamra turned only a few pages in the book before she found the baptism, endowment, and sealing dates of Alexandra Byrnehouse-Davies. Her heart sank a little. She was thrilled to know that the work had been done, but the feelings that had guided her suddenly made no sense. *Why?* she asked herself, and in response was that adage she'd heard many years ago, repeating itself in her memory: *Don't waste time with asking why, just ask what you can do—and eventually the why presents itself.* But in this case, she wasn't certain *what* she could do. She felt as if she'd come here for a reason, and now the reason made no sense. Did Sadie simply need some help taking care of the home and little Evelyn? Or was there more? *Was it because of Jess?* she had to ask herself. But such questions had no answers when she had only been here so short a time. Tamra closed the book and tucked it back into the drawer, praying that the *why*, or at least the *what*, would present itself soon.

"Good night," she said to Jess and left the room before he could respond.

* * *

Jess Hamilton gave up on trying to sleep and wandered quietly downstairs and out to the yard. Walking aimlessly around the house, feeling the cool grass caress his bare feet, he found an abstract comfort in this tangible connection to his youth. He longed desperately to turn the clock back, to be able to start over at a time before he'd made bad choices, defied his upbringing, and taken the first steps down a path that had eventually led to such utter disaster. Beyond the abstract security of moist grass between his toes, he'd only found two points of constancy in his life these last couple of years. One was his parents; they loved him and he knew it. But the very reality of what he'd done made it difficult to even think of facing them again. How could he not be a stark reminder of the pain he'd brought into their lives? Their absence now was a keen relief to him, in spite of missing them desperately.

The other point he'd been able to count on had been Heather. She had been there for him as he'd emerged from a rebellious stage in his youth. She had helped guide him toward a mission and had supported him faithfully through the two years he had served. She had been there for him when he'd returned, and he'd had every hope that they would be together forever. And she had been there for him through his brush with death and the subsequent horror of facing what he'd been responsible for.

But now she was gone. And while a part of him was not surprised, he couldn't help feeling angry and resentful for this sudden abandonment he felt, knowing she was, at this very moment, preparing to marry another man. Or had she married him already? He'd lost track of time completely.

He'd spent weeks in Utah attempting to cope with this loss that seemed the final straw, and then something had snapped and he knew he couldn't face another day surrounded by the memories they'd shared. He'd left Utah with hardly a glance over his shoulder. But he'd arrived home to find that the pain had followed him, threatening to smother the life right out of him. But pain was a familiar companion, and he'd learned how to live with it. Or had he? It was more likely that he'd become an expert at pushing it neatly into a dark corner of his consciousness, where he didn't have to look at it. But he wasn't willing to admit to anything.

Upon returning home, Jess had barely begun to acquaint himself with the emptiness of his own room that seemed to encourage the hollow, vacuum of his unfeeling heart, when he'd walked downstairs to find Tamra Banks staring back at him. He'd barely gotten a good look at her freckled nose and brown eyes, before he'd found her intruding upon cloudy thoughts that only Heather had dominated for years. *How dare she?* he snarled inwardly for the fiftieth time since he'd met her. He had a willful desire to indulge his wounded heart with obsession over Heather; she was the woman who had held it for so many years. But every passing hour found him more and more likely to see the face of this Ms. Banks in his mind, obscuring his memories of a face that only days ago had sworn to never leave his memory. And it made him angry. While something inside him wanted to scream at her to go away and leave him alone, something deeper ached to just be in the same room. And they were practically strangers. It simply made no sense.

Jess paused his walk when he noticed a light on in an upstairs bedroom. He knew Sadie's room was on the other side, right next to the nursery. Even at this simple evidence of Tamra Bank's existence, his heart involuntarily quickened. And it made him angry! Still, he gazed for several moments toward the light, wondering what was keeping *her* up so late. Did she too have trouble sleeping? Were there ghosts from *her* past that haunted her during the loneliest hours?

Jess was startled to see the light go out. He stood in the ensuing darkness, feeling more alone than he'd felt since Heather had first told him it was over. Feeling the pain creep into his conscious mind, he shoved it back into the abyss of his subconscious—where it belonged. Then he wandered back to his room and tried, in vain, to sleep.

Chapter Three

The following morning Tamra ate breakfast with Sadie and Evelyn, realizing that she'd come to feel very much at home here in a short time. She asked Sadie what she might do to help her today. While Sadie was contemplating her answer, Jess appeared in the kitchen; his wet hair and the clean aroma surrounding him made it clear that he had just showered. The vague scent of his shaving lotion brought back memories of their encounter the previous evening. He wore dark green slacks and a white shirt—and shoes on his feet. *He's adorable,* Tamra thought and attempted to allay the quivering in her stomach.

"Good morning," Sadie said brightly. "Would you like some breakfast?"

"Yes," he said, "thank you."

He sat down and Sadie quickly turned the stove on to cook him some eggs. Tamra put some bread into the toaster then responded to Evelyn's demand to get her hands washed and get down to play. She felt Jess watching her speculatively while he sipped a glass of orange juice. Tamra went into the other room to get Evelyn interested in her toys. She returned to see Sadie putting a plate of eggs, bacon, and toast in front of Jess. "Thank you," he said, more humbly and politely than Tamra had heard since she'd arrived.

While Tamra washed some pans and Sadie loaded the dishwasher, Jess asked, "Hey, Sadie, were you going into town today?"

"I wasn't planning on it. I went yesterday, but . . . I can be flexible. Why?"

"Well . . . I was just wondering if I might ride along. I need a few things, and—"

"If I'm not mistaken, there are a number of vehicles out there that you could—"

"I know that, Sadie," he said, sounding tense. "But I . . . would prefer going with you. Just let me know when you're going. If it's not today, fine."

Tamra sensed embarrassment from Jess, and compassion from Sadie. In fact, the woman's eyes hinted at tears. "I can take you later, Jess. I just need to get some things done this morning." She turned to Tamra and asked, "Do you think you could stay with Evelyn later while she takes her nap, so I could—"

"I'd be happy to," Tamra said. "Or I could just . . . " She quickly evaluated whether her idea was practical, or simply an excuse to spend time with him. Concluding that it was both, she went on. ". . . Well, I need a few things in town myself, but I really don't know my way around. Why don't I just go this morning? Jess is welcome to come along."

She couldn't tell if he was pleased or not, but he simply said, "That would be fine." And Sadie seemed immensely relieved.

Once breakfast was cleaned up, Tamra said to Jess, who seemed impatient, "Would you mind helping me carry a few things upstairs from my car? And then we can go."

"No problem," he said and followed her out to where she'd left it parked since she'd arrived. She opened the trunk to reveal an assortment of bags and boxes. She was amazed at how much he managed to load in his arms before he started toward the house. Tamra picked up what she could and followed him. Going up the back stairs, he said, "Just how long were you planning on staying?"

"Who knows?" she said. "Maybe till next week. Maybe next year. As long as I can earn my keep, I wouldn't mind staying. If I start feeling like a freeloader, I might have to move on."

She heard him chuckle, but he offered no explanation. He went straight to her room, and she wondered how he knew which one she was staying in when there were so many. With her stuff deposited on the bed, they went back down to the car. As he opened the passenger door, she said, "Do you want to drive? You probably know the way better than I do."

"No thanks," he said tersely. "I can tell you where to go."

"Yes, I bet you could," she muttered under her breath and got in the car.

They said very little as they traveled nearly an hour into the nearest city. She was amazed to think this was the same man who had so openly touched her hair and gazed into her eyes the previous evening. She asked him questions about the landscape and climate. He answered them tersely.

Once in town, he guided her to a Woolworth's. She parked the car and they went in together. They split up to get what they needed. She got some pantyhose, nail polish remover, cotton balls, and sunscreen. They met back in the drug section where she picked up something to have on hand for a headache. She noticed him picking up a box of sleeping pills, and she asked, "Having trouble getting enough sleep?"

"Quite," was all he said.

They waited in line together, saying nothing. They each paid for their purchases and returned to the car.

"Anywhere else?" she asked and he guided her to the other side of town. He told her to park in front of a shopping center, and she followed him into an expensive shoe store. He went straight to a display of fine riding boots and told the salesperson which size and style he wanted to try on, even though they all looked the same to Tamra. She'd seen such boots in historical movies, and wondered if they had changed at all in a century—or more.

She perused the store while he waited, then she sat close by while he tried them on. "Going riding?" she asked, hoping to be funny.

With no hint of humor he replied, "Yes, actually. If I don't, I will lose my mind."

"And you couldn't go riding without those boots?"

"No, actually, I couldn't," he said. "I had some great, very old, broken-in boots. But I left them in the States—along with a number of other things."

"I see," she said and turned in her chair to try and make some sense of the leather boots displayed at her side—red with two-inch platforms.

"Why don't you get some of those?" he asked, bending over to press his fingers over his toes and examine the fit.

"Thank you, no," she said. "It's just a wee bit too flashy for me."

"A wee bit?" he echoed and actually chuckled. "Do you know how to ride?" he added.

"A horse, you mean?"

He sighed and rolled his eyes. "Yes, I mean a horse."

"I have some minimal experience," she stated. "But it's been a very long time. I fear I might be a bit awkward."

"Well, if you're going to live at BD&H, you're going to have to get on a horse."

"BD&H?" she questioned.

"Byrnehouse-Davies and Hamilton," he said and she felt a brief shiver from hearing the name spoken aloud. *Alexandra Byrnehouse-Davies.* Had this woman ridden horses over the same land that Tamra could now see out her bedroom window? Something compelled her to believe that she had. The idea of getting on a horse sounded suddenly very inviting—in spite of her fears that she'd likely forgotten how to ride at all. And in order to ride, she would have to have a chance to see the stables.

"I'd very much like to get on a horse," she said. "Although I might need a few reminders. It's been a while—a *long* while. Will you be around to give me some tips?"

"I suppose I could be," he said as if it would be a great inconvenience. But he seemed to sense the obvious, that he owed her a favor since she had driven him into town, and she was waiting for him to pick out the perfect pair of boots. "And what were you going to wear to ride?" he asked. "Those?" He pointed to the leather sandals she was wearing.

"No, of course not."

"Do you have any boots?" he asked.

"No," she insisted. "There isn't a big demand for them working in the city. Besides, I wouldn't pay half of what those boots cost for any pair of shoes. I'm sure I can manage with what I've got."

"What are you implying, Ms. Banks?" he asked when the sales person took his boots to the counter. "That I'm spoiled?"

"I didn't say that. But since you brought it up . . . " She gave him a sideways smile that she hoped would let him know this conversation was meant to be light.

"Maybe I am," he said too seriously. "But just for the record, I want you to know I was raised to work for what I get."

Tamra was attempting to find a retort when he said to the sales person, "Find some of the same style in her size."

"What?" Tamra said. "I can't afford to—"

"I'm buying them for you, Ms. Banks. Consider it a thank-you gift for putting up with me and bringing me into town."

"That's ridiculous," she said. "I'm staying in your home and—"

"Just be gracious and accept a simple gift," he said with eyes that were almost angry. "Is that possible?"

Tamra said nothing as she tried on the boots. But her concern over accepting such an expensive gift was quickly overshadowed by a sense of excitement that encompassed her when she looked at herself in the mirror, wearing those boots. She watched as they were put into a box, and then a bag with handles. Jess signed the receipt and took both bags out to the car.

"Thank you," she said as he tossed the bags into the backseat.

"You're welcome," he said, and they got into the car.

He told her to stop at a burger place close by, and he bought her lunch. She was grateful for the loud music in the place, which removed the pressure of having to fill silence. Occasionally she just had to glance at him and remind herself she wasn't dreaming. Just being with Jess Hamilton stirred feelings in her she couldn't begin to understand. He had a way of calming the restlessness she'd felt since her mission, but at the same time, his troubled attitude evoked a deep concern, as if she were somehow responsible for his sorrow, or maybe capable of fixing it. The very idea was completely absurd.

The drive home began even more quietly than the drive out, until Tamra felt like she'd scream. She finally asked, "So, where did you serve your mission?"

He chuckled and said, "The classic ice-breaker question among Mormons worldwide."

She turned to meet his eyes as long as she could safely manage before turning back to the road. Responding to an unspoken challenge in his eyes, she retorted firmly, "Tell me, Mr. Hamilton, were you born with that chip on your shoulder, or is it something you brought back with you from the States?"

His astonishment was as startling as it was gratifying. She waited for him to snap a caustic reply, but he turned to look out the window and said, "I served in Salt Lake City."

"That's ironic," she said, ignoring the past tension as he was obviously doing. "Serving a mission in the Mormon capital of the world."

"Ironic, yes. But not necessarily easy." While she was hoping to stir him into talking about his mission, he asked, "What about you? Oh, never mind. I know. The Philippines. That's where you met my parents."

"That's right," she said.

"I understand there were many challenges," he said, almost sounding compassionate.

"Yes, but . . . I'm certain every mission has its own unique challenges."

"Some more than others," he said.

Silence settled again and she decided to fill it by rambling on about her mission experiences. After talking for a while she was surprised to hear herself admitting, "Over all I think my mission was good, but I wonder if it was more for my own growth."

"How so?" he asked, almost tenderly.

"I'm not sure I really did anything significant that ever led anyone to Christ."

"Perhaps you planted some good seeds along the way," he suggested.

"Perhaps," she said and felt a need to change the subject. She told him how she had met his parents.

When she mentioned that his father had cooked a great meal for her and her companion, he chuckled and admitted, "Yeah, my dad is a great cook."

"You must miss them," she said and his eyes darkened.

"It's been a long time," was all he said. "How about your family?"

Tamra didn't like that question at all, but she figured opening up about her circumstances might eventually get him to open up about his—more specifically about that chip on his shoulder. She told him the situation of her family, and noticed him showing more keen interest than she'd seen in him throughout their brief acquaintance. But he said nothing.

Once they had arrived home, he thanked her for the ride and gathered his packages. She thanked him for the boots. He nodded and walked away. Tamra took her things to her room, then found Sadie, who was resting with her feet up while Evelyn was taking a nap.

"Why don't you come sit with me, dearie?" she said. "And we can visit."

"I'd love to," she said. "But I'd feel a lot better about sleeping under your roof and eating your food if you'd give me something to do."

"It's not *my* roof," Sadie said.

"No, but . . . still . . . I need to earn my keep."

"Very well," Sadie said with a warm smile. "There are some things piled on the stairs going to the basement that need to be taken down and put away. I just open the door and put them there, since it's hard on my knees going down those stairs—which are steeper than the others in the house. If you could take everything down, that would be a big help. Even if you can't figure out where all of it goes, I could come down later and help you. But then I'd just have to make one trip down, instead of several."

"Just tell me where to find these stairs and I'll get right on it," Tamra said.

Sadie gave her directions and Tamra went to the base of the back stairs, looking for the door. Only then did she recall that she'd wanted to ask Sadie about Evelyn. Every time the opportunity presented itself, Evelyn was around. She was only two, but Tamra still felt hesitant to talk about her when she was in the room. She made a mental note to ask Sadie later and opened the door. She flipped on a light and noticed a number of odds and ends piled on several steps, leaving barely enough room to walk down one side. One load at a time, she took the items down. There were empty canning jars, and some bags of canned and boxed food that obviously went with the food storage. It didn't take much effort for Tamra to figure out that the newly purchased food needed to have the date written on it with a handy marker, and it was to be put at the back of the shelf, with the older stuff pushed forward. She found where the empty jars went, then she searched out the shelves where some rarely used kitchen appliances and special dishes were kept. She wondered how long it had been since the punch bowl had been used as she put it onto a shelf that was clearly marked to hold it, inside its box.

Through her search to put away a number of odds and ends, Tamra found a well-organized storage room, with detailed labels on the end of plastic tubs, neatly stacked. She was able to find the places for items that needed to be put away and couldn't help but be impressed with the organization. Having grown up with a mother who couldn't even organize a kitchen drawer, she was especially amazed.

Exploring the basement a little further, she found it to be rather small in contrast to the house above; she'd be more prone to call it a cellar. But she felt certain that houses had been built much differently more than a century ago. She found nothing but storage, until she entered the smallest room. This room housed an entirely different mood than the others. On some shelves she saw a number of boxes and odds and ends that looked extremely old, including a couple of saddles. Where the other storage rooms had been for food and infrequently used items, this room was more like the proverbial attic. She could almost literally feel the heritage of many generations in this room. She felt a desire to explore every item in the room, but her eye was drawn to six fine wood chests, with highly polished finishes, lined against one wall. They were the size of a typical cedar chest, but proportioned higher and deeper, more like a traveling trunk, but with no apparent purpose for travel. On each chest was a beautifully carved name. They had obviously been made by the same person, with a specific purpose. She was reminded of a Christmas when she'd been about eight or nine and her stepfather at the time had given her, her brother, and her stepsisters each a little wood jewelry box, with their names burned into the top. She could almost imagine a member of the family here undertaking a similar project for a Christmas long, long ago.

Tamra blew the dust away enough to clearly see the names engraved there, saying them aloud, "Tyson. Lacey. Emma. Michael. Jess." She chuckled, thinking how those last two names popped up over and over. Then she brushed her hand over the last one and her heart quickened as she said aloud, "Alexa." *Could that be short for Alexandra?* Tamra held her breath and lifted the latch that was long unused. The lid creaked open to reveal what looked like an old sheet folded over the top of the chest's contents. The chest itself was lined with a rich, red fabric. Tamra carefully folded back the sheet and let out a delighted laugh to see something wrapped in white paper and tied with a faded pink ribbon, and a stack of leather-bound books. She picked up the one on the top and opened the cover to read in an elegant hand, *Alexandra Byrnehouse.* Turning another page, she could see that it was a journal. At the top of the page was written a date in 1888. The first entry began: *I've never chosen to record my thoughts and feelings, but now I feel that the book in my hands may be my only friend, my only ally. The shock of my father's death has been coupled with the realization that I am without home, without family, without a place to go. I can do nothing but put my life into God's hands, with the prayer that He will lead me to a way to provide for myself, and with time, that He will lead me to my destiny.*

Tamra didn't realize she was crying until she felt the tears trickle down her cheeks. She quickly wiped them away before they could spill onto the precious pages in front of her. She could never put into words the comfort she had found in those few sentences. Here was a woman, writing from her heart more than a hundred years ago about feelings that Tamra had perfect empathy for. *"Alexa,"* she murmured, pressing her fingers over the delicate handwriting that appeared to be extremely well preserved. While she wanted to sit there indefinitely with this woman's words and explore her every keepsake, she felt suddenly concerned that Sadie might find her here and consider her snooping inappropriate. And maybe it was. But she couldn't rid herself of the feelings stirring inside of her that seemed to have compelled her to this place at this time. If she wasn't here to do this woman's temple work, then perhaps there was something she was meant to learn from this woman's life.

Tamra closed the book she was holding and impulsively picked up one more from the stack, assuming they would be in order. She also carefully picked up whatever was sitting beside them, wrapped in white paper that felt more like fabric when she touched it. Gently closing the lid of the chest, she turned out the light, shut the door, and hurried up the basement stairs. Seeing no one in the hallway, she hurried on up the back stairs to her room and slipped the items into one of her drawers, beneath her pajamas.

Harboring a deep excitement for the adventure she might find when she returned to her room, Tamra hurried back to the basement and finished her work. Once finished, she found Sadie in the kitchen preparing supper and giving Evelyn a snack.

"You know," Tamra said, "it's really not necessary for you to cook for me. I hope you're not going to extra trouble on my account."

"Oh, I love to cook," Sadie said. "But I freeze extra portions and use them often. There are many days, however, when I don't cook, and put my time to other things."

"Well, all right. Just remember, I'm capable of finding my way around in the kitchen, and canned soup or microwave pizzas work anytime."

Sadie chuckled. "Perhaps we could all have that when it's your turn to cook."

"I'll look forward to it," Tamra said. She then reported that she'd easily found where to put everything away, and Sadie expressed keen relief at having that chore taken care of.

Tamra helped deep clean some kitchen cabinets until supper was ready. While they were eating, Jess appeared in the kitchen with sweat glistening on his face. He wore a blousy white shirt, riding jodhpurs, suspenders—and those boots. Most striking of all, however, was the low, flat-brimmed hat he pulled off his head and tossed onto a chair. He pushed a careless hand through his hair, dampened by sweat. He'd obviously been out riding, and she couldn't deny that his attire suited him well. Taking in his appearance, she felt a tingle begin somewhere inside of her.

"Oh, hello," Sadie said eagerly. "You're just in time."

"I was hoping," he said, sitting next to Tamra.

She caught the subtle aroma of his aftershave, combined with warm leather, horses, and mountain air. The combination was almost hypnotizing. She glanced toward him and the tingle inside her intensified. She looked away abruptly, feeling her face turn warm. *What is wrong with me?* He was coarse, rude, and self-absorbed. But the very idea of just sitting next to him at the kitchen table made her fluttery.

Through a relatively quiet supper, aside from Evelyn's typical chattering, Tamra attempted to analyze her feelings. Since becoming a member of the Church, she couldn't recall, even once, entertaining the slightest romantic notion about *anyone*—not even Jason—in spite of all the dating she had done. Was that what she felt? A romantic notion? Well, whatever it was, she had to keep the situation in perspective. He was rich, handsome, and brooding. But that didn't mean falling for him had any positive logic. She told herself that she was simply caught up in fanciful notions that had been spurred from being in this house and feeling a closeness with his great-great-grandmother.

Tamra was relieved to have the meal finished, but she was surprised to have Jess linger at the table while she helped Sadie with the dishes. He seemed lost in thought and relatively oblivious to what was going on around him for several minutes. Then out of nowhere he said, "So, Ms. Banks, are you ready to try those boots out? There's still some daylight left."

"Right now?" Tamra asked, shooting a quick glance toward Sadie. Her approval and encouragement were pathetically obvious.

"Run along," Sadie said. "I can manage here."

Jess stood and left the room, saying, "I'll meet you in the main stable."

"Well," Tamra said to Sadie, "it would seem I'm going riding."

"Have a good time, dearie," she said and waved comically.

Tamra quickly changed into jeans and a dark green, button-down, oxford shirt. And, of course, her new boots. They felt surprisingly comfortable for being new, and she decided she really liked them.

She found Jess alone in the stable—wearing that hat. But she was momentarily distracted by the structure itself. Horses in stalls lined most of both walls, and neatly arranged tack and saddles dominated the section closest to the main door. The stable had the same historical feel as the house, and it was equally well kept. She wondered if Alexa had graced this place, as well as the home she'd lived in. A tingle of goose bumps suggested that she had.

"Do you know how to put a saddle on?" Jess asked, bringing her from her thoughts. She noticed him urging a horse out of its stall.

"I used to," she admitted. "But it's been many years. I told you I'd need some reminders."

"Well, you'd better come and watch," he said gruffly. "Next time you're going to have to do it yourself."

Tamra watched him put the saddle onto a fine stallion, while he explained each step with an air of condescension. She bit her tongue to stop from calling him arrogant and obnoxious, reminding herself that some thoughts were better kept to oneself.

"Are you ready?" he asked.

"As ready as I'll ever be," she said, wishing she hadn't sounded so hesitant. But she felt certain it was Jess's company that made her uneasy, far more than her concerns about handling a horse.

Jess bent one knee and patted his thigh with his gloved hand. "Put your foot right there," he directed, then held out his hand.

"What for?" she asked, certain he was joking.

"I don't know," he said tersely. "My father told me that was how to help a lady into a saddle; he said his father taught him. I think most of the ladies in our family have been short."

"Well, as you can see," she said, mimicking his curt tone, "that's not a problem for me."

He pushed his hand impatiently toward her and said, "Just let me help you get on the horse and get it over with. You haven't done this for years, and I'm not having you break your neck while you're riding with *me.*"

"Your sensitivity warms me, Mr. Hamilton," she said with light sarcasm, putting her hand into his.

Jess felt her long fingers slip into his gloved hand and he became momentarily frozen. She looked into his eyes, as if to question his hesitation, and he had to wonder if she had felt the same electricity. Did she have any idea how just touching her sparked something in him that he'd never felt before in his life? How could she spur such feelings when the woman he had loved for years had spurred nothing for longer than he could remember?

She put her foot onto his thigh as he'd told her to, and he lifted her deftly into the saddle. Once she was seated, she looked down at him as if to silently question his inability to stop looking at her.

Tamra forced herself to look away from Jess's penetrating gaze. Realizing there was no other horse saddled, she wondered if he expected her to sit here and wait for him. She was just about to ask when he said, "You okay?"

"I think so, but . . . maybe I should have a little refresher course before you put me in charge of a—"

"Not to worry, Ms. Banks," he said. "Around here we have a well-proven method of learning to ride. So, just sit tight, and I'll give you that refresher course."

She wondered why he was urging her foot out of the stirrup until he put his own foot there and mounted behind her. She gasped to feel his chest against her back, and to see his gloved hands come around her and take the reins. Tamra checked herself against betraying what his nearness did to her. As he smoothly guided the horse into the open air and broke into an easy gallop, she felt a rush of exhilaration unlike anything she'd ever experienced. Rather than attempting to analyze the reasons, she simply enjoyed the moment.

When they were a considerable distance from the house, Jess urged the reins into her hands, saying, "Okay, now it's your turn." Tamra delighted in the repeated tremors caused by his voice close to her ear as he repeated basic instructions, then complimented her. She quickly remembered her childhood training and found she enjoyed having the horse under her control—especially with Jess Hamilton sitting behind her.

Jess loved the excuse he'd found to share the saddle with Tamra, almost as much as he loved the opportunity to put his arms around her waist now that she had the reins in her hands. He suspected that he could have put her on her own mount and she would have done fine. But this was far more enjoyable for reasons he chose not to analyze. Her initial lack of confidence disappeared within a few minutes, and it was easy to see she had an innate ability that far outweighed her lack of training.

"Where to now?" she asked, and he guided her through the foothills for nearly half an hour before he finally asked, "You okay?"

"I'm great, why?" she answered.

"Do you want to keep going?"

"I think I can handle a little farther," she said. "I may not be able to walk tomorrow, but for the moment, I'm rather enjoying myself."

"Good," he said and they pressed on.

Tamra forced her thoughts away from speculations about the man seated behind her and turned to admire her surroundings. The peaks above, the hills surrounding, and the endless meadows below, all circled around her with the fragrance of mountain air. The confidence of the well-trained stallion beneath her and the presence of the man whose arms were around her waist, all combined to lift her spirit with an exhilaration she had never before experienced. And just when she felt certain she could absorb no more without bursting from perfect elation, she found herself on a plateau ridge, where Jess told her to bring the horse to a halt. He dismounted and held up a hand to help her do the same. She tried to ignore the fresh tingling that his touch elicited, but when she turned to take in the view, she momentarily lost her breath.

"Welcome to Australia, Ms. Banks," he said with a wide sweeping motion of his arm.

Tamra inhaled deeply, as if that would help her absorb the moment more fully into her memory. She was surprised to find his hand still holding hers, but she impulsively squeezed his fingers as she admitted, "How blessed you are to have grown up surrounded by such beauty."

He said nothing for a full minute, then he turned toward her and asked, "And what did you grow up with, Ms. Banks?"

"My name is Tamra," she said.

He lifted one eyebrow and said with false diplomacy, "Forgive me . . . Tamra."

Tamra ignored his condescension and continued to absorb the view. "I grew up in a dumpy apartment in downtown Minneapolis. Even as a child, I hated my surroundings. I felt sometimes as if the city would suffocate me. And I always felt entirely out of place in my home. I had a friend who lived outside the city; her family had horses, and the time I was able to spend there constitutes the only really positive memories of my youth." She sighed and felt compelled to admit, "What I see now is what I might have dreamt of calling home in my youth, except that I doubt I could have ever imagined such beauty."

Jess allowed her words to sink in and wondered why he almost felt tempted to cry. He'd not cried when he'd regained consciousness from the accident that had turned his life upside down. And he'd not cried when Heather had told him it was over. So, why would he feel prompted to emotion over this woman's response to a scene he'd come to take for granted? He glanced toward her and managed to convince himself that there was only one possibility—there was only one plausible explanation for feeling what he felt for someone who was practically a stranger. He'd completely lost his mind.

Tamra was reluctant to return, but she took careful notice of the landmarks they passed, hoping to be able to find her way back should the opportunity present itself. Back at the stable, Jess let her remove the saddle, then they worked together to curry the horse without a word spoken between them. While she couldn't help puzzling over his thoughts, she felt certain she likely wouldn't want to know what they really were. He had a belligerence and anger about him that left her wondering if she should detest him or feel sorry for him. He left the stable without a word and Tamra tried to comprehend this man being raised by the Hamiltons she had known in the Philippines. His selective moments of congeniality were far outweighed by his regular bouts of sulkiness. The fact that she found him attractive seemed completely irrelevant. Such behavior and moodiness were anything *but* attractive, and she'd do well to focus her thoughts elsewhere. Recalling the items that she had tucked into her drawer, she felt a keen anticipation to get to her room and enjoy whatever Alexa might have written in her journals. But once inside the door, she heard Sadie call to her. She followed her voice to the lounge room near the front of the house, where she found Sadie doing some kind of needlework and Jess stretched out on a long sofa, appearing to be asleep. Knowing he was only a couple of minutes ahead of her, she knew he had to be wide awake, but he kept one arm over his eyes and the other over his chest. One booted foot was planted on the floor, and the other hung over the end of the sofa.

"Did you have a good time?" Sadie asked.

"Very much so, thank you," Tamra said, feeling the need to sit down, if only to be polite. She didn't add that her excursion—as exhilarating as it had been—had ended on a sour note with Jess's rudeness.

When nothing more was said, Tamra searched for a topic of conversation to break the silence. Since Evelyn had obviously gone to bed, and the nursery monitor was on the coffee table so that Sadie could hear her, Tamra broached a question that had nagged at her since her arrival. "Forgive me," Tamra said. "There's something I've meant to ask you, but I thought it might not be appropriate with Evelyn around, and . . . " Sadie's needle became still and she looked toward Tamra expectantly. Jess showed no sign of life. "I can't help being curious," Tamra continued, "as to why you're caring for Evelyn. Is she . . . " Tamra stopped when Sadie's expression showed alarm. She glanced quickly toward Jess, as if to gauge his reaction. As if he sensed her looking at him, he dropped the arm from over his eyes and turned toward her. His expression was hard.

"I'm sorry," Tamra said, hoping to break the tension that she had apparently created. "I'm obviously being too nosy, and I should just—"

"No, of course not," Sadie said in a gentle voice that didn't match the distress in her eyes. "Evelyn is Michael and Emily's granddaughter. She only arrived a couple of days before you did, since her aunt was no longer able to take care of her. I'm caring for her until Michael and Emily return."

Jess let out a disgusted grunt and sat up. "Why don't you just tell her the truth?" he growled. "Why don't you stop tiptoeing around me as if you fear I'll go over the edge if you say something wrong?"

Tamra was proud of Sadie when she retorted firmly, "Your mood would imply that you might."

His scowl deepened and Tamra sensed him searching for a sharp comeback. Before he could, Tamra said, "Well, Jess, since you obviously want us to be forthright and open, why don't *you* tell me about Evelyn?"

He turned toward her with an expression that seemed to say he'd like to bite her head off, while his eyes hinted at something raw and painful. In a voice that was relatively toneless he said, "Evelyn's parents were killed; hit a truck head on."

Tamra bit her lip to hold back a sudden gust of shock and emotion. Was that the emergency that had called Michael and Emily home from the Philippines? She couldn't even comprehend how difficult that must have been. Two deaths in the family. But it was evident from the pain in Jess's eyes that she had only heard a very tiny tip of a very big iceberg.

Following a painful silence, Sadie said in a gentle voice, "It was an accident, Jess. Accidents happen. When are you going to learn to accept that?"

Jess turned to Sadie as if he'd like to bite *her* head off. In a voice that was barely calm, he said, "Yes, it was an accident, all right—and it accidently killed the wrong man."

He left the room, leaving in his wake a familiar dark cloud. "I'm sorry," Tamra said when he was gone. "I should learn to satisfy my curiosity when he's not around."

"No apology needed, my dear. He's right in the respect that we need to stop tiptoeing around him, but addressing it head on doesn't seem to bring positive results, either."

Tamra had to ask, "By what he said, I have to assume he was in the car, as well."

Sadie sighed, her eyes saddening. "He was driving, dearie." Tamra sucked in her breath. Sadie sighed again. "They tell us the truck was in the wrong lane. Apparently Jess saw it coming, hit the brakes and tried to move out of the way, but the truck was attempting to pass a car, so both lanes were taken. The car spun and hit the truck on the rear passenger side. The other three were all killed. Jess was—"

"Three?" Tamra interrupted. "Who else was—"

"There was James and Krista, Jess's younger brother and his wife."

"Evelyn's parents."

"That's right. And there was Byron. He and Jess had been friends since they were teens." Tamra squeezed her eyes shut as she began to perceive the magnitude of Jess Hamilton's situation. She felt physically sick to her stomach as Sadie continued. "Jess was comatose until long after the funerals were over. We didn't think he was going to make it either. He was in the hospital for seventeen weeks, and it was long after that before he was up and about with any strength at all. He'd been engaged to be married when the accident happened. He'd met Heather in the States, and she'd waited for him when he went on a mission. They went so well together. But the wedding was postponed because of the accident. When he was sufficiently recovered, he postponed it again. They were both going to school, working toward being married." She shook her head. "But apparently that's changed now. Michael and Emily felt strongly about going on this mission. They put it off until Jess left for the States and their daughter Amee was given legal guardianship of Evelyn. They made me promise that I'd contact them through the mission president if they were needed. I think they both know that Jess is far from healed, but . . . obviously no one can fix what he doesn't want fixed." She sighed once more. "I fear he will simply never recover from what's happened. It's tragic, truly tragic."

In Tamra's opinion, tragic was a gross understatement. She put aside her concern for Jess long enough to say, "Forgive me if I'm being too nosy, but . . . if Michael and Emily's daughter has guardianship of Evelyn, then why is she here?"

"Oh, you're not too nosy at all, dear. Amee had a baby not long ago and had some physical challenges with the birth. Her husband travels with his job and isn't home as much as he'd like to be. She simply couldn't handle Evelyn any longer. The child was only here with me for a couple of days before you arrived. Michael and Emily have cut their mission short to come home and take care of Evelyn. It was difficult for Amee to let her go, but they all knew this was the right thing."

"I see," Tamra said thoughtfully. "You mentioned that Michael and Emily would be home soon, but I didn't realize that . . . "

"They got permission to stay a week or so and finish up with a situation they were involved in, but they'll soon be on their way home. I told them I'd be only too happy to take care of Evelyn until they could get here. I've got lots of experience with my own grandchildren, although it's been a while since I've had the chance to look out for one this size. In that respect, your coming here certainly has been a blessing. I wanted to get the house looking nice for their return, but with watching out for Evelyn, those extras just don't get done."

"Well, I'm glad to help out wherever I can," Tamra said, feeling near tears. "Evelyn's a joy to be around."

"She is indeed," Sadie said before she heaved a long sigh. "If only Jess could . . . " Her words drifted off while Tamra's mind wandered back to the tragic situation she had stumbled into. Having said good-night to Sadie, she walked slowly up to her room feeling a tangible heartache for this man she had known so briefly. And what of Michael and Emily? They had already lost so much, but she could only imagine that standing back and seeing Jess suffer so deeply had to be at least as difficult for them.

Tamra slipped into her favorite pair of white cotton pajamas and sat on the edge of her bed for a long while, lost in thought over what she had just learned. She felt an overwhelming tolerance and compassion for Jess Hamilton, when only an hour ago she had deemed him rude and intolerable. In need of a distraction, she opened the drawer where she had hidden the treasures she had removed from Alexa's chest in the basement. Opening the journal she had barely read a paragraph from earlier, Tamra pressed her fingers over the handwriting of Jess's great-great-grandmother. She wondered if Alexandra Byrnehouse-Davies was aware of the heartache this particular descendant of hers was suffering. Somehow, Tamra felt certain that she was.

Chapter Four

While Tamra felt drawn to Alexa's journals, her curiosity urged her more toward the white fabric parcel, tied with a faded pink ribbon. She carefully set it on the bed and slipped the ribbon off without untying it. Folding back the fabric, she realized it was more like paper—a cotton-rag parchment, she guessed. Beneath the first fold, she found a piece of paper with something written in Alexa's hand.

Soon after my marriage to Richard, Mrs. Brown, the housekeeper, gave me a lovely wrapper and nightgown set as a gift. She had made them herself, specifically for me, and the gift meant a great deal to me. Though little was said between us, I knew she was well aware of my concern for Jess, and the heartache of the situation. I wore the set the morning Jess left the station at dawn, in search of answers that might mend his broken heart, a situation that was poignant at best. Gratefully, Richard understood how difficult it was for me to say goodbye. But I could never again wear the set without thinking of that day. And so it is enclosed, forever put away with the memories associated. Alexandra Wilhite.

"Wilhite?" Tamra repeated aloud. Recalling that Alexa's name on the pedigree had been Byrnehouse-Davies, she couldn't help wondering about the circumstances she was describing. And who was Richard Wilhite?

Tamra finished unwrapping the package and found the clothing items mentioned in Alexa's letter. She carefully lifted each piece up, amazed at how well preserved the fabric was. She realized that what Alexa had called a wrapper was a flowing robe with a fitted bodice and yards of fabric in a circular skirt that hung longer in the back than the front. The nightgown had long sleeves and a pleated bodice that buttoned to the throat. It was positively the most modest night-gown she had ever seen—and absolutely the most beautiful. She felt completely in awe of the reality of how old it was, and that it had been handmade with care as a gift. Tamra held the nightgown up to herself in the mirror, noting that the fit looked about right, except that Alexa had obviously been several inches shorter.

Tamra laid the nightgown and robe over the bed and pulled out the journal she'd started reading earlier. Perhaps it would provide some answers. She felt no desire for sleep as she became completely consumed with Alexa's written words. She told of being disowned by her father in his will, and how she had gone to Jess Davies in search of work. He had hired her to train his race horses, and Jess and Alexa had eventually fallen in love. But Alexa's journal entries gradually revealed her heartache and frustration as it became evident that Jess was a deeply troubled man. Tamra was moved to tears as she read about a man who shared the same name—and the same blood—as the deeply troubled man living under the same roof at this very moment.

Alexa's entries in her journal were not necessarily frequent or lengthy, but they painted a fairly clear picture of the progression of her life. Tamra finished the first leather-bound journal, and started into the second one. Eventually Jess had completely shut Alexa out of his life, and she had made the difficult decision to marry another man—who just happened to be Jess's closest friend. And that man was Richard Wilhite. Now the note enclosed with the robe and nightgown made sense. She read it again, paying special attention to particular phrases: . . . *My concern for Jess, and the heartache of the situation . . . In search of answers that might mend his broken heart . . . Poignant at best.*

Tamra was shocked to look at the clock and see that it was past four in the morning, and yet she didn't feel the least bit sleepy. She pressed her hand over the beautiful, soft, cotton nightgown and robe and felt suddenly compelled by the idea of putting the robe on—very carefully—just to be able to wear something that this woman had worn. Tamra first carefully examined the fabric and the seams, making certain there were no weaknesses that might encourage damage. Then she slipped the robe over her pajamas and fastened the buttons. Looking at herself in the mirror, she felt warm and tingly from the inside out. While it hung only a few inches past her knees in the front, the fit was otherwise close to perfect. The circular skirt hung longer in the back and flowed outward when she turned quickly. Tamra laughed at the sensation, feeling like a child again. She sat at the dressing table and brushed out her hair, trying to imagine the life Alexa had lived in this home, then it occurred to her that she wouldn't have lived in this home until she had married Jess Davies. She returned to the journal and read about the sudden death of Richard Wilhite. She wrote of her mourning and eventual healing, and then the journal ended. Tamra knew the next book was in a chest in the basement, but this was not the time to go searching for it.

A quick glance around the room revealed a hint of predawn light competing with the lamp that had burned all night. And Tamra felt a sudden urge to see the sun rise. Knowing she couldn't see the east horizon from her window, she eased into the hall and moved quietly down the stairs, and out the side door. On the sloping lawn she had a perfect view of the eastern sky that was gradually becoming lighter. While she waited for the sun to appear, she couldn't resist turning circles and laughing as the skirt of Alexa's robe flew out around her. She spun until she was dizzy, then she sat down on the slope of the lawn, taking care to lift the robe up behind her to prevent it from becoming soiled. She looked toward the spinning clouds above her, in hues of purple, in awe of such beauty.

When she sensed the sun coming closer, she stood up and faced east, waiting expectantly for that moment when the subtle light of dawn became the brilliant light of morning. And then she felt it. She wasn't alone. But what she felt was not the bizarre sensation of the veil being thin. She felt as if she was being watched. And a quick glance found her gazing back at Jess Hamilton's very alive, very human eyes gazing back at her from the window of his bedroom. He made no attempt to hide the fact that he'd been watching her, and she found no reason to not return his gaze. She felt a renewal of that extraordinary affinity between them, as surely as she felt a silent battle of wills. And she found herself wondering if she might actually be able to penetrate the walls around his ailing heart. Something warm inside lured her to believe that she had to try. Perhaps that was the very reason she felt the way she did.

Tamra felt the sun come over the horizon while she continued to stare at Jess. She turned to look briefly at the sun, and when she turned back, he was gone. Feeling suddenly exhausted, Tamra went slowly back into the house. On impulse, she passed through the kitchen, leaving a note for Sadie.

I wasn't able to get any sleep last night, so I'm going to try to catch up for a while this morning. Make a list of things I can do and I'll make it up to you later. Have a great day. Tamra.

By the time Tamra got to the top of the stairs, she felt completely overcome with exhaustion and paused only long enough to remove Alexa's robe before she crawled into her bed and fell immediately to sleep. She woke in the early afternoon, her stomach growling with hunger. She closed her eyes again, thinking about the robe, trying to imagine what this woman might have been like. Amazed at the subtle, but undeniable, closeness she felt to Alexa, she was grateful for the knowledge she had, through the gospel, that helped her understand such feelings.

Reluctantly Tamra slipped out of bed. She checked the robe carefully to be certain she hadn't damaged or soiled it. Then she carefully folded it and the nightgown together, just as she'd found them, wrapped them back in the rag parchment, slipped Alexa's note inside, and eased the pink ribbon around them. After taking a shower and getting dressed, Tamra made her way down to the basement undetected. She returned the package and journals she had read to their proper resting place, and picked up another two journals from the stack. She quickly ran up the two flights of stairs to her room and placed them in her own drawer.

Tamra recalled Jess watching her out on the lawn early this morning. She went to the window, realizing his room wasn't far from hers. And she felt embarrassed to see what a clear view he must have had of her carefree display. Her eye caught something unusual in the distance and she moved her focus. Coming out of one of the distant stables were several boys of varying sizes, each leading a horse; some moved into one of the corrals, others went onto the track. She could see a few adults mingling with them, and she wondered what the situation might be. She'd seen a number of adults coming and going from the stables during regular working hours, and much activity with horses around the grounds. But this was different. It took her a minute to remember that connected to this house was that large building with the gabled roof—a home for wayward boys.

"Of course," she said aloud, and watched several minutes as these boys were obviously being guided in caring for and training the horses. She wondered how many years such things had been going on here, and contemplated the possibility that Alexa might have witnessed similar scenes in her lifetime. The thought gave her pleasant chills.

Tamra felt a real need to get some exercise and realized she had let go of a long-time habit in the days that she'd been here. But her stomach growled to remind her it had been long unfed, and she decided that getting something to eat was her first priority. She went down to the kitchen to find Sadie there, putting together a pot of spaghetti sauce. Evelyn was taking her afternoon nap.

"Did you get some rest?" Sadie asked.

"Yes, thank you. If it's all right I'll just fix myself a sandwich, and then I can get to work."

"You're welcome to eat anything you can find, but it's Saturday. There's no need to be doing extra work today. Why don't you just settle in and get better acquainted with your surroundings."

Tamra couldn't help being pleased with the suggestion. "Will you be going to church tomorrow?" she asked.

"Of course. But we need to leave right after breakfast."

"I'll be ready," Tamra said.

They chatted while Tamra fixed and ate a sandwich. Tamra asked questions about the boys' home. Sadie knew little beyond it being a part of the family for generations, and that she enjoyed watching the boys come and go. She said that Michael remained highly involved with the work at the boys' home when he was around, but it was only at Christmas that the family had any direct involvement. She told of the tradition of sharing a Christmas feast and gifts with those boys who had no family. Tamra felt warmed by the idea and wondered if she might be here for Christmas. With the holiday not far behind them, it would be quite a few months before it came again. She couldn't help hoping that she might have cause to be here that long. She felt especially intrigued by the boys' home and kept thinking about how she'd felt when she'd first seen the gabled roof. But she was completely taken off guard when Jess entered the kitchen and Sadie immediately said, "Tamra's been asking about the boys' home. I think you know a lot more than I do. Maybe you could give her a tour."

Tamra turned to meet his eyes, unable to tell if he was pleased or disgusted—or if one was trying to disguise the other. When he held her gaze, she knew he was remembering their silent encounter at dawn this morning. Tamra pressed a hand over her stomach to quell what felt like a swarm of butterflies and turned abruptly away.

"I'd be happy to," he said in a voice that didn't necessarily sound happy. "Only if she wants to, of course. But there is something I need to do at the moment. Perhaps in an hour or so."

"I would love to," she agreed, welcoming the opportunity to see the boys' home almost as much as the opportunity to spend time with Jess. Having a new perspective on the reasons for his abrasive nature, she felt a strong desire to get to know him better.

Jess left the room and Tamra seized the opportunity to ask Sadie, "Is there a place in the house where I could put in a CD and exercise without disturbing anyone?"

"Oh, the girls always did that in the upstairs hall. There's a stereo system up there. Make yourself at home."

"Thanks," Tamra said and hurried to her room to change into her most comfortable dance wear, including soft leather slippers. The wrap-around tricot skirt helped her feel a little more modest in case she came upon anyone in the hallways coming or going. Approaching the huge upstairs hall, Tamra felt a flutter of anticipation. She'd taken some dance classes through her teen years and had really learned to love it through several college courses. Rhea's basement lounge had given her adequate space to get a good workout three or four times a week, and now her body's need for some activity felt long overdue.

Tamra had only passed through the upstairs hall a couple of times, marveling at its size and elegance in contrast to the rest of the house. While the house was certainly large and fine, this room almost had the feel of a small ballroom, with beautiful windows and a polished floor. As she came into the room now, she saw an entertainment center that she'd overlooked before. It was the only piece of furniture beyond a number of chairs situated symmetrically around the perimeter. She opened the wood doors of the center to reveal a full entertainment system for sound and video. She quickly figured out how to work the CD player and slid her disc into it. Glancing up, she noticed several speakers situated around the room, against the ceiling. *Perfect,* she thought and moved into the middle of the floor as the music began. She hurried back to adjust the volume, not wanting to draw attention to herself. She was glad to know that Jess had left the house to do whatever he'd needed to do.

Tamra stretched and warmed up to the music, loving the way it cleared her head. Her muscles, sore from riding, groaned at first, but they gradually loosened up and began to feel better. She then started into a simple aerobic dance routine that gave her the workout she needed with an enjoyment that she'd never been able to get from jogging or playing sports. She was taking a deep breath with her arms above her head, when an arm came around her waist, startling her so that she let out a scream.

Jess chuckled behind her ear without relinquishing his hold on her. Tamra felt her surprise merge into an eager excitement at feeling him so close.

"What are you doing?" she demanded. "With such a big house, I would think I could exercise with some privacy."

"That's pretty fancy exercising," he said and she looked down to see him place one hand purposefully on the front of her waist, at the same time drawing her other hand out to the side.

"What are you doing?" she asked again as he began to move his feet behind hers.

"The samba I believe . . . from the music we're listening to." He dropped the hand at her waist and twirled her with the other hand until she was facing him. Then his hand came to her back just as he led her into a comfortable dance step that took no effort to follow. She knew the samba well. The thrill of dancing with a capable partner was something she'd not experienced since before her mission; combined with having his face so close to hers, the exhilaration made her almost heady.

"Very good," he drawled after she followed him perfectly through a series of intricate steps. "Now how about the rhumba?" he asked and she only missed a couple of steps before she picked up what he was doing.

"Where did you learn to dance like this?" she asked, wishing it hadn't sounded so dreamy.

He actually grinned, revealing a demeanor she'd never encountered before. "Brigham Young University," he said dramatically. "Ballroom dance class. It was one of my favorites."

"Really?" she said, unable to hide her interest.

"Really," he said. "How about you?"

"The same," she said, then clarified, "I mean . . . not BYU, but college. But it's been so long."

"Then you must be a natural," he said, looking into her eyes in a way that was as alarming as it was intriguing.

She started to laugh when he urged her into a tango, which she didn't accomplish nearly as well as the others. After she had messed up several times, which he obviously found amusing by the smile that danced more in his eyes than on his lips, she finally eased away from him and declared, "I think I need a little more practice with that one."

He gave a quick bow from the waist, like some regal courtier, and said with a straight face, "Another day, perhaps."

"Perhaps," she said and watched him walk away. He hesitated long enough to say, "I'll be in the library, whenever you're ready for that tour."

Tamra stood as she was for a full minute, just trying to absorb their encounter—and the way it had affected her. She convinced herself that dancing with a wealthy bachelor certainly had its appeal, but the way she was feeling likely had no more substance than some ridiculous infatuation. She forced her mind back to some measure of logic and returned to her room to change her clothes.

* * *

Tamra found Jess in the library. He glanced up from a book and set it aside as if the idea of taking her on this tour was tedious at the very least. She found his variable moods disconcerting but she ignored his subtle disdain and followed him down the hall where he opened a closet door at the foot of the stairs and took out a ring of keys. He led her to a part of the house she'd never seen before, and put a key into a door. "We could go around to the front door," he said, "but this *is* the shortcut."

They stepped into an adjoining hallway that held an entirely different feel from the house they'd just left. He locked the door behind them, and she followed him over polished wood floors. They stopped at a little office just off some huge double doors that Tamra realized were the original front entrance. Jess stuck his head in and said to the woman sitting there, "Hello, Madge."

"Jess? When did you get back?"

"A few days ago. How's it going?"

"Good, as always. When are you going to come and take over?"

He grunted and said, "Sadie's got a friend staying for a while, and she wanted a tour, so we'll be wandering around a bit; didn't want to alarm you."

"Not a problem," Madge said, her eyes turning to Tamra. "Hi, I'm Madge."

"Hello," Tamra said, stepping forward to shake the woman's hand. "I'm Tamra Banks."

"You're American," Madge said with obvious interest.

"Yes," Tamra said.

"And you're a friend of Sadie's?" she asked.

"Actually," Tamra drawled, "I met Mr. and Mrs. Hamilton in the Philippines, and they invited me, so . . . here I am."

"Well, that's great. Look around all you like. Most of the boys should be in classes or the library. They always love to see Jess." She winked and waved as Jess led Tamra back into the hallway.

"Wait!" Tamra said, noting two large, rather old, paintings on the wall. "Who is this?" she asked just before her eyes moved to the plaque between the portraits of a man and a woman.

Jess didn't answer, figuring she could read. *Jess and Alexandra Byrnehouse-Davies, Founders of the Byrnehouse-Davies Home for Boys.*

"They're you're great-great-grandparents," she said.

"Yes," he said in a condescending tone, as if to say she had stated the obvious.

"Doesn't it make you feel pride in your ancestors to see what they've done?"

His answer was toneless. "I haven't thought about it for a while."

"Well, maybe you should," Tamra said, looking up at Alexa's portrait. That same familiarity brushed over her senses as she looked into this woman's eyes. For a moment she became so dazed by the image before her that she had to remind herself it was simply a mixture of oils on canvas. Still, she knew beyond any doubt that this woman lived on in spirit. She moved her gaze toward the portrait of Jess, and once again stated the obvious, "He's your namesake."

"Yes," Jess said again, sounding even more patronizing.

Tamra ignored his tone. "He must have been a great man," she said, then she recalled Alexa's description of him in the journals she had read. *Deeply troubled. Self-absorbed.* She wondered what might have changed to cause Alexa to marry this man, and how he could be the founder of such a wonderful place. She looked forward to reading on in the journals, but thought it might be better not to stay up all night.

"Let's get on with it," Jess said, walking down the hall. He let her peek through the little darkened windows in the classroom doors so that she could see the rooms without disturbing the lessons taking place. She was surprised to see only two classes taking place, with small numbers of students. But Jess told her the total residents were usually less than thirty, and they were kept in small groups. "With the lives most of these boys have led, they need more focused attention from their teachers and counselors."

"So," Tamra questioned, stepping into the library that was currently devoid of boys, "what brings a boy here?"

"Some of them are orphans; most have been brought here through a process that begins with being picked up by the law, either runaways or involved in crime. If they haven't got a decent home life, or are unable to fit into the foster program for any number of reasons, they have the opportunity to come here. The director works very closely with government and social workers to bring the boys here who need it the most and will be benefitted the most."

"That's amazing," Tamra said, absorbing the beauty of the room in which she stood. Like the house, the boys' home was obviously a very old structure, but it was in perfect condition. She looked directly at Jess and said, "I have some education in social work."

"Really?" he said, actually sounding interested.

"I never got my degree, because I went on a mission. But I was majoring in psychology, and minoring in business."

He made a noise to indicate he was impressed, then he asked, "So, do you think a career in such work would suit you?" He motioned with his hand to indicate their surroundings, and all they represented.

"I do, actually. Although I've always hoped that raising a family would be a top priority."

"Of course," he said, "but in the meantime, maybe Madge could get you a job—if you ever get tired of being Sadie's hired hand."

The subtle sarcasm in his tone implied that he was teasing her—and not very kindly. While Tamra felt intrigued with the idea of working in such a place, she chose not to respond to his comment. He showed her the cafeteria, introduced her to the kitchen help, and took her upstairs to show her the dormitory rooms. Then he stopped outside a door in the upstairs hall and said with aplomb, "And now . . . the grand finale."

He threw open the door and motioned her inside. Tamra felt almost breathless as the room itself seemed to speak to her of the past. It was large with sloped ceilings, a polished, clean-swept floor of wood slats, and three large gables with window seats, facing east. There were no furnishings beyond a pile of blankets stacked in the corner.

"It's incredible," she said, stepping into the center with Jess just behind her. "What do they do here?"

"Oh, all kinds of things. Group discussions, parties, activities. Tradition says that the room is special, I suppose."

"A well-founded tradition, I assume," she said, rubbing the goose bumps from her arms. "The gables," she added and moved toward the center one as her mind made the connection. These were the gables she'd seen when she'd first arrived. They had felt almost familiar to her, and the feeling had strengthened her belief that this was where she was supposed to be. She turned to Jess and asked a question she had posed to Sadie, but had gotten no satisfactory answer. "Do the gables have some significance?" She sat in the window seat to face him.

"Yes," he said, and she leaned toward him expectantly, "but I have no idea what it is."

She sighed in frustration and he chuckled, as if he found delight in leaving her hanging.

"I only know," he added, "that my great-great-grandparents designed the home around this room. That the gables—and their facing east—had some meaning for them. But I don't know what it is. I suppose I should."

"Yes, you should," she scolded. "Surely the story behind them must be recorded somewhere."

"Well, I know there are journals and such somewhere. If you keep snooping like you were in the library the other day, I'm sure you'll find them eventually. And then you can tell me the story."

Tamra didn't admit that she'd already been snooping with excellent results. Instead she replied, "I just might do that."

That elusive sensation which seemed to speak of generations past permeated Tamra once again and she moved to the center of room, closing her eyes as if she could somehow make the veil even more thin than it already felt. She rubbed the tingle from her arms and couldn't hold back a little burst of laughter.

Jess chuckled dubiously, bringing her back to the present. "I take it you like this room," he said, eyeing her skeptically.

"Oh, I do," she said.

He said nothing as he motioned her out of the room, and they went downstairs.

"Can we take the long way back?" she asked, noting the front door.

"Sure," he said. "I've got nothing to do."

"And why is that?" she asked once they'd stepped outside.

"You're terribly nosy, Ms. Banks."

"Curious is the appropriate term, Mr. Hamilton." He said nothing, so she added, "I know you left school in the middle of the term and came home. But . . . what were you studying?"

"I was majoring in psychology and minoring in business."

Tamra stopped walking. He took three steps before he caught on and did the same, turning to look at her. "You're pulling my leg," she said, astounded at the coincidence.

"No, actually. I'm quite serious. In truth," he started walking again and she hurried to catch up, "I once dreamed of being in charge of this place." He glanced up at the gabled attic of the boys' home, just above them.

"And now?" she asked.

"Now . . . everything has changed so much that . . . I don't know what I want anymore."

"But surely . . . you're still the same man, and—"

"No, Ms. Banks, deep changes have taken place right here." He briefly touched his chest, then he stuck both hands in his pockets.

She felt some tension in the conversation, but she sensed that he was being more honest with her—and himself—than he had previously been. Hoping to lure that honesty further into the open, she began to say, "Don't you think that—"

"Could we talk about something else, please?" he interrupted curtly.

"Okay," she said, but she couldn't think of anything to say. Her mind wandered back to the feelings she'd experienced standing in the gabled attic, and similar feelings that had touched her a number of times since she'd come here.

"So, what are you thinking about, Ms. Banks?" Jess asked while they ambled slowly around the house, side by side.

"If I tell you the truth, you might think I'm crazy."

"You couldn't possibly be any crazier than I am," he said, perhaps a little too seriously.

Tamra took a deep breath and asked, "Do you believe in ghosts?"

"No," he laughed.

She laughed with him. "Not like . . . haunted-house ghosts, rattling chains, and stuff like that. I mean . . . it's not ghosts, really, it's like . . . there are some people who have passed through the veil who might have some special assignment to oversee something on *this* side of the veil, so they linger in certain situations . . . as if they've been assigned to them, or something."

He chuckled as if he thought she *was* crazy, but she persisted with her explanation, as if it might convince him. "I've done a great deal of genealogy and temple work for my ancestors, and with some in particular, it felt as if they were calling to me . . . luring me to do the work for them. Some were especially impatient, others were a strength to me. They all had their own personalities, and I could feel them . . . only sometimes, of course."

"So, you *do* believe in ghosts," he said, only slightly jeering.

"In that respect, I suppose I do."

"You're entitled to your opinion," he said with another scoffing chuckle.

Tamra scowled at him and said, "You're not necessarily pleasant to talk to, Mr. Hamilton. You asked what I was thinking, but perhaps I should just learn to keep my mouth shut over things that are close to my heart."

He looked at her as if he had no idea what she was talking about, and she added curtly, "Does the term *casting pearls before swine* mean anything to you?"

He chuckled, but it was more good-natured. "Oh, so now I'm swine."

"Only sometimes," she said. "There are moments when you're almost pleasant company."

He met her eyes and she waited for him to turn hard again, as if to declare that he did not want to be pleasant company—especially not for her. But his voice was almost soft as he said, "The feeling is mutual, Ms. Banks."

Jess discreetly watched Tamra Banks walking beside him and wondered how he had managed to become practically obsessed with her in the hours since he'd seen her dancing on the lawn in the predawn light. To see her now, her hair twisted tightly and clipped to the back of her head, he found it difficult to comprehend this being the same woman who had danced with her hair hanging free, surrounded by white, like some kind of angel.

They went their separate ways inside the house, right after she smiled and said, "Thanks for the tour, Mr. Hamilton. I'll see you over spaghetti."

Jess went up to his room and kicked off his boots. He replayed their encounters in his mind, attempting to analyze how he felt. It was not a surprise to realize that he'd become so accustomed to feeling nothing at all that such soul-searching was difficult, if not impossible. He knew that his feelings for Heather had dwindled slowly over time, and her leaving had not been the shock that Sadie believed. But still, the very notion of entertaining romantic thoughts for this woman he barely knew seemed ludicrous, even crazy. But crazy was something he'd felt close to for a couple of years now.

Jess pondered what Tamra had said about ghosts. Memories of his youth had stirred with her comments and he realized he hadn't been completely truthful with her. If he was any kind of a man, he'd have to make a point of rectifying that the next time he saw her.

He drifted to sleep and later woke up with a gasp, sweat covering his face and drenching his palms. If he could ever stop seeing that accident over and over, he might have the slightest inkling of hope that there could be life beyond it. As it was, even this attraction he felt to Tamra Banks was hopeless and pathetic. What could a man like him ever offer a woman like her? He turned to his side and curled around his pillow, wishing for the millionth time that he had been allowed to die in the stead of his dearest friend.

Hunger startled Jess out of a stupor and he glanced at the clock. It was becoming increasingly more common to find himself losing track of time while knowing he'd not slept. He roused himself and put on his boots before he wandered to the kitchen without so much as a glance in the mirror. He found Sadie, Evelyn, and Tamra at the table eating, and by the way the women looked at him, he knew he must be a sight. But he didn't care. During these moments when he felt himself barely clinging to life, whether or not his hair was combed seemed irrelevant. He sat to eat, tuning out the conversation around him, and focusing mostly on Tamra. She was a pleasant distraction to the pain he was trying to hide from. When supper was over he wandered out to the veranda and sat down, putting his booted feet up on the rail.

"You okay?" he heard Tamra say and turned to find her looking at him.

"Yeah, why?" he asked.

"You didn't seem altogether with us at supper."

Jess panicked. The last thing he wanted was to discuss his state of mind with this woman. He quickly searched for an alternative topic and was relieved when he came up with one. "I think I owe you an apology."

"Really?" she said, as if she thoroughly enjoyed the idea.

"I'm sorry for scoffing at your idea of ghosts. The truth is . . . well, I used to believe in them, in the very way you were talking about."

"Really?" she said, her eyes brightening eagerly.

"Through a certain stage of my youth, there were certain places I would go when I felt down . . . and I could feel the past around me . . . almost like a blanket I couldn't see . . . like it was comforting me." He chuckled and glanced down, stuffing his hands into his pockets. "I remember hearing once about how in some Oriental cultures, the people pray to their ancestors to guide and watch over them. And I know we certainly don't pray to anyone but God Himself, but . . . I must confess that in my youth I had a certain fascination with the very idea that this house . . . this land . . . had been in my family for generations. And there were times . . . even certain places . . . where I could imagine them very close to me. But I'd honestly forgotten about that until . . . you said what you did earlier."

When Tamra said nothing, he looked up to see her gripping the rail post as if it might keep her from falling. Her face looked a little pale, her eyes wide with unmasked expectation. "You said . . . places. Are there places . . . that still exist . . . that . . . " She couldn't seem to finish, as if the very idea might sound too absurd.

"That I felt ghosts?" he asked, chuckling. She smiled and he added, "Yeah. And so you don't have to ask, I'd be happy to show you."

Tamra could barely contain her excitement as she followed Jess across the lawn to a structure as old as the house that had a large, very modern looking garage door set into it. There was a high window that implied a second story. "The carriage house," he said. They entered through a regular door and Jess flipped on a light. Nearest the garage door sat three vehicles, two Toyota Land Cruisers, and a sedan. Jess flipped another switch and lights illuminated the back portion of the carriage house, where a handful of historical vehicles were sitting, as if they expected to be harnessed and taken out for use as easily as their contemporary companions.

"They're beautiful," Tamra said, moving closer.

"This, of course, is a carriage," Jess said, pointing to an enclosed vehicle. "And this," he said, pointing to a smaller, open vehicle, "is what they called a trap." He stepped into it and held out his hand to help her up. "And this," he said, sitting on the seat, "is where I used to come when I wanted to be alone and think."

"And where you felt like you weren't alone?" she questioned, sitting beside him.

"Yeah," he said, "I guess that's how you could describe it."

They sat in silence for a few minutes while Tamra's mind attempted to decipher why this felt familiar, but not in the eerie kind of way that the gables on the boys' home had felt familiar. Then she recalled reading in Alexa's journal that she had initially lived in a room above the carriage house, and Richard had been staying in the room across the hall.

"Are there rooms upstairs?" she asked, pointing to a wood staircase against one wall.

"Yes, but a couple of hands live there."

Tamra resisted the urge to laugh at the connection, then she recalled Alexa also mentioning something about the trap. When Tamra had read it, she'd had no idea what she meant. She couldn't hold back a laugh just before she said, "Did you know your great-

great-grandmother used to sit in the trap in the carriage house to think when she wanted to be alone?"

He turned to her, blatantly astonished. "How do *you* know that?"

"Well," she giggled, "I must confess, I did some snooping and I read a bit in her journals."

"Really?" he said, not sounding offended or upset that she would do such a thing. "Well, I didn't know that."

"So, maybe it was her you felt close to you when you came here," Tamra suggested.

"Maybe," Jess said in that dark voice of his as he stepped out and walked away.

Chapter Five

Tamra hurried to catch up with Jess before he turned out the lights and went outside, closing the door behind them. "Was there someplace else?" she asked eagerly.

"Yes," he said, "but we need the key."

He walked toward the house, saying, "Wait here. I'll be right back." He returned with a very old looking key in his hand. She followed him toward the home where the Murphys lived. Assuming she didn't know, he said blandly, "The stable master lives there with his mother, who is the widow of the previous overseer."

"So the job goes from father to son," Tamra said.

"Well, at least it does in that family. As I understand it, Murphy's great-great-grandfather worked for my great-great-grandfather."

"Amazing," Tamra said. "Do you know Murphy well?"

"He's almost like family," he said, then chuckled, "even though he's an ornery old bloke." He didn't offer any explanation, but Tamra sensed the description was laced with sarcasm. She'd come across Murphy a couple of times and he seemed kind and decent, albeit a little rough.

Tamra followed Jess around the corner of the house where she could see a stairway that went up the outside. Her heart quickened as she followed Jess up the stairs, then watched as he turned the key in the lock and pushed the door open. It actually squeaked.

Tamra stepped through the door ahead of Jess and caught her breath. The room appeared to be some kind of studio. There was a partially finished painting on an easel, with a stool in front of it and oils and brushes scattered as if they had been used that day. Thick dust was the only evidence that it had sat untouched for years. But she had no idea how many years.

Other than the painting paraphernalia, there was little else in the room. A small sofa and a couple of chairs were the only furnishings. The ceilings sloped nearly to the floor, except for a single gable with a large, curtained window. The curtains were practically in shreds, obviously worn from the sun, and the room was heavy with cobwebs. In spite of its aura of disuse, the room had a certain coziness to it. But there was a haunting quality that sent a shiver through Tamra.

She turned to Jess and found him watching her more than taking in his surroundings. But then, he had seen them before—likely many times. "Tell me about this place," she said, turning to look around once more.

"I know very little, actually. The gables in the boys' home were created as some kind of symbol related to this particular gable. They all face east. The only other thing I know for certain is that nothing in this room has been moved since 1879."

Tamra laughed, certain he must have gotten the date transposed or something. "1879?" she repeated.

"That's right," he said severely.

"But you don't know the story behind it?"

"I don't," he said.

Jess watched Tamra turn once again and take in her surroundings as if they could speak to her—literally. He recalled once feeling that way when he came to this place, and he wondered why he was presently incapable of sensing something that he'd once sensed. He felt suddenly cut off. From what, he didn't know. But he felt more lonely and more filled with an indefinable despair than he had felt in his life.

"Jess, what's wrong?" Tamra asked, her voice sounding distant. She touched his arm and he looked into her eyes. Her touch, her voice, her very presence somehow gave him the tiniest belief that life might be worth living. What was it about her that made him just want to be near her? It was as if his spirit, even his very soul, cried out to hers—as if she could somehow save him from the cloud of doom and despair that had become his constant companion. Perhaps she could. But maybe that's what scared him most of all.

* * *

After Jess had shown Tamra the gabled attic, she felt impatient to return to Alexa's journals, hoping to find the answers to certain mysteries about the places from her life that still existed. But she fell asleep that night before she got very far, exhausted from the previous night's lack of sleep. She woke barely in time to begin the long drive to church following a quick breakfast. While Sadie drove the sedan that Tamra had seen in the carriage house, Evelyn chattered from the back where she was buckled safely in her little car seat. Tamra didn't even bother to ask why Jess hadn't joined them. Her heart ached for him, and she wished there was something she could do or say to comfort him.

Tamra enjoyed the church meeting and found a warmth in the people that made her feel welcome. Every person she met spoke with fondness of Michael and Emily Hamilton, looking forward to their return. It seemed to be common knowledge that they would be back in the country before next Sunday. Evelyn's situation and her recent arrival seemed equally well known.

Tamra didn't see Jess at all the remainder of the day. And she didn't encounter him over the next few days beyond occasionally passing him in the hall, where she received little more than a nod in her direction. While she helped Sadie, spent lots of time with Evelyn, and explored Alexa's journals, she felt a concern for Jess Hamilton that seemed to grow in proportion to a deepening attraction. More than once as she read of Alexa's life and the growth that had taken place in her relationship with Jess Davies, she found herself seeing the events unfold with her and Jess Hamilton playing the parts. Taken aback by such thoughts, she couldn't help briefly fantasizing about the possibility of a future with Jess. Logically she knew it was absurd, but something in her heart longed to see him find peace, and a part of her wanted to be the one to guide him there. He was often in her thoughts, and he was in her every prayer. But as long as he continued to avoid her, she doubted he would ever be anywhere else in her life.

* * *

For reasons he couldn't define, Jess stuck mostly to his room, his mind hovering between an obsession with Tamra Banks and an acute wish to be free from his inner torment. The only time he wasn't wishing to trade places with James . . . or Byron . . . was the time he was preoccupied with this woman who had invaded his mind. He had purposely avoided her, sneaking into the kitchen at odd hours to get something to eat when he hoped she would be busy elsewhere. But late one evening, after dragging himself out of a hot bath that had turned cold, he stood at the window and pushed a hand through his damp hair just as he saw her slipping into the stable. Just seeing her made him somehow believe she could be the link to his sanity, and his feelings for her became consuming. He finished getting dressed and pulled on his boots before he hurried down the stairs and out to the stable, hoping she might still be there. When he walked in to see her currying a horse and talking quietly to it, he wondered how her very presence could almost give him the will to live.

As if she sensed him standing there, she looked up, then she smiled and his heart quickened. She actually seemed pleased to see him. "Hello," she said. "I had begun to wonder if you'd left the country."

"Why would I leave when you're here?" he said, moving toward her. She seemed as surprised as he felt, and he wondered where this sudden burst of honesty had come from. Perhaps she could bring out the best in him. He could only hope there was something good enough left inside of him to be worth bringing out.

He leaned against the stall nearest where she was standing. She narrowed her eyes as she looked at him and asked, "Are you okay?"

"Yeah, why?" he asked, looking away. He wasn't sure he liked her perceptiveness.

"You don't . . . seem okay." While he was attempting to come up with a response that would divert her concern, she set down the brush and took a step toward him. "Listen, Jess, maybe I'm being too nosy . . . or pushy . . . but I know you've been through some horrible things, and I wonder if . . . maybe we should talk about it. Do you talk to anybody about it?" He didn't answer and she added, almost in a whisper, "At times I can almost feel the pain threatening to consume you, and I worry about you."

Jess felt almost dazed by her words. He looked into her eyes, wondering if he wanted to run from her and hide before she figured him out any further, or if he wanted to just take her in his arms and let her soothe his aching soul. Without even thinking about what he was doing, he took her shoulders into his hands and pressed his lips to hers.

Tamra found herself being kissed and wondered why it wasn't entirely a surprise. Logic encouraged her to protest, while her heart made it clear that this was something she'd secretly longed for since she'd first laid eyes on him. For a moment her heart won out, then logic paraded in and forced her to her senses.

"What are you doing?" Tamra asked, stepping back abruptly. Their eyes met and she absently pressed a hand over her heart to quell its quickened beat.

"I don't know," Jess admitted, as if the kiss had surprised him as much as it had her. While she continued to stare at him, as if the moment would somehow explain itself, he shot his arm around her waist and kissed her again. Tamra couldn't help but succumb to his affection. As startling as the kiss itself was the raw sincerity she felt from him. His kiss held an honesty that rarely showed through his pain and anger. When he eased back and looked into her eyes, she caught a glimpse of that same honesty, but it was coupled with confusion and distrust. Knowing his unstable state of mind, she was determined to not allow him to toy with her emotions. While she knew her own feelings well, she was not naive enough to think that an impetuous kiss would suddenly erase the emotional baggage he was hauling around.

Tamra waited for him to back away and express some embarrassment over such an impulsive display. Instead, Jess whispered with intensity, "I think I love you."

Tamra sucked in her breath and put distance between them. While she had indulged in speculations over some future romantic possibility between them, she never would have expected—or even dreamed—that he would issue such a confession when they had known each other so short a time. Part of her wanted to throw her arms around his neck and declare the words hovering on her tongue: *I love you too, Jess.* But logic quickly intruded, reminding her of this man's emotional instability. And one fact stood out strongly.

"Jess," she said, maintaining a gentle voice, "not so many days ago, you were stricken with grief over losing Heather. How can you—"

"I don't know," he said, tightening his hands over her shoulders, "but I do. All of a sudden, everything that seemed right before seems all wrong . . . and everything seems right as long as you're there. So what else can I think . . . except that I love you?"

Tamra shook her head as if that would make sense of the situation. "There are a number of possibilities, Jess. How can you *think* you love me? Either you love me or you don't."

"Then I love you," he insisted.

Tamra resisted the urge to call him a fool, and she quelled the temptation to accept his declaration at face value and melt in his arms. Fighting for some measure of reason, she stated tenderly, "Jess, listen to me. If you love me, fine. But don't love me because I'm a convenient rebound after losing Heather. Don't love me because I'm the only single female under fifty that you've had any contact with since you came home. Don't claim to love me because you need my friendship, or companionship, or just because you need a shoulder to cry on. If you want me to return what you feel for me, then you're going to have to be honest about what it is exactly you feel. And you can't be honest with me, until you can be honest with yourself. If you're attracted to me, fine. If you just want a friend, fine. I can live with that. And if you love me from the heart, for the right reasons, I can live with that, too. But don't go labeling feelings you don't even understand." She finished by adding firmly, "I don't know how you could possibly love me, when you don't even know me. And I don't know how you could possibly get to know me when you see nothing but yourself."

Tamra regretted the severity of those last words when she saw a familiar hardness rise into his eyes. She knew her response was tied into the defenses from past hurts in her own life, but how could he understand that when he was so vulnerable? While she was searching for words to soften her declaration, he turned and walked out of the stable.

Tamra nearly ran after him, but she felt certain that any attempt she made now to speak to him would never penetrate the familiar wall she had seen go up in his eyes. She didn't see him again until late that evening when she was searching the kitchen for something to snack on. He appeared in the doorway, obviously shocked to see her there.

"Sorry," she said, "I didn't mean to intrude on one of your secret missions to collect food."

"Not a problem," he said, going directly to the refrigerator.

"Jess," she said gently, "about what I said earlier, I want you to know that—"

"Forget about it," he said harshly, and she couldn't find the will to say anything else while he fixed himself a sandwich.

"I thought I heard someone in here," Sadie said, appearing in the room. "I've been meaning to tell you, Jess, that your parents will be home in a couple of days."

Tamra's heart quickened when she saw an unmasked terror rise in Jess's eyes. He froze for a long moment before he said, "Please tell me you're joking. Their mission can't be over already. They should be out another six months," he protested.

"Yes, they should," Sadie explained gently, "but they've had to cut their mission short to care for little Evelyn. Amee was caring for her, but since she's had her baby, she just hasn't been able to handle Evelyn as well. Your parents have just been finishing up a few things while I took care of Evelyn. They'll be home soon."

"Well, that's just great," Jess said with sarcasm and left the room with his sandwich.

An hour later, Tamra was sitting in her room, replaying her encounter in the stable with Jess. Recalling his kiss she felt a spontaneous tingling, but instinctively, she felt that she had handled it all wrong. She knew that her feelings for him were far closer to his confession than she'd let on. In truth, knowing that Jess held such feelings for her prompted unspeakable joy. And weighing all she knew of the present situation and her feelings for Jess Hamilton, she knew that whatever the future might bring, it was important for him to know that she had been thinking about him the way he'd been thinking about her. Resolved to talk to him at the first opportunity in the morning, she opened a drawer to pull out her pajamas. She had barely picked them up when a thought burst into her mind: *Tell him now.*

Tamra's first response was that she needed more time to think about what she might say. It was a delicate situation and she felt so unprepared. He wasn't an easy man to talk to. How would she approach him? What could she say to get him to listen with an open heart?

Tell him now! The thought repeated itself with such intensity that Tamra practically ran down the hall. There was only one other time in her life when she'd heard the Spirit speak to her with such urgency.

And the prompting had kept her and her mission companion from going into a situation where they had later learned a heinous crime had occurred. With no thought to what she might say, she knocked at his bedroom door.

"What?" he called, sounding groggy.

"Can I talk to you?" she called back.

"I'm tired," he growled. "We can talk tomorrow."

Tamra's anxious heart raced even faster when she recognized a definite slur in his voice. "Jess, are you all right?" she asked.

"Go away," he snarled. And a silent voice responded in her head: *Open the door.*

She momentarily hesitated. What if he wasn't dressed? What if he got angry? What if—*Open the door!* she heard again and she obediently turned the knob.

Her eye was first drawn to Jess, sitting low in an overstuffed chair, his head back, his eyes closed, oblivious to her presence. By his side on the floor was a little bottle of water, left open and tipped over, with water soaking into the carpet. And next to the water was a little box that she recognized—the package of sleeping pills he'd purchased on their trip to town, barely a week ago. Her dread turned to full-fledged panic as her eyes took in evidence that she refused to believe until she knelt on the floor and picked up the box, noting the number 32 printed there. And scattered around it were blister packs to house that many pills—all empty.

"Oh, God help me," she murmured and turned to grab Jess's shoulders. He mumbled indiscernibly like a drunk man. She pressed both hands to his flushed face. "Jess!" she shouted.

"I'm tired," he mumbled and his head lolled to one side. "Just go away and leave me alone," he added in a voice she barely understood.

On impulse, she slapped him, hoping to startle him to his senses, but he only groaned and his head lolled the other direction.

"Oh, God help me," she repeated and ran from the room, nearly tripping over her own feet as she scrambled to Sadie's bedroom door. She pounded with her fist and hollered, "Help me, Sadie. Come to Jess's room. Hurry!"

She returned to find him closer to unconsciousness. She grabbed the cordless phone from his bedside table and quickly dialed three zeroes. The voice at the other end seemed like a lifeline. She saw Sadie appear in the doorway, tying a robe about her waist, looking aghast just as Tamra said into the phone, "I'm with a man who has overdosed on some sleeping pills."

"Good heavens," Sadie gasped, moving to Jess's side to shake him, as if she might convince Tamra that she was mistaken.

Tamra calmly answered questions, then said to Sadie, "You go wake Murphy and tell him to get out on the lawn to show the helicopter where to land. Don't come back until he's dressed and outside!"

Sadie nodded and hurried away. Tamra was grateful that the dispatcher kept her on the phone. But once the necessary information had been exchanged, fear took hold of her and she started to cry. Shaking Jess made it evident he'd completely lost consciousness and she resisted the urge to scream at him, only because she had the phone against her face.

"I can't believe he did this," she said. "I just can't believe it." She kept touching his face, his hair, his hands, as if she could get him to respond.

The stranger on the other end of the phone offered soothing words that kept Tamra from crumbling for what seemed an eternity. The dispatcher kept reminding her that the helicopter was on its way, but Tamra cursed the distance of their location from the nearest hospital. She felt certain she would go mad from the waiting until she declared, "I can hear the helicopter! It's here."

Barely a minute later she heard Murphy bounding up the stairs, leading the paramedics to Jess's room. Tamra finally hung up the phone when she saw two men and a woman enter the room and surround Jess. They spouted information back and forth while they assessed the situation, and within seconds he was strapped to a stretcher and being carried toward the stairs. Tamra thought he looked dead already, and she wondered how she would ever tell Michael and Emily Hamilton that they'd lost another son.

Between Sadie's help and the paramedics' directions, Tamra was in her car on her way toward town within seconds after the helicopter lifted off. With a promise to call Sadie the moment she had any news, she focused on the road ahead, praying and crying so hard at moments that she could barely see.

"Oh, please don't let him die," she prayed over and over. "Please, God, please. Please don't let him die!" She tried to have faith that her prayers would be heard and answered, but a part of her felt prepared to arrive and find him dead. She had absolutely no idea how long it took for such drugs to fully absorb. But if they had absorbed enough to render him unconscious, then . . . No, she couldn't think of that!

When Tamra finally arrived at the hospital and ran through the emergency room doors, she was prepared to be told the worst. If he wasn't dead, she just knew he had to be comatose, or doomed to permanent brain damage. After giving his name at the desk, she was led to a room and told by a nurse, "You can go on in. The doctor will come and talk to you in a few minutes."

"Thank you," Tamra said and slowly pushed open the door. She gasped softly to see Jess, apparently sleeping, hooked to monitors and an IV. A sheet lay over him to his chest. The hospital gown he wore had black smudges on it. Hints of the same black were around his mouth. The shock and disbelief she'd felt during her drive crystallized into the harsh reality before her. She felt a burning in her chest that threatened to erupt at the slightest invitation. She stepped hesitantly toward the bed, wanting to just touch him, to know for herself that he truly was alive. The warmth of his hand tempted her emotions closer to the surface, then she heard the door and quickly swallowed them.

"Hello," a woman about forty, with blonde hair in a ponytail said, "I'm Doctor Hill. Are you his wife?"

"Uh . . . no," she said. "He's not married. I'm just . . . a friend of the family, but . . . he has no family close by at the moment."

"You're the one who found him, then?" the doctor asked.

"Yes."

"Your name?"

"Tamra Banks."

"Well, good work, Ms. Banks. He's going to be just fine."

"He is?" Tamra squeaked.

"Yes, he is," the doctor repeated with a little smile. "Physically, at least. They pumped his stomach en route, and the charcoal helped absorb the rest. We'll be admitting him to the psychiatric ward, and what happens beyond that depends a lot on his state of mind."

The doctor glanced toward Jess and motioned Tamra into the hall. "Do you know why he did this?"

Tamra did her best to succinctly explain what she knew of the accident a couple of years ago and the more recent loss of his fianceé. She said she wasn't certain what exactly had driven him over the edge, but in her heart she had to wonder if her firm words to him in response to his declaration of love had contributed to the problem. When the doctor had finished asking questions, Tamra said, "May I stay with him?"

"Yes, I think that be would good. You can give him the bad news when he comes around."

"The bad news?"

"That he's still here," the doctor said and walked away.

Tamra stepped back into the room to see him still sleeping. Her emotions threatened to surface again, but she recalled her promise to call Sadie and once again forced them down while she found a phone and made the call. She heard Sadie crying on the other end of the line as she repeated what the doctor had said.

"I don't know when I'll be home," Tamra said. "Someone needs to be with him. I'll keep you informed." She hung up the phone and returned to Jess's room to find nothing changed. She put her purse on the floor and scooted a chair close to the bed where she could sit and take hold of his hand. "Oh, Jess," she murmured and her tears needed no more encouragement. She pressed her face to the bed at his side and sobbed without control. She was embarrassed to still be crying when they came to move him to another room. But one of the nurses put a hand on her shoulder and said quietly, "It's going to be all right, honey."

Tamra followed his bed as it was rolled down halls, into an elevator, and into a restricted area of the hospital. Once he was settled, with everything attached to him being checked carefully, a different nurse said to her, "He'll likely be a bit confused when he comes around. If you need anything at all, just press that button. His vitals are being monitored down the hall." Tamra nodded and was left alone with him. The lights were dim and she attempted to get comfortable in a recliner close to his bed. She was trying to talk herself into getting some sleep when she heard him groan.

Instinctively she moved closer to him, sliding a chair close to the bed and taking his hand into hers. He groaned again and she brushed his hair back from his face. "It's all right, Jess," she murmured. "Everything's going to be all right."

"I'm not ready," he muttered in a fearful tone. "I'm not ready . . . It's too soon."

His words tugged at Tamra's heart. She tried to comprehend what kind of inner agony would have provoked him to do what he'd done. She couldn't even fathom the depth of emotional anguish that might cause such desperation. Her own emotions rose again, a combination of intense relief that he was alive and going to be okay, and a deep compassion for the heartache that had led him to this point in his life—a heartache that would not easily be put to rest with one more traumatic event to deal with.

"It's too soon," he muttered again with a fear in his voice that prompted her to put her arms around him and put her face close to his.

"It's all right, Jess," she said again and felt him take hold of her arms. She wept into the pillow beside his head, attempting to keep the tears silent.

"Tamra," he whispered and turned his head toward her. She lifted her head but was unable to move with the way he held her arms. Their eyes met, but she could tell he was having difficulty focusing. "Tamra," he repeated. "You're here. I'm here."

"That's right," she said and sniffled. He moved one hand to touch her face, then he rubbed his fingers together, as if to verify that they were wet with tears. "Everything's going to be okay."

"Where . . . What . . . " He couldn't seem to put his questions into words.

"You're in the hospital, Jess. You almost died. Do you remember?"

He squeezed his eyes shut and furrowed his brow, as if he were having difficulty connecting his thoughts. Several moments later he moaned and muttered, "Heaven help me." He tightened his grip and pulled her close to him. She felt his hands begin to shake, and a noise of anguish erupted from his throat. "What . . . have I done?" he moaned and began to cry. Tamra pressed her face into the pillow and cried with him.

Long after they slipped into silence, Jess held to her arm with one hand, and kept the other at the back of her head. Tamra might have believed he'd fallen back to sleep, except for the way his fingers moved lightly through her hair.

"Tamra," he murmured, "I need you. Don't leave me. Don't ever leave me."

Tamra lifted her head to look into his eyes. Under the circumstances, she knew she was in no position to make promises that were beyond her capacity to keep. In spite of all she felt for him, and what she believed he felt for her, she could not commit her future to any man under such circumstances. In response to the expectancy in his eyes, she said gently, "I'm here, Jess. And everything's going to be okay."

Chapter Six

While Jess seemed to be weighing whether or not to believe what Tamra had said, the door came open and Doctor Hill entered. Jess turned toward her but kept his hand tightly in Tamra's.

"Hello, Jess," the doctor said, pulling a chair close to the other side of his bed. "I see that you're awake. I'm Doctor Hill. You're going to be seeing a lot of me until you're ready to go home. How are you feeling?"

"Not real great," Jess said with an edge to his voice that was more typical than the humble display Tamra had seen the last few minutes.

"Well, that's understandable," the doctor said. "What do you remember?"

Jess moaned and squeezed his eyes shut, as if thinking was an immense strain. "A tube . . . in my nose . . . down my throat . . . and . . . I don't know if I remember anything, or if it was a dream."

"Well," the doctor said gently, "that's understandable as well. An emergency helicopter brought you from your home. Your stomach was pumped en route, and several pill fragments were found. You were given charcoal to help absorb the remaining medicine in your stomach."

"I think I remember that," Jess said and moaned again.

"I'm sure it wasn't very pleasant," the doctor said. "And now that you're here, there are some things you need to be thinking about." She leaned forward and put a hand on his arm. "But first I need to ask you a few questions. I know you're still a little groggy and confused, but do the best you can, and we can talk more later." He nodded and attempted to focus on her. "Do you remember how many pills you took, Jess?"

Tamra saw him squeeze his eyes shut tightly, as if to block out the horror of what he'd done. His expression reeked of self-recrimination. He made a noise akin to a whimper and tightened his hand around Tamra's. Doctor Hill said, "Jess, do you remember how many pills you took?"

"Uh . . . I . . . don't know how many . . . were in the box . . . "

"Thirty-two," Tamra provided. "And he'd had the box for about a week."

The doctor nodded and turned back to Jess. "Had you been taking the pills to help you sleep?"

"Yes," Jess said.

"More than one a day?" she asked.

"No . . . just one . . . at bedtime . . . but sometimes they didn't help much."

"Did you take what was left in the box before you came here?" Doctor Hill asked.

Jess hesitated a moment before answering. "Yes."

The doctor's voice was warm and compassionate, without the slightest hint of reprimand. "Why did you do that, Jess?"

"I . . . I . . . " His voice broke with emotion. "I . . . just didn't want to . . . hurt anymore."

Tamra saw the doctor pass her a quick glance of concern before she asked Jess, "What were you hurting about, Jess?"

Jess groaned and shook his head. Doctor Hill said, "I see you have a very good friend here." Jess seemed to relax at the change in conversation. He squeezed Tamra's hand as if to echo the doctor's statement. "Tamra here saved your life, Jess."

Jess turned to look at her, his surprise evident. While he held Tamra's gaze, the doctor asked, "Do you remember Tamra being there after you took the pills?"

"I think so," he said, but Tamra saw something confused come into his eyes. She could almost imagine him weighing whether or not to be grateful or angry.

"Jess," the doctor said, "can you tell me about what was hurting that made you want to end your life?"

He turned to look at her, apparently bewildered. Tamra wondered if he could even acknowledge the accident without falling apart. But perhaps that's what Doctor Hill wanted. Tamra knew enough about psychology to know that he needed to acknowledge the problem before he could ever work toward healing. But the only acknowledgment she'd ever heard from him had been cursory and bitter.

When he said nothing, the doctor asked, "Does Tamra know what the problem is, Jess?"

"I think so," Jess said, closing his eyes.

"Do you want her to tell me?" Tamra met the doctor's eyes, recalling their conversation in the hall earlier. Perhaps she wanted her to repeat what she knew in front of Jess, so that it could be brought into the open and addressed.

"I don't care," he said, but Tamra sensed a subtle relief, as if he knew it had to be said, but he didn't want to be the one to do it.

"Tamra," the doctor said, "do you know what Jess has been hurting over?" She nodded slightly with meaning in her eyes, as if to encourage her to repeat what she'd said earlier.

Tamra swallowed carefully. "I only know that he was in an automobile accident a couple of years ago."

She hesitated when Jess made that whimpering noise again. The doctor glanced at him, then back to Tamra. "Was someone killed in the accident?" she asked.

"Yes," Tamra said. "I wasn't around at the time, but I've been told that . . . " she glanced at Jess and tightened her hand in his, "he lost his brother, his sister-in-law, and a close friend."

Doctor Hill looked directly at Jess and said with compassion, "That must have been horrible for you." His eyes responded to her validation. "Were you hurt?"

He nodded and said, "I was . . . in the hospital for about . . . four months."

"Goodness," the doctor said, "you must have been in pretty bad shape. But you made it. You were obviously very lucky."

"No," Jess shook his head, "not lucky. It should have been me."

The doctor's voice remained even and gentle. "Is that why you wanted to die? You believe it should have been you?"

Jess didn't answer and she continued, "That accident was a long time ago, Jess. What happened in the last twenty-four hours that prompted you to make this choice now?"

Tamra nearly expected him to glare at her with silent accusations of how she had spurned his confessions of love. Her heart quickened as he turned to meet her eyes, but it wasn't accusation she saw there. It was raw vulnerability. He turned back toward the doctor and said, "I just couldn't face them . . . after everything that's happened, and . . . my fianceé . . . left me . . . to marry somebody else."

"Okay," the doctor said, "that can certainly be tough. But who couldn't you face?"

His voice broke as he said, "My parents . . . are coming home, and . . . "

Again the doctor exchanged a brief glance with Tamra, then she asked Jess the very question that Tamra had on the tip of her tongue. "Do you think they would prefer to come home and find you dead or alive, Jess?"

He groaned and said, "I'm so tired."

"I know you are," the doctor said. "I appreciate your talking to me. I'm going to let you get some rest, and we can talk some more tomorrow. Will that be all right?"

Jess nodded and the doctor added, "Tamra's going to go home and get some rest as well. We'll take very good care of you, and she can come back for a while to visit you tomorrow."

The doctor left the room with a quick glance toward Tamra that seemed to say she should be brief. It wasn't difficult to figure that whatever they needed to accomplish on his behalf, both physically and emotionally, would be better accomplished without her around. She wasn't even family. And barely a friend, for that matter. But oh, how she didn't want to leave him!

"I guess I have to go," she said, coming to her feet to look down at him. He met her gaze while she smoothed his hair back from his face. "We need to talk, Jess. There are things I need to say . . . something I was coming to tell you when . . . " She stopped that thought and sighed. "Anyway, now is not the time, but when you get feeling better, we need to talk, okay?"

"Okay," he said.

"You get some rest and I'll see you tomorrow . . . I promise." As an afterthought, she felt the need to clarify, "Do you want me to come back, Jess?" He looked surprised and she added, "I mean . . . if you look at how short a time we've known each other, we're practically strangers, but . . . we're not because, well . . . we'll have to talk about that, but . . . I just have to know if you want me to come back."

"Yes, oh yes," he said, holding tightly to her hand.

Tamra smiled and pressed an impulsive kiss to his brow. "I'll see you tomorrow, then," she said and, loosening his grip from her hand, hurried from the room.

Tamra walked slowly back to her car, dazed and exhausted. It was only when she turned on the car that she saw the clock and realized it was the middle of the night. She prayed to be able to make it home safely, and kept the radio turned up loud to keep her awake. She arrived at the house feeling like the last several hours had been a bad dream. Sadie met her at the top of the stairs.

"You haven't been up all this time, have you?" Tamra asked.

"I've been in bed, but I've hardly slept. Are you okay? Is he okay?"

"Physically, he's fine." Tamra moved toward her room and Sadie followed. "But I can't even comprehend what must have been going on in his head to bring him to something like that."

"Oh, I've thought exactly the same thing," Sadie said with emotion in her voice. "And how are you?"

Tamra sat on the edge of her bed and kicked off her shoes. "I'm . . . in shock. In some ways, I feel like Jess and I are strangers, and yet I feel so . . . connected to him. I just don't know what to think." Tamra contemplated confessing the heart of her concerns, that her reaction to him in the stable had, at the very least, contributed to this downfall. But she couldn't bring herself to say it aloud. "I think we both need some sleep," she declared.

"Is Jess—"

"He's been admitted. They're taking very good care of him, but I get the feeling he'll be there at least a few days. I don't think they'll let him go if they have any reason to believe he might try it again."

"Well, that's good, isn't it?"

"Yes, I believe it is. I was there while a doctor talked to him about what he'd done. They didn't get very far, but I think they can help him."

"Oh, I do hope so," Sadie said. Her voice became emotional again as she added, "I'm so grateful you were here, Tamra. I don't know what we would have done if he'd . . . " Her voice faded into tears and Tamra stood to embrace her.

Sadie got control of herself and went off to bed. Tamra crawled into her own bed and felt the shock turn, once again, into emotion.

She cried herself to sleep and woke late in the morning with the sensation of emerging from a nightmare. Then she had to admit that her sleep had been dreamless; the nightmare had occurred before she'd gone to sleep. Her thoughts went to Jess and she took a quick shower. Afterward she found Sadie playing with Evelyn and said, "I'm going to the hospital to see him. I promised him I would be there."

"Oh, he called," Sadie said. "It was so good to hear his voice," she added with a dramatic edge. "But he asked for some of his things. I've got them together in a bag on the kitchen table. And I've fixed you a sandwich that you can take with you."

"Oh, you're an angel, Sadie. I'm starving but I didn't want to take time to eat."

"Give him my love," Sadie said.

"I will, and . . . " A thought occurred to Tamra. "Is there anyone that should be called? I mean . . . I'm not even close to being a family member, and . . . maybe you should be with him, Sadie. You've known him so much longer, and—"

"No, no. I'm just a housekeeper, Tamra, and—"

"You're much more than that. It's evident you're very close to the family, and—"

"Yes, but . . . I need to be with Evelyn, and I don't think I'm the right person to be with him. Three of his sisters are in the States. His other sister lives in Adelaide and she has a new baby. I know she couldn't come, and I don't feel like it's my place to call her. Michael and Emily will be home the day after tomorrow. They'll know what to do."

Tamra blew out a long breath. "Yes, I'm sure they will. But I wish they didn't have to come home to this."

Sadie silently agreed and Tamra went to the kitchen to find a complete lunch packed with a little bottle of orange juice, a sandwich, some crisps, and an apple. She also found a bag that was obviously meant for Jess.

The drive went more quickly than the previous night, and she wondered if this growing sense of dread had anything to do with it. Instinctively she knew that she was not going to find Jess Hamilton in good spirits.

Once Tamra got into the psychiatric ward, a nurse thoroughly searched the bag she had brought for Jess, including every pocket of his jeans. While the nurse was doing her inspection, Tamra noticed a woman walking down the hall with bandages around her wrists. She felt a little sick as she realized why the bag was being searched. *Please God,* Tamra prayed, *keep him alive until he can get a grip. And please . . . guide my words and help me handle this right. I can't do this alone.*

Tamra followed the nurse to Jess's room. She peeked in to check on him, then motioned Tamra inside and went back down the hall. His bed was empty and rumpled. He was sitting in the chair she had occupied the night before, his long legs stretched out and crossed at the ankles. His feet were bare. He wore the jeans he'd come in and a hospital gown on backward and left hanging open in the front to show hints of his bare chest. He seemed oblivious to her presence until she closed the door. He turned to look at her and she immediately recognized the dark clouds in his eyes.

"Sadie sent some things," she said, holding out the bag. "She sends her love."

"Thank you," he said, jumping to his feet as if she'd brought food to a starving man.

He tossed the bag on the bed and opened it as she said, "They searched it before I could bring it in."

"They told me they would," he said, rummaging through his things, "so I didn't ask for any pistols or razor blades."

"Good thinking," she said, attempting to match his sarcasm.

He pulled a couple of clothing items from the bag and removed the hospital gown. Tamra reminded herself that seeing his bare back from the waist up was nothing more than she might see at a swimming pool, but she glanced away nevertheless, feeling embarrassed. Perhaps, she reasoned, her uneasiness was caused by the racing of her heart, a stark reminder that she found him attractive. She was aware of him pulling on a garment top and a T-shirt. And she wondered if those he had worn to the hospital had become soiled during the procedures.

Once he was dressed, he turned to Tamra and said, "You've got to get me out of here."

"Me?" she retorted. "What am I supposed to do?"

"They won't let me go until someone signs for me."

"I'd wager that *someone* has to be a family member."

"Well, that's not possible, is it? I know they'll let you take me. Doctor Hill likes you. She thinks you're responsible and levelheaded."

"Imagine that," Tamra said.

"So, just tell them you'll sign for me, and get me out of this place. I *hate* it here."

"What's the problem, Jess? Are they making you talk about your problems?" He scowled at her and she added, "You do have problems you know, Jess. Or at least that's the general assumption when a person attempts suicide. The rest of us have to assume that something's bothering you, and maybe talking about it might help."

"Well, I don't *want* to talk about it," he growled. "How can I talk about it when I can't even *think* about it?"

Tamra softened her voice and asked, "And thinking about it made you take twenty-five sleeping pills?"

He looked appalled that she would face the issue so boldly. He put his hands to his hips, shook his head, and said with cynicism, "Who are you, anyway? What are you doing in my life?"

"I'll tell you who I am, Jess. And I'll tell you what I'm doing here. I'm the one who *saved* your life."

"So, if you had stayed away, I'd be out of my misery."

Tamra swallowed her initial response and forced an even voice. "No, Jess, you would be facing a different kind of misery. I wonder how it might have felt for you to be on the other side of the veil and see your parents and your sisters grieving for you and trying to understand how you could do something so . . . *selfish.*" He looked away and she saw the muscles of his jaw twitch. "And I wonder how it might have felt to face your ancestors, and even your brother, with the accountability of taking your own life."

Jess turned back to face her with more anger showing in his eyes than she had ever seen. "Why don't you just get out of here, and go back to wherever you came from?"

"I plan on it," she said. "But remember, I came from where you did. For the time being, I live at Byrnehouse-Davies and Hamilton, and if you don't like me there, you can take it up with your parents. Maybe when they get back, they'll be willing to sign for you. I'm certainly not going to."

Tamra saw the color drain from his face, and the humility returned to his eyes. "No, please, Tamra," he said. "You've got to get me out of here. Don't let them come home and find me here . . . like this."

Tamra went with her instincts, praying they would not make the problem worse. But she knew she couldn't be accountable for him.

And she knew he had to face up to the repercussions of the decisions he'd made. With a gentle voice she said, "No, if it were up to you, they would have come home to find you dead."

He squeezed his eyes shut and his expression showed regret, but it seemed quickly gone when he looked at her hard, saying, "I need to get out of here, Tamra."

"As difficult as it is, Jess, I think you need to stay. You need help, and I can't give it to you."

"You can get me out of here," he insisted, reminding her very much of her mother when she wanted a drink.

"And then what?" she asked. "I can't stay with you every minute of every night and day. How do I know you won't just slit your wrists or shoot yourself in the head?"

He looked shocked, but it quickly melted into anger. "Maybe I will," he said like a spoiled child.

"Fine," she said, knowing she needed to leave—for her sake as well as his. "You can just stay here and rot, for all I care. But at least you'll be alive."

She walked out of his room and closed the door. She had to lean against the wall and will herself to calm down. She felt such a torrent of fear and hurt and anger that she could hardly see straight. Certain her emotions would not be easily subdued she determined she needed to just get out of the hospital. She turned the corner of the hall and came face to face with Doctor Hill.

"Hello," she said.

"Hello," Tamra replied.

"From your expression I would assume you have been to see our mutual friend." Tamra just nodded, fearing she might start to cry if she tried to speak. "Let me guess," the doctor said, "he was entirely different from the man you left last night." Tamra nodded again. "He was fairly open last night, but his walls have come back up. He's confused, and scared, and at some level I think he's just plain ashamed of what he's done. But we're going to take very good care of him."

Tamra nodded again, wondering if this woman was impressed with her ability to articulate her thoughts. Doctor Hill then asked, "Do you know when his parents are due back?"

"Not exactly, but . . . soon," Tamra managed to say, unable to recall exactly what Sadie had said.

"If you'll let them know what's happened, I'd like to visit with them before we make any firm decisions on how to handle the situation. And in the meantime, we're going to see what we can accomplish with him."

"I'll let them know," Tamra said. "And thank you . . . for everything."

"I know it can be rough," she said. "But I really think he's going to be okay."

Tamra nodded once more and hurried away, knowing she couldn't control her emotions much longer. The moment she shut the car door, she started to cry. She asked herself why she should be so upset over a man she hardly knew, but the answer was immediate and obvious. She had feelings for Jess that could not be denied. And perhaps her attempt to deny them had contributed to his downfall. She reminded herself that it was far more complicated than that, but she still felt guilty. And now what? It was ridiculous to think of hoping for a future with such a man. What she felt for him would never be enough to counteract his challenges. She had to keep her head on straight. She just had to. She only hoped her heart could survive.

Tamra found herself driving around town, wondering why she didn't want to go home. She determined that she wanted to go back and see Jess. But for what? To have him get angry and yell at her again? Or was she hoping to somehow soften the anger between them? After more than an hour, she decided that she did need to go back, and there was something she needed to say.

Once she'd made up her mind to go back, she remembered that visiting hours were limited and she couldn't go in for another two hours. She got herself something to eat and wandered around town, doing some window shopping and picking up a few odds and ends that she needed. When it finally came time to go back to the hospital, she had almost convinced herself that it wasn't necessary. But in her heart she knew it was. She couldn't allow the sun to set without clarifying one point, even if she didn't know exactly how to do that.

The moment she walked into his room, Tamra felt so thoroughly glad to see him that she had to question what was happening to her. Was she simply caught up in a drama that had shaken her? Or was there really more to her feelings for this man? She knew the answer to that question in the deepest part of her heart, but she wasn't certain Jess was ready to hear that answer—not all of it, at least.

For a long moment she stood and watched him, staring out the window, one arm above him, leaning against the frame. Noting his bare feet sticking out from beneath his jeans, she determined that he had an aversion to shoes. He turned around to see who was there and she caught a brief glimpse of pleasant surprise. *He was glad to see her!* That was a good start.

"Hello, Jess," she said.

"Hello, Tamra," he said, turning back to the window. "Did you change your mind about letting me rot?"

"I didn't come to take you home, if that's what you're wondering."

"Well, at least we're clear on that point," he said.

"But there is something I need to say."

He glanced over his shoulder then back out the window. "I'm listening."

Tamra wanted to see his eyes and moved to stand beside him. "It's not a very pleasant view," she said.

"No," he agreed.

Tamra took a deep breath and forced herself to begin. "We need to talk . . . about what happened . . . in the stable."

He turned to look at her slowly, his eyes skeptical.

"You do remember, don't you? Those sleeping pills didn't fry your memory cells, did they?"

"Oh, I remember, all right."

"Well," Tamra glanced down to her wringing hands, "I think perhaps . . . you misunderstood me. I think you should know that . . . you're not alone in the way you feel."

Tamra stole a quick glance to gauge his reaction, but she found it difficult to look at him. He looked dubious, perhaps even amused, and she wondered if she'd opened a can of worms.

"Oh?" he said cynically. "So, the problem then, would be in establishing exactly what it is *we* feel. And according to what you said in the stable, whatever we might feel for each other couldn't possibly be love."

"What makes you so sure?"

"*You* told me that," he insisted.

"I don't know what you heard, but that's not what I said."

"How convenient for you to twist it all around, now that things have turned ugly."

"Yes, it's turned ugly, all right. But you can't blame me for that. And don't be so sure that I'm the one who has it twisted. Whether you want to live or not, there are people who love you who would be torn apart to lose you. So maybe you should stop thinking about yourself long enough to think about the people who care whether or not you live or die—even if you don't."

"And I suppose you're going to claim that you're one of those people."

His expression made it clear he expected a belligerent response, but she softened her voice and said, "Yes, Jess, I'm one of those people."

"But we're practically strangers," he retorted, turning his face away.

"Strangers don't kiss and make confessions of love," she said, wishing her voice hadn't betrayed the emotion she felt.

He turned to look at her as if he might scream at her and tell her to leave. With more raw hostility than she'd ever seen in his face, he snarled quietly, "Well, you were right about that. It was likely just some pathetic rebound after Heather dumped me. What else could it possibly be . . . when we're *practically strangers?*"

Tamra bit her lip, determined not to cry and give him any other reason to mock her. "I was under the impression that we'd become friends . . . at the very least."

"Or at the very most," he snapped. "But don't be calling yourself my friend when you did exactly what I asked you not to do."

"And what's that?" she asked, wondering if she wanted to know.

"I told you to go away and leave me alone. Well, you didn't. And I woke up here."

Tamra squeezed her eyes shut and prayed. This was going all wrong. In a gentle voice she said, "Please stop being angry, Jess, and try to hear what I'm saying." She opened her eyes and focused on him, relieved to see that he was paying attention. "What I said in the stable . . . I, well . . . it doesn't matter what I said, really. What I meant to say . . . what I want to say now is just that . . . we both need some time, Jess, to be able to know for certain what we feel . . . and what to do with it."

She glanced down and held her breath as he pressed a hand to her face and murmured softly, "What is it about you? One minute I think I should run away from you . . . far and fast. And the next I can believe that I will die if I don't have you with me every minute for the rest of my life." He moved his fingers to the other side of her face and she drew the courage to meet his eyes. "What is it about you that can make me so angry with you . . . and so needy for you . . . all in the same minute?"

"I don't know, Jess," she said. "But it would seem we're suffering from the same illness, because we certainly seem to have the same symptoms." That pleasant surprise showed again in his eyes just before he kissed her. Just as with his previous kiss, she felt something honest and sincere come through. But it went deeper, so much deeper. He drew her fully into his arms and she eagerly returned his embrace while his kiss went on and on. She could almost literally feel his pain and desperation seeping into her, and she felt eager to take them if it would only free him from his torment.

"Tamra," he murmured, spreading kisses over her face until he found her lips again. She marveled at the pure, unbridled joy she felt from the experience, as if their spirits had momentarily connected on a higher plane, completely detached from all of the fear and pain and heartache of the world. From this innocent display of devotion, Tamra caught a glimpse of his potential, of a man willing and able to love with his whole heart, a man freed from the tethers that bound him to his crippling grief. *And she loved him!* She couldn't bring herself to admit it outright—not yet, not here like this. But as he drew back and looked into her eyes, she felt certain that he knew what she had been alluding to.

They were both startled when the door came open and Jess let go of her. A nurse stuck her head in and asked, "How you doing, Jess?"

"I'm great," he said while looking at Tamra.

"Good," the nurse replied. "You should be all geared up for group therapy. Five minutes."

She left them alone and he snarled with sarcasm, "Oh, great, another hour or two with all the other crazies."

"You're not crazy, Jess," she said.

"I *feel* crazy," he said, "especially being in here." His gaze tightened on her and she felt it coming. "Take me home, Tamra. Get me out of here."

Tamra reminded herself not to let her emotions override her common sense. "I can't do that, Jess."

"Oh, I see," he said with a cynicism that let her know his walls had gone back up, as Doctor Hill would have said. "We're back to 'you can just rot, Jess.'"

"I don't want you to rot, Jess. I want you to live."

"Well, that makes one of us," he said, moving toward the door. She concluded that group therapy suddenly seemed more appealing than staying in the room with her.

Tamra questioned her own judgment as she blurted the retort that came to her tongue. "Maybe you *are* crazy."

One corner of his mouth twitched upward as he said, "At least we agree on something."

Chapter Seven

The following day Tamra decided firmly against going to see Jess. She simply couldn't handle the roller coaster of emotion he put her through. After taking advantage of the opportunity to exercise without any distraction beyond the memory of doing the samba with Jess Hamilton, she spent the day working herself into exhaustion, and the night sleeping as much as she could. Either way, she could almost keep from thinking about Jess and imagining him pacing the halls of a hospital psych ward, eating himself alive over pain and guilt that was not warranted, as far as she could see.

Tamra pulled weeds along the edge of the veranda for most of the next morning, while Sadie played with Evelyn on the lawn. She went into the house to get something to drink and entered to hear the phone ringing. She was tempted to ignore it, wondering if it might be Jess, begging her to come and get him. But she felt more compelled to pick it up.

"Hello," she said.

"Who might this be?" a man asked. Tamra thought for a moment that it was Jess, except that this voice sounded positive and chipper.

"I'm a friend of the family. Could I—"

"Then you must be a friend of mine," he said. "This is Michael."

"Michael?" Tamra said eagerly. "I don't know if you will even remember me, but I hope you do . . . because I've imposed myself on Sadie and moved in. You did invite me . . . but it was a long time ago, and—"

"Don't tell me," he said. "Let me guess. Tall, red-headed American missionary from the Philippines." Tamra laughed with relief. *He'd remembered her.* "But I'm afraid I can't recall your name."

"Tamra Banks," she said.

"Of course," he laughed, "Sister Banks. Well, it's about time you showed up. We'll look forward to seeing you. Hey, I've just got a minute. Can you give Sadie a message for me?"

"Of course."

"I just wanted to make sure she'd gotten the word we were coming. We're actually in Sydney now, and I'm flying my plane in. We'll be leaving in about half an hour, so we should be there about four or five. We'll fly low to let you know we're there. Sadie knows the drill—so does Murphy."

"I'll tell her, of course." Tamra was glad to know he was in a hurry. She didn't want to feel obligated to tell him that his son was in the hospital—for reasons that would likely break his heart.

"Thank you, Tamra."

"I'll look forward to seeing you, Michael," she said. "Oh, I'm sorry. I've only known you as Elder Hamilton . . . but Sadie calls you Michael, and—"

"As long as we're not serving in the same mission, Michael will be just fine. I'll see you soon."

Tamra put down the phone and uttered a silent prayer—that they would travel safely, and they would be strengthened to face what they were coming home to.

Tamra got something to drink and went back outside to give Sadie the message. It was easy to detect that Sadie shared her mixed feelings. It would be good to have them come home, but they would not be met with the homecoming they expected—and deserved.

"I'll tell Murphy to be on alert," Sadie said, "and he can drive out to get them."

A thought occurred to Tamra and she felt compelled to say, "And is Murphy going to tell them about Jess?" Sadie looked concerned but didn't answer. "Are they going to want to come home at all when they know Jess is in the hospital?"

Sadie was quiet a long moment and said, "Then you should go for them. You know more than anyone about the situation, and you're familiar with what's going on at the hospital."

Tamra wanted to protest, but she knew Sadie was right. "How did I get in the middle of this?" she asked, and immediately she felt the answer come to her mind. She could never explain how she knew, but she knew—beyond any doubt—she'd been led here to help keep Jess alive, and to help Michael and Emily deal with the repercussions of their son's actions and behavior. She knew that Sadie was a good woman, but she needed to be with Evelyn, and she didn't have the emotional strength to handle something like this. And Murphy was just an *ornery old bloke,* as Jess would have said—and he needed to be close to his mother. Everyone else around here were simply employees. Perhaps Tamra was new enough to the situation to not be biased, and still emotionally involved enough to care. Knowing what had just been impressed upon her mind, she felt somehow privileged to be chosen by Alexandra Byrnehouse-Davies to do work that she was unable to do from the other side of the veil. She must have known that Michael and Emily were doing the Lord's work halfway across the world, and there was no one else who could be involved enough to ensure that Jess didn't succeed with his attempt to die. Was that the reason for her attraction to Jess? Had she simply needed to be emotionally involved enough to pay attention to what was going on? Or could there be more that she had yet to understand? Either way, she felt a fresh determination to see Alexa's assignment through. As difficult as it was, she was the right person to pick Michael and Emily up at the hangar, and she would remain involved as much as she needed to be—as much as the Spirit guided her to be. And perhaps when this family was patched up, she would move on to find her own life. Or perhaps she already had.

"I don't know why you're here," Sadie answered, startling Tamra to realize that she'd encountered a huge amount of information and insight in a single moment, and Sadie was just now answering her question. "But I'm sure glad you are. I think you might be an answer to our prayers—even if we hadn't known what to pray for. God obviously knew."

"Well, I'm glad to be here . . . if I can make a difference," Tamra said. "I'm going to get cleaned up. I don't want to end up going to the hospital all sweaty and dirty—if that's what they decide to do."

Tamra cleaned up and got ready, then she straightened her room and ironed some blouses. She called the hospital and left a message for Doctor Hill to let them know that she would likely be coming this evening with Jess's parents. She hoped the message got through and the doctor would be there.

Tamra went outside to find Sadie sitting on the veranda with a book, listening to the nursery monitor while Evelyn slept. She sat close by and they visited, exchanging speculations about how Jess might be doing, and how Michael and Emily were going to feel when they got home.

"They've not seen Evelyn in a year, and she's changed so much. They'll sure be happy to see her. Of course they've seen pictures, but still . . . "

Tamra's heart quickened at the sound of a small plane in the distance, then coming closer. Sadie laughed and hurried down the steps to the lawn, waving her arms as the plane flew so low that Tamra could see every detail, including a familiar logo painted on the side: BD&H.

"So, Michael flies his own plane?" she asked Sadie while moving toward the Cruiser that Murphy had left parked in the drive for her to take.

"He does," Sadie said, obviously thrilled that they were actually home. "Jess and James had their pilot's licenses as well. But Jess hasn't flown since the accident and . . . " Their eyes met and the reality descended. Sadie added sadly, "Tell them I've cooked roast chicken and my special gravy, and I'll heat it up for them no matter what time they get here."

"I'll tell them," Tamra said and got into the Cruiser, praying that she could represent Alexa well in caring for her posterity. She drove around the house, through the trees, and beneath the iron archway. She gained speed on the stretch of pavement, a speed that didn't relent when she hit the dirt road. She glanced at the cloud of dust in the rearview mirror, wishing it could veil the ugly scenes playing over and over in her memory. She attempted to rehearse several possibilities of how she might give Michael and Emily the news, but nothing felt right. She finally settled for praying that the Spirit would guide her. And she simply had to accept that she had unwittingly become the messenger with bad tidings.

When she saw the plane approaching, she couldn't keep her heart rate steady. She got out of the Cruiser, pacing and praying as it came in for a landing and pulled neatly into the hangar. She saw pleasant surprise in both their faces as they recognized her. They had known she was around, but they likely hadn't expected her to pick them up. When the engine was turned off, the contrasting silence let Tamra know her heart was pounding in her ears. She watched Michael help Emily out of the plane, while he was saying, "Is that you, little Sister Banks?"

"It's me," she said, amazed at how familiar they looked when it had been so long. "Like I said on the phone, I decided to take up your offer. I should have known you'd be out traipsing around the world again."

Emily laughed as she stepped down and moved toward Tamra, meeting her with a familiar embrace. "Oh, you sweet thing," Emily said. "I'm so glad you came."

"How long have you been here?" Michael asked, taking a turn to embrace her as well.

"Less than two weeks, is all," Tamra explained while Michael closed up the hangar and the three of them each carried luggage to the back of the Cruiser. "Sadie's been wonderful. She took me right in and put me to work. She told me you'd be back soon, and any letter telling you I was here wouldn't get to you before you left, so . . . here I am." Her voice wavered slightly.

"Well, I think it's wonderful," Emily said as they picked up the last pieces of luggage from near the hangar. "It's such a nice surprise to . . . " Her words faded into an expression of concern as she studied Tamra's trembling hands fumbling with the keys. A quick glance at Michael showed that he'd sensed the same anxiety.

"What's wrong?" Emily demanded, pressing a hand over her heart. Tamra couldn't even imagine what thoughts might go through her head after what they'd come home to following the previous mission. "Please don't tell me that—"

"Everyone's fine," Tamra hurried to say. "Relatively speaking, that is."

"Out with it," Michael said firmly. When she hesitated he asked, "Why did you come to get us? Where's Murphy? Is Sadie—"

"I volunteered," she said. "Murphy didn't want to be . . . Well . . . and Sadie is with . . . Evelyn. And she thought it would be better if I were the one to tell you about . . . Jess."

"Jess?" Michael and Emily both said together, then Michael added, "Jess is supposed to be in the States."

"What's wrong with Jess?" Emily asked, her voice trembling.

"Perhaps we should talk on the way," Tamra said, moving toward the Cruiser.

Emily put a hand on her arm and repeated with moisture glistening in her eyes, "What's wrong with Jess?"

Tamra gazed at Emily, then Michael, then Emily again. She cleared her throat and forced herself to give a quick explanation. "Apparently he arrived just a day before I did. All I know is that Heather left him to marry somebody else." Emily pressed a hand over her mouth and Tamra wondered if she might have some sense of what was coming. She forced herself to go on. "To say he's been depressed would be a gross understatement, but . . . " Tamra bit her lip. "He took some pills, and—"

"Merciful heaven," Michael muttered. "What? When?"

"A few days ago," she said, following them to the Cruiser as they suddenly seemed anxious to get moving. "They were just . . . over-the-counter sleeping pills. He's in the hospital, but he's fine."

Michael grabbed the keys from her and opened the driver seat door, but Emily stopped him and held out her hand. "You drive too fast when you're upset," she said. Michael scowled but handed over the keys and Emily got into the driver's seat. Michael opened the passenger door of the front seat, but he motioned Tamra in and closed her door before he got in the backseat.

"Is he . . . " Emily began to ask as she pulled onto the road. She turned pleading eyes toward Tamra. "Tell us . . . is he . . . all right . . . really?"

"Physically, he's going to be fine. Emotionally . . . he's got a long way to go."

"I can't believe it." Emily started to cry. "If only we had known . . . "

"Calm down, Emily, or I'll have to drive," Michael said in a tone that was obviously meant to ease the tension, but Emily simply said, "I'm just fine. So leave me alone and let me drive."

Tamra turned toward Michael and said, "It's okay. I drive fast when I get upset too." Their eyes met and he offered a wan smile. He reminded her so much of Jess that she felt almost startled. He seemed to silently question her staring at him, and she simply said, "He's so much like you."

Michael turned toward the window and a muscle in his jaw twitched—just like Jess. He shook his head slightly and said, "I don't know if that's good or not." He took a deep breath and turned back toward her, asking, "So, how bad off is he?"

"I haven't seen him since the day before yesterday," Tamra said, "but he was . . . " She heard her voice crack and attempted to get it under control. Emily reached a hand over and touched her arm. "He's angry with me because . . . " The words became stuck behind the emotion in her throat.

"Why?" Emily asked.

"Because I'm the one who found him," Tamra cried. "And he said if I had stayed away . . . he would be . . . out of his misery."

Emily began to cry again. Michael groaned and hit the seat with his fist. Emily wiped at her tears and murmured, "I thank God that you *were* there."

"Amen," Michael muttered, and Tamra realized Emily was driving faster than she would ever dream of driving.

"Tell us what happened, Tamra," Emily urged. "Tell us everything you know."

Tamra did her best to repeat everything she knew about Jess's emotional state leading up to the incident, leaving out his confessions of love in the stable. It was most difficult to tell them that he'd admitted to finding it hard to face his parents.

"Why would he feel that way?" Emily asked Michael, as if he'd have the answer.

He just shook his head and said, "I don't know. But I pray we can find out." He motioned for Tamra to go on.

"That night," she said, "I was feeling badly about something that had been said between us, and I was thinking I would talk to him in the morning and smooth it over. I actually heard a voice in my head tell me to tell him immediately. It told me twice."

Emily put a hand over her heart and her chin quivered. Michael sighed loudly. "You know," Emily said, "there have been thousands of times in my life when I've been grateful to have the gospel . . . and to have the gift of the Spirit in our lives, but . . . "

"That's got to be the top of the list," Michael finished for her.

"Yeah," Emily said. Then she motioned toward Tamra with her hand. "Go on. We need to know what we're dealing with before we get there."

She told them how the Spirit had prompted her to open the door, and what she had found. Emily cried silent tears as the story unfolded, and a quick glance at Michael revealed that he was doing the same. She couldn't even comprehend their heartache. Tamra went on to tell them of their encounters at the hospital, and his different moods, and all Doctor Hill had said. Following a lengthy silence where they seemed to be taking it all in, Michael said, "Do you remember, Emily, what I said to you more than once about a particular sister missionary in the Philippines?"

Tamra turned toward him and found him gazing at her, even though he was speaking to his wife.

"I remember," Emily said, glancing toward Tamra.

"What?" Tamra demanded when they obviously weren't going to tell her.

"I just had a feeling about you," Michael said. "But I never dreamed . . . "

"That you would save our son's life," Emily finished for him.

"Yeah," Michael said, and she wondered how close two people had to be to finish each other's sentences and think each other's thoughts.

Emily pulled the Cruiser into the hospital parking lot and turned off the engine. "Well, here we go," she said and they all got out.

"Lead the way," Michael said, putting a hand on Emily's arm.

Tamra led them into the restricted area of the hospital, once the nurse knew who they were. She was relieved when they were told, "If you'll wait right over there for a few minutes, Doctor Hill asked us to page her when you arrived. I think she wants to be there when you go in."

"Is that a bad sign?" Emily asked Tamra as they were seated.

"I don't know. Maybe, but . . . it's probably better if she's there. I don't think he's going to be happy to see any of us."

Tamra felt some relief to see Doctor Hill approaching. She felt confident that this woman could handle just about anything—even an angry Jess Hamilton. They all stood and Tamra introduced her to Jess's parents. The doctor urged them to sit back down and she sat to face them.

"I understand," she said to Michael and Emily, "that you've been out of the country for several months, and you've not seen him at all."

"That's right," Michael said. "We've been exchanging letters weekly, but we had believed he was still in the States."

"Well, I'll be frank with you; he's not happy about seeing you. It's been difficult to get him to be completely honest, but I believe it boils down to one thing: he's ashamed because he believes he's let you down, he's failed you. He believes the accident was his fault, and he wishes that he would have died instead of his brother, or his friend."

Emily started to cry, saying, "I'm sorry. I just . . . "

"You're welcome to cry, Mrs. Hamilton. Better that you release some of the pressure out here. I don't mean he shouldn't see you cry, because that could be good. But you don't want to get really upset." Emily nodded.

"So, what now?" Michael asked the doctor.

"Well, we're going to go in there and talk to him. Depending on how he responds, you can take him home with you. I really believe that, deep down, he's grateful that he survived, and it scared him enough that he's not going to try it again. But I want to see how he actually responds and interacts with you. I think he'd be better off at home. You don't have to babysit him twenty-four hours a day, but there are signs you need to watch for, and we need to set up some regular appointments for counseling through the coming weeks."

Doctor Hill went over some of the warning signs of depression that could lead to suicidal tendencies. She gave them some literature to read, which Emily stuck into her large purse.

"So, are you ready?" the doctor asked.

"Yes," Emily said firmly.

"Uh . . . " Tamra said, "Maybe I should just wait out here, and—"

"No," the doctor said, "from what Jess has told me, your involvement here is important, Tamra. You need to be there."

The doctor put a hand on Tamra's arm and walked with her toward Jess's room, while Tamra bit her tongue to keep from asking what Jess might have said about her.

The doctor pushed open the door to his room, holding up one finger to indicate that they wait just a moment. Tamra heard her say, "Hello, Jess. Guess what?"

"What?" he retorted and Tamra saw Emily squeeze her eyes shut briefly.

"You've got company."

The doctor opened the door wide and the three of them slipped inside. There was no light in the room beyond the glow of the evening sun, coming through an east window. Jess was seated low in a chair near the window, his legs stretched out, his feet bare. He saw Tamra first, but his expression was unreadable. Then he saw his parents and abruptly looked away, closing his eyes. While everyone else in the room seemed unsure what to do, Emily dropped her purse and rushed to Jess's side. She knelt beside him and touched his chin. He turned further away. She moved closer, took his face into her hands and forced him to face her. But he kept his eyes closed. Tamra noticed his hands gripping the armrests of the chair as if they could save him.

"Jess," she said with firm gentleness, "look at me."

He slowly opened his eyes to find his mother's face within inches of his own. She could see him clearly expecting to be reprimanded, but Emily simply said, "I love you, Jess." Tears trickled down her face. "You have no comprehension of how thoroughly precious you are to me. And I am so grateful that you're alive. Nothing else matters, Jess . . . just that you're alive. There is *nothing* we can't work out . . . as long as you're alive."

Tamra watched Jess's hard expression falter into that raw childlike vulnerability that showed itself rarely. She pressed a hand over her mouth to hold back her own emotion as she saw the shame and regret rise into his eyes along with a glisten of tears that slid down his cheeks. He sobbed and crumbled in his mother's arms, crying like a child against her shoulder. Emily looked up at Michael and he moved a couple of chairs toward them. When Jess's emotion quieted somewhat, Michael urged Emily into a chair beside him. Michael sat directly facing his son and put his hands on Jess's shoulders.

"I can't say it the way your mother can, Jess. But I echo her words exactly. I love you, son, and nothing else matters."

Jess wiped away another stream of tears and embraced his father.

"How do you feel, Jess?" Doctor Hill asked.

"Better," he said and sniffled. "But . . . I can't go home and pretend that everything's all right, and act like nothing ever happened. I don't want everybody tiptoeing around me, afraid to say certain things."

"So, what do you want to do?" the doctor asked.

"I want to feel normal. If somebody wants to talk about the accident . . . or James . . . or anything else to do with it, I want them to talk about it. I hate it when conversations stop as soon as I come in the room, or when . . . they look at me as if I'm going to go over the edge or something."

"Okay," the doctor said, "but you've exhibited some pretty strong behavior over the things you're talking about. If your family and friends talk openly about such things, can you handle it?"

"If I can't . . . I'll say so."

"That sounds fair," the doctor said and turned to his parents. "Does that sound fair?"

"Absolutely," Michael said and Emily nodded.

"Is there anything else?" the doctor asked Jess. He hesitated, but Tamra sensed his need to say something. "When we talked earlier, you had some concerns. I think they should be addressed before you leave, don't you?"

"Yes," Jess said.

"So, now's your chance."

"Well, I . . . " he looked at every occupant of the room, then looked at the floor. "I tried to kill myself, and I was prepared to succeed. I'm glad I didn't. I really am. But I know that you," he nodded toward his father, then his mother, "and you," then he nodded toward Tamra, "and even you, must have some pretty strong opinions about what I did." He cleared his throat loudly and sighed. "I don't want to go home and have to wonder what you're thinking about what I did. I want to clear the air right here . . . right now. And if something comes up later about it, I want it said straight out." He looked at Tamra again and added, "You're very good at that, Ms. Banks. Maybe you should start."

Tamra was taken so off guard that she could hardly think straight. She finally said, "I told you how I felt the other day."

"Do you remember what she said, Jess?" the doctor asked.

"Oh, I certainly do. She told me that I had problems, and that I needed help. And she told me that taking twenty-five sleeping pills was a good indication that I had problems . . . or words to that effect." He looked at Tamra with something close to respect shining through his cloudy eyes. "She told me she was the one who saved my life, and I should be glad she had because I would not want to face my brother or my ancestors as a coward. And she told me . . . Oh, this is my favorite part. She told me I was selfish."

Tamra shot a quick glance at Michael and Emily to gauge their reaction to this. Emily looked amazed, and Michael actually looked proud of her; he was almost smiling.

"And," Jess went on, "she said she would not be responsible for me and have to wonder if I would slit my wrists or shoot myself in the head. And the grand finale was when she said that I could stay here and rot—but at least I would be alive. Did I miss anything?" he asked Tamra.

Tamra warded off her embarrassment and said, "I think you covered it pretty well, except I didn't call you a coward."

"Not in so many words," he said and she wondered how much time he'd spent pondering that conversation in order to remember it so accurately.

"Is there anything else you want to say to him, Tamra?" the doctor asked, standing up long enough to turn on a lamp.

"Not that I can think of at the moment," she said. She felt relieved that he had left out any conversation they'd had in reference to their personal feelings.

"Okay," the doctor said, "who wants to go next?"

"I do," Emily said and leaned close to Jess, taking both his hands into hers. "I'm glad you asked us to clear the air. I think that's a good idea. Because there's a thought that just won't leave me . . . ever since Tamra told us what you'd done. And I would like to share it with you so that I can let it go." She leaned a little closer and said, "I gave you life, Jess. I felt you moving inside of me. I felt your spirit with me as you prepared to come to this world. And the moment you were born was one of the greatest of my life. I have treasured every moment of your life. You have brought unspeakable joy to me and your father. Your life has purpose and meaning, Jess, no matter how difficult it might be. And no one but God has the right to say when your life will end. *No one!*" Emily cried as she added with vehemence, "How dare you! How dare you be so selfish as to think you could take another son from me when I have already lost two?"

"But," Jess choked the words out, "it's my fault you lost James . . . and it should have been me, and . . . "

"No, Jess," Emily said. "It was an accident. And I know in my heart it was his time to go. But it's not your time to go, Jess. It wasn't then, and it's not now." Tamra felt a fear that she suspected his parents shared when she saw the blatant disbelief in Jess's eyes. He simply didn't believe what she had just said. But his expression softened when she added, "You are loved and needed and you have much to be grateful for. And you will not leave this earth until God takes you."

Tamra saw Jess wipe a stray tear from his face. Emily leaned back and said, "That's all I have to say."

"Anything you want to say to her, Jess?" the doctor asked. Jess shook his head and Doctor Hill motioned toward Michael. "I think it's your turn, Dad."

Tamra noted that Michael looked subtly angry as he crossed an ankle over his knee and nervously rubbed his fingers over his lower pant leg. "I was with your mother when you were born. And it was the most amazing experience of my life, up to that point. You know I married your mother when she had three daughters. I quickly grew to love them as my own. But you were *my son*—my firstborn. And seeing you come into this world is something I will never forget. It was a miracle. But let me go back a few months. I had never imagined what a woman goes through in pregnancy to bring a child into this world. Her misery and pain and sickness were all for you. And that was nothing compared to the actual reality of childbirth. Until you see your own child come into this world, son, you will have no comprehension of the true miracle of life. And yet that was only the beginning."

Jess turned away and Michael said almost sternly, "Look at me, son. This is important." Jess met his father's eyes again, but Tamra could see the shame and regret there that were heartbreaking.

"When you and your brother were not very old, your mother had a miscarriage. I barely got her to the hospital before she hemorrhaged and her heart stopped." Jess's eyes widened. He'd obviously never heard this story. "She died, Jess, if only briefly, trying to bring a child into this world. And it could have been you. I realized then the full spectrum of what they mean when they say that a woman walks through the valley of the shadow of death when she gives birth." Michael sighed and added, "I just want you to think about that. And I think you owe both of these women an apology—the woman who gave you life, and the woman who saved your life. And you owe them both a great debt of gratitude. But I don't think you should attempt that right now. I believe you should think about it, and when you're ready, you do what you feel you need to in order to make it right with them. That's all I have to say."

Following a minute of silence, Doctor Hill said, "Jess, is there anything else you want to say?"

Jess's voice cracked as he said, "I want to live . . . and I want to go home."

"I think that's what we all want," the doctor said. "Jess, why don't you get your things together while your parents take care of some paperwork, and then you can go home with them."

Jess slumped with an audible sigh of relief. "It would be a pleasure," he said and came to his feet. Emily and Michael each embraced him tightly then left the room with Doctor Hill. Tamra met Jess's eyes, wishing she could read his thoughts. As she turned to follow the others out, Jess said, "Wait." She stopped but left her back to him. "I owe you an apology. You must believe me when I tell you that I'm truly sorry for what I put you through. You told me the other night that we needed to talk, and yes . . . we do. Not now, but . . . soon."

Tamra turned toward him and managed a smile. "I'll look forward to it." Seeing his humble countenance, she ventured to clear a point that she wished had been cleared when the doctor was in the room. But she thought it would be better now than to wait. "You remembered what I said the other day, but you didn't tell me how you *feel* about what I said." He hesitated and she added, "Should I be embarrassed . . . or sorry . . . for being so obnoxious with a man who has . . . " Her voice broke. She glanced down and cleared her throat. " . . . who has more pain in his heart than I could possibly comprehend?"

He seemed touched by her compassion. "No," he said. "I think you said exactly what I needed to hear . . . even though I didn't want to hear it. I've thought a great deal about what you've said. And I think you are a very courageous . . . and amazing woman."

Tamra met his eyes, startled to see the sincerity there. Seeing him so open, so humble, so honest, almost made her melt into the floor. And he'd called her courageous and amazing. This was the Jess

Hamilton she had hoped to find behind the clouds of his pain. While she wanted to spill her every feeling, her every hope, she simply smiled and said, "It's nice to have you back, Jess. Put your shoes on. Let's go home."

Chapter Eight

Tamra left the room and walked down the hall where she found Emily going over papers with one of the nurses, and Michael standing close by. When he saw her he motioned her toward him and put his arms around her in a fatherly embrace. Pulling back he put his hands on her shoulders, saying, "You're the best thing that's ever happened to him. Things could be rough for a while. But don't give up on him too easily." By the way he said it, Tamra wondered if he'd sensed her attraction for Jess—or his for her.

She simply nodded and turned toward Emily when she too, offered an embrace. "Thank you, my dear," Emily said, "for everything."

Tamra felt suddenly ridden with guilt, knowing she had omitted something very important from what she knew of Jess's situation. In spite of what she had attempted to clarify with Jess—and feelings she simply didn't feel ready to bare—there was something Michael and Emily needed to know. They couldn't work together to help Jess if everything wasn't laid out on the table.

When Emily had signed the last paper, Tamra urged Michael and Emily to a private corner of the waiting area, saying, "There's something I need to tell you . . . before we go." The emotion threatening to erupt made her realize how deeply this had been eating at her. But she attempted to choke it back and forged ahead. "You need to know that his concern over facing the two of you when you came home was only part of what hit him that day."

"What do you mean?" Michael asked.

"That same day, I . . . " She became too emotional to speak and Emily guided her to a chair.

"What is it, dear?" she asked.

"He . . . he kissed me, and . . . he told me that . . . he loved me, and . . . " She saw their eyes widen in unison. "And I told him that I . . . was probably just a convenient rebound after losing Heather. I told him that if he needed a friend, I would be there for him. And if he was attracted to me, that was fine, but . . . I told him not to be labeling feelings he didn't understand." She whimpered and sniffled. "And I told him that I didn't know how he could possibly love me, when he didn't even know me. And he couldn't possibly get to know me when he saw nothing but himself."

With her confession finally spilled, Tamra wrapped her arms around her middle and sobbed. She felt Emily's arm around her and gratefully accepted her shoulder to cry on. "What is it, dear?" she asked. "Why are you so upset?"

"I was too hard on him," she said. "If I had known . . . he was so depressed . . . I could have been more careful, and . . . "

"Hey," Michael said, putting a hand on her shoulder, "you said all the right things, Tamra. You had no way of knowing. And being dishonest with him isn't going to help him."

"But . . . if he had died . . . I don't know if I could have forgiven myself."

Emily looked into Tamra's eyes and said, "Which is exactly Jess's problem." Tamra felt her eyes widen. "You have to be stronger than that, Tamra. Whether it ever comes up or not, he needs to know that you would have gotten over it, because it was out of your hands. Just like that accident was out of his hands. Do you understand?"

Tamra nodded and Emily handed her a tissue. She stood and Michael wiped at her tears. "You gonna be okay?" he asked and she nodded, feeling as if she'd known these people forever.

They all turned together to move toward the hall, then stopped when they saw Jess standing across the room, holding his bag, watching them speculatively. Tamra felt momentarily panicked until she reasoned that he couldn't have possibly overheard anything that had been said. But she wondered what he thought about her crying to his parents.

"You ready to go?" Emily asked, approaching him with a smile.

"Extremely," he said.

The final order of business was Doctor Hill handing Jess a card with an appointment written on it. "My office address is on there," she said. "I'll see you in a couple of days."

He nodded then extended a hand to the doctor, saying, "Thank you."

"You're welcome, Jess. You take care of yourself." She glanced at Michael, Emily, and Tamra, then back to him. "You have much to live for."

"Yes, I know," he said and led the way to the elevator.

Little was said as they walked outside into the dark. Tamra noticed Emily holding Michael's hand, but it seemed too natural between them to be a result of the day's drama. She suspected it was a common habit when they were together.

As they found where the Cruiser was parked, Tamra said, "Oh, Sadie told me to tell you that she'd made roast chicken and her special gravy, and she would heat it up no matter what time you got home."

"Oh, that is divine," Michael said.

Emily handed Michael the keys and said, "You're driving—now that we're not in a hurry."

"Oh, but I am in a hurry," Michael said, opening the front passenger door for Emily. "I need to get home to Sadie's special gravy."

Tamra walked around to get in the backseat, but Jess followed her and opened the door. She glanced at him and he motioned her in before he closed the door and walked back to the other side to get in.

After driving a few minutes in silence, Jess said to his parents, "So tell us about your mission. Tell us all the things you never had time to put in letters."

Tamra was relieved to hear them start talking, and she sensed Jess's need to feel some normalcy and distraction. She was surprised to glance toward him and find him looking at her. She saw him smile through the darkness before she smiled and turned away. A few minutes later he reached for her hand and squeezed it gently, a gesture that warmed Tamra through.

Tamra tried to focus on the stories Michael and Emily were telling, but she felt more preoccupied with the feel of Jess's hand in hers, and all it represented. She felt hope in putting behind them the ugly scenes of the last few days. And having something as drastic as a suicide attempt in the picture, as difficult as it was, had brought about some good in getting Jess to open up more. And he would be going to counseling for quite some time. Feeling his hand in hers reminded her of the kisses they'd shared in the hospital—and the stable. She put her other hand over her stomach in response to a swarm of butterflies. He had told her he loved her, and when he squeezed her hand, as if to remind her that he was still there, she felt certain that he did. It was becoming easier to imagine a day beyond his healing when they could embark on a future together. While she reminded herself not to be presumptuous, she couldn't help indulging in such an incredible fantasy.

Tamra leaned her head back on the seat when she began to feel sleepy. The next thing she was aware of was Jess's shoulder easing beneath her head as his arm came around her, and she realized she'd fallen asleep. She opened her eyes long enough to see that he'd moved over to sit beside her, and she shifted her weight to get more comfortable. Succumbing to this warm security, she closed her eyes and relaxed again but she didn't go back to sleep. Her hand inadvertently came to rest in the center of his chest, and she was surprised to feel his heart beating quickly when he was apparently relaxed. Was there some reason he would be feeling anxiety? She shifted her head in an effort to see his face, but it was hidden by shadows. He pressed a kiss to her brow and tightened his arm around her. Tamra decided to enjoy the moment and not try to analyze him too deeply.

"Hey," Michael said, "is there a cell phone in here?"

"In the glove box," Tamra said and Emily found it.

"Here," Michael said, handing it back over the seat and Tamra took it. "Call Sadie and tell her we're taking her up on that promise. She can take a nap tomorrow."

Jess took the phone from Tamra and made the call. She smiled to hear his jovial tone as he said, "Are you awake, Sadie? Well, good, because we'll be home in about twenty minutes and we're *starving!*" He chuckled and said, "Yes, it's good to hear you too, Sadie. Yes, I'm fine actually, so don't go starting any nasty rumors about me." He chuckled again and said, "No, Sadie, I'm not calling you a gossip. But you *are* a great cook. Tamra told us you had roast chicken and gravy, and I do believe she's a relatively honest person, so we're counting on it." He listened for a minute and said more seriously, "Thank you,

Sadie . . . Yes, I agree. I'll tell her you said so . . . Yes, she's with me. And yes, my parents are with me too."

"Hello, Sadie," Michael and Emily both said loudly and Jess laughed.

"She's hyperventilating," he said to his parents. "You'd better hurry."

Jess got off the phone and handed it back to his mother.

"Tell me what?" Tamra asked softly.

"She said she was glad I was alive, and she was grateful that you'd been around when we needed you. Like I said, I agree."

"Amen," Michael said, then it was silent until he pulled the Cruiser up beside the house. The outside lights were on, and Michael had barely stepped out before Sadie came running out the door and over the lawn. He barely got Emily's door open before he turned and swept Sadie into his arms with a hearty laugh. He actually lifted her feet off the ground and turned her around once before he set her back down.

"Glad to see us, eh?" Michael said.

"You have no idea," Sadie replied, and turned to embrace Emily.

Jess slid out the door and reached out a hand to help Tamra. He held onto it as they followed the others into the house, while Sadie assaulted them with questions.

Following their late-night feast, they all sat around the table and visited for another hour before they all worked together to clean up the kitchen enough to last until morning.

"Well, I'm going to bed," Jess said, moving toward the door.

"Wait," Michael said. "Would you let me give you a father's blessing?"

Jess looked surprised but said, "Sure. I could use all the help I can get."

Jess sat on a chair and Tamra wondered if it would be more appropriate for her to be absent. She moved discreetly toward the door, saying, "I'll just go on and—"

"No, you'll stay right here," Jess said, grabbing her arm as she went past him. He pointed to a chair and she sat beside Sadie.

Tamra was glad she had been invited to stay when she saw Michael put his hands on Jess's head, and a sweet spirit filled the room. She closed her eyes and listened as Michael poured out his love and concern through his priesthood authority. He spoke of Heavenly Father's love for Jess, and the power of the Atonement that was there to heal his wounds and remove his pain, if he would just reach out and take it. Tamra discreetly wiped away her tears, praying that Jess would be able to take those words to heart.

When the blessing was over, Jess stood and embraced each of his parents, saying, "Thank you. It's good to have you home . . . and to be home."

"Amen," Emily said.

* * *

Jess awoke to find his room filled with bright sunlight. He had the sensation of waking from a very long, very bad dream. He groaned as the memories assured him that it really had happened. He had completely lost his mind. Thinking of the possibility that he could be dead right now, he felt an inner trembling that had been a common companion following the accident. But this time, it had been no accident. He really had gone over the edge. How else could he ever justify doing what he'd done? He was grateful to be alive; he truly was. But the very fact that he'd done something so *insane* only seemed to contribute to his sense of inadequacy that seemed to block his every effort to get on with his life.

Jess tried to force his mind to a pleasant thought that might block out the images of group therapy in the psych ward, hazy segments of having his stomach pumped, and perhaps worst of all, facing his parents with the shame of what he'd done. He talked himself into believing that the worst was over and forced his mind to the one bright spot in this drama he had created: *Tamra.*

Jess had completely gotten out of the habit of praying, but when he pondered the reality that he was alive and Tamra was living down the hall, he felt compelled to utter aloud, "Thank you, God." He couldn't manage to get anything out beyond that.

Feeling hungry, Jess took a quick shower, put on a denim shirt and his oldest jeans, and pushed a hand through his wet hair. He went downstairs to find the house completely quiet. He first peeked in the kitchen, then walked up the long hall toward the front of the house, looking into every room. He finally found life in the lounge room. His heart quickened just to see Tamra stretched out on the sofa, apparently asleep, a book left open on her chest, her stockinged feet dangling over the end. He couldn't help smiling. The opportunity was just too good to pass up.

Jess quietly put a hand on the back of the sofa for leverage and bent over with the intention of waking her with a kiss. Her eyes opened just before he tilted his nose to miss hers and he stopped.

"Hello, Sleeping Beauty," he said, his lips almost touching hers, but not quite.

"Hello, Prince Charming," she replied.

Jess chuckled. "You must have the wrong guy . . . wrong fairy tale. I'm more like . . . Beauty and the Beast."

She laughed softly and lifted her lips to his. "The beast became the hero in the end," she said, looking into his eyes. Jess saw the unmasked adoration there and marveled at the hope she gave him.

"I know," she added as he stood up straight, "because I've watched the Disney video with Evelyn about twelve times. It's her favorite."

"I'll have to join the two of you one of these days."

"I'll make popcorn," Tamra said, sitting up.

"What you reading?" he asked, taking the book before it fell. He looked at the front of the old leather-bound book and read aloud, "Alexandra Byrnehouse-Davies." He added to Tamra, "You're reading my great-great-grandmother's journals?"

"Yes, I told you I was last week."

"Did you?" he asked. "I'd forgotten. Is it any good?" he asked, setting it on the coffee table.

"Best thing I've ever read," she said, "beyond the Book of Mormon, of course."

"Of course," he said. "Where is everybody?"

"Your parents are outside taking Evelyn for a walk before her nap. Sadie's already taking *her* nap. We kept her up way too late, and Evelyn didn't let her sleep in."

"Well, I'm starving," he said. "Have you eaten?"

"I had a piece of toast when I first got up, but I'm pretty hungry myself. I'm sure we can find something to make a great sandwich."

"Sounds perfect," he said and offered a hand to help her stand up.

She took a few steps toward the door until he tugged on her hand and said, "Wait a minute. There's something I need to say."

She turned to face him eye to eye. He glanced down to see that she'd slipped some clogs onto her feet. With his feet bare, he had absolutely no advantage in height. "I'm listening," she said when he hesitated.

"My father was right," he said, "I owe you an apology."

"You apologized last night, Jess. And you did it very well."

"Well, thanks, but . . . I don't think I covered everything."

"Okay, but . . . whether or not your dad was right, don't say anything to me if you don't mean it."

"No," he said, "I think I've come to know you better than that. I think you would know if I wasn't sincere. But just so you don't have to wonder, this is sincere. I'm truly sorry, Tamra."

She blew out a long breath. "I must admit it's nice to hear you say that—again; it helps. But I have to know . . . what exactly you're apologizing for."

He snorted a laugh. "Where do I start?"

"The beginning."

"I'm sorry for . . . being so obnoxious with you . . . for being angry . . . for saying anything I might have said that was hurtful, because . . . I really do owe you my life, and . . . now that it's over I . . . " His voice broke and he hung his head. "I really am glad to be alive . . . and were it not for you . . . I wouldn't be." He lifted his head to look at her again. "So, thank you, Tamra." His voice broke as he touched her face and added in a whisper, "I'm so grateful to be alive."

Seeing tears glistening in his eyes, Tamra found it impossible to hold back her own emotions. A sob erupted from her throat. The moment Jess's arms came around her, the full torrent of her fear on his behalf came bursting into the open. She felt his lips on her brow and his hands at her back, urging her closer. She pressed her face to his throat and pulled the fabric of his shirt into her fists while she wept without control.

"I thought I had lost you," she finally managed to say. "I had barely found you, and I thought you were lost to me forever. Just when I had realized that I loved you . . . I thought I had lost you."

The tears overcame her again, but Jess took her shoulders into his hands and looked into her eyes. "What did you just say?"

Tamra tried to recall her words. She shook her head and choked back a sob. And then it came to her. The hope and expectation in his eyes compelled her to admit, "That's what I had come to tell you . . . that night . . . and what I tried to tell you in the hospital."

"What?" he asked.

"I came to tell you that . . . I had been harsh and insensitive. I think I was afraid of my own feelings as much as what you were telling me. But when I thought you were gone, I . . . " Her emotion rose again. "I realized how petty pride and fear really are." She touched his face. "I love you, Jess. And I can only say that because it's true. And whether or not you meant what you said to me is something that—"

"I *did* mean it, Tamra," he said, his eyes soft. "I know my life is a mess. I know I'm confused, and lost. But I want to be the kind of man you deserve. And hearing you say what you just said . . . I could almost believe that such a thing is possible."

Tamra laughed more than cried as she wrapped her arms around him. "Just stay alive, Jess. Anything is possible . . . if you'll just stay alive."

"I promise," he said. "At least . . . well, as far as it's in my control." He looked into her eyes and admitted, "I really don't want to die, Tamra. If there's one thing I've learned from this, I'm more afraid of dying than of staying alive."

"Why?" she asked, feeling concerned.

He chuckled tensely and glanced down. "As you pointed out a few days ago, there are people on the other side that I'm not ready to face. Not now—not like that."

Tamra smiled and touched his face. "Let's get something to eat," he said. Tamra picked up the journal she'd been reading and they walked together to the kitchen, holding hands.

Jess watched Tamra open the fridge and start pulling sandwich items out to place them on the table. Her confessions of love and her anguish on his behalf, swirled in his mind with an almost surreal quality. While he had trouble convincing himself that he'd actually attempted suicide and ended up in the psych ward, he found it equally difficult to fathom that this incredible woman had come into his life just when he'd needed her so desperately. And while his feelings for her were something he'd simply accepted without question or analysis, her feelings for him left him baffled. He wanted to talk to her about these feelings they shared, but the very idea of approaching such a topic seemed like a foreign language. He reminded himself of

Doctor Hill's repeated admonition through their many counseling sessions at the hospital. *You've got to talk about your feelings and concerns, Jess, especially with the people you care about most.*

Jess figured he'd been given a second chance at life, and while he found it difficult to believe he could ever really make much of it, he certainly had to try. Perhaps learning to talk openly with Tamra about his feelings was a good place to start. Watching her fix some sandwiches while he filled two glasses with ice and found the potato chips, he decided now was just as good a time as any.

"Tamra," he said while she artistically arranged thin slices of turkey on a slice of bread, "why do you love me?" She froze and he added, "How do you know it's love?"

Tamra turned slowly to look at him, wondering if he was questioning the validity of her feelings—or his. That recently familiar vulnerability rose in his eyes, prompting her to realize the answer to his question was extremely important. And she was glad that he'd asked it. Still, she had to admit, "I need a minute to think about that; some things are difficult to put into words."

Jess could certainly agree with that. "Of course," he said.

But he was taken off guard when she asked, "If I tell *you,* will you tell *me?*"

He thought about that for half a minute before he said, "I'll do my best; some things are difficult to put into words."

Tamra offered a slight smile and finished fixing the sandwiches while he got a couple of sodas and put everything on a tray.

"How do you know what I like on my sandwich?" he asked as she put them on two plates and cut them in half.

"I've watched you make a sandwich more than once," she said and smiled again.

Jess picked up the tray and she picked up the journal she'd been reading. He followed her out to the veranda, feeling for the first time in years that perhaps there really was a God. What other reason could there be for such an angel to show up in his life?

After Tamra offered a blessing over their meal, they began to eat while she contemplated the questions he'd posed to her in the kitchen. Her sandwich was half eaten when a point of reference occurred to her that would help her explain the way she was feeling. And with the idea came a warm tingling that left her briefly dazed. But Jess remained completely silent, as if he was allowing her the time she needed to ponder his questions. All of her sandwich was gone before she found the courage to admit what she'd just realized. But still, she was hesitant.

"It's been more than a minute," he finally said when they were both completely finished eating. "Have you thought about it?"

"I sure have," she said and turned to look directly at him. He leaned his elbows on the table and pressed his clasped fingers to his mouth. "You know, Jess, in every logical way, it seems ludicrous to feel this way about you, so to try and explain it is . . ."

"Ludicrous?" he guessed.

"Perhaps, but . . . I'm going to try, and I trust that I won't be casting pearls before swine." She gave him a teasing smile and he smiled back, letting her know that he recalled a previous conversation where the attitudes between them had been much different.

"You know," she went on, "this idea of analyzing love is new to me. I had a few boyfriends in high school and college—before I joined the Church. But I was too young for love to ever be an issue. I had one boyfriend who frequently claimed to love me, but I remember thinking it was just puppy love—an infatuation based more on physical attraction than anything else. I dated quite a bit after my mission, but I never felt much of anything."

While she was gathering words to go on, he said, "So how do you know that what we feel isn't just that? Infatuation? Physical attraction?"

"I'm trying to get to that," she said.

"Sorry."

"There's no question about the physical attraction here," she admitted, unable to look at him directly. "My stomach quivers when you walk into a room. My heart quickens when you look at me. And when you kiss me . . . I feel like I'm going to melt into the ground."

"Yeah, I know what you mean," he said and she turned to look at him just as he leaned back lazily in his chair, his eyes penetrating hers in a way that provoked all three of the sensations she had just described. He smiled subtly as if he'd felt it too. And she wondered if he could read her mind when he said, "Yeah, just like that."

Tamra took a deep breath, attempting to suppress emotions that lured her away from the practical aspects of this conversation. Still holding his eyes, she said, "I'm not naive enough to believe that such feelings could carry two people through a lifetime. I'm certain the breathtaking excitement of new love eventually subsides, and if there's no substance there to take its place, that attraction dissipates into disillusionment. Perhaps there's a difference between being in love and loving someone."

Jess thought about that for a minute and asked, "And which would best describe my parents, do you think? Are they in love, or do they love each other?"

"Both," she answered quickly and he knew she was right. Their commitment and respect were as evident as the adoration and attraction they felt for each other.

"So," he pressed, feeling vaguely nervous, "which is it with us, Tamra? Are you in love with me? Or do you love me?"

"Both," she said just as quickly.

Perhaps trying to provoke her—or perhaps needing some clarification—he said, "But we're practically strangers, Tamra. How can what we feel be any more than . . . infatuation? Maybe we're both forging ahead into something that has nothing substantial to hold it together. Perhaps we're just fools in love, Tamra, with no reason to believe we should even consider going on another day with declarations of love between us."

"Is that what you think?" she asked, an edge to her voice.

Jess leaned forward abruptly and lowered his voice to a coarse whisper. "No, Tamra, I want you to explain to me why every time I look at you—or even think of you—I feel something so thoroughly . . . *compelling,* something I never even dreamed of feeling again." He took her hand across the table and his voice became as intense as his eyes. "I want you to tell me why what I feel for you makes me almost believe that life without you would simply not be worth living."

Tamra took a sharp breath as she perceived the implication. She had to ask, "Is that why you took those pills? You believed I didn't share your feelings?"

He let go of her hand and leaned back, apparently unsettled by the question. But he answered it straightly. "No. It was much more complicated than that. I don't know exactly why I did it. Maybe when I do, I won't need any more counseling. But I think I was close to that point before I came home."

Tamra gauged her feelings and decided she'd get no better opportunity to clear up a point that had troubled her. "Well, I'm glad to know it wasn't me who drove you to the edge, Jess, because we both know we can't predict the future. The outcome of this relationship remains to be seen. The circumstances between us need time. I can't have an honest relationship with you—to any degree—if I have to fear that its outcome might drive you to the edge again. Forgive me if this sounds harsh, Jess, but I'm sitting here talking to you this way because I know in my heart it's the best place for me to be right now. I will always do my best to be fair and honest with you. And I expect the same in return. But if it doesn't work out between us, whatever you choose to do is your choice."

"In other words," Jess said, "whatever happens between us, if I choose to kill myself, it's my problem."

"Exactly."

"And you wouldn't rush to save my life again?" he asked.

"Oh, I would," she said firmly. "But it would never change my feelings or my decisions."

"So, you'd save me, but then you'd leave me to rot."

"Whether or not you rot, Jess, is completely up to you," Tamra said, feeling her palms sweat. He stared at her hard and she almost expected him to get up and storm away. Gradually a reluctant smile crept into his countenance and she realized he'd been teasing her—at least to some degree.

"You rogue!" she growled then laughed softly.

"Yes, I am," he said proudly. "It runs in the family . . . or so I'm told. But seriously, Tamra." He reached for her hand again. "I'm glad you said what you just did, because I have to admit that I've wondered in the last half an hour if you would tell me you love me just to keep me from going over the edge. And I could never have any kind of relationship with you if I felt like you were tiptoeing around my emotions. So thank you. Your strength may actually get us both through whatever might lie ahead." He looked out over the view and said in a sad voice, "I want to believe I can get beyond what I'm dealing with, Tamra. But the truth is, I can't even begin to understand what I'm dealing with. I have an illness. It's like there's some . . . raging emotional cancer growing inside of me. I don't know how to fix it, and I don't know how long it will take. I don't even know if it's possible to ever fix it." He turned to look at her and added with passion, "But you make me want to try. You must believe me when I say that whether we have a chance of ending up together or not, your being in my life right now gives me the strength and the hope I need to get out of bed tomorrow, and the next day, and the next. A man in my position can't make any promises, when I can't even take care of myself."

Tamra squeezed his hand and said, "One day at a time is good enough for me, Jess . . . within reason, of course."

He smiled at her and echoed, "Of course."

"So," he said a minute later, "you still haven't told me how you know you love me."

"And you're hoping I can explain how *you* know you love *me.*"

"That's right," he said.

"Well, what if I don't have an answer? What if it simply has no logical explanation?"

Jess couldn't come up with an appropriate reply. Following a few minutes of silence, Tamra finally said, "If I tell you something, will you promise not to think I'm crazy?"

"You're asking *me* to not think *you* are crazy? Oh, Tamra, that is precious. Out with it."

"Well, do you remember when I told you about my genealogical work, and the feelings I'd get at times . . . as if someone were calling to me from the other side of the veil to do their work?"

"I remember," he said. "You asked me if I believed in ghosts, then you told me you were casting pearls before swine."

"Well," she laughed softly, "you redeemed yourself when you took me to the carriage house and the gabled attic."

"I could take you again," he offered, "especially if it might redeem me a little more."

"Couldn't hurt," she said. "Now, stop changing the subject. I'm trying to tell you something."

"Okay. I'm listening."

Jess watched Tamra put a hand over the top of the journal lying on the table. Her eyes deepened and so did her voice. "I've felt that way with your great-great-grandmother, Jess. It's subtle . . . but undeniable." He felt his brows go up as she added, "I know it sounds crazy, Jess, but I believe she lured me here."

Jess allowed her words to sink in and mingle with memories of his early youth. He wanted to tell her there had been a time when he'd believed that Alexandra Byrnehouse-Davies was his guardian angel. He wanted to tell her he'd felt all she was describing and more in relation to many of his own ancestors. He wanted to admit that he envied what she felt, that he'd lost that privilege when he'd allowed his life to go down the drain in his youth. But all he could bring himself to say was simply, "I don't think it sounds crazy."

"So, do you think," she asked, leaning toward him, "that such a feeling is somehow . . . a thinning of the veil? Do you think there are moments when we somehow feel some . . . connection we had before we were born, or perhaps . . . a connection with someone who has passed on?"

"Makes sense to me," he said.

Tamra laughed softly and said, "You know, anyone who was not LDS who heard this conversation would think we were nuts."

Jess chuckled. "Maybe we are."

Tamra looked at Jess with a severity in her eyes that seemed out of place for the nature of the conversation. "Maybe we are," she said, "but . . . " Jess focused more intently on her. He sensed something profoundly important in what she wanted to say, even before he saw a hint of moisture glistening in her eyes. "Jess," she said in a hushed whisper, as if the breeze might overhear, "that's the way I felt when I first saw you; that's the way I feel sometimes when I just think of you."

Jess felt his heart quicken a moment before he perceived the implication. While he was trying to convince himself that she'd not meant what he thought she meant, she added in that same whisper, "I feel like I should already know you, Jess." She reached farther across the table and pressed a hand to his face. She sighed and smiled, then said with a tremor in her voice, "And that's how I know I love you."

"Amazing," Jess said when he finally found his voice.

"How's that?" Tamra asked, wondering how such a confession would affect him. If he scoffed, even vaguely, at such a deep admission, she doubted that she could cope.

But the sincerity in his eyes was evident even before they brimmed with moisture. His voice quavered as he admitted, "Yeah, I know exactly how you feel." He touched her face and laughed softly. "You really did explain how I know that I love you. And I didn't think you could do it . . . because I couldn't even make sense of what I was feeling, let alone put it to words."

Jess contemplated briefly her presence in his life as little puzzle pieces began to settle together in his mind. He couldn't predict the outcome, but he knew in his heart that when all was said and done between them, whether they ended up friends at the very most . . . or the very least, he knew that they had been brought together now for a reason. He didn't understand it, but instinctively he believed it. And he was grateful.

Chapter Nine

Jess and Tamra were both distracted when Michael and Emily appeared, walking toward the house, each holding one of Evelyn's hands. From a distance they heard Evelyn giggle and take off running toward the house. "I wunning, Gwampa," she said. "Come on, Gwampa! Wun wif me."

"I'm running," Michael said, then he tickled her and ran the other way.

Emily laughed and watched while Evelyn ran after Michael and pushed on his leg, as if to tickle him back. He purposely fell backward on the lawn with a dramatic howl. Evelyn giggled and jumped on his chest.

Tamra's attention was drawn to Jess when he laughed—a hearty, genuine laugh that she'd never heard before. "It looks like Evelyn's warmed right up to Grandma and Grandpa."

"Yes, she sure has," Tamra said.

Evelyn squirmed away from Michael and ran once more. Michael shot to his feet and ran, but instead of going after Evelyn, he grabbed Emily from behind, making her squeal with laughter. "I'm too old for that," Emily scolded and laughed again as she tried to break free, but he tickled her briefly then turned her in his arms. "You rogue!" she said and laughed again, just before he kissed her.

"See," Jess said, reaching for Tamra's hand, "I told you it runs in the family."

A few minutes later, Michael came up the veranda steps, holding Evelyn in one arm, and holding Emily's hand. They exchanged greetings before Jess said, "I see you and Evelyn have been having a good time."

"Evelyn is a princess," Emily said as she sat down and put the child on her lap.

"I a pwincess," Evelyn said, then she turned and put her little hands on Emily's face. "Gwamma a pwincess."

"No, Grandma's the queen," Michael said.

Evelyn furrowed her brow and spoke to Michael in a scolding tone. "No, I da queen!"

They all laughed and Michael said, "It would seem you *are* the queen." He took her from Emily, saying, "Come along, your highness, it's nap time."

"For Evelyn or Grandpa?" Jess asked.

"Both," Michael said with a chuckle. "I think the jet lag is hitting me."

"It hit me on the way home," Emily said. "That's why I slept all the way from Sydney."

"Yes, well I was flying the plane, darlin'," Michael said with a chuckle and moved toward the door.

"Don't forget to change her diaper," Emily called.

"Change a bapper, Gwampa," Evelyn said to him.

"Excuse me?" Michael said to Emily. "How long have you lived in this country?"

Emily smiled. "It's still a diaper to me. But whether it's a diaper or a nappy or a napkin, or whatever you want to call it, just change it."

"Change a nappy, Gwampa," Evelyn said.

Michael chuckled and carried Evelyn into the house.

Emily put her feet up and nodded toward the tray. "Lunch on the veranda?"

"Yes, it was nice," Tamra said.

Emily looked around herself and sighed. "Oh, it is so good to be home."

"You say that now," Jess said, "but before long you'll be off to some other godforsaken place to change the world."

Tamra heard a subtle bite in his words. Emily turned toward him, her brow furrowed; she had obviously picked up on the same undertone. But Jess was looking the other way. "Actually," Emily said as if nothing were wrong, "I have a feeling we've done our share of traveling the world to do missionary work. Maybe there are some souls that need saving right here at home."

Tamra felt a soft chill from the meaning in her words—a meaning that seemed lost on Jess. He likely wouldn't want to acknowledge that his soul needed saving. She couldn't help thinking that the timing of Amee not being able to care for Evelyn, which had prompted Michael and Emily's early return, was a direct blessing in regard to Jess. It was evident he needed his parents, but having to actually cut their mission short because of his emotional problems could have made the issues more complicated for him. It was evident that God was truly looking out for this family.

"What's that you're reading?" Emily asked Tamra, motioning toward the book on the table.

Tamra picked it up to show her. "Alexa's journal. I hope you don't mind. I confess I did some snooping, and I've felt rather drawn to Alexa."

"Really?" Emily said, seeming pleased. "Of course I don't mind. You know, Michael transcribed all of those journals on the computer, and there are now printed journals that might be easier to read."

"Oh, I like the original," Tamra said, pressing her fingers lovingly over the aging leather binding. "I promise to treat it well."

"I'm sure you will," Emily said with a warm smile before she added, "There is something compelling about Alexandra Davies, isn't there?"

"Oh, yes," Tamra said.

"Remind me sometime to tell you my experiences with Alexa," Emily said.

"What's wrong with now?" Jess asked. "Did you have an appointment or something?"

"No, but . . . I didn't know if the two of you had plans or—"

"We're just a couple of lazy bums," Jess said.

"Speak for yourself," Tamra said, then she chuckled. "Actually . . . today I suppose I am feeling pretty lazy."

"You had a rough week," Jess said, discreetly squeezing her hand. "So, tell us about Alexa," he added to his mother. Then to Tamra, "I think she believes in ghosts, too."

"I believe there are times when the veil between this world and the next is very thin," Emily declared firmly. "And Alexa seems somehow to be . . . Well, it's difficult to describe, but I've felt at times as if she was perhaps assigned to be the one to watch over this family."

Tamra felt a distinct chill. She glanced at Jess and found evidence in his expression that he appreciated what was being said.

"Well, tell us, Mother," Jess said, a touch facetiously. "We can't bear the anticipation."

Emily gave him a comical glare and said with laughter, "You're just like your father."

"Thank you," Jess said and leaned his head back against his chair.

"Well," Emily began, "I first came here during college, after Michael and I had dated for several months. I remember being fascinated then by the genealogy and family stories, but there was something about Alexa that stayed with me. Of course, I made the decision to marry someone else, and I didn't see Michael for several years."

"I knew you had been married before," Tamra said, "but I didn't realize you and Michael had known each other previously."

"Oh yes," she said. "And those years apart were very difficult on both of us for different reasons. He'd never been able to fully get over losing me, and my marriage turned out to be somewhat of a disaster."

"So why didn't you marry him in the first place?" Jess asked.

Emily turned toward him, surprised. "I thought you'd heard that story dozens of times."

"Well, maybe I wasn't paying attention," he said with a subtle bite to his voice. Tamra wondered if the bite was directed toward himself or his mother.

"Well, pay attention this time," Emily said lightly. "I felt hesitant to marry your father because he wasn't a member of the Church. Ryan was a returned missionary and we were married in the temple. Of course, your father joined the Church later, about the time Ryan was killed, and we came back together." She said more to Tamra, "I can tell you more about that some other time, if you're interested . . . "

"Oh, I am," Tamra insisted.

"But I was getting to a point about Alexa."

"Of course."

"I reached a particularly low time in my marriage to Ryan when I was pregnant with my third daughter. I remember very clearly lying on the couch, holding Amee while she slept. For some reason I started thinking about Alexa, when I hadn't thought of her at all for years. I recalled how the family journals had indicated that she was such a strength and a positive influence; she brought about so much good in her life. That was all, really. I just felt better. And that's when I decided to name my baby Alexa if it was a girl—which it was."

"Really?" Tamra said then turned to Jess. "You have a sister named Alexa?"

"I do," he said as if it were nothing, but Tamra felt almost envious at the thought of having such a great namesake.

"I can't wait to meet her," she said and turned back to Emily. "So . . . do you think Alexa was somehow close to you at that time?"

She saw Emily's eyes light up along with a subtle smile. "It's interesting that you would ask that," she said, "because at the time the idea never occurred to me. But much later, after Michael and I had gotten back together and I began to perceive that I had been destined to be a part of this family, in spite of certain necessary detours, I looked back at that experience and somehow knew that she had been pulling for me from the other side."

Tamra felt a warm chill at the same moment Jess squeezed her fingers. Was the timing coincidence? Or could he see, as she had, the relation to Emily's words and what Tamra had said only a short while ago?

"And there have been other moments since then," Emily said, apparently oblivious to the warm spell she was weaving around Tamra, "when I've known beyond any doubt that Alexa was directly involved with our family." She laughed softly. "I've speculated over it a great deal. They say that spirits on the other side are very busy, and we can't expect those who have passed on to be hovering around us while they have so much work to do. But I have to believe that Alexa has somehow been . . . assigned or something, to look out for her family. I don't think it's a constant thing, but I believe there are times when God knows we need her, and she's been there."

Considering her own experiences, Tamra felt too moved to speak and was relieved when Emily went on. "The experience that stands out strongest for me was related to Tyson and Emma."

Tamra recognized the names from the journals and records she'd been exploring. "You mean Alexa's twins?"

"No," Emily laughed, *"my* twins—named after Alexa's twins."

"Really?" Tamra said, loving the rich heritage of this family more by the minute.

"After Jess and James were born, I had a miscarriage that was quite serious, and after that we had a number of difficulties in trying to have another baby. But I knew in my heart that I was supposed to bring another child into the world. When I lost that first baby, I had a dream where I saw Alexa holding a baby boy and telling me she would care for him until I could. At the time, I believed she meant the child that hadn't been born yet. Years later, after we finally got Tyson and Emma, and Tyson only lived a very short time, I understood that Alexa had known he would die in his infancy, and she would care for him until we were able to."

"That's incredible," Tamra said and felt her eyes become moist. She vaguely recalled Emily telling her in the Philippines about losing a child in infancy. She marveled at all Emily Hamilton had endured in her life, and she was equally amazed at the bridges that existed in this family from one generation to the next. On both counts, she had a feeling she had only scratched the surface and there was a great deal more to learn. She looked forward to every day she might spend here and all she could glean of a history and heritage that was rich with courage and commitment. She glanced at Jess and prayed that she might actually be privileged enough to share her life with him and become a literal part of this family. While it seemed too incredible to comprehend, it also felt completely natural and comfortable. She could almost believe she had been born to be here now, and she could only hope that this was not just a brief step toward her destiny, but her destiny itself.

The conversation shifted to trivialities for a few minutes before Emily asked Jess if he could help her with something. They went into the house together, leaving Tamra with time to enjoy Alexa's journal. Every page she read deepened her love for this great woman, and she only had to lift her eyes to see a view that she felt certain had been familiar to Alexa. She had sat on this veranda and graced the halls of this home. She had raised her children here, lived and died here, and Tamra could only be grateful for the glimpse she had been given of her life.

* * *

Tamra went to the kitchen a little before supper time to see if she could help. She found Michael standing by the stove with a dishtowel tucked into the front of his jeans. Emily and Sadie were both sitting at the table, chatting comfortably. Telltale noises let her know that Evelyn was playing in the next room. They had barely exchanged greetings before Jess appeared and started teasing his father about using foreign guests as guinea pigs for his cooking.

Jess winked at Tamra. Michael chuckled and said, "She's already eaten my cooking, if you must know. And I tried this recipe on you years ago, boy."

"Oh, so your children were your guinea pigs."

"That's right," Michael said. "And you all grew up just fine—in spite of my cooking."

"Or maybe because of it," Emily said. "I never found pleasure in the kitchen the way Michael did," she added more toward Tamra.

"Well," Tamra said, "if it tastes as good as it smells, I'm only too happy to be a guinea pig—whether Michael gets any pleasure out of it or not."

Tamra loved the way Jess took her hand when he sat beside her. The meal progressed with comfortable small talk and laughter, and Tamra appreciated seeing Jess and his parents together this way, after all that had happened. Long after the meal was over, and Sadie had taken Evelyn upstairs to bathe her and get her ready for bed, they sat at the table and visited. Tamra loved hearing about Michael and Emily's mission experiences, some of which she had been a part of in the Philippines.

Following a lull in the conversation that Tamra feared would end this delightful experience, Michael said, "We wrote and told the girls we would call them tomorrow after church." He added more to Tamra, "With the time difference between here and there, we have to plan the calls so we're not waking anybody up in the middle of the night. Anyway," he said more to Jess, "we have to check with the bishop tomorrow to make certain, but we believe our mission report will be next Sunday. The girls all have tentative flights arranged, so we'll call them tomorrow to make more concrete plans."

"So, they're all coming?" Tamra asked, excited with the prospect of meeting the rest of the family.

"Well, the girls are coming," Emily said. "Last we heard, none of them had much hope of having their husbands get that much time off work, so they'd decided to just make it a sibling excursion. They'll be bringing some of the kids, but I believe the ones in school will be staying at home. But Michael and I are planning on going to each of their homes for a good visit. We'll likely set out in a few weeks."

"That sounds great," Tamra said. "I'd be happy to help Sadie with Evelyn. We've gotten to be pretty good friends, and—"

"We appreciate that," Michael said, "but we're taking Evelyn with us. Sadie could use a break, I think. And Evelyn needs to get to know her cousins."

"Of course," Tamra said, thinking how she would miss little Evelyn. Her opportunities to help with the child had become a bright spot in her life.

Tamra saw a look of concern come into Michael's eyes just before he leaned toward Jess and said, "Your sisters need to know what's going on, son. While we're all together, we're going to need to talk about it."

Jess sighed loudly and clasped his hands over the table. "Is that really necessary?" he asked, but he didn't seem angry.

"Yes, love, it is," Emily said. "We're family, and we don't keep skeletons in the closet."

"And," Michael added, "Doctor Hill told us that the more family could be involved in your counseling, the better it would be."

Jess groaned. "What? The whole family talking about me trying to kill myself? Oh, that sounds great." His sarcasm rang deep.

"I know it's not pleasant, Jess," Michael said, "but it will help; I know it will. Your sisters love you dearly."

"I know they do," Jess said, "and I love them, but . . . that's just it. I don't want to drag them into this mess. It's all so ugly, and . . . "

"Embarrassing?" Emily suggested.

"Well, yes," Jess said. "Since you put it that way, yes."

"You're far from the first of our children to struggle, Jess," Emily said. "Amee's divorce was difficult for all of us. But she got through it, and she's happily married now. At the time, however, she told me she was mortified to think of admitting to the family that her marriage was falling apart. When all was said and done, she said it was the family that got her through. And surely you remember the grief Allison put us all through when we lived in Utah. We didn't know where she was, or if she was even alive, for over two years. She sank about as low as a person can get."

Jess admitted humbly, "I'd honestly forgotten about that."

"Well, we're family," Michael said, "and they need to know what's going on. We're not trying to embarrass or humiliate you, Jess. We just need to pull together as a family to get you through this. Okay?"

Jess nodded resolutely. "Will you tell them over the phone, or—"

"No, I think we should talk about it when we're together," Emily said. "But they need to know that they're going to have to set aside some time on your behalf." Jess nodded again and rose from the table.

"Are you okay?" Michael asked.

"I'm fine," he said and seemed to mean it, but his eyes said otherwise. He glanced at Tamra and asked, "You coming?"

"I was going to help with the dishes and—"

"Oh, don't you worry about that," Emily insisted with a subtle nod that seemed to say her efforts on Jess's behalf would be much more appreciated. "Why don't the two of you take a walk or something. It's a beautiful evening."

"My thoughts exactly," Jess said and took Tamra's hand, urging her to her feet.

"Thank you for the lovely meal," she said, moving toward the door. "It was wonderful."

"You're very welcome," Michael said.

"Yeah, thanks," Jess said and led Tamra into the hall and out the side door of the house.

They were only a few steps onto the lawn before he said, "Tell me you love me, Tamra."

"I love you, Jess," she said, letting go of his hand to put her arm around him. He did the same and pressed a kiss to her brow. When he said nothing more, she asked, "Are you really concerned about this thing with your sisters?"

"The thought of having to tell them what I did makes me sick to my stomach," he admitted as they strolled slowly around the back of the house.

"I can see why it would be difficult," Tamra said, "but would you really want to live with keeping it a secret from them for the rest of your life?"

Jess sighed and said, "No, I wouldn't."

"So, do you think your parents are right, or—"

"Yes, I do. I really do. And I'm not angry with them or anything. I just . . . dread it."

"Okay, that's reasonable," Tamra said.

They came back around the front of the house and sat on the steps, remaining in silence until Jess said, "I'd dread it a lot less if I knew you'd be there to hold my hand."

"If you want me to be there, I will," she said. "I promise."

Jess looked into her eyes and pressed her hand to his lips. He couldn't deny that her promise made him feel much better. He wondered what he'd ever done without her, which made him wonder if he would have ever sunk so low if she had been in his life much sooner. But such speculations were ridiculous. He could only be grateful that she'd come along when she did, and he could only hope that she would have the tenacity to stick with him in spite of his idiocy. She put her arms around him and hugged him tightly, expressing silently a complete acceptance that left him in awe. Attempting to comprehend the depth of what he felt for her, he wondered how he could have ever believed that what he felt for Heather was unsurpassable. What he'd shared with her was no small thing, and his feelings had run deep. But Tamra Banks had a way of putting his past into an entirely new perspective. She was incredible. And it was easy to admit, "I love you, Tamra."

She tightened her arms around him and he could almost believe that everything was going to be okay—someday, somehow.

* * *

Tamra was relieved when Jess appeared Sunday morning, ready to join them for church, but he seemed slightly nervous. Walking out to the Cruiser, she asked him quietly, "Are you okay?"

"Yeah," he said with a tense chuckle. "It's just that . . . I haven't been to church for several months . . . I think. I've lost track."

Tamra gave his hand a reassuring squeeze while she contemplated one more clue to the cause of his depression. While she felt certain going to church in itself could never solve deep emotional problems, if Jess had cut himself off from the avenues of spiritual support in his life, it certainly wouldn't have helped the situation.

The drive was pleasant while Michael chattered comically with Evelyn, amidst conversation of catching up on all that had happened during their absence. Michael and Emily received a warm welcome from ward members, and the meetings were without event beyond the well-meaning gentleman who said to Michael, "I understand you had an emergency helicopter out at your place last week. Is everything all right?"

Tamra saw shame rise in Jess's eyes just before he glanced down. But without missing a beat, Michael said, "Oh, Jess had a little accident. But as you can see, he's fine." Michael then smoothly changed the subject. Tamra briefly caught Jess's eye and felt gratified to see his subtle smile. Each hour her hope deepened that he was going to be all right.

After church, while Evelyn napped and Sadie worked on dinner, Michael and Emily went to the *office,* as Emily called it, to phone their daughters. They invited Jess to join them so he would know exactly what was said about him.

"And you can have a chance to stick up for yourself," Michael said lightly.

Jess just scowled and took Tamra's hand, making it clear that he wasn't going to do this without her.

Tamra caught her breath when they entered the office. She'd never been in this room before, but she loved the feel of it. Its most prominent piece of furniture was a highly polished blackwood desk that had to be at least as old as the house.

"This was Jess Davies' office," Emily whispered to Tamra while Michael sat behind the desk and dialed the number.

"Really?" Tamra said, recalling from Alexa's journals that when she had come here to ask Jess Davies for a job, the meeting had taken place in his office. "Incredible," she said, more to herself than anyone else, before they were seated around the desk.

"Who are we calling first?" Jess asked.

"Emma and Allison," Michael said.

Emily explained quietly to Tamra, "Emma's going to BYU and staying with Allison, who is married to Ammon. They have five children, and they're all in school now." Tamra nodded, appreciating the explanation when she felt like such an outsider. When she heard the phone ringing she realized they were using a speaker phone.

"Hello," a man said with an American accent.

"Hello," Michael said, and heard laughter as a response.

"It really *is* you," the man said. "Emma was laying bets, so I beat her to the phone."

"It's really me," Michael said. "How are you, Ammon?"

"I'm great. How are you?"

They could hear a woman squealing with excited laughter in the background.

"I'm fine," Michael laughed. "But what is that horrible noise?"

"That would be your daughter."

"It's Emma," Emily said.

"Oh," Ammon said more to Emma, "they're on that dreadful speaker phone. Here, you'd better talk before you hyperventilate."

"Hello," Emma said.

"Hello," Michael and Emily both said together and she squealed again.

"It's really you," Emma said. "You're really home."

"We really are," Emily said.

"Oh, it's so good to hear your voices."

"And yours," Michael said.

"How are you?" Emily asked.

"I'm fine," Emma said. "Allison ran a quick errand that couldn't wait. She said if you called to keep you on the phone until she got back. She should be here in a few minutes."

"Okay, we'll wait," Emily said.

"Mom, Dad?" Emma said, sounding concerned. "I don't want to worry you, but . . . I can't get hold of Jess. We haven't seen him for a few weeks, which isn't unusual. But I tried to call him a few days ago and haven't gotten any answer. I've left messages. I've e-mailed him, but—"

"It's okay," Emily said. "Jess is here."

"There?" Emma practically shrieked. "He went home without telling me?"

"Yes, but he had his reasons." Emily glanced toward Jess. "He's been having a rough time, but he's home and he's fine."

"What's wrong?" Emma asked.

"We'll talk about it when we're together," Emily said, then to Jess, "Say hello to your sister, Jess."

"Hello, Em," he said and she laughed in response, as if just hearing his voice gave her extreme relief.

"You really are there. Are you okay?"

"I'm fine," he said.

"Oh, Allison's here," Emma said. Then away from the phone, "Pick up the extension. It's them. And Jess is already there."

Again they heard excited laughter in the distance before another phone picked up and Allison said, "I'm here."

"Hello, sweetie," Emily said and Allison laughed again.

"Oh, it's so good to hear your voice. Are you well?"

"We're great," Michael said and she laughed again.

"Hi, Dad," she said, sounding emotional. "I've sure missed you— both of you." Tamra was amazed to hear the difference in the way the two sisters spoke. It was evident that in spite of the time they'd both spent in Australia and the States, Allison had learned to speak in America, and Emma had learned to speak in Australia. The difference gave Tamra a perspective on Emily's first marriage and the daughters that had been born to her before she'd married Michael.

"We've missed you too," Michael said.

"So, what's this about Jess being home already?" Allison asked.

"He just needed to come home," Emily said. "We'll talk more about that when you get home."

Tamra listened while they discussed plans for the following weekend. Flights had been arranged. Allison would be coming without any children since they were all in school, and she was looking forward to a vacation, even though she would miss them. Emma had made arrangements with her professors to bring a great deal of her school work with her so she wouldn't get too far behind. Emily encouraged Jess to talk to his sisters. At first he seemed tense, but as they joked and laughed together, she felt him relax and could see that he was truly enjoying the phone call. They finally hung up and called Dale and Alexa, who lived in California and had five children, including twin boys. All were in school except for Bridger, who was three. The conversation went much the same as it had with Allison and Emma, including a chance for Jess to talk lightly with his sister. Alexa would be meeting her sisters in L.A. when she got onto their connecting flight to Sydney. She would be bringing Bridger, and

Dale would look out for the other children with the help of some neighbors and ward members.

Finally they called Randy and Amee in Adelaide, and the entire ritual was repeated a third time. Amee had one son from her first marriage, and three more children with Randy. The youngest was little Beth, who was about a month old. Michael and Emily were terribly anxious to see this youngest grandchild that had been born in their absence. Amee had gotten a flight from Adelaide to Sydney that would put her there in the same hour her sisters would arrive from L.A. Michael would pick them all up there in the private plane. Along with the baby, Amee would be bringing Katie, who was nearly four.

Listening quietly to the conversations, Tamra found it interesting that Alexa and Amee both spoke with thick Australian accents, even though they had both been born American. But they had moved here at the age of one and two.

They had barely ended the final call when Sadie hurried them into the kitchen to eat. Evelyn was already seated at the table, rearranging the dishes.

"So, who is coming?" Sadie asked as soon as they'd had the blessing. "And when will they be here?"

"The girls will all be arriving in Sydney Friday morning," Emily answered. "Michael will fly them home from there." Sadie giggled like a child. "It will just be the girls and the children who aren't in school."

"Which would be Katie and Bridger and the new one," Sadie said.

"Beth," Michael said with a smile of anticipation.

"Hey there, Evelyn," Michael said. "Do you want your cousins to come and stay and play with you?"

"I pway my dowy," she said.

"Yes, you can play with your dolly," Emily said, kissing the child's head. Emily then said to Tamra, "Katie, Bridger, and Evelyn were all born while we were in the Philippines. It will be nice to spend some time with all of them and get to know them better. Before our missions we were able to spend more time with the kids, in spite of the miles between us."

"Then this will be a wonderful visit," Tamra said.

Jess made a disgruntled noise to indicate he had reason to feel dubious on that count, but the conversation went elsewhere. When the meal was finished, Tamra stood and said, "Jess and I will be doing the dishes tonight. Why don't the rest of you go . . . play with Evelyn or something."

It took little urging to get them to leave the kitchen, once they'd teased Jess a bit about making himself useful. Tamra wondered if he might not be thrilled about being left with such a monumental task, when it was evident that Sadie had dirtied a great many dishes in cooking a wonderful meal. But he quickly began unloading the dishwasher and filling the sink with soapy water to start washing the pans while Tamra cleared the table. It was evident he'd been raised doing this task by his practiced efficiency, but she became concerned when he said nothing and she sensed a subtly dark mood.

"You okay?" she finally asked, sidling up next to him at the sink.

"Yeah, why?" he asked.

Tamra sighed. "Don't skirt around the truth, Jess. You're concerned, at the very least, and I think you should talk to me."

Jess stopped washing and turned to look at her. She couldn't tell if he was disgusted or teasing when he said, "What gave you the ability to read my mind, Ms. Banks?"

Tamra just smiled and said, "I'm just a good guesser. I *can't* read your mind, Jess, so you're going to have to tell me what you're thinking. Holding all of it inside has not proven to be effective."

"You got me there," he said, tossing the dishrag into the sink with a healthy splash.

"So talk." He said nothing and she pressed, "Are you upset about this thing with your sisters?"

"Not upset," he said, "but . . . dreading it."

"That's understandable."

"I suppose I'm just feeling a little unsettled to think that . . . " He met her eyes and she saw sincerity there. "Talking to my sisters actually made me feel better, in a way. Getting all of this out in the open isn't going to be easy, but if anything, I'm grateful to have a family that's loving and supportive—even if it's usually long distance." He glanced down and briefly bit his lip before he added, "I just keep thinking of what you said about . . . my sisters grieving for me and trying to understand how I could . . . " Emotion broke his voice and she put her arms around him. He returned her embrace, pressing his wet hands to her back. "As hard as it will be to tell them what I did," he said, "I'm just grateful that I'm alive to tell them. It breaks my heart to think of my parents having to call and tell them that I . . . "

When he couldn't finish, Tamra took his face into her hands, saying gently, "We're all grateful you're alive, Jess. But I'm even more grateful to know you feel that way too. As long as you keep sight of all the people who love you, you'll get through this just fine."

He nodded and bit his lip again before he said, "Yesterday when Dad said my sisters were coming home and they needed to know, I was cursing the timing of all of this. But today I actually think it's a blessing. I'm looking forward to seeing them, even if what I have to tell them will be tough."

Tamra cherished the maturity and healthy attitude she was hearing, grateful for the progress he had made. She prayed that it would hold out until his healing was complete.

"Besides," he said, "you told me you'd be there to hold my hand, so it can't be too bad."

Tamra smiled and kissed him quickly. "No," she said, "it can't be too bad."

Chapter Ten

The following morning, Tamra was helping Emily put breakfast on the table when Jess appeared, wearing jeans and a T-shirt—and hiking boots on his feet. Knowing his aversion to shoes, she knew he had plans of going out; his attire suggested he had some kind of work in mind.

"Good morning," Tamra said.

"Good morning," he replied, giving her and his mother each a quick kiss.

"How are you today?" Emily asked.

"I'm fine, Mother, thank you. No suicidal tendencies or debilitating depression."

Tamra knew he was trying to provoke his mother, but she simply smiled and said, "Good, I'm glad to hear it."

Michael arrived with Evelyn, announcing that Sadie was still asleep. "I think the last couple of weeks with Evelyn have worn her right out," he said, putting Evelyn at her place at the table.

Jess ate quickly and rose from the table. "Where are you off to?" Michael asked.

"There's a whole lot of fence line that could use some maintenance," he said. "I thought I'd get started since the hands all seem to be too busy to get to it."

"Well, I've had the same thought," Michael said. "If you wait a few minutes, I'll join you."

"I'll get the stuff together," Jess offered, moving toward the door. He turned and winked at Tamra, saying, "I'll see you later, darlin'."

"I'll be counting on it," she said, loving the way he called her what she'd often heard Michael call Emily.

"Jess," Emily said with a tone that indicated he wouldn't like what she had to say, "don't forget about your appointment in town this afternoon. We'll be going with you."

"Don't worry," he said with chagrin. "In spite of great effort to forget, I haven't been able to."

He grabbed one more piece of sausage and headed out the door. Sadie appeared and Emily insisted on heating up some breakfast for her.

"Oh, you mustn't do that," Sadie said. "I work for you, remember?"

"You're practically a member of the family," Emily said. "And we could have never paid you enough to take care of Evelyn until we could get home. So just be quiet and enjoy your breakfast," Emily finished by hugging Sadie quickly. The women visited while Sadie ate, then she offered to take Evelyn outside to play on the lawn.

A few minutes later, while Tamra was scouring a pan, she noticed from the kitchen window Michael and Jess driving across the fields on a couple of four-wheelers. Tamra couldn't resist saying to Emily, "I bet Jess Davies never imagined riding something like that out to fix fences."

Emily chuckled. "No, I'm sure he didn't. But the four-wheelers are much more patient than the horses when it comes to getting work done. Although I understand Jess Davies did live to drive a car. I know Alexa did."

"Really?" Tamra said.

"She died after World War II, not so many years before Michael was born."

"That's an interesting perspective," Tamra said.

"Michael's mother knew Alexa very well, and spoke of her often. She passed away not long before we went to the Philippines. Once she didn't need us to care for her, and Emma had made the decision to go to the States to finish high school, there was nothing holding us back from serving a mission."

"I'm sure glad you did," Tamra said.

Emily laughed softly. "Yes, so am I . . . in spite of certain . . . hardships; I know it was the right thing to do."

Tamra felt slightly chilled when she caught on to Emily's meaning. They had been called home from that mission with the news that James and his wife had been killed and Jess was in a coma.

When a tense silence descended, she wondered whether to change the subject or open it up. She opted for the latter, hoping she wouldn't regret it. "That must have been so difficult for you," she said gently, keeping her attention on washing the dishes that were too grimy or too large to go in the dishwasher.

Emily stopped loading the dishwasher and said, "It's absolutely the hardest thing I have ever faced." She chuckled without humor, "And I must admit I've faced some pretty tough things." She seemed to appreciate the opportunity to talk, as she continued easily, "My first marriage was difficult at best, but losing my husband in a car accident was . . . incredibly hard. Before Tyson and Emma were born, Michael and I were in an accident that nearly killed *me,* and the heart malfunction that only allowed Tyson to live a couple of days was likely a result of what I went through from that accident."

"This accident thing has touched your life far too much," Tamra said, hoping she didn't sound insensitive.

"It certainly has," Emily agreed vehemently. "But in each case, I have known beyond any doubt that, as horrible as it was, each of these *accidents* were . . . Well, if it hadn't been that, it would have been something else because I know it was their time to go. I knew it with Ryan. I knew it with Tyson. And I knew it with James and Krista. And Byron for that matter. Jess's friend was almost like a son to us. He spent so much time in our home, and he made such an enormous difference in Jess's life. Losing him was hard in itself."

Emily sighed and sat down at the table, as if the conversation were exhausting and required her full attention. But still, she seemed eager to talk. Tamra turned from the sink and dried her hands, leaning against the counter to listen. "I can't even begin to put into words my gratitude for the gospel and the knowledge it has given me that life goes on, that we will all be together again, that we will be able to continue the relationships that we shared here on earth. And I'm especially grateful for the gift of the Holy Ghost." She shook her head with a sense of awe. "To call Him the Comforter seems such an understatement to me. The comfort I have been given through the years is incomprehensible. And the personal revelation that has helped me understand a bigger perspective is equally incredible." Tears finally came to Emily's eyes as she looked up at Tamra and said, "But oh, how I miss my sons!" Her voice cracked as she added, "All three of them."

Tamra sat beside Emily and took her hand as she continued. "I've had the most difficulty, not in losing James, but in seeing how losing him has affected Jess. As much I miss James, I know he's well. He's with his sweet wife and I'm certain they are engaged in a glorious mission. But Jess . . . Oh, Jess. I look into his eyes and my heart breaks. I've not seen any measure of peace in his eyes since he came out of that coma and I had to tell him that James and Krista and Byron were gone."

Tamra passed her a clean dishtowel to wipe her eyes and waited for her to go on, not knowing what to say. A minute later, Emily said in a composed voice, "Michael and I had both felt strongly about going on another mission before we'd even left the Philippines. We'd prayed about it, and talked it through, and felt right about going once Jess had recovered. Amee was eager to take guardianship of Evelyn, and we felt like it was the right thing to do. Of course, she hadn't anticipated this pregnancy, or that her husband would be required to work out of town more. It just became too much for them to handle."

"Will Amee take Evelyn back once she adjusts?" Tamra asked.

"Oh, I don't believe so," Emily said. "I think it's better that Evelyn remain here now where she can be completely settled and have more attention to compensate for so many changes in her young life. I think it was a good experience for Amee, and I feel that Michael and I served the time in Africa that we needed to. But I can't help believing that it worked out this way so that we could be here for Jess."

"I've wondered that myself," Tamra admitted.

"When we left we knew he was still struggling emotionally, but it was evident that no amount of talking about it was helping, and we just figured that he needed time to sort it through. When he made the decision to go back to the States to continue his schooling, we felt good about going on a mission. I worried and prayed constantly for Jess, but I knew we were where we needed to be, and I had to believe the Lord would look out for him—much better than we ever could have." Emily lifted her eyes to meet Tamra's and added with fresh emotion, "My first thought when you told us what had happened—combined with the timing of your being here—was how directly my prayers had been answered. The Lord did look out for Jess, and He guided you here to be there for him through his darkest hours."

Tamra felt a little emotional herself at Emily's observation. She took the opportunity to share the feelings and experiences that had led her to come there, and they both agreed without question that Alexa was working on behalf of her descendants from the other side of the veil. The Spirit had undoubtedly had a hand in bringing Tamra into their lives. They shared a tearful embrace before they forced themselves to finish the dishes.

When the kitchen was in order, Tamra said, "You know, in spite of feeling like I belong here—at least for the time being—I really came here expecting to work. I think you need to give me something to do."

Emily laughed softly. "My dear, let me tell you, in essence, what I just told Sadie. We could never put a price on what you have done for us, already. Besides, Sadie tells me you've put a great many hours into helping her. And it's evident you've spent a great deal of time watching over little Evelyn. Again, I have to believe the timing was not coincidence. Sadie was eager to cover the time between Amee's husband being able to bring Evelyn here, and our being able to get back. We felt confident that Evelyn would be well cared for, but with everything else that happened, you were a great support to Sadie in ways that are priceless."

"Okay, but that's irrelevant to my staying here. If *you* won't give me a job, I'll have to go into town and get one and start paying you rent, or something."

Emily laughed. "Not to worry, Tamra, there is plenty you can do around here to help. And we should be discussing some kind of salary and giving you something specific to do. You certainly need to be making some money of your own on top of room and board. But let me clarify something." She leaned closer and lowered her voice. "I'm not one to make comparisons, but I would like to share a little perspective. Heather stayed here three different times. Or was it four? I don't remember. Anyway, each time she was here for several weeks, and I don't recall ever seeing her do *anything* to help beyond occasionally washing a few dishes. She seemed to take the attitude that we were rich and there were servants in the house and we didn't need her help. The truth is, we didn't. But it apparently never occurred to her that every member of the family worked at least as hard as the people we hire to help us keep everything under control." Tamra opened her mouth to comment but Emily held up a finger and apparently had read her mind. "Now, I understand that she came here as a guest, and you came here expecting to get a job. But in my opinion, you feel more like a member of the family than she ever did, and she was a part of Jess's life for years. And let me clarify that Heather really was a good woman. She had many fine qualities, and she would have made Jess a good wife. I'm simply trying to make a point."

Emily leaned even closer and took Tamra's hand. "Jess loves you, Tamra. And so do we. I'm not going to speculate aloud on where I hope that might lead. There is too much uncertainty in Jess's life right now, and we both know that. But I want you to know that whatever job you might be assigned, or whatever task you might take upon yourself, don't ever let that work interfere with the *real* reason you're here. If Jess needs you, I want you to be there for him. And we'll just let the rest work itself out."

Tamra just nodded, feeling suddenly too touched to speak. She'd believed when she made the choice to serve a mission that she would be blessed. She'd been told as much in a priesthood blessing. But to look at all that was surrounding her now, as a direct result of an encounter from her mission, she felt too humbled and in awe to even begin to express her gratitude.

"You know," Emily said, "I don't get to see my daughters very often. It's nice to have you here . . . if only for the company." Tamra just nodded again, not knowing what to say. She wanted to tell her how she'd grown up with a lousy mother and no father at all, and being a part of this family—for any time at all—had already taught her so much about life and love and being a part of something bigger than herself. But there was a lump in her throat and she determined that she'd just have to save that conversation for another day.

"Let's go sit outside for a few minutes," Emily suggested. "Maybe you could help me make some plans."

Emily pulled open the drawer of a little desk built into the corner of the kitchen and pulled out a notebook and pen. Then she led the way out to the veranda where they sat beside the table there. "If it's all right with you," Emily said, "I could use your help most right now in getting ready for our little celebration this weekend. We'll not only be having the girls coming to stay, but there will be many friends and relatives that we haven't seen for more than a year coming either Saturday or Sunday. A few will be staying over. Michael and I have been making calls to let everyone know. Now we have to get the house ready and plan some meals that won't keep us in the kitchen when we could be visiting. So . . . " Emily laughed, "I think your helping me get through the next week sounds like a full-time job."

"Just tell me what you want me to do," Tamra said eagerly. "I can clean anything that needs to be cleaned, and I'm not bad in the kitchen, either—as far as basics go."

Emily verbally shared her thoughts on what needed to be done, making lists as she went. Sadie had kept the house up relatively well, and most of the extra rooms in the house were always kept prepared for guests. Living so far from friends and loved ones made overnight guests a common occurrence. Emily figured a quick dusting and a little airing out would be sufficient in that area. The extra work Tamra had already done for Sadie since her arrival took care of many of her other concerns, so they concluded that the biggest hurdle was the food. They discussed possible menus while Emily made notes and a very long grocery list.

"Michael can help cook a lot of this stuff," she said, "but it will have to be done in the next couple of days and frozen because he's leaving Thursday to fly to Sydney. He'll stay there that night and bring the girls home Friday."

"You're not going?" Tamra asked.

"No, there's not room in the plane, actually. But that's okay. It's an awfully long flight, and I can look forward to seeing them when they get here."

The hum of four-wheeler engines drew their attention to Michael and Jess returning and Emily glanced at her watch. "Oh, good heavens. It *is* nearly lunchtime already."

The vehicles were parked in a way that suggested they would be used again after lunch. Tamra watched Jess walking across the lawn with his father and felt a familiar warm quiver. Seeing them together was stirring, somehow. They were so visibly father and son—near the same height, same build, same coloring beyond the hints of gray in Michael's hair. They dressed the same. And they even walked the same.

"They're so much alike," Tamra couldn't resist saying.

"They certainly are," Emily said. "Looking at Jess often reminds me so much of Michael back in college. It's incredible. Of course, Michael has said the same about Allison—that she looks so much like me. I have trouble seeing it, myself, unless we're comparing photographs or something."

Tamra was surprised to see Jess playfully slug his father in the shoulder, then start dancing with his fists poised like a boxer in the ring. Michael laughed and she barely heard him say, "I could still take you, boy."

"Oh, good heavens," Emily said then laughed. "They've been doing this since Jess was crawling. Here it comes," she added just before Michael wrestled Jess to the ground to begin a haphazard brawl that lasted the better part of ten minutes. Once she quit fearing they might actually hurt each other, Tamra had to admit they were probably pretty even; first one seemed to have the advantage, then the other. She could hear their laughter and light-hearted banter floating over the lawn, and she couldn't help laughing herself when Emily said in a bored voice, "Male bonding—I'll never understand it."

"I guess it's their version of crying together in the kitchen."

Emily smiled and briefly squeezed Tamra's hand.

"Or . . . " Tamra added, "maybe it's like shopping and going out to lunch."

Emily laughed again, as if Tamra had just spouted a great epiphany. "How true," she said, "and when the girls get here, we are *all* going to do just that. We'll leave the macho team here in charge of the kids."

"I'll look forward to it," Tamra said.

Emily called loudly, "If you children are finished yet, we could all go get a sandwich."

The men both laughed and walked toward the house, brushing the grass off their jeans.

"You know," Tamra heard Jess say to his father, "one day you're going to be too old to take me."

"Don't bet on it," Michael said lightly.

Emily stood up and met Michael with a kiss at the top of the veranda steps before they went into the house together. Tamra held out a hand for Jess and he kissed her much the way his father had just kissed his mother.

"I could spend the rest of my life living like this," he said.

Tamra smiled. "It wouldn't be a problem for me." The idea warmed her deeply.

After lunch the men went back out and worked for a while, then they came in and got cleaned up. Tamra stood on the veranda, holding Evelyn, watching Michael, Emily, and Jess drive away in the Cruiser. She uttered a silent prayer on Jess's behalf, actually feeling grateful that she didn't have to be involved with his counseling from here on out. She'd been there for the suicide attempt, but she'd had nothing to do with the accident or the events surrounding it. She only hoped it would go well and Jess could continue to make progress.

Tamra played dollies with Evelyn while they watched the *Beauty and the Beast* video. Tamra laughed at Evelyn's commentary on the movie that was the same every time. They read storybooks once the movie was over, then Tamra left her to play in the room next to the kitchen while she searched the available items to see if she might actually be able to cook something presentable. She found a basic recipe book and perused it until she came across a lasagna recipe similar to one she'd made at home, then she pulled out all the ingredients to be certain she had everything before she started. When that was in the oven, she made a tossed salad and brownies from a boxed mix. Sadie came into the kitchen to get a casserole out of the freezer, concerned because she'd been reading and lost track of the time. She was delighted to find supper nearly ready, and they sat and visited until they heard the Cruiser pull up outside.

Tamra checked on Evelyn, expecting the others to follow the smell of lasagna to the kitchen. She heard the side door slam and footsteps bounding up the stairs. A minute later Michael and Emily appeared in the kitchen, both looking concerned.

"What?" Tamra demanded, wishing she hadn't sounded so panicked.

Emily blew out a long breath and sank into a chair, saying, "I have a feeling it's going to get a lot worse before it gets better."

Sadie slipped into the other room with Evelyn, and Tamra noticed she had a way of distancing herself from the family problems. Michael sat down and said nothing. Tamra had to ask, "Is it none of my business?"

"There's not much to tell," Michael said. "We spent most of the hour just talking about our family. You know, birth order, personalities, circumstances—just the basics. Everything was fine until she asked him to talk about the situation of the family prior to the accident. He told Doctor Hill that we had been out of the country on a mission, and he had just returned from his mission. That seemed fine. She asked some questions about this mission thing and seemed impressed. She went back to the subject and asked about the situation of his relationships with the people who had been in the car. He swore at her and left the room. She told us to give him a few minutes to calm down and then to just let it rest until our next session."

"Which is when?" Tamra asked.

"Thursday morning," Emily said.

Following a strained minute of silence, Michael rose and opened the oven. "Something smells divine." He hollered into the other room, "Sadie, what have you been up to?"

"I didn't do it," she said, appearing in the kitchen now that the topic was not family psychology. "Tamra's been cooking."

"Ooh," Michael said, sounding impressed.

"It's just basic lasagna," she said. "Nothing gourmet like the great Michael Hamilton could produce."

"It smells wonderful," Emily said, "and in spite of the drama, I'm starving."

After the blessing was said, Tamra felt compelled to say, "I'm going to at least try to get him to come down."

"You go for it," Michael said. "He didn't say a word the entire drive home. If you can get him to talk, I'll make your favorite dessert tomorrow. If you can get him to come down to dinner, I'll be your slave for an hour."

"That *is* great incentive," Tamra said and hurried upstairs.

She stood at his door and finished a silent prayer that she'd begun on the way up. She took a deep breath and knocked, hating the memory of the night when he'd tried to end his life. "Jess?" she said.

"Yeah?" he called.

"May I come in?"

"Sure," he said and she pushed the door slowly open to find him standing at the window, his hands in the back pockets of his jeans, his feet bare. He'd obviously been in a hurry to take off his shoes.

"You okay?" she asked, closing the door and leaning against it.

"I will be . . . I hope . . . eventually."

"Counseling can be pretty deplorable," she stated.

He turned toward her, looking surprised, and she realized she'd never told him certain things about herself. She felt as if she knew him so well that she could almost believe he knew everything about her. She really didn't feel like getting into it at the moment and hoped he wouldn't ask. She was relieved when he turned back toward the window and simply said, "Yeah, it's deplorable. But I suppose it's necessary."

Tamra crossed the room and gently placed her hands against his back. "Anything you want to talk about?" she asked.

He sighed. "Not at the moment . . . but I guess I'm going to have to eventually. Maybe if I'd talked about it a long time ago, it wouldn't have gotten so out of control."

"Maybe," she whispered. When he said nothing more, she added, "I cooked supper."

"Really?" He turned toward her, apparently grateful for a distraction.

"I can't compete with Sadie or your dad, but I believe it's edible. Do you think you could stand coming down to eat with us, or do you want me to bring some up for you and give you some time alone?"

Jess hugged her tightly and said close to her ear, "I think I'm sick to death of being alone. Let's go eat." He took her hand and led her into the hall.

"I was hoping you'd come down," she said, "but I didn't want to be too pushy."

"Why were you hoping?" he asked, going down the stairs at her side.

"Because when I said I was going to talk to you, your dad offered me a great incentive to get you to come down to dinner."

"Really?" he said with a smirk.

"Does he know anything about cars?"

"He can take care of the basics pretty well. He taught me. Why?"

"Just wondering." She smiled and they entered the kitchen together.

"Oh, hello," Emily said with obvious surprise. "Tamra cooked."

"So, I heard."

"And it's wonderful," Sadie said with her mouth full.

"Tamwa cook," Evelyn said and Jess chuckled as he took his seat.

Tamra sat between him and Michael, leaning toward the latter to say, "My favorite dessert is chocolate mousse, and my car could really use an oil change."

Michael chuckled and shook his head. "Did the two of you conspire over this, or what?"

"No," Jess said, scooping lasagna onto his plate, "but we might next time."

"Don't count on it," Michael said.

The following day, Tamra returned from a lengthy shopping trip with Emily to find Michael pouring fresh oil into her car. She and Emily got out of the Cruiser and walked over to admire his work. He finished and closed the hood as he announced, "Fresh oil, new oil filter and air filter. Murphy just happened to have the right ones on hand; we do keep a reasonable supply. Washer fluid filled and battery checks out okay. And," he leaned toward Tamra and smirked, "the chocolate mousse is chilling in the fridge."

"A man of many talents," Emily said, going on her toes to kiss him.

"I'm impressed," Tamra said. "I do hope you've trained Jess."

"He knows how to take care of a car," Michael said. "But I'm not sure he knows how to make chocolate mousse."

"We'll have to work on that," Tamra said and kissed Michael's cheek. "Thank you. You're a pretty good guy to have around."

"Well," he said, wiping his hands on a rag that he pulled out of his back pocket, "if you can continue to lure Jess out of his bad moods the way you did last night, the feeling is mutual."

"I can try," she said. "But if you must know, last night was a piece of cake. It didn't take much effort. But like you said, Emily, I have a feeling it's going to get worse before it gets better."

Tamra felt as if her words had been a prediction when Jess came in from working on fences, wearing a dark scowl. She and Emily had just finished putting away all the groceries that Michael had carried in from the Cruiser, and Sadie was taking a casserole out of the oven. They all sat to eat as usual with the conversation centering around their plans for the coming weekend. But Jess didn't say a word. The moment he was done eating, he stood and began unloading the dishwasher. Michael started helping with the dishes and Sadie took Evelyn upstairs to give her a bath. Tamra hovered at the table with

Emily and was relieved when Michael finally broke the silence by saying, "What's eating at you, Jess? You need to talk about it."

Jess continued working as if he hadn't heard, then he stopped abruptly and put both hands on the counter. He hung his head and sighed. "I'll tell you what's eating at me," he said. "I killed my brother. *That's* what is eating at me."

Tamra held her breath, wondering if Jess had been stewing over this since the counseling session yesterday, and he'd reached a point where he couldn't hold it inside any longer. Following a minute of astonished silence, Emily said firmly, "No, Jess, you did not! It was an accident. It was their time to go."

He turned toward her and growled, "How can you *know* that?"

"You grew up with the gospel, Jess. You know how the Spirit can guide us, comfort us."

"I understand how that's supposed to work," he said. "But I don't get those kinds of answers. I'm not sure I ever have. As I see it, if somebody else had been driving that car, the outcome would have been different."

"It was an accident, Jess."

"And how do you know that?" he countered.

"Because I know you would have never done *anything* to hurt them—never!"

"How do you know *that?* How do you know I was paying attention to what I was doing? Maybe I was playing with the stereo. Maybe I was paying more attention to what Byron was saying than my driving."

"There isn't a person alive," Michael said, "who hasn't had moments of distraction when they're driving. Most of them are simply fortunate to not have a truck coming in their lane when that happens."

Jess shook his head. "Okay, but . . . maybe if I had been paying attention, I could have avoided it."

"Were you distracted, Jess?" Emily asked. "Is that what's bothering you?"

He shook his head with a humorless chuckle and sat down hard. Michael sat as well. "I don't remember," Jess admitted. "I have absolutely no idea what I was doing. I remember Byron saying something about those headlights coming straight at us. I remember Krista screaming, and the tires squealing, and I was turning the wheel. And that's it." He seemed to startle himself out of a daze and added, "But maybe if I had turned the wheel the other way, the impact point would have been me, instead of . . . " He pressed a hand over his eyes. " . . . Instead of my brother." He hung his head and muttered, "Why me? James and Krista had a life; they had a child. And Byron was such a good guy. He had everything going for him, you know. He was the one who pulled *me* out of the gutter. And there's no question that it would have been better for Heather if Byron had lived instead of . . . " He stopped abruptly and glanced at his parents, then Tamra, as if he realized he'd let something slip that he hadn't wanted to say.

"Where did that come from?" Michael asked. "What on earth makes you think that Heather would have preferred for you to die instead of Byron?"

"She told me!" he shouted.

"What?" Emily countered. "Surely she would not have even alluded to something so insensitive. Tell me what she said."

Jess dragged a hand abruptly through his hair. Tamra could see that this was difficult for him, but she prayed it would get some things in the open—once and for all—that would help him heal and get on with his life.

"Jess," Emily urged more gently, "please tell me what Heather said."

Tamra feared he would simply storm out of the room. But he leaned his forearms on the table and pressed his hands together. "She . . . uh . . . well, a couple of weeks before the accident . . . maybe ten days, I don't know. She told me we needed to talk. She told me that she'd had some feelings about us . . . that maybe we weren't meant to be together after all."

"This was before the accident?" Michael asked, as if he couldn't believe it.

"That's right," Jess said.

"But . . . she was staying here when it happened," Emily said. "She'd been here . . . for weeks; that's what I remember from what we were told."

"That's right," Jess said. "She didn't go with us that night because she wasn't feeling well, or so she said. I believe she didn't go because she didn't want to be with me and Byron at the same time."

"What are you saying?" Emily asked.

"She was completely honest with me, Mother. She wasn't being flaky or two-timing or anything. She just told me that . . . she'd had some strong feelings for Byron, and . . . "

"Oh, good heavens," Emily muttered breathlessly and exchanged a hard glance with Michael. Tamra hadn't known Heather or been around when all of this had transpired, but she could feel the deepening of the irony—and one more level of Jess's inner turmoil.

"She said," Jess went on, "that it had actually frightened her to realize what she was feeling, and in spite of all the years we'd been together, she couldn't marry me unless she knew it was right. She said she just . . . needed to step back a little and . . . search her feelings . . . and pray about what she needed to do. I do know that she met Byron in town more than once while she was staying here. She told me she was going to. She was never unkind or dishonest, but . . . it still . . . was hard to take, and . . . " His voice cracked only slightly. "When I came out of the coma . . . and found out he was gone and I wasn't . . . I just had to believe that she would have preferred it to be the other way around." He gave a bitter chuckle. "After that, she was sweet, and she did and said all the right things. But I could feel it. She had gotten me by default, and nothing could ever be the same between us. I think we both hoped that with time we'd fall in love again. But it just didn't happen. And when she told me she'd found somebody else, it wasn't really a surprise. And I knew it was likely for the best. I don't think I was so much brokenhearted over losing Heather by that time—I just . . . felt sorry for her . . . because I think she really loved him. I know I did." He shook his head in disbelief. "A man could have never asked for a truer friend."

Michael leaned forward and asked, "Jess, did Byron talk to you about Heather? Do you know how he felt?"

"Yes. He told me soon after Heather had talked to me that . . . he'd started feeling attracted to her after he got home from his mission and was at BYU, and I was still on my mission—less than an hour from BYU most of the time. But he'd never let on to her about the way he felt, and he'd always remained true to me. He had figured that time would work it all out for the best as long as he had integrity. And he *did* have integrity. When he realized that Heather was feeling the same way, he came and talked to me. He said he wouldn't see her without my knowing. I was hurt . . . needless to say. But you can't tell somebody not to feel something they feel. I never felt angry. I really didn't—not with either one of them. I only felt angry with myself for not working it out so that Byron could have been here for her, and I could have been out of my misery."

Following a minute of silence, aside from Emily sniffling, Jess erupted to his feet and left the room, declaring, "I think I'm tired."

Chapter Eleven

Tamra stood up and pulled the chocolate mousse out of the fridge, saying hopefully, "We forgot to have dessert. Maybe chocolate will make us feel better."

They ate in silence for a few minutes before Emily said, "When I was married to Ryan and we were pathetically poor, I would go to the mall once in a while and scrounge all of the change in my purse to buy an orange truffle. It always made me feel better."

"Where did that come from?" Michael asked.

"She said chocolate might make us feel better. I was illustrating a point to tell her that I agreed."

"Well *I* don't feel better," Michael said, pushing his dessert dish away.

"I do," Tamra said. "It tastes wonderful."

"I feel better too," Emily said.

"It must be a female thing," Michael growled and jumped to his feet.

"Sit down, Michael," Emily said and he did. "We're not making light of what just happened. But if we don't get a little relief from the tension once in a while, we're all going to lose it."

Michael groaned and pushed his hands through his hair. "You know," he said, "when Tamra first told us that Heather had left him, I was certain I knew exactly how he felt, and I could actually understand—to some degree—how he could be suicidal. But now there's a whole different twist, and I realize I have absolutely no idea how he must feel."

"How were you thinking you knew exactly how he felt?" Emily asked in a tone that made it evident Jess's struggles had put some strain on their moods. He looked at her hard and Tamra wondered if she should get up and leave. She attempted to stand and Emily put a hand over her arm to stop her. "How?" she repeated.

"You're going senile, Mrs. Hamilton," he said. "Surely you must recall how I left BYU in the middle of a term because the woman I loved had told me she was going to marry another man."

Emily squeezed her eyes shut. "Yes, I must be going senile," she said softly. She opened her eyes and reached for Michael's hand. "I'm sorry. I know how hard that was for you. But as you just said, what Jess is going through has an entirely different twist."

Michael sighed and shook his head. "I just don't know how to help him, Emily."

"The best thing we can do is pray."

Michael nodded and stood up to finish the dishes. Emily tried to help him but he said, "Let me. I need to do something to get things out of my system."

Tamra slipped into the hall and moved toward the side door, wondering if they needed to talk without her. But a moment later she felt Emily's hand on her arm. "Can we talk?" Emily asked.

"Of course," Tamra said and they stepped outside. Walking over the lawn, she asked, "He was talking about you, wasn't he?"

"What?" Emily asked.

"You're the one who left him in college to marry another man."

"Yes, he was talking about me," she said. "When I put all the puzzle pieces of my life together, I know I did what was right at the time, and it had to be that way. But those were difficult years for both of us. Knowing something is right doesn't necessarily make it easy."

They walked around the side of the house while Tamra waited to hear what she wanted to talk about. Emily finally said, "Has Jess said anything to you about Heather?"

"Nothing," she said. "I knew she had left him. But that was more my happening to be there when he told Sadie."

Emily sighed loudly. "She really was a sweet girl, in spite of certain things I mentioned earlier that really have no bearing. I never really felt like she was right for Jess, but they loved each other and there are many things a mother has to accept that have nothing to do with her."

"So you're relieved it didn't work out?" Tamra asked.

"Yes, I must admit that I am. I'm only sorry that the entire thing has caused so much grief for Jess. I had no idea there were so many complications tied into what had happened."

"Do you think what he said tonight is the heart of what's been eating at him?"

"I think it's part of it," Emily said. "But . . . there's something else—something that doesn't make sense. I can't figure what, but . . . I just pray he can come to terms with whatever it is, before it ends up hurting him any further."

"And everyone who loves him," Tamra added.

"Yes," Emily agreed, "and everyone who loves him."

* * *

Jess stood in a familiar spot to stare out his bedroom window. He wasn't surprised to see Tamra and his mother walking across the lawn, arm in arm. He figured they could come up with plenty to talk about, given that they were so much alike. But he strongly suspected they were talking about him. He wondered what percentage of his life he had been the main source of concern and speculation for his family. And perhaps that's what troubled him most of all.

When he lost sight of the women, he lay back on his bed and stared at the ceiling, pondering all he'd revealed to Tamra and his parents this evening. He hadn't intended to let it spill like that, but now that it was out he had to admit a degree of relief. They knew now that he had lost Heather's love a long time ago, and they didn't have to wonder if the accident was the wedge that had driven them apart. Rather, it was the hammer that had driven the wedge deeper.

As the memories crept closer, Jess resisted his habit to push them away and instead invited them into his mind. The years prior to his mission were difficult to look at, but he'd finally come to his senses and put his life back together. Byron had had a lot to do with that. He'd befriended Jess in spite of his mean disposition and dark lifestyle. He'd talked Jess into going to BYU with him, where he had met Heather. And he had filled Jess with a desire to serve a mission. The mission itself had been a relatively positive experience. There had been challenges and disappointments, and there had been rewarding moments. But the consistent stream of letters he'd received from Heather and his family had given him a strong foundation of support. He'd come home from his mission filled with hope for a bright future. His feelings for Heather had remained strong and true, and he was ready to marry her and take her back to Utah where they could both get their degrees before they returned to his home in Australia and took over management of the boys' home. And then the axe had fallen. He'd barely absorbed the shock of Heather's love for his best friend when a truck in the wrong lane had shattered all of their lives. But James, Krista, and Byron were out of their misery. Heather had found happiness elsewhere. And he had been left holding the baggage. And oh, what baggage! He couldn't even begin to fathom how he might unwind the tangled, complicated mess his emotions had become. He felt as if his mind had been fogged over with shock and regret for so long that it had lost its ability to think. There was only one thing he knew for certain, only one thought that he clung to with any kind of consistency: he loved Tamra Banks, and her love for him was the one bit of hope that he might be redeemable.

Jess smiled at thoughts of her, and closed his eyes to bring a clear image of her to his mind. He loved the way he'd never caught a hint of makeup on her lightly freckled face beyond a subtle wine color that she frequently applied to her lips from a tube she carried in her pocket. She could smooth it on perfectly in a matter of seconds without a mirror or any fuss. It was as if she had too much life to live to be fussing with incidentals like trying to change the way she looked, and he admired such self-confidence in a woman. That same attitude was manifested in the way she wore her hair. Only his memory of watching her dance on the lawn let him know that it was long and luxurious, full of rich, reddish-gold waves. Occasionally she wore it in a simple ponytail, but it was more often twisted and clipped to the back of her head in a way that seemed to beg him to just steal that silly little clip and set her hair free.

Jess was thinking about doing just that, and of kissing those wine-colored lips, when he was startled by a light knock at the door. "Yeah?" he called.

"It's me," his mother said. "May I come in?"

"Sure," he said, but made no effort to move from his comfortable position.

In the late-evening light he saw her peer around the door as it opened. "Just wondered what you're up to," she said, closing the door behind her.

"I'm looking at the ceiling," he said flatly. "But tell the truth, Mother. What you're really wondering is how I'm doing after I left in the middle of an extremely miserable conversation."

"That's part of the truth," she admitted.

"What's the other part?"

"I just wondered what you're up to," she repeated, and sat on the edge of his bed.

"Just thinking," he said.

"Well, that gives us something in common. And I bet there's a good chance we're thinking about the same thing."

"Really?" he said. "Were you thinking that cold fried chicken and potato salad sounds good right now?"

Emily laughed softly. "No, but it does sound kind of good." A moment later she added, "I had no idea, Jess . . . that you were struggling with such feelings all this time. But I'm glad to know now. And I just wanted to say that . . . well, I keep thinking about a time when your father was struggling with some feelings that he had trouble talking about, and it ended up bringing a great deal of grief into our lives." He turned more toward her, hoping she would expound on that, but she just pressed a hand to the side of his face and added, "You're so much like him, Jess. And that's good. But I hope you can learn to talk about the things that are troubling you more easily than he did." She took his hand and squeezed it. "We have so much to be grateful for, Jess."

"I know we do, Mom, but . . . sometimes that almost makes it worse."

Her brow furrowed. "I don't understand."

"Sometimes I wonder why I have to feel the way I do when I have so much to be grateful for."

"I don't know, honey," she said, "but we're going to keep working on that until we figure it out. And maybe those antidepressants the doctor prescribed will make a difference when they kick in."

"I would like to believe that *something* will make a difference," he said, "because I'm not sure I remember what it was like to feel completely happy."

Jess heard his mother sigh, but she said nothing. She pushed his hair back off his face the same way she had done for the whole of his life, and impulsively he rolled toward her and put his head in her lap. "I love you, Mom," he said.

"I love you too, Jess," she said and they remained in comfortable silence until the room became completely dark. He had to admit that there was one other point of consistency in his life—the love and example of his parents was something he needed to appreciate. He truly was blessed, in spite of his idiocy.

"I should let you get some sleep," Emily said at last, and a moment later there was a knock at the door.

Jess sat up and turned on the lamp before he called, "Come in."

Tamra peeked in and said, "Oh, I'm sorry. If the two of you are—"

"I was just leaving," Emily said, moving toward the door, "honest."

Tamra came into the room with a spoon and a little bowl. "You forgot your dessert," she said to Jess.

"Isn't she sweet?" Emily said. "Chocolate will make you feel better. Good night."

"Good night," Jess and Tamra both said at the same time.

"You *are* sweet," Jess said, taking the bowl of chocolate mousse. He kissed her before he took a bite. "Mmm, you should get my father to bribe you more often."

"I'll see what I can do."

"Did you eat yours?" he asked.

"A long time ago," she said, but he gave her a couple of bites of his.

When his dessert was finished and the dish was set aside, he took both her hands into his and said, "I'm sorry about that scene in the kitchen."

"Sorry? Why?"

Jess looked down and sighed. "I was just thinking how pathetic all of this must seem to you. It seems pathetic to me. When you came here I'm sure you weren't expecting to get pulled into some ridiculous soap opera with the Hamilton family."

"No, but . . . I'm glad that I'm here, Jess. I know I'm where I'm supposed to be." She touched his face, much like his mother had a while ago and he wondered how he could be so blessed as to be loved by two such incredible women. How had his father put it? *The one who gave him life, and the one who saved his life.*

"I love you, Jess," she said and kissed him. "Every step you take toward coming to terms with what's hurting you is one step closer to your happiness. And your happiness is my happiness. Therefore, it's not pathetic."

"I love you too, Tamra," he said and impulsively put his head in her lap. She pressed her fingers through his hair and the next thing he knew he was wakening in the dark and she was gone. The clock on the bedside table read half past three. He hated the feeling of being alone, and it occurred to him that he should just ask Tamra to marry him. A scoffing laugh broke the darkness as the thought was immediately followed by the reality of his life. How could he take responsibility for a wife when he could barely cope with living from one day to the next?

"Face it, Jess," he said to himself as he shuffled into the bathroom, "your life is a mess, and she deserves better."

* * *

Jess had trouble getting back to sleep and went down to the kitchen early the next morning. He found his parents there working on different cooking projects that he knew were for the grand event this weekend. He had to ask, "Is that chicken I smell cooking?"

"It is," Emily said. "I don't know what you had planned today, Jess, but your dad can't help you fix fences because he's going to be busy in the kitchen all day. And Tamra can't be helping here because you know how grouchy your dad gets when he's crowded in the kitchen." Michael passed Emily a comical scowl and she laughed. "So, I'll have lunch for you and Tamra all ready about ten and you can take her on a picnic; ride up into the mountains, make a day of it. How does that sound?" When Jess said nothing she looked up at him and smiled. "You did say cold chicken and potato salad sounded good."

"Well?" Michael said, prompting Jess out of a stupor.

"It sounds great," Jess said. "But I'm getting the impression you're trying to do a little matchmaking here."

Emily faked an innocent expression. "Did we need to?" she asked. "I was under the impression you were doing just fine all by yourself. I think you've already realized she's an adorable girl—among other things."

Jess chuckled and grabbed a couple of rolls that had just come out of the oven. "If I'm going on a picnic, I'd better go back to bed for a while. I'll set my alarm."

* * *

Following a hasty breakfast, Tamra quickly accomplished the tasks Emily had asked her to do in some of the bedrooms upstairs. Then she returned to the kitchen to find Michael and Emily still working, and Jess standing next to the table, dressed in riding attire, complete with suspenders and boots—and that hat. He had a large set of leather saddlebags flung over one shoulder, and she wondered where he might be headed. She was about to ask when he said, "Hey there, gorgeous."

Jess noticed her eyes going wide and he couldn't help but smile as he put on his sunglasses. "Why don't you go put on those pretty little riding boots I bought for you and meet me in the stable in five minutes?"

Tamra felt a rush of butterflies, wondering what he might be up to.

"Did you buy her riding boots?" Emily asked.

"I did," Jess said proudly.

"Your father bought me riding boots when he brought me here during college. That's when I knew he was madly in love with me."

"Yes, I know," Jess said, winking at Tamra. "I *do* remember that story. And Grandpa bought Grandma riding boots when he came home to make her his wife after trying to join the Air Force. I remember *that* story too."

Tamra had to wonder over the insinuation. They had barely known each other a few days when Jess had bought her those boots. Had there been some deep underlying message in their meaning—at least from his perspective? She could only suppress a fresh tingle inside and say, "I'd like to hear those stories."

"Well, let's go," Jess said. "I haven't got all day."

Tamra looked to Emily, ready to say that she'd catch up on helping her later, but Emily laughed and said, "Everything's under control. Have a good time. No need to hurry back."

Jess leaned toward Tamra and whispered loudly enough for his parents to hear, "They're matchmaking." He kissed her quickly and added, "It's working. Go put your boots on."

"I'll hurry," Tamra said and ran up the stairs. She quickly changed into a pair of narrow jeans that could be worn inside the boots, the way Jess wore his riding breeches. She put on a button-up white shirt and a tapestry vest her aunt had made for her, then she smoothed her hair and twisted it into a clip at the back of her head. Glad that she'd put sun-screen on already, as she did every morning, she stuffed her lipstick in her pocket and hurried back down the stairs. She found Jess still holding the saddlebags, shifting through a pile of mail that sat on the top of the little desk in the corner of the kitchen.

"You have a letter there," Emily said. "I told Jess to find it before you go."

Jess glanced up to look at Tamra, then he straightened his back and lowered his sunglasses, giving her a long gaze from head to toe and back again. "You're right, Mother," he said.

"How's that?" she asked absently.

"She *is* adorable—more now than ever, I believe."

Michael and Emily both turned to look at her and she felt suddenly conspicuous. "I thought you were in a hurry," Tamra said to Jess.

"Just have to find this letter of yours," he said, turning back to look through the mail. "Oh, here it is," he said then laughed as he held it up. "Tamra Sue?"

"Oh hush," Tamra laughed and tried to grab it but he moved it beyond her reach and read aloud, "Tamra Sue Banks. That certainly would be you, now wouldn't it."

"It's from my aunt," she said. "She's always called me Tamra Sue. Now give it to me, *Jess Michael,* or you can go riding by yourself."

He quickly handed it over, as if her threat were truly a concern. She stuck the letter in the back pocket of her jeans and took Jess's hand.

"Have a good time," Emily called.

"Oh, we will," Jess called back and led the way to the stable.

They arrived to find two horses already saddled. "You prepared ahead. I'm impressed," she said, and he tucked his sunglasses into his shirt pocket as they entered the dimly lit stable.

"I assume you can handle your own mount this time," he said.

"I believe I can," she said, not admitting to a subtle disappointment as she recalled how she had enjoyed riding with him. He gave her a warm smile just before he bent his knee close to the stirrup to help her into the saddle.

She slipped her hand into his and put her foot briefly on his thigh, deciding she liked his method of helping a lady onto a horse. He put the reins into her hands and looked up at her, saying with gentle sincerity, "You look beautiful, Tamra."

She looked down at him, wondering what gave him the ability to touch her so deeply with such simple words or a fervid gaze. She'd been told before that she was beautiful, but never had she felt so prone to believe it. Never had she felt so beautiful as when Jess Hamilton looked into her eyes.

"You're very sweet, Jess," she said, taking his hand.

"Just honest," he said nonchalantly and mounted the other horse after he'd transferred the saddlebags there from his shoulder.

"Lead the way," she said. He put his sunglasses back on and headed toward the stable doorway. They galloped across the open fields then slowly meandered up into the hills, saying little as they absorbed the scenery with silent appreciation.

Tamra watched Jess ride ahead of her and couldn't help admiring the fine picture he made with a spirited stallion at his command. There was a certain dignity and refinement about him that couldn't be ignored. She was pleased to see that they were returning to the spot he'd brought her to before, and they dismounted to admire the view. As he put his arm around her and pressed a kiss to her cheek, she marveled at how far they'd come in so short a time. She hated the memory that crowded into her mind of finding him after he'd taken those pills. But she pushed it away and hugged him tightly, grateful that he was alive and they were together. Briefly analyzing all she felt for him, she found it difficult to comprehend how she'd lived her life without him until a few weeks ago. She'd heard stories of people finding the love of their life quickly and irrevocably, but she'd never imagined the intensity of such feelings.

After a few minutes he said, "Come on, let's go. There's another place I want to show you."

"Ooh," she said dramatically. "I can't wait."

They rode again for a long while. Tamra enjoyed the excursion, but she began to feel hungry and a little saddle sore, and she wondered if he might have anything to snack on in those saddlebags. He finally stopped in a grassy clearing surrounded by trees, where a clear stream ran over smooth stones.

"It's breathtaking," Tamra said and Jess chuckled.

"Yes, it is," he said, taking hold of her waist to help her down. When her feet touched the ground he hesitated to let go. She took off his sunglasses in order to see his eyes, now that they were in the shade. He smiled subtly as she tucked them into his pocket, then he tilted his face to kiss her. Oh, how she loved it when he kissed her!

He smiled again and stepped away to tether the horses where they could graze and drink comfortably. She watched him remove a blanket that had been tied behind her saddle—and she hadn't even noticed.

"What are you going to do?" she asked. "Take a nap?"

"Eventually . . . perhaps," he said, spreading the blanket on the ground. "But first I'm going to eat. I don't know about you, but I'm starving. It's past noon, isn't it?"

"Yes, it is," she said. "And yes, I'm starving, too."

He picked up the saddlebags he'd been carrying earlier and she asked, "What you got in there, Hamilton? Peanut butter and jelly sandwiches?"

"Don't you wish," he said. "I thought you should have a real Australian lunch. Vegemite sandwiches for you, my dear."

"Oh, please no," she said as he knelt on the blanket.

He laughed. "It's an acquired taste, my love."

"I've lived in Australia for more than two years, and I've tried it several times. If I haven't acquired a taste by now, I'm not going to."

Jess laughed again and watched her wrinkle her nose as he began to unload the contents of the saddlebags onto the blanket. He brought out two bottles of water, plastic forks and knives, little paper plates. She said with distaste, "Please tell me you have something in there besides Vegemite sandwiches."

He purposely hesitated before he pulled out a little bag of fresh, raw vegetables. She let out a laugh of relief. "Well, that's not much," she quipped, "but at least I won't starve to death."

"Would I let you starve to death?" he asked and produced two plastic containers, which he opened with a great deal of aplomb to show her the chicken and potato salad his mother had sent. "And cookies," he said, pulling out another bag.

"It looks wonderful," she said, laughing. "How did you ever manage?"

"I confess . . . it was my mother's idea and my parents did the cooking. I fear the more you get to know me, the more you'll realize I'm really not terribly clever."

"But you are terribly adorable," she said, sitting down across from him. He smirked and tossed the empty saddlebags off the blanket.

While Tamra spooned potato salad onto a paper plate, Jess removed his boots and stockings. "You *do* have an aversion to shoes," she observed.

"Yes, I do," he said. "Shoes are a necessary evil. And if you have to wear them, they'd better feel pretty darn good."

"Like these?" she asked, pointing to her own boots.

"Yes, like these," he said, pulling her boots off as well.

When her feet were bare he picked her up and carried her to the stream where he stepped into the water before he set her down. "Ooh, it's cold," she laughed.

"Invigorating," he corrected and kissed her. "Now we can eat."

He led her back to the blanket and they sat close together before he said, "My father told me many years ago that this particular spot has a great deal of history in my family."

"Really?" Tamra said.

"Really," he echoed, realizing she said that a lot—and he liked it. "As I understand it, Jess Davies' father came from Europe and claimed this land. He discovered this spot early on and came here often, and subsequently brought Jess as a child. Jess wrote in his journal about this place, and how he loved to come here and find solace. He brought Alexa here, and so it goes—one generation to the next."

"Incredible," she said and he chuckled. She said *that* word a lot as well—and he liked it.

"Would you like me to bless the food?" she asked. He nodded and she spoke a prayer over their meal before they began to eat. "Oh, this is wonderful," Tamra said. "Your parents really are very clever."

"Yes, they are," he admitted.

"After all, they produced you," she added and he smirked again.

"So, who produced you?" he asked and she looked surprised by the question. Had he been so self-absorbed that he'd never bothered to find out anything about her before now? The thought made him a little queasy. But it was never too late to start.

Tamra groaned. "If I start telling you about my life, you may decide you don't want to hang around with me anymore."

"No chance of that," he said.

"Well," she sighed, "there's not much to tell, really. I grew up in Minneapolis. My father left my mother when I was very young. I've only seen him twice, very briefly, and a very long time ago. My mother's been married several times, to deadbeats who would move into our dumpy apartment until they were tired of us and then they'd move on. I have lots of step-siblings, but none that I know well. I have only one blood brother."

"Where is he now?" Jess asked.

"He works with my mother, which is what she wanted *me* to do. She owns a bar. When I made the decision to go on a mission, my mother told me that if I did, I could no longer consider myself a part of the family. She was angry when I joined the Church, but when I told her I would serve a mission, she was furious. She had always wanted me to help run the business she had spent her life building, but I just . . . couldn't." She sighed and her eyes became distant. "I told her I respected her and her life, but it wasn't for me, and I knew in my heart I needed to serve a mission. She told me to never come back."

"You're joking," he said, even though her eyes made it evident she wasn't.

"I wish I were." She looked away and added, "I suppose that's one of many reasons the acceptance your family has given me means so much." She met his eyes with a timidity that he'd never seen before. "I guess you were right about me; I'm just another one of those lost souls who gets taken in."

He briefly touched her face and said, "We've never taken in anyone like you before." He forced his attention back to his food and added, "We have, however, taken in someone else who was disowned when they joined the Church."

"Really?" she said.

"Really," he chuckled.

"Tell me about her."

"Him," he corrected. "He became a sort-of foster brother when we were living in the States. My parents took him in and helped him through a number of challenges, I believe. Although, I was just a kid at the time. We still keep in touch regularly."

"You lived in the States as a child?" she asked.

"Yeah. Mother wanted to get her degree at BYU, so we lived there for . . . I don't know . . . three or four years, maybe."

"Did you like it?"

"It was all right, I guess. I think I'm more suited for Australia, however."

Tamra looked around herself and said in a wistful voice, "I think I could say the same about me."

Jess just couldn't resist saying, "So you think you could actually marry an Australian man? Raise Australian children?"

She looked at him abruptly, with eyes that seemed to read his soul. "Absolutely," she said.

Jess returned her gaze, while the thrill of such a prospect filled his entire being. But it was quickly squelched by the reality of what kind of man he was. *She deserves better,* he reasoned and looked away.

Chapter Twelve

"So," Jess said, leaning on one elbow while he continued to eat, "what lured you to Australia in the first place?"

"The only family I have beyond my mother and brother is an aunt—my mother's sister. She lived near the elementary school I attended, and I visited her nearly every day after school. We were very close, although she was much like my mother in many ways. They both smoked and drank too much. But she had a way of understanding me that my mother never had, and she always had a certain level of integrity that my mother lacked. She married an Australian and moved here several years ago. She invited me to stay with her after my mission, since my mom had turned me out. I was worried that it might not work out and I wouldn't be able to get back to the States. But your parents offered me an option, so I decided to go for it."

"Does your being here mean it didn't work out?"

"It worked out well enough. I just felt like I needed to . . . move on."

"And here you are," he said.

"Yes, here I am."

"Would this be the same aunt who wrote you a letter . . . Tamra Sue?"

She gasped and pulled it out of her back pocket. "I forgot all about it."

"Here, I'll read it to you," he said, grabbing it from her quickly.

He expected her to protest, but she just said, "Okay."

He opened the letter and cleared his throat elaborately before he began to read, *"My dear Tamra Sue, It was so good to hear from you, and to hear that things are going well for you with the Hamiltons. It's been pretty . . . 'Oh,"* he laughed, "your aunt has some rather colorful language."

"Yes, she does," Tamra said. "Sorry, I can just . . . "

"No, no, no," Jess said. "I'll censor it for you, and spare your pretty little eyes from these four letter words." He began to read again, *"It's been pretty* bleep *lonely without you."* Tamra laughed but he ignored her and forged ahead. A few sentences later, he made his *bleep* noise again and she laughed so hard that he had to stop reading, if only to laugh with her. "What's wrong with you?" he demanded. "Don't you like the way I censor?"

"Oh, I love it," she said. "But I'm not sure you should be exposing yourself to such worldliness for my sake."

"You can't contaminate what's already been contaminated, darlin'," he said and ignored her questioning gaze in order to read on. When the letter was finished he put it back into the envelope and set it aside.

Tamra contemplated Jess's last statement while they cleaned up their picnic beyond the water bottles and the cookies, then she sat across from him and said, "I think there's a difference between being contaminated and being tough. Even before I joined the Church, I always found certain things offensive. But it was impossible for me to get away from those things. So I just . . . tried to be tough and learned to look past them."

Jess made a contemplative noise and rested his forearms on his knees. "I tried to be tough, and for a long time I really thought I was. But I think I was just pretending to be tough." His eyes shifted to meet hers. "I think you really are."

Tamra shrugged her shoulders, wishing she could read his mind. She was about to ask exactly how he had pretended to be tough, when he glanced around himself and said, "So, what makes you so tough?"

Tamra sighed and reminded herself that she could talk about this without having to dredge up all the memories. And perhaps talking about her less-than-perfect past might inspire him to tell her the ingredients of his troubled heart. She cleared her throat and watched him closely as she said, "I was twelve when I decided that I was either going to have to shrivel up and die, or I was going to have to be tougher than my mother's string of husbands and live-in boyfriends— many of whom had abused me."

Jess turned toward her, startled. "Are you saying what I think you're saying?"

Tamra turned away, hating the familiar inner trembling that erupted each time she thought of her childhood. "If I admitted to the worst, would that make you think any less of me?"

"Of course not," he insisted. "You were a child . . . a victim."

"Well, yes I was. But that doesn't mean I didn't waste a great deal of time feeling guilty for what had happened. I think I believed that if I could be accountable for it, I could be in control of making the pain go away."

"So, you *are* saying what I think you're saying," he stated.

"If you can imagine the worst . . . that's what I'm saying. But don't try to imagine it. Don't even think about it; it's far too ugly."

Jess sighed and hung his head forward. "Obviously you didn't shrivel up and die."

"No, I didn't. I wanted to. But there was something deep inside me that knew it was wrong, and no one was going to stop it but me. When I told my mother what had been happening, she was eager to put blame on the men who had gone out of her life, but she refused to do anything about the one who was still living with us. So, I went to him myself and told him he was never stepping foot in my room again, and if he tried I would scream loud enough to wake the entire apartment building. And if that didn't work, I would call the police and tell them everything. And if that didn't work, I would kill him. He never bothered me again. In fact, no one ever bothered me again. Some months later, after that guy had left her, my mother actually got me into some counseling. It saved me, I'm certain. At least it laid the groundwork for me to come to terms with the whole thing. But the real healing came for me when I joined the Church. I learned that applying the psychology to strengthen ourselves emotionally is an important thing, but it can only work to its fullest potential when it is coupled with the Atonement."

Her voice broke with emotion as she added firmly, "Once I shifted the burden to my Savior's shoulders, I no longer had to hate and resent those who had hurt me. I knew that they would be judged fairly. Justice would be met, and mercy would be served. And when I was able to give the Savior all the suffering that He had already endured for me, I finally stopped hurting over what had happened."

She turned and looked into Jess's eyes, seeing a tentative hope there. She wondered if he could hear the deeper meaning in her experiences that could be applied to his own.

"And you never hurt over the memories . . . ever?" he asked.

Tamra sighed and attempted to explain effectively how she felt. "I can't say I never think about it. Those experiences, as ugly as they are, have become a part of who I am. But I made choices in dealing with them that made me stronger and better, instead of allowing the hurt inflicted on me to undo me. Sometimes it comes into my mind and I can feel troubled . . . sad . . . even a twinge of pain. You might call it . . . emotional residue. I'm human. But whenever that happens, I just remind myself of how far I've come, that it's in the past, and the price has been paid. And then I just . . . pray those feelings away. But that doesn't mean it's easy. And sometimes . . . " Tamra turned away, feeling the trembling inside her increase.

"Sometimes what?" he pressed, reaching for her hand.

"Sometimes . . . I wonder if I've completely dealt with it. I'm not naive enough to believe that such abuse won't impact my life just because I've told myself it's put away. I understand that healing comes in layers and . . . at times I wonder if I'm simply in some level of denial." She chuckled with no humor. "Perhaps it's just a sleeping dragon that has yet to be faced."

She was surprised when Jess kissed her hand and murmured, "I believe I know how that feels." He looked into her eyes and added, "Perhaps we will be able to slay those dragons together."

Tamra smiled and touched his face. A moment later he turned away and his eyes became distant. She wanted to question the source of his thoughts, but he turned back toward her and asked, "So, how's my great-great-grandmother?"

Tamra felt saddened by the question. She cleared her throat and answered carefully. "I have to assume she's fine, but I don't feel her close by any more."

"Why not?" he asked, seeming genuinely puzzled—or perhaps concerned.

"Well, I can only speculate, but . . . I believe there was something she wanted me to do, and now that it's done, she's gone on to other business."

"Really?" Jess said. She couldn't tell if he was fascinated with the idea, or amused by her apparent insanity. "And what was it she wanted you to do?"

Tamra looked away and briefly wrung her hands. She wasn't certain how he would respond, but she felt compelled to tell him the truth. "As I said, I can only speculate, but I believe she . . . wanted me to save your life."

Jess reached out a hand to touch her face, caressing her skin with warm fingertips. "You *did* save my life."

"I just acted on a prompting, Jess. If I hadn't been there, someone else would have—"

"Who else?" he asked.

"Sadie was there; Murphy wasn't far."

"Murphy's too ornery to listen to a prompting," he said. "Sadie's a good woman, but she doesn't have the courage you have."

"I don't know," Tamra chuckled. "I've seen her stand up to you quite well."

He chuckled as well. "So, she has. But I doubt she would burst into my bedroom and start slapping me around."

Tamra was relieved to see him smiling. "You remember that part, eh?"

"Oh, I remember," he said, perhaps sadly. His expression turned to subtle mischief just before he reached over and pulled the clip from her hair. She wondered why she felt briefly embarrassed as her hair fell around her shoulders. Jess pushed it back off her face with both hands, then he methodically combed his fingers down the length of it, murmuring with adoration, "Exquisite."

"Is it?" she asked. "I always thought it was unruly and a bit over-whelming. But wearing it in any style but long just takes too much work."

Jess let out a delighted little laugh and pressed handfuls of hair to his face. She was reminded of how he'd touched her hair that evening in the library when they'd hardly known each other. "It's absolutely the most beautiful hair I have ever seen in my life. Turn around," he added and she moved to face the other way. He played with her hair for a few minutes before she realized he was braiding it.

"Where did you learn to do that?" she asked.

"Horses' tails," he said and she laughed. "And I do have four sisters," he added. When he was finished with the braid that had nothing at the bottom to hold it, he touched the tip to her back as if to measure its length. "About three inches above your waist, I'd say. Exquisite."

Tamra chuckled as she recalled something she'd read in Alexa's journal. "What's funny?" he asked.

"I was just thinking about something your great-great-grandmother had written . . . about her hair."

"Do tell," he said, moving to face her.

"In a day when women kept their hair long and wore it up all the time—"

"As you do," he said with a smile.

"Not exactly." She smiled back. "Anyway, she was about seventeen when she cut all her hair off to pass as a jockey, and it was slow growing back. She said when she came to ask Jess Davies for a job, she could barely manage to pin it into a decent bun to be presentable for the interview."

Jess chuckled, as if he truly appreciated the nonconformity of this woman he had come from. "You know," he said, his eyes growing distant again, "there was a time when I believed that Alexandra Davies was my guardian angel. It's not like I had any profound experiences or anything. It was just a feeling. And then one day the feeling went away. I remember resenting her absence in my life, as if she'd abandoned me when I'd needed her most. It was years later before I realized that the way I had been living my life had driven many good things away—including my great-great-grandmother." He turned to her with intense eyes. "I hadn't really thought about it much until you brought it up a while back. I have to wonder now if she went to you because she couldn't get through to me."

At the risk of agitating him, Tamra asked, "And why couldn't she?"

He chuckled with no trace of humor and shook his head, briefly squeezing his eyes shut as if something painful had entered his mind. He forced a smile and said, "That *would* be the heart of the problem, now wouldn't it?"

"Would it?" she asked, wishing with all her soul that they could get to the heart of the problem—whatever it may be.

Jess said nothing. After a few minutes he lay back on the blanket, putting one arm over his eyes. Determined to not allow a pattern of avoidance to establish itself between them, she said, "What are you doing, Hamilton? Hiding?"

He moved his arm and looked over at her, showing a smile that broke the tension somewhat. "Come over here, Tamra Sue," he said, patting the blanket beside him.

Tamra lay down at a ninety-degree angle from him, putting her head on his shoulder. He took hold of her hand and she squeezed it gently. A few minutes later he said, "Do you know what the biggest difference is between us?"

"When did you come up with this?" she asked.

"About five minutes ago. Do you want to know?"

"I'm listening," she said.

"You rose above the worst kind of upbringing to become an incredible and amazing woman. I sank below the best kind of upbringing to become a loser."

Tamra lifted her head and rolled over to look at him. "You're not a loser, Jess. A little lost, perhaps, but—"

"A little?" he scoffed. "Oh, my dear Tamra. Your unconditional acceptance of me is touching. It truly is. But I fear you have no idea what kind of man you've fallen in love with."

"I know you have a good heart, Jess."

"And how do you know that?" he asked, his voice gentle.

"There are just . . . moments when it shows—almost against your will. I've seen it shine in your eyes. I just know."

"You're very sweet, Tamra," he said, touching her face, "but I must confess that I have trouble seeing what you see."

"Why?" she asked. "And don't change the subject or evade the question. Is it the accident? Does it have something to do with what happened with Heather?"

His eyes picked up a hardness that she knew all too well, and she feared he would get angry and put up his familiar walls. But he said in a strained voice, "I believe those things are just the long-term results of who and what I was long before that."

He became silent and she wondered if he would offer any explanation, or let the conversation drop. He turned to look at her and patted his shoulder with his hand, as if to urge her head back where it had rested. She accepted his invitation and quickly relaxed. She was surprised to hear him break the silence by saying, "I don't know what made me start making bad choices early in my teen years. I only remember feeling as if there was something inside of me that felt like it was going to explode if I didn't declare my independence and individuality hard and fast. Living between a home for wayward boys and a bunkhouse full of stable hands, I had all kinds of education available to me on how to go down the wrong path. But I quickly became a pro. Before I was fifteen, I had a smoking habit, I'd been drunk several times, and I had tried marijuana. Before I was seventeen I had experimented with hard drugs, and I . . . " He hesitated abruptly. Tamra squeezed his hand to offer encouragement, sensing his need to share the burdens of his past, just as she had done. "I . . . " he began and hesitated again, "I had taken advantage of a number of girls. Of course, they were the kind of girls that very much wanted to be taken advantage of, but . . . I know that doesn't excuse what I did, and . . . " His voice became subtly shaky, and she could tell this was difficult for him. "The only thing I can say that's perhaps a bit redeeming is that . . . well, I never went all the way. That scared me worse than cocaine." He chuckled tensely. "So, that's the truth of it, Tamra. That's the kind of person I am."

"*Were,* you mean," she said. "What's past is just that—past. Did you not put your life in order and go on a mission?"

"Yes, eventually" he said, with a tinge of sadness. "James left before I did, even though I'm much older. I'm glad I went, but . . . nothing was ever the same."

"Obviously our choices and experiences make up who we are, Jess. But whatever may be in your past doesn't make you a loser." He made a skeptical noise and she added, "If you were *still* doing cocaine and taking advantage of women, *then* you would be a loser." In a lighter voice she attempted to break the tension, "You aren't, are you?"

"No," he chuckled humorlessly, "I just do sleeping pills."

"*Did,*" she corrected. "Even that is in the past."

He was silent a minute then asked, "Do I have to confess to my bishop that I tried to die?"

"I don't know, Jess. You'll have to ask your dad. He'd probably know."

"I'll have to do that," he said and fell into silence until she realized he was asleep.

Her next awareness was a soft kiss against her lips. She opened her eyes to see Jess smiling. He kissed her again and she stretched herself awake. "Ooh, Prince Charming," she said.

"No," he chuckled, "I've told you before, we're Beauty and the Beast."

"And I've told *you* before, the beast became the hero in the end."

"You can hope, I suppose," he said and started putting on his stockings and boots.

"We must be leaving," she said, "or you wouldn't be constricting your feet that way."

"We'll be pushing supper time before we get back, and we ate just about everything except a few cookies."

"So, I'd better be putting *my* boots on, is what you're trying to tell me," she said through a yawn and twisted her hair into the clip.

"You *do* look adorable in them," he said and stood up to put the saddlebags back on his horse.

They returned home to find a production still underway in the kitchen with Sadie, Michael, and Emily all busily engaged in preparations for the weekend. For supper they all went out to the veranda for sandwiches, since they could hardly find the kitchen table. Tamra and Jess both helped in the kitchen and with Evelyn through the next twenty-four hours, until it was declared at the supper table Wednesday evening that everything was basically ready. Michael would be flying to Sydney the following day to bring the girls back on Friday. Jess and Emily would be going into town after they took Michael to the hangar. They had a counseling appointment, and then they would do some shopping and errands. Tamra was put in charge of Evelyn, while Sadie finished up some food preparation.

Tamra felt excitement building inside her as she listened to the plans for the weekend. As they talked about the party they would have Saturday night, she realized it had nothing to do with the mission homecoming beyond the fact that Michael and Emily had been gone for a year, and there were many family and friends that were looking forward to seeing them again. Tamra realized there was an unspoken tradition that this family used any excuse to celebrate with loved ones, and even business associates, who would gather to eat, visit . . . "And dance," Jess declared with a grin. His mother smiled at him and continued telling Tamra their plans, as if she thoroughly enjoyed the prospect of sharing the experience with a newcomer. Emily told her there would likely be far more people in attendance who were not members of the Church, including all of the hired hands and their families, and many associates who would drive from the surrounding area. Some would be coming far enough that they would be spending the night.

On Thursday morning Tamra stood on the veranda with Evelyn, waving good-bye as Michael tossed an overnight bag in the backseat of the Cruiser and climbed in to drive with Emily and Jess, getting into the front seat beside him. She prayed that Michael would travel safely and the counseling session would go well. She hoped Jess wouldn't come home in a bad mood and put a strain on the celebrations ahead.

While Sadie spent the day in the kitchen, Tamra played with Evelyn as she organized the toys in the nursery. With more children coming to stay, she doubted the order would last, but it might help keep the toys in better control. After lunch, Tamra put Evelyn down for her nap and set to work doing some ironing in her room, with the nursery monitor close by. Examining her wardrobe, she wondered what she might wear to the party Saturday evening. She opted for a casual dress she could wear with sandals, which would fit any category from casual to slightly dressy. It was wine colored with a crinkly skirt and floral patterns stitched over the bodice which buttoned up the front. She found a small hole under the arm and pulled out some thread and a needle to mend it. She rose to get the scissors just as a knock sounded at her door. She stuck the needle in her teeth to answer it, and she found Jess leaning against the door jamb holding a pair of black shoes with chunky, high heels and ankle straps that dangled from his fingers. He also had a dress bag draped over the other arm, with a hanger sticking out of the top. He was smiling. She felt relief at this evidence that the counseling had gone well.

"What is this?" she asked, pulling the needle out of her mouth.

"Shoes," he answered, holding them up slightly.

"I can see *that.*"

"And a dress," he said, lifting his other arm.

"What for?" She tucked the needle into the dress she'd been mending and set it aside.

"The party Saturday," he said and she realized it must be a more formal occasion than she'd believed. Did he not want to be embarrassed by having her show up in her everyday, casual clothing? He walked into the room and added, "I knew your shoe size from the boots."

"And my dress size?" she asked skeptically, not certain she liked this.

"My mother peeked in your closet," he admitted and she couldn't deny feeling a *little* better to think that Emily had been in on this little scheme. "Here," he said, holding out the shoes, "try them on." He tossed the dress bag onto the bed.

Tamra sat down on the edge of the bed just as Jess knelt beside her and took off her sandals. "Perfect," he said, fastening the little buckle around one ankle, then the other. "Stand up. Tell me how they feel."

While she was trying to absorb his excitement over a pair of shoes, she stood up and stated the obvious. "Jess, if I wear these shoes I'll be taller than you."

He grinned. "I know—a little, anyway. That's why I like them. Not to mention . . . you have great ankles, and those shoes just . . . " He looked down and chuckled as if he were admiring a work of art. "They just look great," he concluded. "Now look at the dress," he said with the excitement of a child on Christmas morning.

He lifted the bag and pulled it off the hanger before he held it up for her to see. Tamra gasped and took a step back, looking it up and down. The fitted bodice had a sweetheart neck and quarter sleeves, sparsely covered with sparkling beadwork. The satin skirt was full of gathers and hung longer in the back than the front.

"Do you like it?" he asked.

Tamra laughed and had to admit, "I love it, but . . . "

"But what?" He sounded alarmed. "Listen," he said, tossing it to the bed as if it were suddenly nothing, "if you don't like it or you don't want to wear it, that's okay. We can take it back—not a big deal. I know I'm being presumptuous here, but I don't want to be obnoxious and expect something that you're not comfortable with. So just . . . speak up, and be honest—not that I would expect you to be otherwise. But you might not want to hurt my feelings." He smiled again. "I just thought you would look great in black satin."

Tamra appreciated his attitude, but she readily admitted, "I love it, Jess. I really do. It's just that . . . I never even *dreamed* of wearing a dress like that. It looks like something you'd see at the Academy Awards—but much more modest," she observed and he laughed.

"What will you be wearing?" she asked.

"My black tuxedo," he said and she wondered how often this family had such formal occasions that he would *own* a tuxedo. His brow furrowed slightly as he asked, "So, will you wear it, or—"

"Of course," she said. "Thank you." She kissed him quickly. "You're really too good to me, Jess."

"It's not possible to be *too* good to you, Tamra." He kissed her again. "Now, if you'll excuse me, there are some things Dad asked me to do while he was gone. I'll see you at supper."

The following day at lunch, Emily announced that Michael had called earlier to say he had met everyone as planned and they were on their way. With last-minute preparations completed, Evelyn went down for a nap and Sadie decided to do the same. Emily sat on the veranda to read, waiting for the plane to come in. Tamra read from one of Alexa's journals for a short while, then she found some garden gloves and put them on to help Jess pull weeds from along the edge of the veranda. He was in one of his dark, thoughtful moods, and little was said between them. But Tamra enjoyed his companionship nevertheless while her mind wandered with her own thoughts. She wondered how Jess's sisters would react to what had happened in his life since they'd last been together. And she wondered how they would react to her, an outsider who had quickly become involved in a delicate family matter—almost as quickly as she had come to love their brother.

She didn't realize how nervous she'd become until she heard the plane approaching and felt startled. Her heart quickened and she found her palms clammy as she pulled off her gloves.

"They're here," Emily said with excited laughter.

Jess chuckled and pulled his gloves off as well, tossing them onto the veranda before he and Emily moved quickly toward the driveway where both Cruisers had been left, ready to go pick up the family members and luggage that couldn't be held in one. Tamra wondered if it would be more appropriate for her to wait there—or perhaps they didn't have room for her. She felt both relieved and freshly nervous when Jess turned back toward her and said, "What are you waiting for, darlin'? Let's go."

"Is there room for—" she began but he interrupted.

"Of course. Come along."

Tamra set her gloves with his and ran to catch up with him. He opened the driver door and she slid in to the middle seat, but he tossed the keys at her and closed the door before he walked around and got in the other side. Tamra moved back to the driver's seat as a reality dawned on her. She'd never seen him drive. She turned the key in the ignition and said, "Is that why you wanted me to come along? So you could gracefully get out of driving?"

He looked startled as she moved the vehicle forward, following Emily around the house and toward the hangar. "No," he said with a defensive edge. She glared at him and his voice softened as he added, "I appreciate your driving, but that's not why I wanted you to come. I'm looking forward to having my sisters meet you. It's the one bright spot in this reunion for me."

Tamra had to admit, "Well, that's nice to hear, but . . . maybe it would be better for you to drive and—"

"Tamra," he interrupted, only slightly terse, "I'm not out for any pretenses with you. If I hadn't assumed you would be coming along, I would have asked Murphy to go get them."

She turned toward him to check his expression before she looked back to the road ahead. "Are you trying to tell me that you—"

"I haven't been behind the wheel since . . . well, you know."

"Don't you think that's a little extreme?" she said, hoping he wouldn't move past irritated and become angry.

"I know it is," he said. "I don't know if it just . . . scares me, or if it brings the memories too close. I just know I don't want to do it."

"Okay, but . . . sooner or later you've got to drive again, Jess. You can't live your life out in the middle of nowhere and not drive. How did you manage in Utah?"

"I made good use of a bus pass and my own two feet. Oh, and I had a great bicycle." He chuckled, which eased the tension, but Tamra couldn't help feeling concerned. She was pulled from her thoughts when he put a hand on her arm and said, "I love you, Tamra. Don't give up on me, darlin'."

Tamra smiled and shook her head. "I'll never stop loving you, Jess. Never."

He returned her smile and said, "Then everything's going to be fine." He turned to look at the road ahead and added, "Hurry up, girl. My mother's leaving you in the dust." He let out a burst of excited laughter and she knew he was anxious to see his sisters—in spite of knowing they had some difficult issues to discuss.

The two Cruisers pulled up to the hangar just as it swallowed the plane. They had barely stepped out of the vehicles before a young woman with short, wavy hair came running out of the hangar.

"Emma!" Emily laughed her name as the two met with a hearty embrace. Then Emma turned and saw Jess. She literally took a flying leap into his arms and he was obviously well practiced at catching her, a gesture that clearly exhibited the trust and comfort of their relationship. He turned circles with her while they both laughed, then he set her down and they shared a kiss and a firm embrace.

"You look better than I thought you would," she said, pinching both his cheeks as if to mimic the proverbial aunt. "After what Mom said on the phone, I almost expected you to be half dead."

Tamra saw a brief glimmer of nervousness pass through Jess's eyes, but he quickly subdued it with a confident laugh and said, "I'm great."

All eyes turned toward the hangar as Michael appeared, carrying luggage. Three women of similar stature appeared with him, moving toward Jess and Emily, along with two small children and the baby being held by the one in the middle. They exchanged greetings with Emily and Jess amidst frequent bursts of laughter and a few tears. Tamra heard all three make similar comments to Jess about expecting him to look worse. He just laughed it off and told them how glad he was to see them.

After greetings had been exchanged and the laughter died down, all eyes turned almost simultaneously to Tamra, as if they'd all just now figured out that there was a stranger among them. Tamra saw the question rise into the eyes of all four of Jess's sisters in the same moment Emily said, "Oh, girls. You must meet Tamra."

Michael added, "She served in the Philippines with us, and now she's come to stay."

"Tamra, this is Allison, Amee, Alexa, and Emma."

"Hello," they all said in unison.

"It's so good to finally meet you," Tamra said, noting that Allison had a strong resemblance to her mother, while Amee looked nothing like anyone else in the family. And Alexa's appearance seemed a combination of her sisters. It took her a moment to recall that these three girls were not Michael's daughters, and Amee's resemblance was obviously to her blood father. Emma, on the other hand, was obviously

Michael's daughter—a feminine version of Jess, their features and coloring so similar that they could have been twins were it not for the obvious age difference. They were all taller than Emily but shorter than Tamra, with Emma being the tallest of the four. They were all beautiful girls, with obvious confidence and refinement. Tamra felt a bit intimidated—or perhaps just outnumbered. But Emily eased the feeling somewhat when she said, "You girls will all have to get acquainted with Tamra; I know you're going to just love her."

Tamra smiled toward Emily, wishing she could express how deeply her acceptance was appreciated. There was a moment of awkward silence while it seemed that each of the girls was waiting for one of the others to be the first to speak. But before they could, Jess reached out and took her hand, saying with obvious affection, "I know I do."

The surprise in their expressions was blatantly evident. But Tamra was startled to hear Amee say to him, "What happened to Heather?"

Alexa nudged her with an elbow. "Always so tactful," she said with sarcasm.

"No sense beating around the bush," Amee said, mostly to Jess. "Last we all heard, you and Heather were working toward a wedding."

"Well, it didn't work out," Jess said as if the idea was actually pleasant—which made Tamra feel a little better.

"Is that why you came home?" Allison asked.

"That's the biggest part of it," he said.

"Without calling me?" Emma added with a teasing anger.

"Sorry about that," he said with a smile toward her. Tamra could easily see that Jess and Emma shared a closeness that wasn't so readily evident with his half sisters.

"We can catch up later," Emily said. "There's a comfortable house and good food waiting for us. We don't have to stand around in the dust chatting."

"Yes, Mother," Jess said and moved to help his father with the luggage. Michael and Allison brought baby safety seats of different sizes out of the plane and fastened them into the Cruisers before the girls put the children into them. Michael took a moment to introduce Tamra to Bridger, who was barely three, and Katie, who was nearly four. Tamra concluded that Bridger belonged to Alexa, and Katie belonged to Amee, as did five-week-old Beth.

When everyone was settled and the hangar had been locked up, they drove back to the house. Tamra was relieved when Michael drove the vehicle she had been driving, which diverted any attention being drawn to Jess's aversion to being behind the wheel. Emma and Amee, along with Amee's children rode with them, and Tamra enjoyed listening to their comfortable banter. She was surprised when Amee asked, "So, where are you from, Tamra?"

"I grew up in Minneapolis," she said, "but I have an aunt who lives in Sydney, and I've stayed with her the past couple of years."

"So, what do you think of Australia?" Emma asked.

"Oh, I love it," Tamra said with exuberance and Jess put his arm around her. She saw a sly glance pass between Jess and Emma, as if they had a secret way of communicating. She hoped whatever they were saying was good; it seemed to be.

"I was born in the States, you know," Emma said. "But of course, we moved back when I was a baby, so I don't remember anywhere else."

"Oh, but she's got an insatiable American streak," Michael said. "We can hardly keep her away from there anymore. She'll end up marrying an American—just wait and see."

"*You* did," Emma said to her father, and he grinned.

"Best thing I ever did," he said.

"It's not likely she'll meet many Australian men in the States," Jess added.

"Personally, I prefer Australian men," Amee said and Tamra knew she had to be the one living in Adelaide. She hoped that before long she could keep them all straight.

The remainder of the day ended up being a flurry of commotion and activity that Tamra was content to mostly observe from the sidelines. Having Jess's hand in hers kept her from feeling too much like an outsider. The girls were all gracious and kind to her, but she sensed their being disconcerted to have a new woman in Jess's life when they had all expected him to still be attached to the one who had been in his life for years. Michael and Emily smoothly kept her included in the conversation enough to make her feel welcome, but she preferred to just observe.

Tamra was relieved, as she sensed Jess was, to see that they were all far too busy getting settled in and catching up to bring up the problem with Jess. Once Emma said, "So what's been going on that we need to talk about?"

Emily simply said, "We need to discuss that at a more appropriate time, dear." And the subject was dropped.

The following day was equally busy while they all worked together to prepare for the party and look out for the children. Evelyn enjoyed having her little cousins to play with, and they did relatively well together in spite of an occasional confrontation over the possession of certain toys. Tamra appreciated the way each of Jess's sisters made an effort to engage her in bits and pieces of conversation in an obvious attempt to get to know her better. She sensed the same goodness in each of them that she had found in their parents and couldn't helping liking them. She only hoped they would like her as well.

Chapter Thirteen

When it was time to get ready for the party, Tamra was seized by a fresh bout of nerves. She took a quick shower and fluffed her hair to encourage its natural curl, rather than attempting to smooth it out as she usually did. She loved the feel of the black satin dress as she slid into it and managed to reach back and fasten the zipper. She was glad to find that she had some black pantyhose, realizing she'd not even thought about any accessories she might need to go with the dress and shoes. She found a pair of silver earrings that worked well enough, and decided the ensemble didn't require any other jewelry. She pulled her hair into a clip that left the bulk of it cascading down from the back of her head in a mass of curls. Looking at herself in the mirror, she couldn't deny that she felt more beautiful than she ever had in her life. But she wondered if that was partly due to the knowledge in her heart that Jess Hamilton loved her.

Tamra barely had her shoes on when he knocked at the door. She'd come to recognize his knock, and her heart quickened as she stood to open it. She caught her breath to see him in the classic black tuxedo, complete with a black bow tie. While she was completely absorbed with how incredibly good looking he really was, she was surprised to realize that he was gazing at her with unmasked adoration sparkling in his eyes.

"You look incredible," he finally said.

"Thanks," she said and glanced down briefly before she met his eyes and added firmly, "So do you."

"Are you ready?" he asked, holding out his arm.

"Oh, just a minute," she said and picked up her lipstick, then she realized that she had nowhere to put it.

Jess grinned and took it from her, tucking it into his jacket pocket, saying, "I'll never be far away, I promise."

Tamra put her hand over his arm and closed her bedroom door. In the hall he hesitated and just smiled at her again, approval and adoration shining from his eyes. Tamra loved the way he didn't seem the least bit chagrined over her height advantage in these shoes, however slight. She'd dated at least a few men who were disconcerted by such an unconventional situation. But Jess seemed almost proud of her height as he walked her toward the stairs. His silent approbation inspired her to pull her shoulders back and be confident in who and what she was.

Standing at the top of the stairs, with her hand over his arm, she could see a number of people gathered in the entry hall below—all dressed very casually.

"Jess," she whispered frantically, "don't you think we're just a wee bit overdressed?"

He chuckled softly, close to her ear. "That's what's so fun," he said. "If everybody was dressed like this, it wouldn't be any fun."

Tamra turned around and moved away from the top of the staircase, attempting to adjust to a situation she hadn't been prepared for. It only took a moment to realize that it was his motive that mattered.

"Listen," he said, taking her arm and looking into her eyes, "I said it the other day and I'll say it again: if I'm being obnoxious and you're not comfortable with this, all you have to do is say so. It won't hurt my feelings. I'm not trying to embarrass you or anything, but you're just so beautiful, and I . . . "

"What?" she asked, wishing it hadn't sounded so angry. "I'm an ornament? Something to show off, to bring attention to yourself?" The shock in his expression made her regret an assumption that she sensed was way off base.

"Listen to me, Tamra," he said, sounding angry as well. "I don't care what people think. This is about you and me. If we were the only two people at this party, it would be all right, because it's just . . . for fun. But if you want me to go put on a pair of jeans, I will. And we can have a good time either way. I can take the dress back Monday if you don't want it, and I won't be offended." He gave a wan smile. "Disappointed perhaps, but not offended."

Tamra sighed. "I just . . . need a few minutes to . . . think."

"Okay," he said, his disappointment evident. "I'll . . . be in the kitchen."

Tamra nodded and hurried back to her room. By the time she was leaning against her closed door, she realized why the situation was making her so uncomfortable. She put a hand over her stomach, attempting to quell a sudden nausea over memories that had nothing to do with Jess. She was so startled by a knock at the door just behind her that she gasped. She took a deep breath and opened the door to see Emily standing in the hall. Her face lit up when she saw Tamra in the dress. After a long appraising gaze, she said, "You look lovely, my dear. I dare say you've fulfilled Jess's every expectation."

"Not *every* one," she said, opening the door wider as an invitation into the room.

Emily closed the door and said, "He didn't send me up here, in case you're wondering. But he did tell me that he'd blown it with you this evening. You can wear anything you like to the party, Tamra, and it won't make any difference to anyone here—especially Jess. There's just something I want to tell you about Jess." She sat on the edge of the bed but Tamra remained standing, almost afraid of wrinkling the dress.

"Through his preteen years Jess was a relatively quiet boy, always in the background, often seeming subtly unhappy. Then almost overnight he became a teenager, boisterous and obnoxious, defying us right and left, driving us crazy. His behavior gradually became worse until we knew he was smoking and drinking, even trifling with drugs. It went on for years while all we could do was love him and pray that somehow he would come back to us before he ended up in the gutter. And then he started hanging around with Byron. And one day he and Byron just showed up at one of these parties wearing tuxedos. And everything started to get better. It took me a while to figure out that Jess just had a need to be . . . *different.* Trust me when I tell you that tomorrow after church when we have a much less colorful gathering of ward members who stop by for punch and cookies, he will be wearing his rattiest jeans and a T-shirt, while everyone else is wearing their Sunday best. He's very showy, very funny when he wants to be—but it's never for the purpose of drawing attention to himself. It's just as if he's trying to declare that he doesn't have to think the way everybody else does. When I commented to Byron about the tuxedos, he just smiled and said, 'Better that than cocaine.'"

Emily smiled more to herself and added, "It seems that Byron had an insight into Jess that I had missed somewhere along the way. Jess is just full of this incredible need to be a nonconformist, I suppose. And this amazing energy, this . . . zest for life that he needed an outlet for. When he found a way to put all that energy and individuality into positive avenues, he came out of his rebellion. When he focuses on something good, he soars. He did amazing things in college, and he was a phenomenal missionary. But he's relatively oblivious to such achievements. He just wants to be . . . " she shrugged her shoulders and smiled, "different."

Emily stood and added, "I'd better get back to that party. It's pretty crazy down there. You come down when you feel comfortable."

Tamra stood alone in her room for only a few minutes before she took a deep breath and opened the door. She suddenly needed nothing more than to be with Jess and to explain all that she was feeling. She hurried down the back stairs, loving the way the yards of gathered satin flew out behind her and rustled on the steps. She stopped abruptly when she saw Jess step onto the bottom stair, obviously heading up. He stopped just as suddenly when he saw her. She saw him briefly search her face, then he smiled.

"You okay?" he asked.

"Yes, actually," she said, "but . . . I need to tell you something. Do you think we could talk someplace private before we . . . make an entrance?"

"Absolutely," he said and continued up the stairs, taking her hand as he passed her. They slipped into the sitting room adjacent to his bedroom. He turned on the light and they sat on a little sofa, still holding hands.

"I'm listening," he said while she was trying to gather her thoughts into words.

Tamra cleared her throat. "I've told you about my childhood, and when I told you that I'd come to terms with all of that, in spite of some *emotional residue,* I didn't clarify a certain point. There are moments when a memory will catch me off guard, and it kind of . . . throws me off balance. There are some things that I think I may have simply . . . blocked out, and when it comes back to me, I just have to take some time and come to terms with it before I can move on. Does that make sense?"

"Absolutely," he said with compassion.

"Well, I'd forgotten until we were standing at the top of the stairs that . . . whenever my mother would bring home a new man, wanting to impress him so that he'd move in and help pay the bills—marriage was optional—she'd always dress me up in the best she could afford. She'd spend a ridiculous amount of money for a dress I didn't even like, but she couldn't afford to pay for piano lessons, which I had desperately wanted. It was like she wanted me to be some kind of ornament to make this guy think we were just a sweet and cozy little family. After he took the bait and moved in, she became oblivious to the fact that he was a jerk just like the last one . . . or two or three. I lost count after a while. So . . . anyway, that's why I reacted the way I did, and I apologize for getting upset."

"Hey," he said, regret evident in his eyes, "I'm so sorry. I had no idea that—"

"It's okay, Jess," she said, putting her fingers over his lips. She smiled and added, "I love the dress, and I love the way you look in that tux, and . . . there's a party waiting, so kiss me and let's go downstairs."

"You don't have to ask me twice," he said and pressed his lips to hers. He eased back and smiled before he pulled her lipstick out of his pocket and said, "I think you need some of this."

Tamra wiped her fingers over his lips to remove the residue of lipstick she'd left there. "I think the color looks pretty good on you."

As they came down the front staircase together and moved through the different rooms of the house that were occupied with guests, Tamra felt eyes turn toward them, but not in surprise or shock at their being overdressed, as she might have expected. It was evident that these people all knew Jess well, and seeing him this way was no surprise. While they mingled and chatted, Tamra felt a deepening pride and inexplicable joy to be the woman who had claimed Jess Hamilton's heart. At moments she tried to convince herself that this was all temporary, that he had a passing fancy for her that would eventually fade, and she would need to move on. But something deeper inside, something rooted firmly in her truest instincts told her that their love was meant to be, and she had truly come home. She pondered the idea that these people who were obviously well acquainted with the Hamiltons would eventually become equally familiar to her. It occurred to her that one day she would likely take on the role of matriarch of this home, and such social gatherings would be under her jurisdiction. She found the idea surprisingly comfortable and realized she was truly enjoying herself.

After Jess had introduced her to a few dozen people whose names completely escaped her, he escorted her to a buffet table that had been set out on the veranda. They sat to eat at one of the many long tables that had been put out on the lawn, where they visited with more people. Tamra enjoyed seeing Jess in a different light as it became evident that he was socially competent, and there was a confidence about him that seemed a stark contrast to the emotional turmoil she had seen him struggling with.

After they had eaten, Jess took her hand and, with no explanation, led her to the upstairs hall, which was dimly lit and void of any people. She watched him program the CD changer to play randomly from several CDs that he had obviously put in earlier. Then he turned to her and said dramatically, "All set for hours of great dance music."

"Really?" she said, and he chuckled.

"Really," he said and eased her to the middle of the floor as the music began. "Have I ever told you how I love it when you say that?"

"What?"

"Really?" he perfectly mimicked the tone of voice she usually said it in and she laughed as he led her in a slow version of the swing to accommodate the tempo of the music. As they continued to dance, one song after another—everything from the samba, to rock and roll, to the tango—she realized more fully that he had meant what he said. He didn't need an audience to *notice* that he was different. He just wanted to have fun, and he did it by being different from the crowd. She was comforted to know that at least he didn't wear jeans to church. It seemed he could conform when he needed to.

Tamra felt a little self-conscious when a small group of guests came upstairs and started dancing as well. Their comments made it evident that dancing was expected in the upstairs hall, as long as Jess was around. When Alexa and Emma appeared, they sat against the wall and teased Jess loudly. He just kept dancing and teased them back. Tamra finally admitted, "My feet are killing me. Dance with your sisters."

"Take off your shoes," he said while he was kicking off his own shoes. A few minutes later, Tamra found herself dancing with Jess *and* his sisters, at the same time. His feet were bare, his jacket hung over the back of a chair, and his tie hung unfastened around his neck. They all laughed and did their own thing, oblivious to the need for any specific partner. Before long Allison and Amee joined them, and Tamra realized this was a long-time tradition. The hall became steadily more crowded, and eventually Michael and Emily appeared, coming close enough for them to hear when Emily said, "Only *you* could manage to dance with five women at the same time."

"All *beautiful* women," he said and took his mother's hand. "And make that six."

"Oh no you don't," Michael said and took Emily's other hand.

A slower song began and Michael put an arm around Emily's waist, holding her other hand near his shoulder. Jess took hold of Tamra much the same way, saying with mock condescension to his sisters, "Sorry, girls, there's only one of me. You'll have to sit this one out."

About halfway through the song, Michael turned toward Jess with a humorous scowl and asked, "Where did you dig up this music?"

"Dig up is right," Jess said. "This is *your* music, old man."

"Be careful who you're calling old," Emily said. "He's not much older than me."

"But you're much better looking than he is," Jess said.

"And you look just like him," Tamra added which made Michael laugh as he waltzed Emily to the other side of the room.

"I love you, Tamra," Jess said, looking into her eyes. "And I know you love me, too."

"How do you know that?" she asked.

"Because you came to the party terribly overdressed." He smiled and added, "Thank you. It was fun."

"My pleasure . . . and don't put it in past tense just yet. We're still dancing."

"So we are," he said and kissed her quickly before the next song picked up tempo.

He laughed as he eased away and motioned to his sisters to join them. Then Tamra realized what they were listening to and groaned.

"Oh my gosh," she said. "You would think I could move to Australia and get away from music like this."

Jess just laughed and proceeded to lead the entire crowd into doing the international arm motions to the chorus of YMCA. Michael and Emily found them again and Michael shouted to be heard above the music, "You didn't dig *this* out of my music. Disco was against my religion."

"You didn't have a religion when this song came out," Jess called back and Michael laughed again.

When that song ended Jess put everyone in lines and started the Macarena. Seeing Jess this way, Tamra felt almost in awe of this incredible gift he had to find joy and share it. Everyone around him seemed to naturally gravitate to his energy and enthusiasm. He was incredible. And she loved him.

Gradually the crowd filtered away, and once again it was just the two of them, but she had yet to hear any song twice. She wondered how much planning over the years had gone into his little tradition of the upstairs dance event. They finished with a song that was slow and romantic while he looked into her eyes and started syncing the lyrics so well that she could almost believe it was his voice she was hearing as he sang: *I can see a new horizon that will keep me realizing you're the biggest part of me.* He led her in a flamboyant turn and a deep dip that made her laugh, then he returned to the tempo and silently sang: *Need your loving here beside me, need you close enough to guide me, I've been hoping you would find me; you're the biggest part of me.*

When the song came to an end, he kissed her with a meekness that made the moment perfect. He held her hand while he turned off the stereo, picked up her shoes, and dangled them on his fingers while he walked her back to her room. At the door he kissed her brow, as if he didn't want to dilute the kiss he'd given her at the end of their last dance.

"Thank you for a perfect evening, Ms. Banks."

"Thank *you,* Mr. Hamilton," she said. "I'll see you bright and early for church."

"So you will," he said and walked away backward, blowing her a kiss before he turned and disappeared down the hall. Tamra drew in a deep sigh as if she'd just watched the end of a romantic movie, then reluctantly got ready for bed.

The following morning was a mad rush as several people hurried to get ready for church and get on the road in order to arrive on time. Jess sat beside Tamra in the Cruiser and held her hand, but he said little and she sensed that he was feeling down. As they walked into the chapel, she asked, "You okay?"

"Yeah, why?" he said and she just shrugged her shoulders. But his solemn mood hovered through the meeting, while his parents gave a heartfelt report of their mission and bore their testimonies with emotion.

Jess didn't perk up through the remainder of the day as they returned home and quickly put the house in order before many people came to visit. Tamra was amazed at Emily's prediction when Jess left for a few minutes, then returned with his church clothes exchanged for jeans with holes in the knees and an old T-shirt. Tamra followed his example and went to her room to change into her most comfortable jeans and a short-sleeved, gray sweater. When she found Jess on the side lawn where a crowd was gathered visiting, his eyes took in her attire—and her bare feet—which provoked a brief grin. But it quickly faded into the dark mood that was more typical of the Jess she'd come to know, and such a disconcerting contrast to the fun-loving man she had seen the last few days. He hung around his sisters and parents, but seemed prone to stay in the background and remain uninvolved. She wondered if having to face his sisters with the facts of his life had intruded upon the celebration. Or was there more?

Tamra went to bed, consumed with exhaustion, long before all the visitors had left. And since Jess stuck close to the crowd, she'd found no opportunity to ask him about his mood. She fell asleep praying for him, and woke up doing the same. After a quick shower, she went down to the kitchen to find breakfast nearly ready, with Michael working at the stove while Sadie mixed orange juice and Emily helped situate the children at the table.

"Oh, good morning," Emily said when she saw her.

"Good morning," she said, and the girls all greeted her as well.

"What will you have?" Michael asked. "A cat, a bunny, or Mickey Mouse?"

"Excuse me?" Tamra asked with a chuckle.

"He's making his specialty," Allison told Tamra. "Animal pancakes."

"Oh," Tamra said with an exaggerated enlightenment that provoked a giggle from the girls. "I'll take Mickey Mouse."

She stepped in to help set the table and sat down when everything was apparently ready and everyone else was sitting, except for Michael who slapped a perfect Mickey Mouse pancake onto her plate.

"Very impressive," Tamra said.

After the blessing they began to eat, even though Jess hadn't arrived. Tamra felt an urge to go make certain he was all right, given his mood yesterday. A few more minutes passed while she became steadily more nervous, wishing she had checked on him before she'd come down. When Emma said, "Is Jess still asleep, or what?" Tamra jumped to her feet and took a step toward the door before Emily put a hand on her arm and said quietly, "He's fine. I checked on him a while ago. He's taking a shower."

Tamra didn't realize how apparent her concern must have been until she sat back down and took in the stunned expressions on the girls' faces. Tamra focused on eating her breakfast, hoping they would all do the same. A minute later, Amee asked, "So, what *is* the problem with Jess?"

"We'll not be talking about it while he's not present," Emily said.

"That's somewhat of a relief," Jess said, coming into the kitchen with damp hair and bare feet. He glanced at the food on the table and said to his father, "Where's mine? I want a bunny."

Michael chuckled and said, "As soon as I finish eating my very ordinary round pancakes, I would be happy to make you a bunny. Sit down and eat some eggs."

"Good morning, girls," Jess said to his sisters as he sat down next to Tamra. He nodded toward Emily and Michael, "Mom, Dad."

"Good morning, Jess," they both said before he turned to Tamra and surprised her with a light kiss.

"Good morning, Tamra," he said, apparently jovial, but she could see the darkness in his eyes. He had a very unpleasant encounter ahead of him, and they both knew it.

"Good morning, Jess," she said, squeezing his hand tightly beneath the table. He returned the gesture with such fervency that she knew he was nervous.

Just after Jess began to eat, Allison said to Tamra, "So, how long have you been here?"

"Uh . . . just a few weeks, actually."

"So," Amee asked, "did the two of you know each other before then, or . . . "

"No," Tamra drawled, wondering if they were implying concern over the briefness of their relationship. Without apology or justification, she said, "We just hit it off rather quickly."

She appreciated Allison saying, "I'd only known Ammon about a month before he proposed."

"Yeah," Amee said, "she brought home a fiancé and we didn't even know she was dating anybody."

The girls began chattering about their experiences of falling in love and getting married, and Tamra was relieved to have the attention drawn away from her and Jess. Then Amee said directly to Jess, "Forgive me, little brother, I'm probably being obnoxious—I usually am—but I can't help being concerned when it wasn't so many weeks ago that you were engaged to Heather. You'd probably prefer that I keep my mouth shut in front of Tamra, but the two of you are obviously very close. Maybe I'm cynical; divorce can do that to you. But I'm just concerned that maybe this is simply some kind of rebound and you should—"

"Amee," Jess leaned forward and looked at her directly, "allow me to clarify a few points. I admit to not being very communicative with my family lately, but just because you haven't heard something, doesn't mean it's the way you believe it to be. Heather and I were never formally engaged. We discussed marriage, but the truth is, we have barely managed to maintain any relationship at all since the accident. And just so you don't have to wonder, I have no secrets from Tamra, so you can say anything you like in front of her. If she still loves me after what we've been through in the last two weeks, there's nothing any of you could say to change it."

A long moment of silence prefaced Emma saying, "What exactly *have* you been through in the last two weeks?" Jess sighed and hung his head. "That *is* what we all need to talk about, isn't it?"

Tamra was relieved, as she sensed Jess was, when Michael said, "We're not going to talk about it around the breakfast table with the children needing attention. After we eat and get the dishes washed, Sadie can watch the kids in the nursery and we'll talk."

Jess pushed his chair back abruptly and said, "Never mind that pancake, Dad. I'm suddenly not very hungry."

He moved toward the door and Emily asked, "Jess, where are you—"

"Don't worry, Mother, I'll be back in an hour."

Tamra caught a subtle glance from Jess and rose to join him, sensing his relief. "Thanks for breakfast," she said.

"You're welcome," Michael said and she left, holding Jess's hand.

They walked outside before he said, "I don't want to talk right now. There's nothing to say that hasn't already been said. I just need to clear my head and get my thoughts straight."

Tamra put her arms around him and hugged him tightly. "It'll be all right, Jess. They love you."

"I know," he said, "even if they are nosy—some more than others."

"They're just concerned."

"And curious," he said.

"You're their brother; they have a right to be curious."

"I suppose they do," he said and they walked slowly around the house in silence.

As Jess's mind circled through the surreal events that he was obligated to share with those who loved him most, he couldn't begin to fathom his appreciation for Tamra's presence in his life. If his great-great-grandmother had truly helped guide her here, he could only be grateful for such a miracle.

When they finally returned to the house, they found his parents and sisters all gathered in the lounge room, obviously impatient for him to arrive. He sat on one of the sofas, keeping Tamra's hand tightly in his.

"Okay," Allison said the moment he was seated, "I must say I'm glad we can finally get to the bottom of this, because my imagination has come up with all kinds of horrible possibilities."

"I'm with her," Amee said. "What's going on?"

Michael said to Jess, "Do you want to tell them, or do you want me—"

"I think I can be man enough to do that," he said, squeezing Tamra's hand and giving her a long glance. His eyes scanned over his family members. He took a deep breath and just said it, "I took an overdose of sleeping pills." There were a couple of gasps. "I tried to kill myself."

"Good heavens!" Allison said.

"Why on earth would you . . . " Amee began but couldn't seem to finish.

"I can't believe it," Emma said. Alexa just shook her head with her hand pressed over her mouth.

Jess looked at his sisters' faces and tightened his hold on Tamra's hand. Their grief and concern was readily evident; they all had tears in their eyes. How clearly he recalled her saying to him in the hospital: *I wonder how it might have felt for you to be on the other side of the veil and see your parents and your sisters grieving for you and trying to understand how you could do something so selfish.*

"Why?" Allison asked.

"I'm going to get to that," Jess said. "This is not easy, so bear with me. I can assure you, if I had been able to predict this moment, I never would have had the nerve to take those pills. First of all, let me clarify, straight up front: I'm very grateful that I didn't succeed, even though at the time I had no intention of failing. I'm glad to be alive, in spite of certain . . . challenges."

"Like facing his sisters," Michael said lightly. Only Jess and Tamra smiled.

"Why didn't you succeed?" Amee asked, her voice shaky. "What happened . . . exactly?"

Jess searched for the words then turned to Tamra and said, "Maybe you should tell them this part. I don't remember much of it."

Tamra was taken off guard, but quickly gathered her thoughts. "Well . . . it was late evening, and—"

"Wait a minute," Amee said. "When was this?"

"A few days before your parents came home," Tamra said. "There was only me and Sadie and Evelyn in the house besides Jess. I was uh . . . thinking about a conversation Jess and I had had earlier that day, and feeling concerned because I was afraid he'd misunderstood me. I was thinking that I would talk to him again first thing in the morning. I was about to put on my pajamas when a voice spoke in my head, saying very clearly: *Tell him now.*" His sisters all showed varying degrees of emotion. "I remember hesitating, not knowing what I'd say, and it repeated the same words. Then I panicked and ran. I knocked on the door and he told me to go away, but that same voice told me to open the door. He was barely conscious, and the empty pill packets were on the floor, so . . . " Tamra felt suddenly a little emotional and glanced at Jess. He squeezed her hand and she swallowed carefully and went on. "I made the call and stayed on the line until the helicopter got here. They pumped his stomach on the way to the hospital. By the time I got there, they told me he was going to be fine."

A torturous silence fell over the room. Two of his sisters were crying. The other two were obviously in shock. Emma asked through her tears, "Why, Jess? Why?"

Jess pushed a hand through his hair and tugged at it briefly. He chuckled tensely and cleared his throat. Looking at the floor he said, "I've asked myself that question a thousand times. It's complicated. And I'm seeing a counselor. I guess that's what we're trying to figure out is why . . . exactly. At the time I just felt so . . . tired of hurting and I knew Mom and Dad were coming back . . . and I just didn't want to face them. I know that sounds ridiculous. I was only with them for five minutes before I could see how they love me. But it's like I just . . . became consumed with this overwhelming . . . fear and . . . helplessness. It was like I just felt completely . . . dark. I could almost hear a voice telling me that this was the easiest way out. And I just wanted it all to go away."

The silence was broken by a variety of sniffles and Jess glanced up to see his sisters passing around a box of tissues. He sighed and turned to look at Tamra; she was crying, too. It was all so pathetic. He was such a *fool!*

"Was it because of the accident, Jess?" Alexa asked. "You said you were hurting. Is that still bothering you?"

Jess wanted to scream at her and tell her that was the grossest understatement of the twenty-first century. He swallowed carefully and said, "I'm sure that's a lot of it, yes."

"And what else?" Allison asked. "Did your break up with Heather have something to do with it?"

Jess put his rising frustration in check and quickly told them the situation with Heather that he'd told his parents last week. He concluded by saying, "Truthfully, my life has been a mess since that accident. But then, it was a mess long before I went on my mission. So, I guess my life is just a mess. Maybe I'm just irrevocably screwed up, I don't know. I only know that I'm glad to be alive, and I'm grateful to have such a great family. And," he turned to look at Tamra and she squeezed his hand, "I'm grateful for this incredible woman who has already lived a lifetime with me."

"So you are seeing a counselor, then?" Emma asked.

"Yes," he said.

"Are you taking any medications?" Allison asked.

"Antidepressants, you mean?" he retorted, wishing it hadn't sounded so terse. "Yes, I am. Sometimes I think they're helping, and sometimes I think they're useless. But then, it hasn't really been long enough to tell one way or another." Fearing he would get barraged with another embarrassing question, he erupted to his feet and said, "I think I need some fresh air."

He moved toward the door with Tamra's hand in his, stopping when his mother said, "Jess, there's one more thing before you go." He turned hesitantly and she added, "Doctor Hill asked you to tell your sisters something."

Jess sighed and hung his head for a moment before he looked up and said, "I have an appointment this afternoon, and she thinks it would be good if any or all of you would be able to come. Personally, I can't think of any earthly experience that sounds more miserable at the moment. But you might as well come, and then I won't have to tell you what happened."

"Jess," Allison said in a gentle voice, "we all love you. That accident was difficult for all of us, but far worse for you. I think I speak for my sisters when I say that we would gladly do anything to help you get past this. We're family, Jess. And we love you," she repeated. The others made noises of agreement. Jess nodded and hurried out of the room with Tamra, suddenly feeling a rush of emotion that threatened to completely undo him.

Jess hurried up the hall and into the library, keeping Tamra's hand in his. Just before he closed the door, Tamra asked, "Do you want me to leave you alone?"

"No," he insisted and closed the door, immediately pulling her into his arms. "I need you," he murmured and pressed his face to her shoulder just before a sob jumped out of his throat, followed by another, and another.

"It's okay, Jess," she said and urged him to the sofa where she held him while he cried like a baby. When he finally managed to calm down, he found his head in her lap while she gently combed her fingers through his hair. He looked up at her and she smiled with complete acceptance. "I love you, Jess," she said earnestly.

"Yes, that's evident," he said, reaching up to touch her face. "But I must admit . . . I'm amazed that you do."

"Why is that so amazing?"

"You have seen me emotionally disemboweled, my dear Tamra. You have seen me mentally dissected and completely broken. But you still love me, and you still treat me as if I'm a man worthy of respect."

"You are," she said.

He made a doubtful noise and she added, "So, do you find that amazing, or is it a rationalization to make yourself believe that we could never make it together?" He was surprised, not only by her ability to be forthright, but by her perception of feelings he could barely define. "Does it wound your pride to think of me seeing you emotionally disemboweled?"

He looked at her hard and had to admit, "Maybe."

"Talk to me, Jess," she said when he left his answer at that.

Jess sighed and sat up. "I just don't . . . understand how you could love someone like me. I mean . . . look at me. I'm a loser, Tamra. I don't have a college degree. I work with the stable hands who work for my father. Inheriting fifth generation wealth doesn't necessarily give me any personal value." He met her eyes with intensity. "So, why would a woman like you actually . . . love a man like me?"

"First of all," Tamra said, folding her arms abruptly, "love is not something we choose. I can certainly choose what I do with my feelings, but what I feel for you is not something I had any choice over. How I let those feelings affect my choices is up to me. And secondly, what exactly is your definition of *a woman like me?* Would that be a woman who came from a home of alcoholics and pedophiles? Would that be a woman with practically nothing to my name, and no family to speak of? I don't have a college degree—yet. And I'm working as a girl-Friday who is living rent free in someone else's house."

"Yes, but you're so . . . " he pressed the back of his fingers over her face, "strong . . . and secure. You know what you want, you expect what you deserve." He sighed and his eyes turned sad. "And I just can't help thinking that you deserve better than a man who would lose his mind and want to die. You told me yourself—it was selfish."

"Yes, it was," she said and he loved the way she never tried to mince words or soften reality for the sake of his feelings. "But you're beyond that, Jess. You're getting better every day. We all have low times when we're more vulnerable and struggling. I've had hard times, and I will again. As I've told you before, I'm certain I still have lingering residue from my abuse that I have yet to face. I believe true love is encompassed by the commitment two people share to help carry each other through such times."

Jess looked into her eyes and had to say, "Thank you for loving me, Tamra. I would be lost without you."

She smiled sadly and said, "The feeling is mutual, Jess." And then she kissed him, and he had to believe that everything would be all right.

Chapter Fourteen

Jess resumed his comfortable position with his head in Tamra's lap, and he was still there when the door to the library opened. Tamra looked over to see Emma, who said, "Hi."

"Hi."

"Jess, are you here?"

"No!" he growled and Emma chuckled.

"Okay, well . . . tell Jess we're eating without him . . . if you see him."

"I'll tell him," Tamra said, "if I see him."

"Very good," Jess drawled after the door had closed.

"Let's go eat," she said, trying to urge him off her lap. "That Mickey Mouse pancake gave up on me a long time ago."

"Well, I didn't even get one," he said like a hurt child. "But I think we should just run away and eat lunch in . . . Brisbane, or something."

Tamra laughed. "Maybe we should get a burger to get us by until we get there."

"Sounds good," he said and jumped to his feet.

"If we went to Brisbane," she said, following him out of the library, "you'd miss your appointment."

"I know. That's the idea, love."

She followed him into the kitchen where he announced to his family, "Tamra and I are going to Brisbane for lunch."

It seemed to take everyone a moment to be certain he was teasing. The tension eased when he sat at the table and Emily said, "You'll have to pack a lunch to get you there."

"I'll just eat this," he said and began making himself a sandwich.

Tamra was relieved when the conversation remained light and trivial, as if the difficulties of Jess's life had not just been laid out in the previous hours. The meal was nearly finished when Emily said, "We'll need to get off soon if we're going to make that appointment. Amee's taking the baby, but the other children are staying with Sadie."

"Lucky Sadie," Jess said with subtle sarcasm. "How about if I stay with the little ankle-biters, and Sadie can go to counseling?"

"Thank you, no," Sadie said. "Being with the little ones is far too much fun for me."

"I knew she was going to say that," Jess said as Tamra rose to help clear the table.

While she was rinsing some dishes at the sink, Jess whispered something in her ear. She nodded and he said to his family, "Tamra and I are going into town in her car, and we'll meet you there. We can't all fit in one vehicle anyway. Besides, if I'm not with you, you can talk about me." He added to Tamra, "I'll meet you outside in twenty minutes."

He had barely left the kitchen when Emma touched Tamra on the arm and said, "Forgive me, but . . . I just wanted to thank you . . . for being here and for . . . " her voice cracked, " . . . helping him through."

She offered a tight embrace that Tamra returned eagerly, overwhelmed with gratitude for the growing love and acceptance she felt from this family. The feeling deepened when Allison said, "It seems you've been able to reach him in a way that none of us have been able to for . . . "

"For many years," Amee added.

"That's right," Alexa said and embraced Tamra as well.

Allison and Amee did the same, while Tamra admitted, "I'm the one who is grateful, I can assure you. Whether I stay permanently or not, I can never tell you how I appreciate being here."

"Why is that?" Amee asked.

Tamra hesitated, not wanting to sound whiny about her situation. Emily explained succinctly, "When Tamra went on a mission, her mother turned her out. She has no family beyond an aunt in Sydney."

"That's horrible," Alexa said. "I can't imagine life without having a family. How would we ever cope?"

"I don't want to think about it," Amee said.

"Well, for many reasons," Allison added, "we're glad to have you here, Tamra. Personally, I hope Jess has the sense to make you a part of the family."

"Amen," the others said with an enthusiasm that almost made Tamra emotional.

"Either way," Emma said, "we're glad Jess has you."

Tamra smiled and turned back to the sink. "It's my pleasure, actually. Jess is easy to love."

The girls all laughed and she turned in surprise. "Don't mind them," Michael said. "It's just that . . . ever since Jess turned thirteen, he's been terribly difficult to love. It's evident you've had quite an impact on him, if that's the way you feel."

"What about Heather?" Tamra asked and a tense silence fell over the room.

Allison ventured to offer an explanation. "Heather was a sweet girl, but . . . we all had the feeling their relationship was not very . . . Shall we say, deep? And that was the way Jess seemed to like it. To see him holding your hand and talk about the things he just talked about is . . . "

"Amazing," Alexa finished.

Michael chuckled and said, "How do you girls finish your sentences when you live on different continents?"

"Life's just never the same when you're without your sisters," Amee said and the girls all heartily agreed.

While Tamra quickly freshened up and went out to meet Jess, she couldn't help wondering how it might feel to have a sister. She found Jess leaning against her car, wearing a white shirt and tweed vest with a pair of jeans. She was frequently taken aback with how thoroughly handsome he was. And she had to comment, "You're wearing shoes."

"There are times when it can't be helped," he said, but at least he said it lightly. He seemed to have maintained a relatively good mood in spite of the impending appointment.

"Are you driving?" she asked and tossed him the keys.

He tossed them back and said, "Not today. Thanks anyway."

Through the drive he kept his hand on her shoulder but said very little. She felt his mood darkening but let him be. When they arrived, Tamra asked, "Do you want me to just meet you when you're done or—"

"No!" he said, obviously appalled at the very idea. "You need to hold my hand."

"I'd be happy to," she said, "as long as I know you need me in your life for more than a security blanket."

His surprise was evident as he said firmly, "I love you, Tamra. You make me wonder what life was like before you came. I'm certain I could survive the forthcoming hour without your sitting next to me, but I would far prefer that you're there."

Tamra took his hand and kissed it. "I love you too, Jess. And I would be happy to hold your hand."

Jess's nervousness was evident as they went into Doctor Hill's private office, but it seemed to decrease dramatically once the session got underway. He was quietly emotional as each of his sisters took a turn expressing their shock over Jess's suicide attempt, and the fact that he would internalize so much grief and guilt. But their comments were made without criticism or disdain. Rather, their love and concern for him came through dramatically. Prompted by Doctor Hill, they each expressed their feelings over the accident that had taken James and Krista from the family. Through varying degrees of emotion they expressed their grief over the loss, but their gratitude for Jess's survival. It was plainly evident that not one of them had even remotely entertained the idea that he might be responsible for his brother's death. But most amazing of all was the conviction shown by each one of them as they expressed their absolute conviction that it had been James and Krista's time to go. Their peace over the matter was unanimous, and Tamra marveled at their spiritual strength, which was as readily evident as their love and acceptance for Jess. Tamra sensed that Jess was appreciative, but she suspected he found it difficult to fully believe what he was hearing.

In conclusion the doctor said, "You should bring them more often, Jess; you didn't have to say much."

"It's hard to get a word in with four sisters," he said lightly.

"Is there anything you'd like to say to your sisters while they're here?" the doctor asked.

"I just want them to know how much I appreciate their love and . . . their not judging or condemning me for my mistakes. I'm truly blessed to have such a family."

"Yes, I think you are," the doctor said. "I've seen some pretty interesting family dynamics unfold in this room. I hope you all realize what a blessing it is to have such a family."

Tamra saw Michael reach for Emily's hand.

When the session was finished, Michael took them all out to dinner where they talked and laughed, reminiscing over memories that Tamra enjoyed hearing. Jess laughed and participated comfortably in the conversation, giving her another layer of hope that he would be able to completely heal and put the pain of the past behind him.

They returned home to find that Sadie had just gotten the children to sleep, and she was off to bed herself, even though it was just past nine. Amee put little Beth to bed as well, since she'd fallen asleep on the way home, and the family then gathered in the lounge room, as if they all had a mutual desire to continue the reminiscing that had begun over dinner. Tamra found it fascinating to hear Allison talk of her memories prior to her own father's death, and how Michael had come into their lives. Amee and Alexa had no memory of their father, and it was only through photographs and hearing Allison and Emily's memories that they had any perception at all of life before Michael Hamilton had moved their family to Australia. And soon afterward, Jess had been born. It was evident that those years had been difficult, and Amee and Alexa seemed pleased to have been too young to know what was going on.

"I knew that marrying Ryan was the right thing to do," Emily said. "It seemed we all needed those years and experiences to be who and what we are. But coming here was like feeling a puzzle fall into place—everything just seemed more right than it ever had in my life. The girls thrived on the Australian air—Allison especially."

"Yeah," Amee said, "Utah didn't do well for her back then."

"It does well for me *now,*" Allison said.

"Yes," Alexa added, "but when we went back for you and Mom to go to BYU, it didn't do well for you at all."

"No, I guess it didn't," Allison admitted. "But then . . . those were some tough years for all of us."

"You missed the worst of that," Amee scolded her sister lightly. "You ran off to Vegas and avoided the *real* drama. By the time you got back, the worst of it was over."

"I had more than enough drama in Vegas," Allison said. "But I must admit, I'm glad I learned about that accident when it was all over."

Putting together what Tamra knew of the family's history, she figured they were talking about the accident that Emily said had nearly killed her. She saw a shadow come into Michael's eyes, and Emily reached for his hand, as if to offer some unspoken comfort.

"Oh, that day was so horrible," Amee said with a visible shudder. "Even before we got news of the accident, it was the worst day of my life."

Jess felt an uneasiness seep down his spine as Amee's words struck something incongruous with his own memories. The day had been horrible for him, too. But only *after* the news of the accident. He was about to question her on that when she said, "You know, Dad, you never did tell us exactly what you were angry about that day."

Jess's uneasiness deepened when he saw his father stiffen visibly, and the muscles in his face tightened. Emily turned toward Michael with stark concern showing in her expression.

"He told *me*," Allison said, apparently oblivious to the tension their parents were feeling.

"How could he have told you?" Amee demanded of her sister. "You were in Vegas when it happened."

"He told me when I got back," Allison explained.

Emily sidled a little closer to Michael before she said, "You know, girls, you need to learn to be a little more tactful."

Amee looked alarmed as she said, "Sorry, I just . . . It's been years. I assumed that it was put to rest."

Jess watched Michael closely as he turned to gauge the faces in the room before saying quietly, "There are some things that never become easy to talk about. I came to terms with what happened that day a long time ago, and I'm certainly not carrying any baggage around over it, but thinking about it always catches me off guard."

Jess recalled Tamra describing her feelings much the same way in regard to the abuse in her childhood. What had she called it? *Emotional residue.* Jess wanted to blurt out a demand to know what had happened that day to cause so much emotional residue. But he wondered if he wanted to know.

Following a torturous length of silence, Michael continued in a firm voice. "The reasons for my anger that day are not important." He passed a silent admonition to Allison, and Jess felt certain she'd never repeat to any of them what she knew. "You all knew I was angry and—"

"*I* didn't know," Jess said and all eyes turned toward him. "I thought it was just an accident."

"It *was* an accident," Emily said firmly.

"An accident that wouldn't have happened if I hadn't been out of my mind with anger," Michael said and Jess's uneasiness merged into heart-pounding alarm.

"What are you saying?" Jess asked, feeling his father's eyes penetrating him with a disquiet he'd never seen before. The emotional residue was visibly evident.

"I'm saying that I was driving like a maniac because I was *angry,* and your mother nearly died."

Following another length of silence while Jess feared his heart would pound right out of his chest, Allison said quietly, "It's okay, Dad. It's in the past. It's all forgiven."

Michael turned toward her abruptly and snapped, "Would all be forgiven if she had died? If you had lived all these years without your mother, would you have been able to forgive me for killing her?" He motioned toward Emma and added, "Your sister never would have been born."

The silence grew deeper and more taut until Michael turned back to Jess and said with a quavering voice, "At least you know you weren't angry when you were behind the wheel of that car."

"And if he had been," Allison said tenaciously, "we would have forgiven him too. Not one of us is in a position to judge why the accident happened or what was behind it. None of us are perfect. We're all prone to fear and anger and making mistakes. I made some pretty big ones myself, and *you* forgave *me*. It's in the past. We love you, Dad, and we know you love us. And it just doesn't matter."

Jess was trying to figure why he felt so uneasy with what she'd just said, when she turned directly toward him and added, "You know, little brother, you and I are a whole lot alike. We have never talked about it too deeply, but we both know that we're the ones who did a lot of stupid things in our youth and brought a lot of grief to this family. But we both came through and made it right, and we have to put it behind us. And just for the record, Jess, I don't care whether or not you were angry when that accident happened. I don't care if you were distracted, or being an idiot, or downright careless. It doesn't matter. Because it was their time to go. And if it hadn't been, they would have been protected somehow. It's in the past. And we're all going to be together again. And it's okay."

She turned directly to their father and added, "It wasn't Mom's time go that day, Dad. But if it had been, it would have been okay. And just for record, Dad, I remember very well when you told me what you were angry about, and once it all settled in my head I don't remember feeling shocked or disgusted. I remember feeling in awe . . . " She hesitated and her voice broke with emotion. " . . . completely in awe of the incredible love you had for my mother—for all of us; a love my own father never could have understood. And I want you to know that I've never—ever—since that day taken that love for granted." Tears trickled down her cheeks, and a quick glance showed that everyone else in the room was crying too as Allison went on. "I thank God every day of my life that *you* came into our lives, and because of you we have Jess and James and Emma—and even Tyson. And we'll all be together. I know it beyond any shadow of a doubt."

"Amen," Emily said, putting her arms firmly around Michael.

"Amen," the girls all said together, and Amee added, "to every word."

Tamra discreetly wiped at her tears, struggling to comprehend the depth and breadth of the love present in this family. She thought of what Allison had said about Michael's love. And while she had no idea of the specifics that were being discussed, she could understand why Michael was the kind of man he was. He came from generations of good people who had lived lives of loving and giving. Alexandra Byrnehouse-Davies would be proud of him—human imperfections and all.

Tamra turned to look at Jess and felt concerned to see that he still seemed upset, when everyone else in the room seemed to be basking in the warmth of a formless but tangible comfort. The conversation gradually merged back into pleasant reminiscing, but Jess's uneasiness remained. When the gathering finally broke up close to midnight, Jess kept hold of Tamra's hand and took her out to the veranda.

"What's wrong?" she asked once they were alone.

He began to pace so she sat down and patiently watched him until he finally said, "I remember so little of that day before actually being told that my parents had been in an accident. James and I were watching a video, and I hadn't even known my parents had left. Penny came downstairs and asked if we were all right. She was a friend of my mother's that lived around the corner. I was vaguely aware of Amee crying to Penny, but she tended to be emotional over everything, and I didn't give it a second thought. Some time later, Penny and her husband sat us down and told us our parents had been in an accident. My dad had gone into surgery for a badly broken leg, but was okay otherwise. But my mother . . . well, they couldn't tell me much, and I knew it was bad. I remember being terrified, but I didn't let anybody know. I remember crying in bed at night by myself, and it was days—I don't know how many days—before we knew that Mom would be okay. But even after she came home from the hospital, she was in bed and struggling for a long time."

Jess gave a humorless chuckle and shook his head. "The whole thing has always been such an . . . uneasy memory, but I never dreamed . . . "

Tamra ventured to guess. "You never dreamed there were emotional issues between your parents that had caused the accident?"

"Yeah," he said and shook his head again. "I just can't believe it."

He continued to pace and she said, "You're obviously upset. What's the problem?" He didn't answer and she pressed, "Are you just . . . disconcerted over learning something you didn't know before or—"

"I feel *angry,*" he admitted and Tamra had to acknowledge the counseling was doing well at getting him to talk about his emotions.

"At who?"

"I don't know. I'm just angry."

"With your dad?" Tamra guessed.

"Well . . . yeah, I guess I am."

"You heard what Allison said. She's right, you know."

He said nothing and she wondered if he somehow disagreed.

"Talk to me, Jess," she said after another minute of silence had passed.

"I just can't believe he'd do something like that. And I don't know if I can just . . . let go of it. Maybe that makes me less noble than my sisters, but—"

"Or maybe," Michael's voice startled them both and they looked over to see him leaning against one of the posts, his hands in his pockets, "you can't forgive me for my accountability behind the wheel of a vehicle when it brought so much pain to this family, because if you did that, you'd have to forgive yourself, even though you have no accountability—because it was an accident."

Tamra watched Jess stiffen visibly and the muscles in his face tighten—much as his father had done earlier when the incident had first come up. She felt chills as she realized that Michael had likely just hit a very big nail right on the head.

When Jess said nothing, Michael added, "You know, son, whether or not you can forgive me for what you just learned makes no difference to me beyond the sorrow I may feel to think that my son would punish me for something that I have already punished myself for excessively. But I know from vast experience the emotional cancer that can eat away at a human soul when that soul is unwilling to forgive things we don't even understand. That's the key, Jess. That's what finally opened the door for me to get beyond my anger and my fear. It's forgiveness. I had to forgive your mother's first husband for all the pain he'd brought into her life—and mine. And I had to forgive myself for being proud, and stubborn—and angry." He shook his head and added with emotion, "It's not worth it, Jess. You're going to have to let go of the burden and give it to the Lord. Because *you* can't handle it on your own. No human being can. And while you indulge your pride enough to think you *can* handle it, you're hurting everyone who loves you. And the hurting just goes on and on, and gets deeper and deeper. And yes, I'm speaking from experience. I only thank God that He was merciful enough to let your mother live—in spite of my pride and anger." He sighed loudly and turned toward the house, saying, "Good night."

While Tamra was trying to figure how Jess had taken what his father had just said, Jess moved abruptly toward the door, saying, "I'm going to bed."

Tamra sat down on the veranda and turned her mind to prayer until she was so exhausted that she barely made it up the stairs to her room. But still, she found it difficult to sleep. Her heart was filled with a complicated mixture of emotions. The gratitude she felt for being where she was, and for her opportunity to be a part of this great family, was equal to the sorrow and concern she felt on behalf of these people she had come to love so quickly. Again she turned her mind to prayer and fell asleep before an amen was spoken.

* * *

The following day at breakfast, Emily announced that all of the women would be going shopping and out to lunch, and Michael and Jess would be looking out for the children, since Sadie would be going as well. Michael seemed pleased with the prospect. Jess seemed indifferent. But with the dark mood he was in, Tamra suspected he would be relatively indifferent to almost anything.

Once Tamra stopped worrying about Jess, she thoroughly enjoyed her outing with the women in his family. They talked and laughed in a way that left Tamra feeling completely comfortable and included. It was one more aspect that made the idea so appealing of being a permanent part of this family. She just had to believe that the love she shared with Jess would be strong enough to withstand the emotional struggles that lay between them.

Tamra felt especially close to Emma and found it easy to understand why she and Jess were so close. She had the vibrancy and sense of humor that Tamra had seen come out in Jess occasionally. Overall, Emma's personality reminded her so much of Jess that being with her gave Tamra some idea of what Jess might be like if he could come to terms with what was eating at him. The main thing Emma had that Jess lacked was spiritual strength and emotional peace.

Through the remaining days of the girls' visit, Tamra grew to love them each deeply and individually. And she felt complete love and acceptance from them. Jess and his father did some work together that left the women time to talk girl talk. She helped them put up a quilt to be tied, which they sat around and worked on while they visited, and she learned that it was common for them to do such a thing at these gatherings. The quilts were then used for wedding or baby gifts for close friends and relatives, or sometimes they were donated to a worthy cause.

Beyond the girl-talk, there were times when the entire family was all together, often reminiscing about experiences in their lives that broadened Tamra's perspective of the family. On Thursday morning, Michael and Emily went with Jess to a counseling appointment, while Tamra helped the girls finish the quilt and take it off the frames. Tamra felt deeply gratified with the accomplishment, even though she had done very little on it herself. And she was amazed at how beautiful it was, when it had been so simple. The back was made from a navy-colored queen-sized sheet, and the top was a print fabric in blues and whites, with mountains and snowflakes, tied with white yarn. Never in her life had she even considered what making a quilt might entail, and she found the experience deeply nostalgic somehow.

When it came time to say good-bye to the girls and their children, Tamra was amazed at how truly sad she felt to see them go. Michael and Emily were obviously sorry to have them leave, but in just a few weeks they would be going to spend time with each of them and their families. Jess said little as he gave each of his sisters an embrace, but Tamra sensed his emotion. It was evident their love for each other ran deep and Tamra considered the idea that it wouldn't be nearly so difficult to say good-bye to loved ones if the relationships were not so meaningful. She couldn't help thinking of how very little she actually missed her mother and brother. It had been difficult to be cut off and to know that she had no family love or support. But in reality, it had only severed something that had barely existed to begin with. She wondered if this family truly appreciated what they had. To some degree, she felt certain they did. Gratitude seemed to be one of the strong threads that bound them together.

The house felt eerily quiet in the days following the girls' departure. Tamra helped Emily and Sadie with some odd jobs around the house to put it back in order after the guests. She reorganized the toys in the nursery, washed little fingerprints off of furniture and walls and windows, and helped wash bedding and replace it so the guest rooms would be ready when they were needed. When that was finished, Emily had Tamra help her organize some family scrapbooks and photographs that had piled up through the last few years. And she also helped organize some mission photo albums, loving the stories that Emily told her associated with the photographs. In the midst of their projects, Tamra was able to help care for Evelyn, and grew to love the child more every day. She especially enjoyed sitting in the rocker in the nursery and holding her while she was still sleepy from her nap, and they would look at storybooks together.

Tamra was thrilled with the opportunity to have Emily and Michael tell her about the dozens of framed photographs hanging in the long hall. Some were portrait quality, many were snapshots. She saw pictures of Jess and his siblings through the years and pictures of Michael and Emily that helped put more substance to their history together. And especially intriguing were photographs of Jess's ancestors—even Jess and Alexa Davies. This facet of the family history put an added depth to the stories she had been reading and hearing about.

Jess kept busy with his father much of the time. Tamra noted that they did some maintenance around the house and grounds, spent time working with the horses, and even many hours at the boys' home. She began to see that Michael—and even Emily—had some involvement in every aspect of the family business. She recalled Jess telling her of his dream to take over the boys' home and run it, and she could easily imagine him doing such a thing. The current administrator, a Mr. Hobbs, did a fine job, but he had some health problems and was approaching retirement age. In Tamra's opinion, having Jess take over his job seemed an ideal arrangement. But much of the time Jess seemed so lost in dark moods that she worried he couldn't be successful at much of anything beyond following his father around and doing what he was told. He showed his fun-loving, cheery side enough to keep her from worrying that the depression was overtaking him. But she couldn't deny her deep concerns on his behalf. He continued to go to his regular counseling appointments with his parents, until Doctor Hill declared that Michael and Emily had done all they could do and Jess needed to go on his own. His appointments were also reduced from two to one a week. Still, one or the other of his parents drove him into town, working in errands and shopping to make the trips more worthwhile.

The weekend before Michael and Emily were scheduled to leave for the States to visit their daughters, they had company arrive Friday evening. Emily had explained to Tamra that Michael's sister Katherine, and her husband, Robert, had been unable to come to their gathering a few weeks earlier because they'd been staying with some grandchildren while their daughter, Stacy, and her husband, had been away on a business trip that they'd combined into a vacation. So Robert and Katherine would be coming to visit them for the weekend.

Tamra immediately liked them, and since Jess hung around while they visited with his parents, Tamra did the same. She learned that they had one other child, a son named Wade, who was also married with a few children. Stacy and Wade had both settled in the Adelaide area, and Robert and Katherine had relocated there a couple of years earlier to be close to their children. Before then they had actually lived here in this home, helping Michael and Emily manage the family businesses—which explained why they were all obviously very close. They talked quite a bit about Amee and her family and it became evident that since they lived in the same area, they kept in close touch.

On Saturday, Tamra had the opportunity to go into town with Emily and Katherine while the men went riding. She genuinely liked Katherine, in spite of a slight hard edge she had that wasn't evident in her brother—or her husband. Emily told Tamra privately that Robert had joined the Church many years earlier, but Katherine had never been interested. Their daughter, Stacy, had joined and was married in the temple. But Wade had also chosen to remain aloof from religion of any kind.

Their visit was a pleasant experience until Saturday evening after supper. Tamra and Jess remained in the kitchen to wash the dishes together, while the others went to the lounge room to visit. Jess was in a relatively good mood as they quickly worked together to put the kitchen in order. He kissed her and told her that he loved her before they started down the hall toward the lounge room. As they approached the open door, Tamra heard James's name and knew that Jess must have too by the way he stopped abruptly and held her back with the obvious intent to hear what was being said before he alerted them to his presence.

Tuning in more carefully to the conversation, Tamra could hear Katherine saying, "I really miss James. It just doesn't seem the same without him here."

"It's not," Emily said. "We all miss him."

"He was always such a good boy," Katherine went on and Tamra felt suddenly nervous. She didn't even have to wonder how Jess would perceive this. "We never had to worry about him getting into trouble or doing something he shouldn't. I don't think he ever gave any of us a moment's grief."

Tamra heard Jess sigh and nearly expected him to turn and walk the other direction, but he stepped into the room, saying with an angry edge, "Unlike Jess, who was *constantly* causing *everyone* grief."

Each occupant of the room sighed in unison before Emily said, "Katherine was not making comparisons, Jess. She was simply making a comment."

"That's right," Katherine said. "We all love you, Jess, and we always did."

"Yes," he said, his scorn evident, "but you can't tell me I was easy to love."

"No, you weren't," Robert said. "And neither was Wade for many years. That doesn't mean we loved either of you any less."

Jess sighed and asked, "Why are we even having this conversation?"

Tamra ventured to say, "You're the one who made it clear a long time ago that you didn't want the family tiptoeing around the issues. And you're also the one who walked in here and turned the conversation into a skirmish."

He glared at her, as if to say: *Whose side are you on?* She just smiled and urged him to sit beside her before she said to Katherine, "So, tell me more about Adelaide. I must visit there one day and see how it differs from Sydney."

The conversation quickly became light and comfortable, but Jess's sour mood remained until Robert and Katherine left. Tamra felt especially disconcerted to realize that it was slowly becoming more sour by the day.

Chapter Fifteen

The day after Robert and Katherine left, Michael said at the dinner table, "I know you've told me a little, Tamra, but remind me about your education and work experience."

"Are you trying to find me a job?" she asked lightly.

"Maybe," Michael smirked.

"Well, that could be good since Emily and Sadie are probably running out of odd jobs for me to do. This house can't get much cleaner."

"So, tell me," Michael said and she wondered if he had something specific in mind, or if he was just gathering general information.

"Well," Tamra said, "I've waited tables and done a little bit of restaurant cooking. I've done some secretarial work, and I worked as a receptionist in a legal office in Sydney. I'd like to get back to earning my degree one of these days—when it feels right."

"And what are you working toward?" Emily asked. "I don't think you ever told me."

"I was majoring in psychology, and minoring in business."

"Really?" Michael said, his interest suddenly keen.

Emily asked Jess, "Isn't that what you were doing?"

"Exactly," Jess said, smiling toward Tamra. "Interesting coincidence, don't you think?"

"I do," Michael said, "especially since I think I have the perfect job for you, Tamra—only if you want it, of course. If you don't, I'm sure we can find something else for you to do, however . . . "

"Yes?" Tamra said. "Don't leave me in suspense."

"Well, it's only temporary," Michael said, "but you just might be the answer to a very big problem that's come up."

Tamra's heart quickened with excitement. She loved working around the house and helping Sadie and Emily, but to have a specific job with real purpose intrigued her greatly.

"You see," Michael went on, "one of the assistant administrators at the boys' home—Shirley is her name—is expecting a baby. While we were out of the country, I kept in touch through letters with Mr. Hobbs somewhat, and he'd told me that they'd been expecting her to go on maternity leave and knew they would have to hire some temporary help. But she's just encountered some unexpected complications and was told a couple of days ago that she has to stay down in bed until the baby comes."

"Oh," Emily groaned, "that's horrible. I know how bad that can be. I'll have to visit her and give her sympathy."

"And some books and videos," Michael added.

As always, Emily quickly filled Tamra in on what she was referring to. "Before I had Emma and Tyson, I had to stay down for several weeks. It was horrible." She turned to Michael, "As you were saying?"

"Well, I think Tamra would be perfect to fill in for Shirley until she comes back—or at least until they can hire someone permanent, depending on how it works out." He looked directly at Tamra, "What do you think?"

Tamra resisted the urge to shout, *I'd love to!* Instead, she asked, "Exactly what would the job entail? Do you really think I could handle it?"

"I know you could handle it," Michael said. "And I think the job entails a little of many things. Mr. Hobbs would guide you, of course. There's a little office work, some overseeing of the staff and teachers, and even a little bit of working with the boys on certain points. If you're interested, we can go talk to Hobbs as soon as we eat."

"I *am* interested," she said. "Very much." She glanced at Jess and felt warmed by his smile, as if to say that he was pleased with the idea.

Mr. Hobbs hired Tamra eagerly and she went to work the next day, staying at the boys' home from right after breakfast until just before supper. She even had lunch in the cafeteria with the boys. She was barely settled into the job when Michael and Emily left for the States, taking Evelyn with them. Tamra was especially glad for her job because the house suddenly felt extremely empty. She enjoyed her time with Jess in the evenings, and he was usually in a favorable mood. But she sensed a growing distance between them that was too subtle to verbalize, but made her uneasy nevertheless. Occasionally he came to the boys' home to share lunch with her and she loved to see him interact with the boys. They had a way of bringing out his charming and comical side.

Tamra quickly felt at ease in the boys' home. The other employees were eager to answer her questions and guide her, and she became good friends with Shirley over the phone, regularly calling her for guidance. She liked and respected Mr. Hobbs, and she quickly grew to like being around the boys—even though there were a few that were obviously a definite challenge. She wondered what kind of heartache had preceded their coming here, and felt eager to learn more about them.

Less than a week after Michael and Emily had left, Jess said to Tamra, "Would you mind going with me into town tomorrow? I've already talked to Hobbs and he needs some things picked up anyway. He said it would be fine."

Tamra couldn't help being concerned with Jess's continuing reluctance to drive, but the prospect of spending some time in town with him was inviting. She loved her job but its restrictions had been an adjustment. She recalled Emily once admonishing her to not let any work she was doing interfere with Jess's need for her.

"That sounds nice, actually," she said and he smiled just before he kissed her. But as they started out the following afternoon, Jess was in an especially aggravating mood. He said practically nothing beyond terse answers to her simple questions.

"You know," she finally said, "you're not very agreeable company these days."

"Forgive me," he said in a voice that was anything but penitent, "I find little in life to be agreeable over."

Tamra couldn't help taking the comment personally and had to say, "And that would include *me*, I suppose, since I *am* in your life." He only tossed her a brief glare and she slammed on the brakes, skidding the Cruiser to an abrupt halt. She turned off the engine and got out, slamming the door.

"What are you doing?" he demanded, getting out as well.

"I am not driving you anywhere, anymore! Not another inch!"

"Why not?"

"You are belligerent and obnoxious and I can't think of one good reason why I should help you with *anything!*"

She expected him to argue that point, but he only growled, "I have an appointment. We're going to be late."

"Then I guess you'd better get in and drive."

"But . . . I can't."

"You've forgotten how? I know your license is still good, because I peeked." She gave him a forced smile.

"Tamra," he said as if she were a child, "just get in and drive."

"Nope." She glanced at her watch, then looked around at the desolation in every direction. "We don't have much water with us. We'd better get going."

Tamra looked into his eyes and could see his anger battling with his fear. She put both her hands to his face and said gently, "Jess, there is no good reason why you can't do this. You are strong and capable and we are not leaving until you get behind that wheel and get us out of here." He looked stunned and hesitant. She added firmly, but with a smile, "I am not going to even consider spending my life with a man who won't drive."

Jess took a deep breath and she felt some relief to see humility rise into his eyes, drowning out the anger. He glanced down and asked, "Aren't you afraid to get in a car with me driving? What if I kill you too?"

"My patriarchal blessing says I'm going to live a full life with many children and grandchildren. If I feel inspired to not get in a car with you, I'll let you know."

He chuckled, albeit tensely. He eyed the Cruiser as if it were some kind of a monster, then he took a deep breath and took hold of Tamra's hand. "Okay," he said, opening the passenger door for her. "You win."

He got into the driver's seat and fastened his seat belt. He gripped the steering wheel tightly for a long moment before he turned the key in the ignition, and it was another couple of minutes before he put the vehicle in gear and moved forward.

"Very good," Tamra drawled and he frowned without taking his eyes from the road. He was visibly tense and nervous through the entire drive, but at least he was doing it. When they got into town where they encountered other vehicles, his nervousness increased, but Tamra encouraged him gently and they arrived safely at Doctor Hill's clinic. When he turned off the engine, Tamra applauded and he actually laughed.

"You did it," she said and kissed him quickly on the cheek. "I'm so proud of you."

Jess turned to look at her and took her hand. "Forgive me," he said, "for being . . . What did you say? Belligerent and obnoxious?"

"I believe that was it."

"Well, you're right; I am. I know it can't be easy putting up with me, but . . . I need you, Tamra. Be patient with me."

Tamra touched his face and smiled. "I love you, Jess. Just keep moving forward, and don't shut me out. That's all I ask."

He nodded and kissed her quickly before he hurried in to keep his appointment while Tamra did a few errands. When they met back at the clinic, he slid easily into the driver's seat and said with triumph, "Doctor Hill told me to tell you she's proud of you."

"Me? Why?"

"Because you made me drive." He smiled subtly as he started the engine. "I conquered a great fear today, she said. And you know what?"

"What?"

His smiled deepened. "It feels good. Thank you."

"You're welcome," she said. "But my services don't come cheap. I'm starving. You have to buy me dinner."

"A small price to pay," he said, "especially since I was planning on buying you dinner anyway."

Tamra enjoyed their evening together, while Jess seemed equally happy and content. She wished that he could always be this way, and prayed that a day would come when he could get beyond his pain and achieve his full potential.

He drove home seeming much less nervous, and she could feel his confidence behind the wheel returning. But two weeks later she almost regretted provoking him to drive on his own. She had watched him grow steadily more independent of her, and she had to wonder if she had, indeed, been little more than a security blanket—something to hold onto when he was feeling lost and afraid. There were moments when she felt his love for her come through, and she had to ask herself if she was simply being impatient with his need to progress through his challenges at his own pace. But there was something deep inside of her that feared a day would come when their relationship would have nowhere to go but apart. She wondered if her fear came from her own seemingly desperate need to connect herself to the love and acceptance she had found being a part of his life. Or perhaps her fear stemmed from the growing evidence that Jess continued to hold onto a bitter anger that kept him distanced from her.

Not certain what the answers were, Tamra forced herself to not think too deeply about their relationship. She focused on her job and quickly learned to love many of the boys she had the opportunity to work with. She felt comfortable with what was expected of her, for the most part, and the challenges were minimal. She thought it funny that she had almost come to see Jess as one of the troubled boys being harbored by Byrnehouse-Davies and Hamilton. And she wondered if Alexa might have perceived such an irony from the other side of the veil.

Tamra saw Jess at breakfast and supper, and they often spent evenings riding together or just relaxing while she read out of a family journal and he read the newspaper. Jess kept busy during the days doing odd jobs around the house and on the grounds, and working with the horses. She was pleased when he made the decision, prompted somewhat by Doctor Hill, to press forward on his education. And she was especially pleased when he determined that he could likely get the bulk of his remaining requirements done via the Internet. He quickly made the arrangements and became thoroughly absorbed in what he was learning. He spent endless hours in front of the computer and studying the books that had been shipped to him. Tamra was glad to see him working hard and being committed to a goal. But his education seemed to be one more aspect of excluding her from his life.

He continued to attend church meetings with her and Sadie, but he managed to evade any effort Tamra made to engage him in spiritual conversation. The darkness she had seen surrounding him when she'd first arrived gradually returned and seemed to settle around him permanently. But he managed to be just agreeable enough to avoid giving her any just cause to address what was wrong.

Tamra continued to remind herself to be patient, longing for Michael and Emily to come back and give her the support she had become accustomed to in handling Jess's fragile spirit. And she missed Evelyn terribly as well. It was almost frightening to realize how quickly she had come to love and depend on being a part of this family, with her love for Jess being the crux of all she felt. Not wanting to address such issues, she was grateful for her job, and she spent much of her free time, when she wasn't helping Sadie, reading the family journals. After she finished Alexa's, she read the journals of Jess Davies, which didn't take long because he'd not written nearly as much as his wife. Tamra then read the journals of their children, Tyson and his wife Lacey, and Emma and her husband—Michael Hamilton. Occasionally she told Jess about the stories she was reading, and of her intense fascination with their experiences. He listened politely, but she sensed he wasn't absorbing much of what she hoped he might learn from his ancestors, the same way he seemed to deflect any comment she might make concerning the Atonement and how it could free him of his inner torment.

Jess continued with his counseling, and while he seemed to be gradually improving in some areas, she sensed he was simply learning how to cope with his pain and pretend to lead a normal life, rather than actually healing and finding a way to put it behind him. There were times when they could talk and laugh and she'd feel hope for a future with him, but the darkness always crept back in. He kissed her frequently, never behaving the least bit inappropriately with her in spite of the many hours they shared alone. And he often declared his love for her, and that he didn't know what he'd ever do without her. But where he had once alluded to sharing a future with her, such references stopped coming up. While Tamra reminded herself to be patient, a growing dread lured her to believe she was banking on something that might simply never happen. She couldn't force Jess to be happy, any more than she could force him to change what he didn't want changed. She could only pray that having her heart invested in him would not leave it broken in the end.

When she finished reading the journals of Jess and Alexa's children, she went on to read those of Jesse Hamilton and LeNay Parkins—Michael's parents. Every page made her feel closer to these people who had gone before, while Jess's growing disdain made her feel further away from ever becoming a part of something that she instinctively believed was meant to be.

When there were no more journals to read and Michael and
Emily still weren't due back for a few days, Tamra filled in some
empty hours with extra cleaning projects. Sadie had mentioned once
that the family video cabinet was sorely disorganized, and Tamra
found it the perfect way to fill up a Saturday morning while Jess was
glued to his studies—as if he could get his degree in record time.

While Tamra categorized dozens of prerecorded videos and dusted
the shelves they sat on, she came across several videos that were labeled,
family video camera, with dates that indicated segments covering a span
of weeks, or even months. Then she found a hand-written label that
read, *Jess's video project,* with a date that she figured would have been his
senior year in high school. She couldn't resist putting it in while she was
working, but she quickly found herself just sitting on the sofa, absorbed
in what she was seeing. Jess was behind the camera, but she could hear
him talking while he was filming different things at his school and
narrating information about his classes, his teachers, etc. Then there
was a segment filmed around the house and grounds, which looked
very much the same. He had footage of his family, although it was
evident the older girls weren't living at home because they were absent.
Michael and Emily hadn't changed too much. She felt chilled to see
James and hear him talking. She guessed he was about fourteen or
fifteen, but tall for his age. The segment ended with Jess's voice saying,
"So, that's my family." Then words came on the screen that said,
Lip-sync music video. Jess Hamilton. Fifth period. "Regular Boys."

"Oh, this I gotta see," Tamra muttered aloud and chuckled softly.
Then she let out a burst of laughter to see a younger Jess Hamilton
holding a microphone, pretending to sing his heart out to a song with
loud guitars and hard rhythm. There were two other boys performing
with him, each pretending to play electric guitars. And they were all
doing a *very* good job. If she hadn't known it was a lip-sync, she
would have believed it was the real thing. The guitarists were dressed
in jeans, T-shirts, and tennis shoes, looking fairly ordinary except for
wigs that made them look like they had long hair. And their faces
were difficult to discern with the flashing lights and shadows. Jess,
however, was in the foreground and in the spotlight, and his image
was clearly visible—which made it quickly evident that *his* long hair
was real. The carefully mussed waves on his head looked similar to the

way he wore his hair now, but it merged into a pony-tail that hung a few inches down his back.

With a professional ease that suggested he'd grown up a rock star, Jess looked into the camera and synced the words, *We're just the thing. We're regular boys.* He wore tight jeans, a shirt left unbuttoned with the sleeves rolled up below his elbows. His feet were bare. And while he uttered into the microphone, *And we're one in a million, and we like the way we are,* she realized there were six little silver rings of different sizes piercing the side of his left ear. Once she got used to this entirely different glimpse at the man she'd grown to love, she had to admit he was amazing. He danced, skipped, jumped, and slid on his knees, while pretending to sing the lyrics with such perfect ease that he didn't miss the slightest nuance in the voice as it sang, *Ooh, shoulder to shoulder. Ooh, gotta stick together.* Tamra laughed again and leaned closer to the TV, wanting to get a better look.

"What on earth are you watching?" Jess growled from behind, startling her.

Tamra just laughed and said, "Oh, I found a treasure."

"It's pathetic," he said, reaching for the remote in her hand, but she held it out of his reach.

"Let me watch it," she said, studying the screen. She laughed and asked, "Is that . . . Oh, my gosh, it is! You have a pierced navel." She laughed boisterously.

"Had," he grumbled. "It was a long time ago."

"And a pierced tongue too, apparently."

"Give me that," he said just as he sang from the screen, *I've got the goal, if I can get the money. Could fall in love with a regular girl; that's no big deal for a regular boy.*

"You've got great rhythm there, Jess, and some real talent. Maybe you missed your calling in life."

"Oh, yeah," he snarled, "I was extremely talented at mouthing other people's music."

"It's incredible," she said. "I mean it. All things considered, you look adorable. Who are the guitarists? They're pretty good, too."

"That's James and Byron," he said and took advantage of her surprise to grab the remote. He clicked the television off, leaving a deadly silence in contrast to the loud music.

He said nothing more, but he stood above the sofa as if he expected *her* to say something. She finally came up with, "It looks like the three of you had a lot of fun together."

"Yeah, we had a great time," he said with sarcasm and tossed the remote at her before he left the room.

Tamra didn't move for several minutes as she tried to understand one more layer of Jess Hamilton's character. She finally forced herself back to work, but she didn't get much further before she found a video labeled, *James and Krista's wedding*. Praying that Jess wouldn't come back in the room, she stuck the video into the machine and turned on the TV. Tamra lost track of time as she became mesmerized by images of a family wedding celebration centering around two people whose lives had been tragically shortened. *Evelyn's parents,* she thought and couldn't hold back the tears. There was footage outside the Sydney Temple, with Michael and Emily and all of the girls. And footage taken at a wedding luncheon that same day, and a reception that was obviously on a later date here at the house. She was struck with the fact that Jess was missing when she saw a cardboard cutout of a life-size photograph of him standing at one end of the receiving line. She had assumed he was behind the camera until she looked at the date and realized he would have been on his mission. And by the time he came home, Evelyn had been born. And then . . . Tamra clicked off the television, suddenly feeling a deep empathy for Jess's grief.

Help me to keep perspective, she prayed silently and forced herself back to her task.

A few days later, on the day that Michael and Emily were due to return, Tamra entered the kitchen to find Jess shuffling through the mail.

"A letter from your aunt," he said, handing it to her while he continued to peruse the small stack. "And what is this?" he asked with a little chuckle, holding up another envelope. "It's for you. From an accountant?" He laughed and waved it in front of her. "Don't tell me. You secretly have massive hidden assets and you have an accountant who—"

"You have a great imagination, Jess," she said, reaching for the envelope only to have him keep it from her grasp. "I don't *have* an accountant. It's personal. He's a friend."

"*He?*" Jess echoed and laughed. "Ooh, can I read it?"

Tamra chuckled and shook her head. "I really don't care, Jess. If you want to read it, you're welcome to do so. And you won't even have to censor."

"Okay," he said and sat down, dramatically opening the envelope. He cleared his throat elaborately and began, *"'My dearest Tamra.'* Ooh," he drawled. *"Dearest* Tamra. Just a friend?"

"That's what I said," she stated and motioned for him to go on.

"'I'm truly glad that you're doing well with the changes you've made in your life, but how can I deny how very much I miss you? It seems like an eternity since you told me good-bye, and I wish there was a way to convince you to change your mind and come back. How can I tell you the full depths of my feelings for you without sounding . . . '"

The subtle uneasiness in Jess's eyes changed abruptly to . . . what? Jealousy? Fear? He tossed her a harsh glare and said in an accusing tone, "This man is in love with you."

Tamra kept her voice steady, refusing to let him rile her. "Yes, I believe he is."

"You *believe* he is?"

"He never came right out and admitted it."

Jess shook his head and his eyes hardened further. "You were having a relationship with another man before you came here and didn't even *tell* me?"

"I told you I had dated quite a bit, and had never felt much of anything. That was absolutely true. Jason is a kind and decent man. But I didn't love him, and he knows it." Seeing the skepticism in his eyes, she added, "You don't believe me."

"Should I?" he asked and she had to will herself to not get angry.

"Listen to me, Jess," she said firmly. "I have never given you any reason to mistrust me. If you want to convince yourself that I'm dishonest to justify your own bad attitude in this relationship, that's your problem. I don't love Jason. I never did."

"But he obviously loves you," he said as if he resented it.

"A fact that has absolutely no bearing on you and me—unless you choose to make a big deal out of it."

"Have you told him about us?" he asked in that accusing tone.

"I haven't told him much of anything beyond, 'this is where I am and I love it here.' He asked me to write, so I did."

"Why didn't you tell him about us?" Jess demanded.

Tamra resisted the urge to scream at him. She closed her eyes and counted to ten before she looked at him squarely and gave him an answer that unloaded every thought that had plagued her for weeks. "And what would you have me tell him, Jess? 'I've met a man that I love more deeply than I had ever imagined possible. I believe with all my heart and soul that he and I are destined to be together, and I know that he loves me too. But he spends increasingly less time with me, and where he once opened his heart and soul to share his deepest fears so that we could overcome them together, he now tells me nothing. His good moods are becoming more rare, and his kiss has become hollow and meaningless.' Is that what you think I should tell him?"

Jess was silent a long moment before he asked, "Is that how you feel?"

"Yes, Jess. That's how I feel."

His eyes hardened further before he said, "Maybe you should write and tell him you made a mistake and you're coming back." He tossed the letter scornfully onto the table.

Tamra felt a swarm of emotion rising up in the wake of the words she'd just spilled. Her voice was barely steady as she asked, "Are you trying to say that you would prefer I leave?"

"No!" he shouted and she took a step back. He squeezed his eyes shut with self-recrimination before he said in a gentler voice, "No, I don't want you to leave. I want you to be happy, Tamra. And maybe . . . I'm not capable of making that happen."

Tamra pressed a hand over the sudden pain burning in her chest. Tears slipped out with her words. "What are you saying, Jess? That you would doom me to a life with a man I don't love because you're not willing to do what it takes to get beyond this?"

"It's not that simple, Tamra, and you know it."

"I know no such thing. There's only one way to be free of your pain, Jess, and Doctor Hill can't give it to you. It's there for the taking, but you're too proud to reach out and take it."

"I have no idea what you're talking about."

Tamra heaved a sigh of frustration. "Only because you hear what you choose to hear. I can testify to the numerous opportunities you have been given to understand that the Atonement is the key that will open the door to free you of this pain. But you are refusing to take hold of it while you bang your head on the door and insist on being a martyr to your own misery."

While she felt him searching for a comeback, they heard the plane circling overhead and knew his parents had returned. "Come on," he said and grabbed the keys to the Cruiser. Tamra grabbed her letters and followed him.

Jess watched Tamra walk ahead of him toward the carriage house. He hated himself for the way he treated her at times. The last thing he wanted to do was hurt her, but he was doing just that, and he knew it. He just felt so thoroughly afraid and confused most of the time that he hardly thought about what he was doing. And what he felt for her was so intense and consuming that it frightened him almost as much as the possibility of losing her. In truth, he had to wonder if letting her go would be better for her, but the very idea of being without her tempted those suicidal thoughts far too close to the surface.

He opened the passenger door for her and watched her slide in. Her expression clearly displayed her mood—and it wasn't good. He got in and put the key in the ignition, but before he started the engine he turned toward her. He couldn't face his parents with every-thing wrong between him and Tamra.

"Forgive me," he said, touching her face. He marveled at how quickly her features softened and her eyes filled with tears. "I love you, Tamra, I do. You must be patient with me."

"I love you too, Jess," she murmured and wrapped her arms around his neck.

Tamra absorbed the love she felt in his embrace, wishing it could be there always. His Jekyll and Hyde behavior was making her crazy, but she resigned herself to patience and relished the moment. He eased back to look into her eyes, his adoration evident. He pulled her closer and gave her a kiss that was anything but hollow and meaning-less. And from it she drew hope that—one day—they could get beyond this and be truly happy together.

Tamra was so happy to see Michael and Emily that it almost fright-ened her. Had she become too dependant on these people? Or was her fear more rooted in the probability that Jess would eventually exclude her from his heart completely and she would have no choice but to move on? She tried not to think about it and just enjoyed having Michael and Emily around again—as well as little Evelyn. Having the child back in the home made everything feel better somehow. They quickly settled back into a comfortable routine, and Jess seemed in better spirits when his parents were around. Although Tamra had to wonder if he was simply more on guard with his feelings in their presence. She felt certain that Michael and Emily were concerned for Jess, and had noticed that he'd regressed somewhat since they'd left. But nothing was said, and she knew they were all praying for him, and that was the best they could do. Tamra focused on her job, spending time with Evelyn, and enjoying the company of the rest of the family, hoping she wasn't deluding herself to believe that she belonged here.

On a particularly hot evening, Tamra was helping Sadie and Emily put supper on when Michael came into the kitchen, apparently angry.

"What's wrong?" Emily asked.

"Well," he said, pulling off his work gloves, "Jess is driving again all right. He just drove out of here like a bat out of—"

"Michael," Emily interrupted.

"Sorry," he said, obviously still upset.

"He's like you, and you know it."

"Yes I know it," Michael said and hit the wall with the side of his fist. "How does that happen? He never once saw me drive fast when I was angry or frustrated. So, why does he do that?"

"I don't know," Emily said, moving to embrace her husband. "And after what happened, such behavior seems so . . . " She hesitated in a way that made Tamra wonder if she couldn't think of the right words, or if she didn't want to verbalize what was apparent.

"Self-destructive," Tamra said, suddenly tired of keeping the burden of her concerns to herself.

"Exactly," Emily said, her eyes clouded with concern.

"How has he seemed to you, Tamra?" Michael asked. "I've wondered, but I think I've been afraid to ask."

Tamra wasn't prepared for the hot tears that crept into her eyes without warning. "There are moments when I feel like he's doing better, but most of the time I feel as if . . . " the emotion crept into her voice, "I'm losing him." She moved to a chair and sank into it. "I don't know what else I can do."

Emily sighed and put a hand over her face, as if that might help her think more clearly. "I keep praying that if there's something I can say . . . or do . . . that will make a difference, that I will know."

"I've prayed for the same," Tamra said. "It all comes down to the same thing. Jess is a free agent, and this is his problem. We can love and support him, but we can't fix it. And for some reason, he just can't see himself as worthy of being free of his pain."

"I just don't understand it," Emily said. "He was raised with love and spiritual guidance. We weren't perfect parents, but he grew up in a positive atmosphere."

"He came to this earth with his own spirit," Tamra said.

"I know, but . . . "

Tamra watched Emily wipe away some stray tears before she hurried from the room, and Michael followed. Tamra choked back her own emotion, afraid if she started to cry she'd never be able to stop.

Chapter Sixteen

A few weeks after Michael and Emily's return, the two of them went into town on a Saturday for an appointment, for which they gave no explanation. Sadie rode with them to be dropped off at a friend's house for the day, and Tamra spent the day with Evelyn, since Saturday was her day off. She thoroughly enjoyed their time together, while Jess was holed up with his studies.

Following Evelyn's nap, Tamra put in the *Beauty and the Beast* video at the child's request and they sat close together on the sofa. It had barely begun when Jess appeared and asked, "What you doing?"

"You're just in time," Tamra said. "You keep telling me you're going to watch this with us, but you keep reneging."

"Hi, Daddy," Evelyn said to him and turned her attention back to the television. Jess ignored her.

He sat beside Tamra and reached for her hand, squeezing it gently. As always, Tamra relished every little evidence of his love. She focused her attention on the movie just as the narrator said, "As the years passed, he fell into despair and lost all hope, for who could ever learn to love a beast?"

"You could take a lesson from that," Jess said.

"What?"

He imitated the narrator perfectly as he repeated, "Who could ever learn to love a beast?"

"I've told you before," Tamra said, "the beast becomes the hero in the end."

She stood up and he asked, "Where you going?"

"To make some popcorn. Don't worry. I know what happens."

He actually smiled. "Yes, I'm sure you do."

Michael, Emily, and Sadie returned a few minutes before the movie ended. Emily commented, "Oh, I love that movie. And it has special significance in this family, you know."

"It does?" Jess and Tamra both said at the same time, turning to look at her.

Emily smiled. "What does the song say? *Tale as old as time, song as old as rhyme; Beauty and the Beast.*"

"And?" Jess said when she didn't explain.

"Hold onto your socks," Emily said. "I'll be back in a minute."

Jess lifted his typically bare feet and said to Tamra, "I don't have any socks."

She laughed and impulsively kissed him, wishing he could always be this way.

Emily returned to the room just as Tamra clicked off the TV and started rewinding the video. "You know," she said, more to Tamra, "you've read Jess Davies' journals, but I don't think you've read his poetry."

"Poetry?" Tamra said, taking the binder reverently. She opened it to see very old pages of hand-written poems placed in sheet protectors. "Incredible," she said and Jess chuckled.

Emily turned a few pages and pointed to one in particular, as if she knew the book well. "Read that one out loud," she said.

Tamra cleared her throat then hesitated at the chill she felt before she'd even read the title. *"In the mirror I see a man, but the reflection shows a beast. Does my soul show through my eyes, or do my eyes only hide my soul? From the distance I watch you there, and I see nothing but beauty. Beauty through and through. I have heard through legend's tongue, from books my mother read, the only thing that changes beast to man is true love, pure love, Beauty's love."*

Tamra felt almost breathless as she glanced up to see Jess Davies' great-great-grandson gazing at her with an intensity that was clearly meant to echo the words she'd read.

"There's a part two," Emily said, turning the page. "Read here."

Tamra swallowed the emotion building in her throat and read, *"Beauty is not afraid of the beast in me. She entices it to come out and show itself. She, with her courage wants to battle it out— The winner takes my heart and soul. Beauty's love can conquer the beast in me.'*

Incredible," she murmured and once again met Jess's eyes. He seemed disconcerted before he stood up and left the room without a word.

The following morning Tamra was relieved to find Jess in fairly good spirits as they all set out together for church. He even drove without seeming the least bit concerned. She pushed away her frustrations and noted what a huge step he had taken; he was willing to drive a vehicle with his parents, and even little Evelyn, entrusted to his care.

Not far into sacrament meeting, Tamra realized they were making changes in the bishopric, and the old bishopric was released. Then she became distracted with helping Evelyn, but she realized that Michael's name had just been announced over the pulpit. She glanced at Jess to see his eyes wide with surprise, then glanced the other direction to see Michael standing to be sustained as the new bishop. Tamra quickly raised her right hand to join in the sustaining vote. After Michael sat down, Jess leaned forward and got his father's attention. Michael leaned forward as well and Jess silently expressed his surprise. Michael just shrugged his shoulders and leaned back.

The new bishopric was asked to come up and take their seats behind the pulpit. Tamra noticed Emily squeezing Michael's hand as he stood up. He was asked to stand and bear his testimony, and Tamra was moved to tears as he expressed his appreciation for the gospel and for his family. He specifically expressed love and appreciation to his wife, then he publicly told Jess how proud he was for the progress he'd made in his life before he bore testimony of the healing power of the Atonement. Tamra was surprised when he mentioned her by name, expressing his gratitude for the light she had brought into their home. Emily reached for her hand and squeezed it, as if to echo his statement. She felt so overcome with emotion she barely managed to keep her tears silent. Jess put his arm around her and discreetly pressed a kiss to her temple. "I'm grateful too," he whispered close to her ear, and she felt a fresh affirmation that she had found her place in life.

When sacrament meeting ended, Jess said to his mother, "So, that was the mysterious appointment yesterday, eh?"

"That was it," she replied.

"Well," Jess added softly, "it does alleviate one problem for me."

"What's that?" Emily asked.

"I was wondering if I needed to confess to my bishop that I'd tried to kill myself."

"And now he already knows," Emily said with a sad smile.

Through the following weeks, Tamra saw definite changes in the household due to Michael's new Church calling. He was gone for several hours two evenings a week, most of the day on Sundays, and occasionally he was drawn away for an emergency. Emily commented more than once how grateful she was to have Jess around to help carry Michael's load at home. She told Tamra of a time when Michael had been branch president, and Jess and James had been small boys. His hours away had been a strain for many reasons. "However," she said, "when I look at the big picture, I'm incredibly grateful for Michael's commitment to the gospel. It's difficult to imagine there was a time when I had desperately wanted him to join the Church, and he had stubbornly refused to even consider it."

Tamra said, "He must not have been a member very many years when he was made branch president."

"About eight, I believe," she said. "And of course, the Church has grown a great deal in the years since, and now we're actually a ward. And we don't have to travel nearly so far for meetings either."

Emily changed the subject and said, "I get the impression you're really enjoying your work at the boys' home."

"Oh, I am," Tamra said eagerly. "It's as if . . . " She hesitated to admit the full depth of her thoughts, fearing she would sound presumptuous.

"You were meant to be there?" Emily guessed and Tamra wondered how they could almost read each other's minds at times.

"Yes," she admitted.

Emily apparently picked up on her concern when she asked, "So what's the problem?"

Tamra sighed. "Sometimes I fear that I'm becoming . . . too comfortable here—that maybe I'm making myself too much at home."

Emily looked so alarmed that Tamra wondered if she sensed the concern between her words. "What are you saying?" she asked.

Tamra took a moment to gather her words. "I just have to wonder if . . . perhaps my lack of family, and the circumstances of my upbringing, have made me latch onto the situation here too easily."

Emily said with vehemence, "And perhaps you instinctively know this is where you belong."

Tamra inwardly cursed herself for being so easily prone to emotion when tears surfaced as she admitted. "But . . . how can I belong here without . . . " She couldn't bring herself to say it, and said instead, "Maybe I'm hoping for something that simply isn't realistic."

"We must not give up hope, Tamra," Emily said, putting a hand over hers. Tears rose into her eyes as well as she added, "And whatever Jess does or does not do, you will always have a place with us. *Always.*"

Tamra appreciated Emily's support and acceptance more than she could ever put into words, but in her heart she knew that she could never bear trying to pretend she was a part of the family without Jess being the one to make that happen.

Overcome with discouragement, Tamra embarked on a fast, keeping a prayer in her heart for Jess, and praying also that she might be guided to the answers for her own life. In the days following, she felt strongly that time was the key. She resigned herself to be patient and not let herself worry so much. Putting the matter into the Lord's hands, she set a goal to be positive and enjoy the life she was being allowed to live—even if it was only temporary.

A few days later, when Michael was actually home to have supper with the family for the first time that week, talk of work at the boys' home eventually led to something about the gables.

"Did you ever find out what they mean?" Jess asked Tamra. "With all that reading you did in the journals, you should have—"

"Actually, I did," she said, "quite some time ago. There must have been a lot going on at the time." She recalled making the discovery in Alexa's journal about the time his sisters had arrived.

"So, what is it?" Jess asked.

"I know there's some meaning," Michael said, "but I've forgotten. We certainly *ought* to know."

"I'll see if I can find it," Tamra said, and the following morning at breakfast she handed the book to Jess and pointed to a particular place.

He cleared his throat and read aloud, *"'This morning I walked through the completed Byrnehouse-Davies Home for Boys, and while every part of it is beautiful and pragmatic there is no question that the gabled attic is the heart of the Home, as we had hoped it would be. When we embarked on building this home as a refuge for boys whose situations have left them at great disadvantage, we wanted the structure itself to be a tangible symbol of all we have endured to bring us to a point where such an endeavor was possible. Through much pondering and discussion, we made the decision to call upon the poetry written by Jess's mother, the key to uncovering the reasons for the heart of our trials and hardships.* Through the gable facing east, I see my source of pain. *By looking east through the gabled window, we found the answers that eventually made it possible to merge the Byrnehouse and Davies names, and to have the means to fulfill Jess's dream of helping boys with no control over the circumstances that have marred their precious spirits. For us, the source of pain is deep and personal, as it is with every human being who fights to rise above the difficulties of this world to make something meaningful and rich of their lives. My deepest prayer is that every boy who has the opportunity to stand at these gabled windows and watch the sun rise, will leave here changed for the better and more capable of finding a life of happiness and peace.'"* Jess sighed and added, "Wow. That's beautiful."

"Yes, it is," Emily agreed. "And it perfectly expresses what the home truly has come to mean."

Tamra wanted to add that it wasn't simply the boys living in the home who reaped such benefits from being here. She felt certain that no matter how long she ended up staying, she would certainly leave here changed for the better and more capable of finding a life of happiness and peace. She thought of Jess once saying that some of the lost souls were just born here, and she prayed that he could somehow be able to let his own soul be healed by the seeming magic that Alexandra Byrnehouse-Davies had bequeathed to her family and the longstanding results of her life's work. Tamra kept the thought to herself and said, "I was thinking . . . when I found it last night, that perhaps we should have the paragraph engraved on some kind of plaque and hang it in the gabled attic."

"I think that's a marvelous idea," Michael said and the others made noises of agreement. "I'll find my typed copy of it and take it into town later today."

A week later, Michael had the family and the administrators of the boys' home go to the gabled attic with him to hang the new plaque on the wall. At the top it said, *The Gabled Attic,* and following

Alexa's words, it read at the bottom, *Alexandra Byrnehouse-Davies.*

"I love it," Emily said after it was hung up and they stood back to admire it. "Tamra just has a way of making everything around here a little bit better."

Tamra glanced down humbly, feeling somehow unworthy of such praise over coming up with a simple idea. Jess reached for her hand as if to silently echo his mother's words. At such moments she actually felt hope that she would find her place among the family.

The following Saturday, Tamra went to the family library in search of something to read since she'd finished all the journals long ago, and she needed something to fill her time and keep her distracted from the growing distance between her and Jess. She perused the shelves for more than an hour, searching the many volumes of fiction, biographies, church books, and history—but nothing appealed to her. She contemplated the idea that after reading such incredible personal histories, nothing could satisfy her. Then her eye caught the spines of a six-book set of hardbound novels. She felt a tingle on her arms before she consciously realized the author's name. Certain her eyes were deceiving her, she pulled one out and stared at the front. *Verity, a novel by J. Michael Hamilton.* She chuckled with disbelief and read inside the cover to verify that this novel, and five others, had indeed been written by Jess's father. She quickly discerned that there were two separate trilogies, and she found the first book of the first set and took it with her. She quickly became immersed in the story, marveling that it was actually very good.

At lunch Tamra walked into the kitchen and tossed the book on the table in front of Michael. "You've been keeping secrets from me," she said.

Michael looked slightly sheepish as he said, "It was something I always wanted to do. I eventually got it out of my system."

"Well, I'm impressed," Tamra said. "So far it's very good."

"Thank you," he said and changed the subject.

Tamra said to Jess, "Have you read these?"

"Actually, no," he said, sounding a bit embarrassed.

"Well, you should," Tamra insisted.

"Yes, I probably should," Jess agreed, and the minute lunch was cleaned up, Tamra returned to the book and stayed up late that night reading.

The following morning at church, Michael asked Tamra if she would come to the bishop's office following church meetings and speak with him. She felt a little nervous with the formal setting as she sat down to face him. While she was prepared for a discussion on his son, she was completely surprised when he asked her to serve as a Relief Society teacher.

"Really?" she asked. "You want *me* to teach Relief Society?"

He chuckled comfortably. "This has nothing to do with you and me, Tamra. The Relief Society presidency prayerfully came up with your name and submitted it to me. The bishopric agreed that it would be a good thing."

They talked for several minutes about what would be expected, and he expressed great faith in her ability to add insight and wisdom to the lessons. Tamra felt good about accepting the call, and then he asked if her temple recommend was valid. She knew it would be expiring soon, and so he gave her the standard interview so that she could keep it current. "Even though we're a long distance from a temple," he said, "I think it's important to have a recommend and know that you're worthy."

Before she left his office, he expressed his appreciation on a more personal level for all she had done for his family, but she felt too emotional to respond, without fully knowing why. She was surprised to step out into the foyer and see Jess sitting there.

"You didn't have to wait," she said, knowing Emily and Sadie had already taken Evelyn home. "I was just going to read until your dad is finished and—"

"I'm not waiting for you," he said, seeming terribly nervous.

"He has an interview with the bishop as well," Michael said to Tamra. Then he smiled at Jess and motioned toward his office, "Shall we?"

Tamra felt a little nervous herself as Jess's interview became rather lengthy. He came out with a calling to assist in the deacon's quorum and a temple recommend. While they were waiting for Michael to finish one more interview before they could ride home together, Tamra ventured to ask, "So, how did the interview go? Is it strange to have your father asking the questions?"

"Yes, but it was fine."

"Then what's wrong?" she asked, certain he would pretend that his dark mood was normal, as he usually did. He said nothing and she added, "Are you unhappy about the calling?"

"No, actually . . . I think it could be good for me; it might even be fun."

"Then what's the problem?" she pressed, hoping she wouldn't regret it.

He sighed and said, "I tried to be honest answering the questions, and he says I'm worthy to have the recommend, but . . . "

"But?"

"I sure don't feel worthy."

Tamra felt chilled by the way he said it, and she wondered if that was somehow the heart of the problem for him. She was searching for words to press him further when Michael declared he was ready to go and they started home.

Later that day she shared Jess's comment with Michael. But it was evident he'd already picked up on the same feeling, and he agreed with her concerns. Although, neither of them knew how to reach him.

At the supper table, Emily commented to Jess, "You didn't make it into town yesterday to get a haircut, did you?"

"No, I didn't," he said, pushing a hand through the thick, wavy mass.

"Just let it go a little more and you can go back to that ponytail look," Tamra teased. He scowled at her and she knew he didn't think it was funny. She quickly added, "Would you like me to cut it for you? My aunt taught me years ago, and I have some experience. If I flub it you can go into town and get it repaired."

"A woman of many talents," Michael said.

Jess smiled subtly at her and said, "Sure. Why not?"

Tamra pinned a towel around his shoulders once she'd dug out her basic hair cutting tools that Rhea had given her two Christmases ago. "How short do you want it?" she asked, combing it through.

"Just . . . keep the top of my ears covered." She met his eyes inquisitively and received another scowl, but as she started cutting she noticed the reason. The scars from once having several holes pierced in his ear were readily evident—and he obviously didn't want them to be seen.

Jess admitted he liked the haircut, and Tamra got a genuine smile and kiss in return. Given the growing rarity of his warmth toward her, she was hoping to fit in a haircut as often as possible.

Tamra was terribly nervous the first time she taught Relief Society, but it actually ended up going rather well, and she received

many compliments on her presentation of the lesson. The following
month she felt a little more confident and realized that she enjoyed
the calling and the opportunities it gave her. She enjoyed her work in
the boys' home more all the time, and as Michael came and went,
keeping himself minimally involved on many levels, she found an
opportunity to get to know him from an entirely different perspective. He was as intelligent in business matters as he was sensitive and
wise in dealing with difficult boys. And it was easy for her to imagine
Jess being so much like him and eventually taking on the full responsibility of the boys' home. She tried to keep that vision clear in her
mind during discouraging moments, certain that Alexa would be
thrilled to see her great-great-grandson living such a life.

* * *

Somewhere in the middle of breakfast, Tamra glanced at the
calendar and realized she'd been here six months. Evelyn had turned
three, and she'd given Jess a haircut once a month. She'd read all of
Michael's novels twice, and Jess had finished his counseling with
Doctor Hill more than two months ago. Dr. Hill had told Michael
and Emily that there was simply nothing more she could do. He had
reached a plateau where he had technically talked through every
aspect of the circumstances that troubled him, and he had followed
through on every exercise she'd challenged him with. Her only
concern was his need to forgive himself and let go of the burden he
had resigned himself to carrying. But only Jess could do that, and she
couldn't help him.

In the weeks since, Tamra had kept busy while she'd kept hope
that he would rise beyond that plateau and take the spiritual steps to
complete his healing. But today she had to admit that, if anything, he
had only regressed. She wasn't concerned about suicidal tendencies,
and he wasn't what she would call depressed. But he seemed to believe
that this weight he carried would always be with him, and he simply
wasn't worthy of being happy. He worked hard at helping keep the
station running, and he'd made great progress on his college credits.
But he had clearly taken the attitude that this was the best life would
ever be for him. And it didn't take much thought to realize that their

relationship had certainly reached a plateau, as well. He seemed content to hold her hand during church or family activities, and to take her into town for a date occasionally.

Tamra began her day at the boys' home with an ease that made her realize she'd become completely comfortable with her job. She loved working here. She loved living here. And she loved Jess. But she felt a hollow sense of despair in facing the fact that something had to change. Instinctively she knew that the path she was on would never bring about anything good for her and Jess.

Confused and distraught, she began a fast right after lunch, knowing she could never face such life-altering decisions on her own. She prayed that Jess's heart would be softened, that something would change to allow him to see the need for them to break out of this debilitating stagnancy and move forward with their lives. By the time she broke her fast the following day, she was still feeling discouraged, but she knew that it was time to make some changes in her life. If only she knew what—and how.

A few days later, while Tamra was consumed with prayer, it occurred to her that Alexandra Byrnehouse-Davies had struggled with having the man she loved caught up in his own pain and unwilling to commit himself to her. She felt drawn back to Alexa's journals and dug them out the minute she was finished with her work at the boys' home. After supper she went to the library and made herself comfortable on one of the sofas there, hoping to glean some of Alexa's wisdom in a way she might not have perceived on her previous reading.

Tamra was surprised when Jess appeared and sat beside her; it was the first time he'd sought her out in several days. "What are you doing?" he asked.

"Just reading," she said, holding up the journal.

"I thought you'd finished all of those."

"I'm reading this one again," she said. "Alexa and I have a lot in common."

She was hoping he'd ask what, but he said nothing. They sat in comfortable silence while she read for more than an hour. He put his head in her lap and relaxed, and she wondered what mood might have compelled him to want the assurance that she was there.

"You okay?" she asked, setting the book aside.

"Sure, why?" He sat up and looked directly at her. "I just . . . missed you." He touched her face and pressed a thumb over her lips.

"That's nice," she said, "because I've missed you too."

"I love you, Tamra," he said and kissed her. Tamra delighted in his simple display of affection and the encouragement it gave her. He drew back to look into her eyes, then he pulled her into his arms and kissed her with more passion than he'd exhibited toward her in several weeks. Initially it sparked a glimmer of hope inside of her. If he could only remember the intensity of what they had once shared, perhaps he could be prompted to make some changes, if only to have the opportunity to share their lives completely. He kissed her again and again until his kiss became unlike anything she'd ever experienced. She began to feel uneasy as she realized he was getting carried away and had no apparent intention of bridling his passion. Warning bells sounded in her head and she sat up abruptly, pushing him away.

"Jess, we have to be careful," she said while he gazed at her, apparently disoriented, as if he had no idea what she was talking about. "If we're *not* careful," she said, forcing a light tone that she hoped would ease the sudden tension between them, "we'll both be needing to confess to the bishop, and under the circumstances, that could be *really* embarrassing."

The intensity in his eyes only deepened before he pushed a hand into her hair and kissed her again, as if he could somehow convince her that what he wanted was worth any consequence.

"Jess?" she murmured, easing away.

He slid toward her to close the distance she had just created. He kissed her cheek and whispered close to her ear, "I want you so badly, Tamra."

Tamra looked into his eyes, momentarily startled beyond words. Tempted perhaps, but she could never go through with it. And she couldn't even fathom what frame of mind would lure him to believe that she would give in to such a temptation. She spoke in a firm voice that she hoped would drop the issue once and for all. "Marry me first, Jess. It's a simple equation, and you're a fool if you think it would ever be any other way." He looked so completely distressed that she had to believe he was simply acting on his impulses without giving any thought to his behavior.

Shame filled his eyes just before he turned away and said, "I'm sorry, Tamra. I don't know what I was thinking. Sometimes I just . . . "

"You just what, Jess?" she urged gently.

"I just . . . get so confused that I almost feel . . . crazy. Or maybe I *am* crazy, and I just don't know it." He looked into her eyes with some kind of fear blatantly showing. "How can I even consider letting you marry me, Tamra, when . . . "

Tamra retorted her first impulse. "How can you even consider *not* marrying me after what we have felt . . . what we have shared?"

The lack of emotion in his expression frightened her even more than his response. "You deserve someone better than me, Tamra."

"I don't want anyone else," she said, hating the way her voice cracked.

That familiar hardness appeared in his eyes, as if it could somehow protect him from the truth he didn't want to hear. His voice was edged with spite as he retorted, "I don't think you're nearly as much in love with me as you are with my family."

Tamra swallowed her temptation to get angry. Her voice was steady as she answered, "I *do* love your family, Jess, but only because you are at the heart of it. *You're* the reason I came here, Jess. Don't start labeling my feelings and assuming you know my heart for the sake of rationalizing the way you've shut me out."

"And what about *my* feelings?" he countered.

"What about them, Jess? Do you even *know* what you're feeling? I don't know how you could possibly even begin to comprehend what you're feeling when you haven't felt anything but pain for years, and even that has been hidden away. You're going to have to learn to feel again, Jess Hamilton. And when you do, you might begin to realize what you're trying to throw away."

His expression only hardened further and she turned and left the room before she broke down and started to sob. Her dignity, barely intact as it might be, was practically all she had left.

Tamra hardly saw Jess at all over the next few days, and she feared he was retreating into the kind of depression she'd seen when she first met him. She discussed her feelings with Emily, but they both felt equally helpless to know what to do or say that might make a difference. They shared a surprised glance when Jess appeared in the lounge room late one evening, looking haggard and unkempt. He sank into a chair as his father asked, "How you doing, son?"

"I've had better days," Jess said.

"Want to talk about it?" Emily asked.

He sat on the sofa beside Tamra and took her hand. "Not especially."

Michael returned his attention to the book he'd been reading. Emily said, "We got a wedding announcement today. Marie is getting married."

Jess made a noise of indifference and Emily explained to Tamra, "Marie is Byron's younger sister."

"I see," Tamra said.

Jess pulled his hand from hers and folded his arms. With no preamble he blurted, "I really don't think I'll ever get married."

Michael lowered his book abruptly. Emily's eyes widened. Tamra sucked in her breath and couldn't let it go when she realized he was serious.

"I think it would be better if I just accepted that I don't have anything to give to a wife and children," he went on. Tamra's breath came in spurts that she fought to keep silent. "I don't want to burden any woman with . . . "

"With what, Jess?" Emily demanded, sounding subtly angry.

"With this pain," he snapped back, hitting his chest with his hand. "I have to accept that it's just never going to go away, and no woman deserves to live with a man who can't love her with his whole heart."

Tamra caught strained glances from Michael and Emily, but it was obvious none of them knew what to say. Tamra fought back tears that threatened to erupt. She was relieved when Emily broke the silence. "Jess," she said gently, "your patriarchal blessing says that you will marry, have children, and carry on a great family legacy."

Jess's voice was angry as he retorted, "Those blessings are on the condition of my worthiness."

"Is there some grievous sin that is presently not taken care of?" Emily asked. "Is there something you haven't told us about?"

Tamra winced when he shouted, "I killed my brother!"

She knew Michael and Emily shared her astonishment in recalling that months ago he'd said those very words. Had he made no progress on that count after all their discussions on forgiving himself and applying the Atonement to his life? Tamra felt physically ill and rushed from the room, fearing she would either start to sob or throw up.

She cried more than she slept, and could hardly find the strength to pray. She couldn't bring herself to accept that it was over between her and Jess, but she felt certain she was only in some type of denial. When morning came she forced herself to get up and shower, determined to be responsible and committed to all she'd been blessed with—in spite of Jess's amputating her from his life.

She was relieved when Jess didn't show up for breakfast, once his mother reported that she'd checked on him earlier and he was fine— beyond his apparent depression.

"And how are you?" Michael asked Tamra.

"I can't answer that and get through the day," she said, fearing the tears would get started again. "But thanks for asking."

"You mustn't give up hope," Emily said, putting her hand over Tamra's on the table. "We have fasted and prayed a great deal on his behalf. We all know he is a free agent, but I truly believe in my mother's heart, Tamra, that he *will* get past this."

Tamra nodded to acknowledge that she'd heard, but she feared attempting to speak.

"You know," Emily went on, "Michael is the only son of an only son of an only son. We have three sons, but Tyson died as an infant, and James left only a daughter behind. If Jess does not marry and have children, the Hamilton line will end with him."

"The Hamilton line is eternal, Emily," Michael said.

Emily sighed, "Yes, I know but . . . "

"But it would be nice to know that it went on in this world. I know."

Tamra forced herself to eat before she went to work, praying it would take away a lingering nausea that hadn't relented since Jess had made his declarations the previous evening. The day dragged for Tamra while she forced herself not to wonder what she would do and where she would go. She couldn't think of that now; not yet. She couldn't give up hope so easily. She wondered what might be going on in Jess's heart, and by late afternoon she had to go to the ladies' room and cry for ten minutes. In spite of his stubbornness, she knew she could never comprehend the depth of his pain. *If only he would let it go!*

Tamra washed her face and put on fresh lipstick before she went back to the office and sat at her desk, attempting to focus on the pile of paperwork in front of her. A few minutes later Madge peeked her head around the partially open door and said, "There's a gentleman here to see you."

Tamra tried to remember if she'd had some appointment related to the boys' home that she'd forgotten. As if Madge sensed her confusion, she clarified, "It's personal. He says he's a friend."

"Oh, help," Tamra said, gripping the edge of the desk. It couldn't possibly be anyone but Jason Briggs. The timing was *horrible!* She'd written him a total of three letters in all the time she'd been here. What could possibly make him search her out this way? And why now? Remembering that she wasn't alone, she cleared her throat and said, "Okay. Tell him I'll be out in about five minutes."

"Will do," she said and slipped away.

Tamra uttered a quick prayer before she forced her thoughts away from Jess and reminded herself that she had long ago established very clear boundaries of friendship with Jason. Not wanting him to believe that she was anything but perfectly happy, she put on a cheerful demeanor and went out to the front office where he was sitting with a magazine.

"Tamra!" he said and came to his feet, opening his arms.

"Hello, Jason," she said, accepting a brief embrace. "What a nice surprise. I can't imagine what would bring you all the way out here."

"I missed you," he said and Tamra caught a glimpse of Madge eyeing them speculatively from where she sat at her desk.

She alleviated the tension by saying, "Madge, this is Jason Briggs, a dear friend. Jason, this is Madge. She's the one who keeps the rest of us on track around here."

"It's a pleasure," Jason said, stepping forward to shake her hand.

"It is indeed," Madge said.

"I think I'll show Jason around a little," Tamra said, stepping with him into the hall.

"Hey," he said, "I know it wasn't fair for me to just drop in like this. If you're busy, I understand. I didn't even know if you'd be around. I could wait until you're off, or . . . I could come back or . . . "

"It's okay," she said. "There's nothing terribly pressing at the moment, but . . . " They ambled slowly up the hall. "I'm just wondering why you drove all the way out here without even knowing if I'd be around."

"I just . . . felt like I needed to," he said. "I had some business a couple of hours away from here, and . . . I just couldn't get you out of my mind." He chuckled tensely and glanced down. "Maybe I should come right to the point and say that . . . I couldn't help hoping that something had changed."

Tamra hated the way her heart quickened with an unexplainable dread. Was God trying to tell her something? Would she be smarter to let go of her intense feelings for Jess that had led her only to a fruitless relationship? Should she simply accept that having a man in her life who lived the gospel and loved her was good enough, even better than many women might ever hope for? Funny that she would recall Jess saying: *no woman deserves to live with a man who can't love her with his whole heart.* And surely Jason deserved a woman who could love him with her whole heart. His visit didn't change what she knew in her heart was right. She just had to keep perspective in spite of the confusion of the present circumstances.

Tamra stopped where the two halls crossed and looked directly at Jason. "You're very sweet," she said, "and it's good to see you, but . . . I must admit that I'm not completely certain where my future will take me, but I *do* know, however, that you and I are not meant to be."

His disappointment was evident, but he smiled and took her hand. "You're an amazing woman, Tamra. I . . . appreciate your honesty, and . . . I truly hope you can find what you're looking for." He turned and looked around. "So, you really enjoy working here— at least you did the last time you wrote."

"I love it," she said. "I think I could be happy working here for the rest of my life."

"It's pretty secluded out here," he commented, as if that were a definite drawback.

"That's one of many reasons I like it," she said.

He nodded and looked around again. "The building is beautiful; it's pretty old, isn't it?"

"It was built in the late nineteenth century," she reported. "But as you can see, it has been maintained very well. The house that it's connected to is a little older."

"And that's where you've been living," he stated, as if to clarify.

"That's right," she said, hating the tension, and hoping he wouldn't stay long. "Would you like a quick look around? Some of the boys are out working with their horses right now, and the others are in the library."

"I'd love to," he said and they started up the stairs. They were nearly to the top when Tamra looked up to see Michael starting down. He stopped and smiled when he saw her, while his eyes showed curiosity concerning her guest.

"Hello," they both said at the same time before she added, "This is a friend of mine, Jason Briggs. He just dropped by and I thought I'd show him around a little."

"Hello, Jason," Michael said, extending his hand. "It's a pleasure to meet you."

Tamra continued her introduction. "Jason, this is Michael Hamilton."

"The one you met in the Philippines," Jason guessed with a smile.

"That's right," Michael said, obviously pleased.

"So, this is your place, then," Jason said.

"It's a family establishment," Michael said humbly. "I just keep an eye on it."

"Well," Jason said, "I certainly don't want to keep Tamra from her work. I'll just—"

"Oh, that's fine," Michael interrupted. "There's nothing too urgent to prevent her spending some time with a friend."

Tamra forced a smile to keep herself from scowling at Michael. She'd been hoping to send Jason quickly on his way, and Michael was encouraging him to hang around. She was preparing to move along when Michael added to Jason, "Supper's not far off. You must stay and join us. By the time you drove back to town, you'd be half-starved."

Jason's surprise was evident, but he smiled and said, "Thank you. I certainly didn't come expecting to be fed, but I'd like that very much."

"Great," Michael said. "We'll see you then." He winked at Tamra and added, "And we'll see you then as well, sweetie."

He hurried on down the stairs and Tamra quickly said to Jason, "Wait just a minute. There's something I've forgotten to ask him; business."

"Michael," she called and he stopped on the landing before it turned. She hurried to stand beside him before she said quietly, "Are you out of your mind? Do you have any idea how Jess would respond to this in his present frame of mind? He turned green when he found out this guy had written me a *letter!*"

Michael smiled and put a hand on her shoulder. "I think Jess could stand to have his feathers ruffled a little, my dear."

Tamra gave him a doubting glare. "The timing is horrible. Didn't you hear what he said last night when—"

"I heard him," Michael said gravely. "And maybe the timing is *good.*" He tightened his gaze on her and said gently, "I don't know what the outcome will be, Tamra. I think we're as afraid as you are. But sometimes it takes some rough waters to get us where we need to go. And maybe it's time we stopped treating Jess with kid gloves; maybe his perspective of marriage might change if he comes face to face with the reality of another man." He chuckled softly. "Stop worrying about Jess and enjoy a visit with your friend. Just treat it as what it is and let Jess stew a little." He walked away to put an end to her argument.

Tamra sighed and went back up the stairs where Jason was waiting. "Everything all right?" he asked.

"Oh, yes," she said, feeling as if she were lying to him once every five minutes.

She showed him through the upper floor of the home, taking her time in the library to visit quietly with each of the boys there and introduce them to Jason. Knowing he was staying for supper, she wanted to drag the tour out as long as possible. By the time they had arrived in the gabled attic, she knew she couldn't take him to eat with the Hamiltons and not tell him something about her feelings for Jess. How clearly she recalled Jess's words in response to reading Jason's letter, *Why didn't you tell him about us?*

While they were standing side by side, looking out of one of the gable windows, Tamra said, "There's something I need to tell you. I didn't include it any of my letters because . . . I just felt like it had no bearing on our relationship. What I feel for you has nothing to do with what's been happening here."

He turned toward her in surprise, as if he sensed where this was headed. Her assumption proved correct when he said, "You've met someone else."

"Yes," she said easily.

"So, why are you telling me now?" he asked.

"Because you're going to be having supper with him," she said and his eyes widened.

"Michael?" he squeaked.

"No, of course not," she laughed.

"Well, that's somewhat of a relief," he said with a chuckle that helped ease the tension. "Since he's old enough to be your father."

"And he's very happily married," she added, then took a deep breath and plunged on. "And I'm very much in love with his son."

Jason seemed momentarily dazed before he turned abruptly to look out the window. She saw his face tighten and added quickly, "Maybe I should have told you before, but I had no reason to believe we'd ever see each other again. I wouldn't blame you for being upset, but—"

"I'm not upset," he said in a sad voice. "Just . . . disappointed, perhaps. You know how I feel about you and . . . "

"Listen," Tamra said following a miserable length of silence, "you don't have to stay for supper. I can understand how difficult it might be to—"

"I'd like to stay, Tamra, unless you would rather I didn't."

Once again Tamra heard herself uttering a white lie. "I don't have a problem with it." She quickly attempted to redeem herself by telling him quite truthfully, "But I can't say that Jess won't. He's having a rough time at the moment, and—"

"Jess," he said as if to acquaint himself with the name. "And you really love this guy?"

"I really do," she said with conviction.

"How do you know . . . for certain?" he asked.

Tamra sighed, recalling Jess asking her that very thing—back when he had been open and honest with her, and his talk of the future had given her tangible hope. She forced such thoughts away and answered his question. "You know, Jason, through many dating experiences I began to wonder if there was something wrong with me. I told you about the abuse in my youth, and . . . I often wondered if I had lost any ability to be attracted to a man, or to feel anything at all—because I never did. But all of that changed when I met Jess. I never imagined that I could feel something so thoroughly intense and consuming. And he felt it too—right from the start."

Jason didn't seem as disconcerted as she might have thought. Either his feelings for her weren't nearly as deep as he claimed, or he did well at hiding them. "And when was that? The start?"

"I met him when I came here," she said and his expression showed surprise.

"Then why aren't you married by now?" he asked and Tamra turned away, hating the way his question stabbed at her deepest fears. While she was searching for a suitable answer, he said, "You told me he's having a rough time. If I'm being too nosy, just say so, but . . . I'm concerned about you and—"

"You've never been nosy," she said and decided to tell him just enough to explain the situation; there were certain things he simply didn't need to know. "The thing is . . . soon after his mission, Jess was driving a car that was hit head on by a truck in the wrong lane." Jason gasped even before she added, "His brother, sister-in-law, and best friend were all killed."

"Good heavens!" Jason said.

"Jess was in a coma for a while, and barely survived himself. He was in the hospital for months, but emotionally he still hasn't come to terms with it. I know in my heart that he is the reason I felt compelled to come here. I can't say for certain that we'll end up together—he's struggling with depression and he needs time. I do know that for now I'm in the right place, and I love him."

Jason was quiet a moment before he smiled and said, "I'll look forward to meeting him."

Tamra responded with a silent, *I was afraid you were going to say that.* Then she led him out of the room and they finished their tour, while the supper hour loomed closer.

Chapter Seventeen

Jess attempted to focus on his studies, but it was becoming increasingly more difficult. When hours of effort yielded no progress, he returned to his room and curled up on his bed. The confusion and fear that had briefly relented in his life in the face of Tamra's love had gradually returned to overtake him with familiar dark clouds that closed in on him more every day. He'd long ago ceased trying to analyze his feelings and how he might change them. He only knew he hated feeling this way, but he felt powerless to change it.

Jess was startled by a knock at the door. "Who is it?" he called and hurried to lean against the headboard and open a textbook.

"It's me," his mother said.

"Come in," he called, and she opened the door.

"How you doing?" she asked.

"I'm okay," he said.

She sat on the edge of the bed and pushed his hair back off his face. "I don't believe you," she said. "In fact, I think we have some good cause to be concerned. Maybe we should call Doctor Hill and—"

"There's nothing she can do, Mom. We've been through all of this."

"At the very least, maybe she could prescribe a different anti-depressant."

"The last three haven't made a difference. What makes you think another one would?"

Emily sighed. "I just want to find a solution, Jess. I want you to be happy."

"I'm fine, Mom, really."

She looked as if she'd like to argue, but she said nothing.

"Did you need something?" he asked. "Or did you just come to discuss my medication?"

"I just wanted to let you know that we're having company for dinner. I thought you should be warned. You might want to make yourself presentable. Anyway, I need to get back to the kitchen and help Sadie."

"Who?" he snarled, thinking he'd just claim not feeling well and stick to his room.

Emily rose and moved toward the door as she said, "Tamra's friend, Jason, stopped by the boys' home this afternoon to see how she was doing. Your dad invited him to stay." She smiled and closed the door.

Jess growled to the empty room, "Oh, that's just what I need." He contemplated the situation for several minutes without coming to any conclusions before he tossed his book on the floor and got up to take a shower.

* * *

Tamra was putting cloth napkins on the table in the dining room when Jess entered the room, forcing her to do a double take. He looked more perky and put together than he had in several days. Emily had told her that she'd warned Jess about their guest, but she had predicted he wouldn't show for dinner.

"Ooh," he said, "we're eating in *the dining room*. This must really be a special occasion."

"Who are you?" she asked nonchalantly and returned to her chore. "No, don't tell me. You kidnapped that scruffy, obnoxious Jess Hamilton, and you're an imposter in his place."

"Oh, that's a good one, Tamra," he said. "Where did you come up with that?"

She chuckled and admitted, "Your great-grandfather's journal, actually. You should read it sometime."

"So," he glanced around, "where's the special occasion?"

"He's in the bathroom. And you'd better behave yourself."

"Of course," he smiled and surprised her with a tender kiss. She resisted the urge to call him a hypocrite and was glad she had when she looked up to see Jason standing in the doorway. She felt her face turn warm as she realized he must have observed their kiss. A quick glance at Jess made it clear he was pleased with himself, and she had to wonder if that was his biggest motive for doing it.

"You must be Jess," Jason said, stepping forward with his hand outstretched. "You look very much like your father."

"Thank you, I think," Jess said with an easy chuckle and shook Jason's hand. "And you must be Jason. I've heard so much about you."

Tamra was stunned speechless as she observed Jess and Jason embark on a witty and comfortable conversation, mostly focusing on the boys' home and horse business. Watching Jess, she realized that she hadn't seen him interact with anyone but family for several weeks. She'd forgotten how absolutely charming he could be. And his knowledge and appreciation for the family businesses became so readily evident that she was struck again with the tragedy of Jess's depression.

Michael and Emily entered the room carrying food that they set on the table. Michael glanced at the two men, conversing casually, then he smirked subtly toward Tamra. She couldn't help hoping that perhaps his theory might be proven right. Maybe Jess *did* need his feathers ruffled a little.

"I'll help you," Tamra said and followed them back to the kitchen, praying the conversation would continue to go well in her absence.

"So far so good," Emily said to Tamra.

"Yes," Tamra said, "and as soon as we figure out who this imposter is that kidnapped your son, we can—"

Emily laughed so hard that Tamra couldn't finish her sentence. "Oh, that's precious," she finally said.

"Well, I stole it from Michael Hamilton's journal." Michael turned with his eyes wide and she clarified, "Your grandfather."

Sadie handed Evelyn to Tamra and said, "She's all washed up. If you'll get her settled at the table, I'll get the gravy dished up."

Tamra returned to the dining room with Evelyn and put her into her booster seat. "Hi, Daddy," she said to Jess.

Jess actually acknowledged the child. "Hi, Evie," he said with a comical wave that made her giggle.

Jason looked mildly alarmed and Tamra said to him, "He's not really her daddy. Her parents were killed when she was a baby." Jess gave her a subtle scowl. She just smiled and said, "Isn't it nice how we can talk about such things without tiptoeing around."

Michael, Emily, and Sadie all entered the room with the remainder of the food and they all sat down to eat. Tamra was amazed at the comfortable conversation and the way Jason fit in so easily. But then, Michael and Emily had a way of making people feel that way. She was more amazed at Jess's affectionate glances toward her and the way he occasionally put a hand on her shoulder or touched her hair. She might have been touched by such a display under any other circumstances. As it was, she only felt angered by his apparent play-acting for Jason's benefit.

When the meal was finished, Michael and Emily insisted on doing the dishes, and Sadie took Evelyn upstairs. Tamra was relieved when Jason insisted that he needed to get going. He thanked Michael and Emily profusely for their hospitality, and Tamra offered to walk him to his car. She was only mildly disappointed when Jess tagged along. Her discomfort in being with both men at the same time was more appealing than being alone with Jason.

"Well," Jason said, opening the door to his car, "I'm really glad I came. It's nice to see this place you've told me about in your letters. And I'm glad to know you're doing so well." He kissed her cheek and squeezed her hand while Jess tensed visibly. "You deserve to be happy, Tamra," he said then turned to Jess and shook his hand. "You're a very lucky man, Jess. Treat her well."

"I'll do my best," Jess said as if it were nothing. He put his arm possessively around Tamra as Jason got into his car and drove away.

When the car was out of sight, Tamra turned to Jess and said, "That was quite a performance, Doctor Jekyll."

He looked so innocently astonished that she wanted to slap him. "I have no idea what you're talking about," he said, deepening her frustration.

"Then go look up hypocrite in the dictionary," she snapped and walked away.

"Tamra, wait," he said, taking hold of her arm to stop her.

"I'm too angry to talk about it right now," she said and wrenched her arm from his grasp.

By the time Tamra got to her room, her anger had dissolved into fear. Her feelings reminded her all too much of the night she had given Jess a harsh declaration and later found him half-dead. She knew she could never sleep if she didn't at least try to talk to him. But first she knelt beside her bed and prayed long and hard. She came to the conclusion that perhaps Jason's visit had been a blessing after all. It had given her some perspective on Jess's feelings in contrast to his declaration the night before. And it had opened up a point where she could actually talk to Jess about the issue in last night's conversation that had wounded her heart. It had been eating away at her until Jason's visit had distracted her. And now, she had to talk to Jess. She had to know.

Tamra walked to his room, hoping he would be there. She knocked lightly and got no response. She turned the knob to peek inside, just to make certain he wasn't there before she went searching the rest of the house. The room was dark, but she distinctly saw his shadow sitting on the floor, leaning back against the side of his bed. She closed the door quietly and leaned against it. Hearing subtle evidence that he was crying tore at her heart. Her accusations of hypocrisy were now overshadowed by concern. She wondered if he'd even heard her come in, and wondered what to say to alert him to her presence. She took a step toward him and he said, "You really should learn to mind your own business, you know." A vague sarcasm in his tone let her know that he wasn't opposed to her company.

"It's not my prerogative to mind my business . . . especially with you. I worry about you too much to mind my business."

"Well, I'm not going to slit my wrists or anything, so you don't have to worry."

"I'm not worried about that," she said, feeling dishonest. There were moments—especially of late—when she had to wonder if he would sink so low again. "But I do wonder if you're all right." He said nothing and she added, "You're not all right, are you?"

She heard nothing but stifled tears and she sat on the floor beside him, putting her arms around him. He took hold of her with desperation and crumbled into heaving sobs. Tamra cried silent tears while she held him and let him cry, running her fingers through his hair.

"You know," he said, "you really should find a man who doesn't bawl like a baby."

"I heard once that it takes a strong man to be able to cry."

"Well, I must really be strong then," he said with sarcastic self-recrimination.

"Why don't you tell me why you're so upset?" Tamra said.

He tightened his arms around her and murmured, "I'm such a fool, Tamra. And . . . I just miss them so much. I don't know why they had to leave me that way. I just don't understand."

"I don't know the answers, Jess. But I know that I love you, and I want more than anything for you to be able to find some peace and be happy."

"I don't know if that's possible, Tam. I've tried. I've really tried. But somehow I always come up short."

"Have you ever considered, Jess, that you're the only one who believes you're not worthy to be free of this pain?"

His voice picked up a familiar cold edge. "That's because I'm the only one who knows the whole truth."

"God knows," she said.

He said nothing for a few minutes, but when he spoke his voice sounded genuine again. "Tamra, I love you. You must believe me."

"I know you love me, Jess. And I love you, but . . . " She didn't want to say what she was feeling, as if not verbalizing her deepest fears would keep them from coming to pass. But she knew it had to done. She couldn't go on waiting—and wondering.

"But?" he pressed and she knew now was just as good a time as any. She got up to turn on the lamp so that she could see his face.

"Jess," she said, "I just have to know . . . What you said . . . about never marrying or having children . . . What am I supposed to assume from that?" He said nothing and she added, "I have spent months with you, Jess, listening to your declarations of love for me. Was I wrong to assume from your words and your actions that we would share a future together? And then tonight you show up and behave as if everything you said last night had been some kind of joke." Still he said nothing. "Talk to me, Jess!" she pleaded.

"I don't know what to say," he said resolutely. "My intention was never to lead you on or deceive you, but maybe I . . . I have to accept that . . . you deserve better than me. Maybe I would be doing you a great disservice to expect you to spend your life with me."

Tamra felt her heart fall like a rock. She steeled her voice enough to say, "So, what are you saying? I should leave here?"

"No," he insisted, "you love it here. You love your work and—"

"But I should find myself another man?" she questioned. He said nothing. "A man like Jason, perhaps?" she said and he visibly tensed. "You *are* a hypocrite, Jess. You sit there and imply that I should find another man, then you make it clear to *another man* by your every action that you love me and I am yours. You're so confused you don't know *what* you want. And while you're trying to figure it out, you're driving me crazy."

"Well, that would make two of us," he said and pressed his head into his hands.

Tamra sat beside him and took his hand. "I love you, Jess," she said, hating the desperation in her own voice.

"I love you too, Tamra."

"Then let's get on with our lives, Jess. We can be happy together."

"I'm just . . . not ready for that, Tam."

"I can be patient, Jess. But I have to have hope. You said last night that you weren't going to marry . . . or have children. Where does that leave me?"

He made no effort to answer the question. He simply tightened his arms around her and said, "I love you, Tamra. I need you." He turned his face toward hers and kissed her warmly. She felt some measure of relief and tried to convince herself that time would make a difference. But in her heart she couldn't be sure.

* * *

The following day Tamra fasted again and prayerfully came to the decision to give Jess a little more time, but she reminded herself that her patience had to be coupled with hope. In her heart she knew that her Father in Heaven would not want her to pine away over a fruitless endeavor. She'd come too far in her life and had risen above too much to become codependent on a man who refused to come to terms with his debilitating emotional problems.

A month later Tamra had no choice but to accept that Jess had become comfortable with being depressed and keeping her at a distance. Again she fasted and felt compelled to try once again to appeal to Jess with the ridiculousness of the situation. Searching her feelings carefully, she was surprised to feel the Spirit's guidance taking a shift. Where she had repeatedly been given the answer to be patient and give the situation time, she now felt strongly that it was time to get on with her life—one way or another.

Michael, Emily, and Sadie had gone into town for a Saturday of errands and had taken Evelyn with them. Tamra found Jess lying in the middle of the floor in the upstairs hall, wearing an old T-shirt and his rattiest jeans. And of course, his feet were bare. He had one arm over his eyes in a way she'd come to recognize as some form of hiding. The music playing from the speakers around the room was far too loud for him to hear her approach him. But a portion of the lyrics caught her with an unexpected chill. *The beating of my heart is a drum and it's lost and it's looking for a rhythm like you. You can take the darkness from the pit of the night and turn into a beacon burning endlessly bright. I've got to follow it 'cause everything I know, well it's nothing till I give it to you.*

Tamra pushed the Pause button on the stereo. He didn't move as he said, "I was listening to that."

"We need to talk," Tamra said and walked toward him. He still didn't move. "Could you at least look at me?"

He slowly moved his arm and looked up at her, like a child defiantly expecting a scolding. She ignored his silent insinuations and forged ahead. "I can't go on like this, Jess. I have to know where we stand."

"I dearly appreciate your patience," he said with bitter sarcasm, as if her bringing the subject up at all was deeply insensitive.

"If, by patience, you mean that I should go on hovering near you while you sulk around and slither further into this abstract dark solitude you seem so comfortable with, then you're a fool to expect me to be here at all."

"Maybe I am," he said like a spoiled child.

Tamra ignored his attitude and stated firmly, "I would gladly be by your side forever, Jess, if I could see evidence that you were progressing, that you actually cared about your life enough to get beyond this. But I will not stand by and watch you steadily digress while *my* life hangs in the balance. Those antidepressants you're taking will only level out the chemical imbalance, Jess. They will not magically heal your spirit or take away your pain. There is only *one* thing that can do that, and you are too proud and stubborn to accept it."

"You're not going to start preaching religion to me again, are you?"

Tamra took a deep breath and counted to ten. "It's not religion, Jess. It's life. But you know what? I think this bad attitude you have is simply a mask. You put this pride up in front of your face to conveniently keep yourself from having to look too deeply at the *real* problem. And I think you're just so blasted comfortable with being miserable that you don't *want* to fix it."

"Well, I'm glad you've got it all figured out. If only it could be so easy."

"It's not *easy*, Jess. But it is simple. And if you'd muck through all the pride and fear you would be able to see that it is actually possible for you to be free of this ridiculous burden you're carrying. The problem is that only you can take those steps, Jess. Only you can fix it. But it's not only you that's hurting. Everyone who loves you is hurting, and you're too *selfish* to do anything about it. And I can't stay here any longer and live like this."

"What are you saying?" he demanded, no less angry. "You're leaving?"

"I don't know what I'm going to do, but I can't make a decision without knowing where we stand."

Jess put his arm back over his eyes and said, "I love you, Tamra. That's all I can say."

Tamra felt such perfect despair that all she could do was switch the music back on, only to hear the lyrics, *I can make you every promise that has ever been made, and I can make all your demons be gone. But I'm never gonna make it without you; do you really wanna see me crawl?*

She hurried back to her room and cried herself into a dazed stupor. More than an hour after the tears had subsided, she found herself drawn to Alexa's journal. Her time for reading had been minimal, but she had kept the journals close, absorbing them in bits and pieces in between her work and her help with Evelyn. She marveled at the timing as she began where she'd left off a couple of days ago, and read, *It is likely the most difficult thing I've ever done, but I knew in my heart I had no choice but to give Jess an ultimatum. If he can't get beyond whatever it is that's hurting him, he will never be able to accept the love I feel for him.*

The tears came again and Tamra cried herself to sleep. She woke up and turned her mind to prayer, resolving to begin another fast. She knew in her heart that nothing short of an ultimatum would make a difference. Her biggest concern was drawing the courage she needed to do it. And she needed to do it right. She had to make a decision she could stand by no matter what he chose to do; she couldn't be bluffing, or he would surely see through her. She had to be prepared for the possibility that he would choose to let her go, and she would have to resign herself to a life without him. She simply had to trust in the Lord that everything would work out the way it was meant to.

Tamra felt it wise to give her decision a few days to settle, if only to be certain she wasn't acting carelessly or on impulse. She felt an affirmation that she was doing the right thing as she felt the Spirit guiding her on the steps to take and the words to say. She prayed that those words would come to her when the time was right.

Tamra reread some sections of Jess Davies' journals, which added one more layer of confidence that she was doing the right thing. Following a supper where Jess didn't utter a single word, or even glance in her direction, she went to his room and knocked at the door.

"Yeah," he called, and she went in, closing the door behind her. "Another lecture?" he asked, barely glancing toward her before he returned his eyes to the view out the window where he was standing.

"No," she said and tossed Jess Davies' journals on his bed, "much worse."

He gave her a surprised glance, then took notice of the books before he asked, "What's that?"

"Your great-great-grandfather's journals. He didn't write much, but what he wrote was powerful. I'd really like you to read them, but obviously whether or not you do is up to you. You've spent a lot of time listening to me talk about your forebears; maybe you should learn to appreciate for yourself what your ancestors sacrificed to give you what you've got. Jess Davies was not even a religious man. But he believed in God, and he had the sense to ask Him for help when he needed it."

Jess glanced once more toward the journals on his bed with an indifference that made her angry.

"Apparently there's something else you want to say to me," he said, turning back to the view.

"It can't go on this way, Jess. I can't stay here, living on a fence."

"What? You're threatening to leave . . . again?"

"It's not a threat, Jess. I can't stay here like this."

"But you have . . . your work. You love it here."

"Yes, I love it here. And I love my work. But it's not enough. You're the reason I'm here, Jess. But you don't want me here."

"But I do," he protested, finally turning toward her.

"Yes, you want me here . . . at arm's length. You've got your heart surrounded with barbed wire, and you don't want me to get close to it. And I can't live like this anymore."

"Live like what?" he asked with an ignorance that frustrated her to distraction.

She forced herself to stay focused on her purpose. "Loving you from a distance. It just can't go on."

"So, what are you saying? You're leaving?"

"If something doesn't change . . . yes. We can't live here under the same roof like this any longer. This is *your* home, so I've got to go."

He looked so thoroughly dumbfounded that she wanted to slap him. Instead she persisted with what she knew she needed to say. "Listen to me, Jess, and listen good. I love you. I love you with all my heart and soul. I know beyond any doubt that my place is with you, that I was guided here for you, because of you. We're meant to be together. But I cannot alter your free agency. And I cannot take responsibility for what you choose to do with what's been given to you. You have to learn that this lack of worthiness you feel comes from within yourself, and you have to come to terms with it. Until you do, you will never be able to see anything beyond your own misery. And I can't live with a man who is so absorbed in his own pain that he has nothing to give me."

"Which is exactly what I've been trying to tell you," he snapped indignantly. "You deserve better than what I can give you."

"No, Jess, I deserve better than what you're *willing* to give me. It's pride and fear that have come between us, and *you* put them there. Only *you* can take them away."

"Pride?" he retorted skeptically. "You have no idea what you're talking about. It is pain that stands between us, Tamra. There is so much pain inside of me that I can't even fathom walking through it to get to a place where I could even think of being free of it. And I can't bring that kind of pain into *your* life."

"Are you trying to tell me that keeping me at a distance is some kind of selfless sacrifice on my behalf?" He didn't answer but she could see it in his eyes. "You are, aren't you? You really believe that. Well, let me tell you the *truth,* because whatever voice you're listening to is lying to you. This is not a selfless sacrifice, Jess, this is *selfish.* You're selfishly holding onto something that's become comfortable for you, because letting go of it is frightening. But you're more afraid of the pain than you are of losing me. And that's the bottom line. That's your choice. You've made it clear. And that's where the pride comes in."

"Pride?" he echoed once again.

"Yes, pride. And since your skull has apparently become too thick to perceive the obvious, I'm going to spell it out for you. In the time I've known you, I have seen repeated opportunities for you to take hold of the power that could get you beyond this once and for all. I have seen people who love you surround you with acceptance and support and the answers. But no one can do it for you, Jess. You're the one who has to reach out and take hold of the *only* thing that can free you of this pain. You don't have to walk through it, Jess. You already have—over and over and over. The price for this pain has already been paid . . . a long, long time ago. But you are too proud to reach out and accept the greatest gift your Father in Heaven could possibly give you. *God so loved the world that He gave His only Begotten Son.* And He gave Him for *you,* Jess. But you've heard all this before—over and over and over. And you choose not to listen. It's pride, Jess, that is—and will be—your downfall. As I see it, you apparently believe that you have more wisdom than God."

"What?" he retorted in a voice so angry that she doubted he had absorbed a single word she'd said.

Tamra took a step toward him and pushed her face forward. "Who are you to say that you know better than God Himself how and where atoning gifts should be distributed? You grope your way through mists of darkness day after day after day, deeming yourself unworthy of the only gift that can make you worthy. But you're just too blasted proud. So make your choice, Jess. I think we can get through anything—together—if we're both willing to live those two great commandments. First, to love God. And second, to love our neighbor as ourselves. Well, I'm your neighbor, Jess. But you can't love me, because you don't love yourself enough to even . . . "

"What?" he snapped again when she didn't finish.

Tamra shook her head, unable to go on. "I've already said too much. You're obviously not with me, anyway. But you could at least think about what I've said."

His only response was a cold glare that prompted a cloud of despair to surround her heart. She'd said what she needed to say, and his response was evident. Once she was beyond the door to his room, she ran into her own and closed the door, as if the pain of her ultimatum would catch up and smother her.

Tamra cried herself to sleep and woke up feeling an instinctive emptiness. She hovered in her bed for more than an hour, grateful that it was Saturday. She couldn't even motivate herself to get out of bed. Even a knock at the door couldn't prompt her to move. She knew it wasn't Jess.

"Come in," she called, pulling the covers to her chin.

Emily stepped timidly into the room. Her teary eyes and the envelope she held in her hand only confirmed what Tamra instinctively knew had happened. She forced her voice past the lump in her throat to say, "He's gone, isn't he?"

"Yes," Emily said, seeming surprised that she knew. "He was gone when we woke up this morning. He left this."

Emily sat on the edge of the bed and held out the envelope. Tamra sat up and reluctantly took it. On the envelope it said: *Mom and Dad.* She felt angry to think that he hadn't even left her a personal good-bye as she unfolded the page and read:

Mom and Dad, I can't possibly explain why I need to leave. I just have to get out of here. I don't know where I'm going, and I don't know when I'll be back. But please don't worry. I love you both and I appreciate all you've done for me. I can only hope you will be able to forgive me for all the grief I have brought into your life. Tell Tamra I love her more than life, and I want her to be happy. That's why I have to go. She belongs here more than I do. Jess.

Tamra squeezed her eyes shut and hung her head. She felt Emily's arms come around her just before the first sob burst from her throat. They cried in each other's arms, then they sat together in anguished silence until Michael knocked at the open door and came into the room. Tamra was grateful to be wearing her typical pathetically modest pajamas, and sitting mostly beneath the blankets. His eyes showed signs that he'd not taken Jess's leaving any easier than she and Emily had. He was carrying a book that Tamra recognized as being one of the family journals that she had read. His finger was between the pages where he'd obviously been reading. Emily asked, "What have you got there?"

"My grandfather's journal," he said, sitting in the chair near the bed. "May I?" he asked.

"Of course," Tamra said.

Michael cleared his throat and explained, "I know you've both read this, but . . . this was after my father had run off and joined the Air Force in the middle of World War II. His father writes, *'I wonder sometimes if there isn't something in a man that has to break free before he can settle down and look at life as it really is. Tyson left. I left. Even Jess Davies left. But we all came back eventually, changed and stronger. Maybe it's that walkabout thing. I wonder if only Australian men are like this, or if we just have a word for it. Knowing what I know of Tyson and Jess, and even myself, I realized that the greatest factor in bringing us home was the innate love we had for this land where we were raised, and the women who hold our hearts. I told LeNay that I really believe Jess will come back, and for me, having her here strengthens that belief. I know how much he loves her, because I've seen the way he looks at her; the same way I look at Emma, and Jess always looked that way at Alexa. I don't consider myself much of a romantic, but I am living evidence of the power of love to change a troubled heart. And I have to believe love will bring him home. LeNay asked me how I could be sure he'd come back when Richard didn't. I told her I had trouble with such questions, but I knew how Alexa Davies would answer it. I can't count the times in my life that I've been saved by imagining what Alexa Davies would say. She would tell us to have faith and believe. And I have to believe her, because no woman on earth has more love to give than my dear, sweet mother-in-law. Where would any of us be without her? I feel confident that her example and strength will guide generations to come, and I pray that my own grandchildren, and great-grand-children—and my dear, sweet Jesse—will always be guided back to this place, knowing that no greater legacy of love exists anywhere on earth.'"*

"Amen," Emily said. Tamra just put her head on Emily's shoulder and cried.

Chapter Eighteen

"You will stay, won't you?" Michael asked, startling Tamra from her tears.

"I . . . don't know," she admitted. "I want to, but . . . I have to think about it. And pray, of course. I just . . . I don't know."

"I understand," Michael said and Tamra was surprised to realize from Michael and Emily's expressions that they had come to care for her as much as she cared for them.

"I hate to say it out loud," Emily said, "but I can't help thinking that . . . well, I hope he doesn't reach such a low that . . . " She became too emotional to speak.

"I've had the same thought," Michael said, and Tamra knew they were referring to his suicide attempt. "We can only pray." His voice broke and he leapt to his feet and left the room, obviously wanting to be alone.

"Come along," Emily said, standing as well. "We can't let ourselves get depressed over this. Let's go get some breakfast and find something to keep ourselves busy."

Tamra reluctantly agreed and met Michael and Emily in the kitchen a short while later. Evelyn's antics perked them all up. She had a way of bringing a simple, perfect joy to her surroundings. After Evelyn went down for her nap, Tamra found Michael and Emily in the office going over some papers at the desk.

"I need to talk to you," she said. "If this is a bad time, then—"

"No, of course not," Emily said, motioning her to an empty chair. "What is it?"

Tamra told them about the conversation she'd had with Jess the previous day, and all of her feelings that had led up to it. She told them about Alexa's example of the situation with Jess Davies and how strongly Tamra had believed it was what she needed to do. But now she couldn't help doubting her decision. They both assured her that she'd done the right thing, but if she hadn't, would they tell her?

When there seemed nothing more to say, Emily told Tamra, "We need to call the girls. Will you stick around?"

"Of course," Tamra said and stayed in the office while they called each of the girls and explained the situation over the speaker phone. Tamra appreciated the closeness she felt in talking with the girls and being actively included in the conversation. Their love and support meant more than she could ever tell them, but without Jess, nothing felt right.

The entire family began a fast together that day, and they decided if Jess hadn't come home or called by the following Sunday, they would do it again. They also made calls to put Jess's name on the prayer rolls of more than a dozen different temples. Tamra felt hope in the personal testimony she had of fasting and prayer. But she had to acknowledge that no amount of prayer could alter a person's free agency.

Through the next few days, Tamra felt as if there had been a death in the family. Jess's absence was keenly felt, and Tamra developed an acute restlessness, not unlike the feelings that had lured her away from her aunt's home to come here in the first place.

Less than a week after Jess had left, Shirley returned to work at the boys' home, following her extended leave of absence to be with her new baby. Tamra almost believed the timing was some kind of sign. Whether or not it was, her temporary job no longer existed. And while the staff of the home tried to find things for her to do to keep her busy, she knew they were just being kind.

In the midst of the second family fast on Jess's behalf, Tamra focused her prayers toward the path her own life should take. Three days later she knew what she needed to do. The hard part would be telling Michael and Emily.

After the supper dishes were finished, Tamra found Michael in the lounge room reading.

"Hello," he said. "Have a seat."

"Where's Emily?" she asked.

"Putting Evelyn to bed, I believe. Did you need something?"

"Well," Tamra admitted, "maybe I need to talk to my bishop." Michael looked concerned as he set his book aside. "Don't worry. I haven't got any grievous sins to confess or anything. I just . . . need some support, I guess."

"I don't need to be your bishop to give that," he said.

"No, but . . . " Tamra cursed her voice for breaking. She hadn't expected to get through this without becoming emotional, but she had hoped to get a little further into it. "Perhaps my bishop would be a little less biased . . . a little less emotionally involved."

Michael sighed loudly and she felt certain he didn't like the implication. "Don't count on it," he said. "So what's up?"

"I've been praying . . . a lot, and . . . Well, I don't know what the future will bring. But I do know that for now . . . I need to go." The silence grew long and she said, "So what do you think, Bishop Hamilton?"

"As your bishop," he said, "I would tell you to pray and do what you feel you need to do. Obviously you've already done that. As Jess's father, I . . . " His voice trembled and Tamra looked up to see him rubbing his eyes with a thumb and forefinger. She saw a subtle quivering of his chin as he said, "I would try to talk you out of going." He looked at her as if he'd resigned himself to being emotional. "I would tell you that having you here makes us miss him less and makes us believe more that he'll come back. I would tell you that you have brought a light into our home that I'm not sure how we're going to do without."

Tamra attempted a comment to fill in the silence, but she was preoccupied with keeping her tears silent. She was relieved when he went on. "I've grown to love my children's friends and spouses, and they've all made great contributions to our family. But . . . none of them have been like you. Even my own children have never had this kind of respect and fascination for the history of who and what we are, and what this place means to us. You're an incredible young woman, Tamra, and I can only say that I believe with everything inside of me that you are supposed to be here."

"I believe it too," Tamra admitted, less concerned about her tears as she watched Michael wipe his face dry with his hand. "But . . . without Jess everything that should be right feels all wrong, and—"

Emily stepped into the room and stopped abruptly. "I'm sorry," she said. "Obviously I'm interrupting something."

"It's okay," Tamra said. "We were just having a little bishop's interview, but I think you should probably be in on it."

Emily met her husband's eyes and asked, "Why is the bishop crying?"

Michael and Tamra exchanged a long glance, as if they were each hoping the other would explain. Emily sat down and said to Tamra, "You're leaving, aren't you?"

Tamra nodded and hurried to finish the explanation she'd been attempting to give to Michael. "I'm not saying that I won't come back. If an opening came up at the home, I think I could be happy working there, no matter what might happen in my personal life."

"More than that, Tamra," Emily said, "you're as good as family. Whatever Jess chooses to do, I believe you were meant to be a part of this family. You will always have a place with us, the same as any of our daughters."

"That's right," Michael echoed firmly.

Tamra nodded again and wiped at her tears. "I know that. I really do. And I could never tell you what that means to me—especially given the circumstances of my own family. Right now I can't try and speculate over the future, because it's just too . . . uncertain. And I just have trouble imagining my life without Jess." Her tears increased and it took her a minute to get control of her emotion enough to speak. Emily moved to get a box of tissues.

Tamra wiped her face and blew her nose before she went on. "There is something I have to say, and it's difficult to explain, so bear with me. I think when I came here, I was so starved to feel some kind of belonging with a *good* family, that I quickly latched on to my feelings for Jess and . . . for all of you. And maybe I became too dependent on the situation."

"Or," Emily said, "as I've told you before, maybe you just instinctively knew that you belonged here."

"Maybe," Tamra admitted, "but . . . I keep thinking about what Michael read from his grandfather's journal about . . . having to leave to be able to see life as it really is. Now that I know what a real family is like, I think I need some time on my own to sort my own life out and find the balance that I need to be completely happy—with or without Jess. As much as I long for him to come back, I have to be realistic enough to accept that he may never come to terms with the situation. Am I making any sense, because . . . it sure doesn't *feel* like it makes any sense, but I know in my heart that I have to take this step. I'll keep in touch. And one way or another, I will come back. I hate to put it the way Jess did, but . . . I honestly don't know where I'm going or when I'll be back. I need to see my aunt, and . . . beyond that I'll just . . . have to see."

"Yes, Tamra," Emily said, "it makes perfect sense. And as hard as it is to see you go, I respect what you're doing, and the reasons you're doing it. Stay close to the Spirit, and you'll be all right. We'll miss you dreadfully," she said with a teary voice, "but I understand."

Tamra spent the following day packing, and decided to leave some of her things there until she knew more specifically what she might be doing. Michael and Emily seemed pleased to have a tangible reason for her to return. Early the next morning, Michael, Emily, Sadie, and Evelyn all walked out to Tamra's packed car to say good-bye. They all shared long, tearful embraces. And Tamra found it most difficult to say good-bye to Evelyn. The child touched Tamra's tears and said, "You cry, Mommy?"

Tamra chuckled and cried harder, holding the little girl close for the few seconds that she would allow before she wiggled out of her arms. She finally forced herself to get in the car and close the door. Through the open window she said, "I'll be in touch and . . . if you hear from Jess just tell him that . . . I'll be in touch."

Emily nodded. "Of course. You'll be in our prayers."

"Do you need any money?" Michael asked.

Tamra smiled and squeezed his hand. "No, Michael. I have more money than I've ever had in my life. That job I had paid pretty well, and I didn't have much to spend it on, since I got room and board as well." She forced another smile, telling herself she could cry more later. "I can never thank you enough for all you've given me."

"It's been a pleasure, dear," Emily said.

"Amen," Michael added and Tamra drove away. She stopped in front of the boys' home and stared up at the gabled attic, recalling clearly how she had felt the first time she had seen it. She turned the stereo up loud and drove on. Once she hit the dirt road, she drove as fast as she dared, not wanting to even glance in her rearview mirror at the cloud of dust she left in her wake, separating her from a life that she feared would be lost to her forever.

* * *

Tamra made her way toward Sydney, since it was the only other place in this country where she had any connections. She took the journey more slowly than before, not feeling in any hurry. She took in some tourist attractions and found she had a deep love for this country. She knew that whatever she ended up doing with her life, she would likely be doing it in Australia.

Her thoughts were most often focused on Jess. She kept a prayer in her heart for him continually, and while she couldn't deny that her deepest wish was to spend her life with him, their history made it evident that nothing short of a miracle would make such a thing possible. And while she wanted to believe in such a miracle, she felt she had to be more realistic.

Tamra tried several times to call her aunt through the stops she made en route, but she only got an answering machine with Rhea's voice asking the caller to leave a message. Tamra left a few and just kept trying. She arrived in Sydney to find Rhea's house locked up tight. Visiting with a neighbor that she'd known well when she'd lived there, she discovered that Rhea had taken a lengthy vacation with a couple of her friends, and she'd been vague on when she might return. This neighbor was collecting the mail and newspapers and taking care of the yard, but she had no way of getting into the house.

Tamra got a motel room and early the following morning she did what she'd been longing to do since her journey had begun: she went to the temple. She spent the day there, doing several sessions, and felt herself become replenished with the closeness to the Spirit that could only be found within those walls. She returned to her motel room late, feeling peace but no definite answers. When Rhea still hadn't returned, Tamra went again the next day. She sat in the celestial room for nearly two hours, mesmerized by the spirit she felt there while she pondered her life carefully, from her earliest childhood memories to the present. She prayed for guidance to know the steps to take in her life at this point, and she prayed to find the strength to move ahead—without Jess. In spite of the sorrow associated with putting him behind her, she felt an undeniable peace in knowing that she would, indeed, be fine—albeit, forever changed. She wondered if she would ever find a love to compare with what she'd felt for him. Perhaps not, she reasoned, but she had to have the faith that there was someone out there who could make her happy, and she him.

Tamra stood and was about to leave the celestial room when she was struck with the enormity of all that took place within these temple walls. She thought of the many ancestors she had done work for right here, and a warmth filled her. She recognized the feeling. It was the spirit of Elijah. She knew the scripture well, and recalled clearly that she had first felt this sensation when reading that particular verse. *And also Elijah, unto whom I have committed the keys of the power of turning the hearts of the fathers to the children, and the hearts of the children to the fathers, that the whole earth may not be smitten with a curse.*

Tamra sat back down, suddenly overcome with an impression that struck her to the core. She had worked very hard to fulfill the promise of Elijah, to turn her heart to her fathers and do everything for them that she could possibly do. But only now did it occur to her that she had done nothing to heal the wounds of her own flesh and blood who were still in this world. She sat in the celestial room for another hour, sorting her thoughts and digesting this profound personal revelation she had just been given. She left the temple and drove straight to a travel agent's office where she made reservations for a one-way flight to Los Angeles, and then on to Minnesota. She was going to visit her mother.

Over the next few days she spent a great deal more time in the temple, visited some museums, and wandered the city, contemplating her life and praying for Jess. The night before she was to leave the country, she left one last message on Rhea's machine and decided she'd just have to see her when she came back. If nothing else, she did know she would be coming back. One way or another, Australia would be her home.

* * *

Jess awoke and took in his surroundings before he groaned and slammed his head back onto the pillow. The cheap motel room had seen endless days of sporadic sleep, and waking hours filled with nothing but a hollow void. The room was littered with fast food containers and empty soda cans. He'd barely met the maid a few times at the door for clean towels. As he tried to figure how long he'd actually been away from home, he was struck with a sensation that had recently become unfamiliar. He had managed rather successfully these last several days to stuff his pain down where he couldn't feel it, but now thoughts of home—and Tamra—lured it to a place where it suddenly threatened to overtake him in one overwhelming swell. And with the pain came a thought that frightened him so thoroughly that he sat bolt upright, grasping the sheets with white knuckles. As plainly as if it had been whispered in his ear, he heard the thought, *Ending it all would be easier, Jess.* He knew that voice, and he knew the full measure of grief he'd endured the last time he'd given heed to it. If he'd learned nothing from that experience, he'd learned that he wanted to live. And if he'd learned anything in the months since, he'd learned that he wanted to be happy. He had deemed himself unworthy of happiness, but Tamra's words had echoed in his mind over and over for days now, until he had to wonder if they could possibly have any substance. *You grope your way through mists of darkness day after day after day, deeming yourself unworthy of the only gift that can make you worthy.*

He'd tried for months to convince himself that the things she'd been telling him—that his parents had been telling him—simply didn't apply to him, that he was somehow beyond hope, a lost cause. But he'd reached this point of desperation one too many times, and he'd gotten sick of it. Could it be possible that they'd been right? In silent answer to his question, Tamra whispered in his memory, *You've heard all this before . . . and you choose not to listen. It's pride that will be your downfall . . . You apparently believe that you have more wisdom than God.*

Jess groaned and rolled back onto the bed, pressing his arms up over his head. She was right, blast her. *Pride.* Was that what it boiled down to? Had he been just too proud all this time to ask for divine guidance? After contemplating the question for more than an hour, he had to admit that pride was part of it. But Pride had a formidable companion that bound Jess with stronger tethers: Fear. Pride and Fear had eagerly taken their place as sentinels, standing guard over his very heart and soul, as if they could protect the pain he harbored there.

Following another hour of stewing over his familiar—but unwanted—companions, Jess felt little beyond confused. Only one thing made sense: he truly *wanted* to be free of the chains that bound him to this debilitating weight he carried. And only one answer stood out above the chaos of his mind and emotions. As if in slow motion, Jess slid to his knees beside the bed, clasped his hands together, and pressed his face to the bed. It took minutes to form those first words in his mind, but when they came at last he became acutely aware of the greatest reason for his misery. He'd forgotten how to pray.

Once he got started, the momentum kicked in and he poured out his heart and soul to God, sometimes silently, sometimes verbally, always with tears. He lost track of the time, going on and on with his one-sided conversation, wondering if God would actually see fit to answer him. He had to believe that He would. He just *had* to! If not, he felt certain the hovering darkness would surround and engulf him irrevocably.

When Jess's knees and back began to ache, he crawled back onto the bed, but his prayer continued until he awoke and realized he'd prayed himself to sleep. With the heavy drapes closed, he could hardly tell if it was day or night. He went into the bathroom then looked at the clock. He peeked through the drapes to determine that it was actually daytime before he curled up on the bed again, contemplating his hours of prayer and the slightest glimmer of hope he'd begun to feel. He felt no desire to eat, as if it were simply a distraction to what he was trying to discern. But he did feel a sudden desire to talk to somebody, as if sorting his thoughts verbally could help them make more sense. He contemplated calling home, wanting to talk to his father. But he feared having to encounter Tamra during the phone call, and he simply wasn't ready to face her—even over the phone. Not yet.

While he was stewing over his need to connect with another human being, he found himself pulling out the journals that Tamra had brought to his room. He felt a sick smoldering to recall their conversation and the way he had hurt her. Deciding he needed to take this one step at a time, he opened Jess Davies' journal and began to read. He quickly felt a growing closeness and kinship with this man and marveled at how many of his emotions Jess was able to relate to. He fell asleep and woke up again, immediately drawn back to the journals. When he'd finished reading all that Jess Davies had written, he lay back on the bed and contemplated his words for a long while before that urge to talk to someone overtook him again.

Calling on his newfound source of help, he prayed specifically for guidance in finding the help he needed to get beyond this abyss in his life. The answer came to his mind so quickly, and with such clarity, that he gasped. Perhaps God was listening to him after all.

Jess reached for the phone, knowing now who to call. Then he glanced at the clock, calculating the time difference from there to Utah. He had to wait at least an hour to make the call, or he'd be waking the family out of a dead sleep. He found the number in the address book he had tucked in one of his suitcases. Then he became so lost in thought that he was startled to look at the clock and realize if he didn't call soon, he'd be having to call the office instead of the house, and he'd be competing with every other psychologically needy patient.

Jess took a deep breath and dialed the number. After just one ring he was startled to hear, "This is Doctor O'Hara."

"Isn't this your *house?*" Jess asked.

"Yes," Sean O'Hara chuckled. "But I know if the phone rings this early, it has to be a patient."

"Well, I'm not a patient, but maybe I should be," Jess said. "This is your baby brother, by the way."

"You think I don't know that?" Sean asked lightly. "Not only do you sound a lot like your father, but I don't have any patients who talk the way you do."

"You do now," Jess said more seriously.

"What's wrong?" Sean asked with a concern that bordered on panic.

"Everything's wrong," Jess admitted. "I really need to talk to you. And I think the idea to call you was an answer to a prayer, which is amazing in itself because it's the first time I've prayed in I don't know how long. I know you're busy, and I can call back any time you say. I'm not going anywhere."

Following a moment of silence, Sean said, "Your timing's good, actually. I have the morning off. I was going to go to the temple, but—"

"Hey, you don't need to change your plans on my account. You can call me some other time, when—"

"No, it's all right. This is more important. You're family, Jess."

"Not really, but—"

"Yes, really," Sean said earnestly and Jess almost felt moved to tears. "So, listen, call me back in . . . say, twenty minutes. Let me make a quick phone call and get settled with some privacy and a better phone."

"Okay. I'll talk to you in twenty minutes then," Jess said and hung up. He sighed and uttered into the quiet room, "Thank you, Lord."

While Jess waited for the minutes to pass, he contemplated the part Sean O'Hara had played in his family. He recalled well the first time he'd come to dinner at their home when they'd been living in Utah while his mother was getting her degree at BYU. His mother's sister had been vaguely aware of a young man who had joined the Church and been turned out by his Catholic family. He'd gone alone to BYU, and Emily had followed her sister's suggestion to look him up and see how he was doing. Sean had quickly become a part of the family. They had helped him get some surgeries he had needed on his hands, and they had supported him on his mission. Jess had clear memories of Sean spending many hours in their home, often playing with him and James, or taking them places. Sean had come to Australia a few times in the years since the family had moved back, and he kept in close touch with the family members living in Utah. Being able to turn to Sean as the brother he no longer had in a technical sense was a true blessing. The fact that Sean was a well-practiced psychologist made Jess wonder why he hadn't called him months ago—or even years. Maybe if he'd been smart enough to ask God for help before now, he would have gotten the idea a long time ago.

Twenty-two minutes after he'd hung up the phone, Jess called Sean back. "So tell me what's been going on," Sean began. "I talked to your parents on the phone a few minutes after they got back from their mission, but they didn't share any drama beyond telling me that you'd gone home unexpectedly."

"Well, yeah, I did," Jess said and proceeded to catch Sean up on all that had happened to bring him to this point, including certain aspects of the accident and events preceding it that had affected the way he'd felt. He finally came to the bottom line, "I just can't get beyond this, Sean. I don't know what's wrong with me. It's like I've spent all this time in some dark void, afraid to even ask God for help."

"And why is that?" Sean asked.

It took Jess a minute to answer, then all he could say was, "I don't know."

"Is it that you don't know, or you don't know how to define it?"

"I don't know," he said again. "It's like I've been so preoccupied with being afraid that I never tried to analyze *why* I was afraid."

"Did you talk about this with your counselor?"

"No. God never came up."

"Well, in my opinion, Jess, no amount of psychology can truly heal the human spirit if it's not coupled with spiritual truths. I know you've been educated on a fair amount of psychology, and you've endured many hours of counseling. Obviously, it hasn't given you the answers."

"Obviously," Jess said with sarcasm.

"I'm not knocking psychology," Sean said. "I wouldn't be doing it if I didn't believe in it. But as I said, it has to be coupled with spiritual truths to be fully effective. So, if it's all right with you, I'd like to share with you some things I've learned through my years in this business that might give you some insight into what you're dealing with."

"I'm listening," Jess said.

"The human spirit is a fragile thing, Jess, easily subjected to pain and fear. Satan knows this, and he uses these things as some of his greatest tools. Experiencing pain can make us afraid of pain, and the one thing that can heal the pain is the very thing that Satan tries to make us especially afraid of. If he can make you believe you're unworthy of God's love and that your weaknesses give you cause to fear Him, then he manages to cut the human spirit off completely from the only source of true healing and peace. But it's all a lie, Jess. A big fat complicated lie. Satan tangles it all up like a wad of fishing line that no human being could ever untangle, making you believe there is no hope, no peace—only pain and despair. Are you with me so far?"

It took Jess a moment to find his voice. "I'm with you," he said, stunned to realize how accurately Sean had just described the very essence of his deepest thoughts and feelings—even though he never would have been able to consciously define them.

"Now, I'm going to tell you the truth, Jess—the only truth that matters, the only truth that can heal all the grief and pain and sorrow you've been carrying around all these years. Are you sitting down?"

"I'm sitting down," Jess said.

"Okay, this is it, kid. God loves you. He loves you constantly, perfectly, and unconditionally. He loves you even when, or perhaps especially when, you mess up. He didn't love you any less when you were seventeen and snorting cocaine than he loved you when you were three and without sin. And He doesn't love you any less now. His love has nothing to do with your performance, or your weaknesses, or even your stubbornness and pride. You are His son, Jess, and He loves you."

Silence ensued, as if Sean wanted to give him time to absorb what he'd just said. And absorb it, he did! The warmth of Sean's words penetrated his frosted heart with an immediate witness that what he was being told was absolutely true. Perhaps the very fact that he'd already opened his heart through hours of prayer had made such penetration possible.

"Are you with me?" Sean asked.

"Oh, yeah," Jess said, unable to hide the fact that he was crying.

"Okay, now: the truth, part two. Are you still sitting down?"

"I'm still sitting down," Jess said and sniffled.

"When God set the workings of this world in motion, He had a very definite plan. A major key in that plan is the fact that there must needs be opposition in *all* things. The good news about that is knowing that for every bit of fear and grief and pain and sorrow, there is equal peace and joy and perfect hope. And do you know how that's possible, Jess? The answer ties directly into part one: God's love. *For God so loved the world that He gave—*"

"*His only Begotten Son,*" Jess finished through a stifled sob.

"And there's your answer, Jess," Sean said in a voice of gentle compassion. "But there's one more thing you need to understand to fully put Satan's efforts against you at bay and take hold of the gift of the Atonement. You have to understand, Jess, that it's personal. *The world* is not some conglomeration of human kind with no individuality. Your Father in Heaven loves *you*, Jess. And when the Savior bled in the garden, and hung on the cross, He was aware of each and every one of us as individuals. There just wasn't room in the scriptures to list us all, so He had to say 'the world.' What He wants you to know, and what He is willing to let you know through the Spirit if you just ask Him, is that it really should say, *'For God so loved Jess Hamilton that He gave His only Begotten Son.'* And Jesus Himself said, *'I have glorified the Father in taking upon me the sins of Jess Hamilton, in the which I have suffered the will of the Father.'* There you have it, Jess. That's spiritual psychology 101."

Jess barely managed to get past his emotion enough to say, "Why didn't I get this class a long time ago?"

"I don't know, Jess. Sometimes we just have to pass through that vale of sorrow before we can be prepared enough to accept the contrasting joy. Your dad could tell you a thing or two about that. Or maybe you *did* get this class and you just weren't in the right frame of mind to absorb it."

"That's highly likely," he said, recalling all of the repeated efforts of the people who loved him to discuss spiritual matters.

"Life can be tough, Jess, and you've been through some tough things. I've seen men fall apart over losing much less than you lost in that accident. But you don't have to suffer any more." Sean was silent for a full minute before he asked, "You okay?"

"Yes, actually, I think I am. I just . . . need some time to take it all in I guess. Thank you. To say that you said all the right things sounds pathetically trite. But . . . thank you."

"I'm glad to help, kid, but I'm just the messenger. It's up to you to get to the Source and learn all of those things for yourself."

"I think I've already got a great start on that, but I'll keep working on it."

"That's great," Sean said, then he changed the subject. "So from what you told me, this Tamra woman must be pretty amazing."

"Oh, she is," Jess said, suddenly missing her so keenly that it hurt.

"So what are you going to do about it?" Sean asked.

"I'm not sure exactly, but I'm going to be working on that too."

"Okay, kid. You know my number if you need to talk it through any more."

"Thank you," Jess said again and hung up the phone. The clock told him they'd been talking nearly three hours. Marveling over all that Sean had said and the way it had made him feel, Jess turned his mind to prayer, in awe of how quickly it had become comfortable and easy. He lost all concept of time while he poured his heart out to God, expressing his regret for his pride and foolishness, for getting caught up in the fears and pain that had held him bound. He specifically asked for a personal witness of the truths Sean had told him, and forgiveness for the grief he had caused for himself and those he loved. And he begged God to take this burden of pain and grief from him so that he could press forward and lead a good life. He fell asleep before the amen was spoken, and woke up feeling changed, somehow. It took him several minutes to recognize what was different, and when he did, warm chills filled his every nerve, as if to confirm that he was indeed a changed man. His burden was gone. And only in its absence did he fully realize how thoroughly heavy it had become. He wept without control as the contrasting joy and freedom penetrated his very soul. He was reminded of the passage in the Book of Mormon where Alma had experienced something that he believed must have been very similar. *And oh, what joy, and what marvelous light I did behold; yea, my soul was filled with joy as exceeding as was my pain!*

Jess's mind went back to the journals he'd read. He felt a renewed appreciation for the life Jess Davies had lived. He was amazed at the similarities of their experiences, even though the events leading up to all they'd felt had little in common. But still, there was one stark difference. Jess Davies had finally turned to God and had been able to turn his life around and be free of his pain, but he hadn't been blessed to have the gospel in his life and all of the understanding that came with it. Still, he seemed to have instinctively been led to the answers he'd needed to get beyond his pain and be happy. He thought of how Alexandra Byrnehouse had been a huge factor in helping Jess Davies make those changes. And his heart filled with fresh awe and gratitude as he realized that Tamra Banks was no less incredible of a woman, and deserved no less credit than Alexa. And suddenly he needed her. He needed to hold her and tell her how very much he loved her, and how horribly sorry he was for all the grief he'd given her. And he had to do it now!

Jess frantically picked up the motel room enough to not leave an absolute disaster for the maid, then he showered and packed his bags. He left the maid a big tip and went out to the Cruiser. Only when he got suddenly dizzy did he realize that he couldn't remember the last time he'd eaten. He stopped for a quick meal, forcing himself to eat slowly and not make himself sick. Then he drove toward home, grateful that he'd not gone far from home to begin with.

Chapter Nineteen

Jess came into the house and found it quiet. Then he heard Evelyn's laughter, which prompted a quickening of his heart. He crept up the long hall and peered into the lounge room to see his parents, both reading, while Evelyn played on the floor with some rag dolls. Overcome with emotion, it took him a minute to find his voice enough to say, "I'm home."

Michael and Emily both gasped as they looked up abruptly. Then they rose to their feet in unison and engulfed Jess with tearful embraces. Emily put both her hands to Jess's face and looked into his eyes. "You're all right," she said, as if she had truly doubted he ever would be again. He had to admit she'd had good reason for such fears.

"Yes, I'm all right," he said and couldn't hold back a little laugh. "In fact, I'm better than I ever have been in my life."

"Really?" Michael said and Jess laughed again.

"Hi, Daddy," Evelyn said and Jess swept the child into his arms, making her giggle. He couldn't recall ever holding her before, except when she was an infant just after his mission—just before her parents had left them. She'd always been a stark reminder of their absence. But now he looked into her little face and saw something different. She was a gift—a tangible remnant of his brother. Suddenly weak, he sank onto the sofa, still holding Evelyn close. The closeness of the Spirit had become familiar through the last several hours, but he was still taken off guard to be struck by an idea that he never would have considered, but suddenly felt completely perfect and natural.

"Of course," he murmured and hugged Evelyn tightly, pressing a kiss into her wispy hair before she squirmed away to go back to her dolls.

"Of course, what?" Emily asked, startling him to the realization that he wasn't alone with the child.

Needing some time to let the idea settle, he just smiled and said, "I need to see Tamra. I assume she's at work this time of day so—"

"She's not there, Jess," his mother said gravely and he shot to his feet.

"What do you mean?" he demanded, a deep dread tightening his stomach into knots. He saw his parents exchange a rueful glance and he hurried to speak his thoughts, as if he could convince them that she *was* here. "She told me she couldn't live under the same roof with me under the circumstances. I thought if I left that she would stay, and . . . " He stopped when he saw tears swell into his mother's eyes.

"She said she couldn't stay here without you," Emily muttered and Jess reached for the back of a chair to keep himself standing. "She told us she would come back . . . eventually, one way or another, but . . . she just had to leave."

"Where did she go?" he asked, his voice shaking. "Where is she?"

"I don't know, Jess," Emily said.

"How can you care so much for someone and not know where to find them?" he blurted. Emily gave him a hard stare and he heard the words reverberate back to him. He groaned and pressed both hands to his head. He dropped his hands to his side and added humbly, "But you're a good person, Mother, and I'm just an idiot."

Emily gave an emotional chuckle and hugged him tightly. "I've got her aunt's number; perhaps she's seen her. Perhaps she's even there."

"Of course," Jess said, feeling hope loosen the knots inside himself. "Where is it?"

He followed Emily to her little desk in the kitchen where she pulled out a little book and found the number, along with a Sydney address. He dialed the number and only got a machine. Not knowing what he'd say when he didn't even know if Tamra was there, he hung up, feeling an instinctive desperation. "I've got to find her," he said and turned around to see his father holding up a set of keys that he recognized. "The plane?" he asked, feeling his heart quicken.

"Your license is still good, and so is the weather. Go find her, Jess, and bring her home. Because we miss her every bit as much as we missed you. This is where she belongs."

"Yes, it is," Jess said firmly and sighed.

"Everything will be all right, Jess," his mother said. "She loves you."

"Yes," Jess's voice cracked, "I know she does. And I love her." He paused and added, "Mom, Dad . . . I'm so sorry. There's so much I want to say . . . to tell you, but . . . I've got to find her."

"We'll talk when you come back," Emily said. "Why don't you pack some clean clothes and get going. Call and keep us posted."

"I will," Jess said, grabbing the keys from Michael. He rushed from the room then hurried back and hugged them each tightly. "Oh, by the way," he said on his way out the door again, "Sean said hello."

He saw his parents smile and exchange a knowing glance. They knew Sean well enough to know that if they'd talked, it had surely contributed to the changes that had taken place.

Jess was quickly packed and his father drove him out to the hangar, talking him through a brief refresher course on flying the plane. "I've called in your flight plan," he said as they pulled up, "so you're set."

They embraced again before Jess got into the plane. "I love you, Dad," Jess said, hesitating a long moment. "I've got the greatest father in the world."

"I love you too, Jess," Michael said. "And I could not ask for a better son."

Jess was amazed to realize that he truly meant it. He nodded, hugged him again, then got into the plane and started the engine. He felt briefly nervous as he pulled it out of the hangar. He'd given up flying for the same reasons he'd given up driving. But by the time he had it up to flight speed, he felt his confidence coming back to him. And how could he not be grateful for the means to travel so quickly to where he hoped Tamra would be?

As the plane lifted into the air, Jess laughed aloud. He circled low over the house and saw his mother out on the side lawn with Evelyn. They exchanged hearty waves and he headed toward Sydney, praying with all his heart and soul that she would be there, that he could find her, and most especially that she would forgive him.

* * *

Jess arrived safely in Sydney and rented a car. He tried calling Tamra's aunt again from the airport, but he only got the machine. Driving toward her home, he wondered what he might do if no one was there. He had to find her. He just had to!

It took Jess a while, but he finally found the home where Tamra had lived with her aunt. And God willing, she would be living here now. He knocked at the door and was startled to have it come open only a second later. The thin woman with bleached hair and flagrant clothing fit perfectly with the words he'd read in Tamra's letters.

"You must be Rhea," he said with confidence.

"That's right," she said, looking him up and down. But her gaze was more intrigued than skeptical. "And who might you be?"

"I'm Jess Hamilton. Tamra was staying with—"

"Oh," she laughed, "you don't have to explain. I've heard all about you in about a hundred letters. Come in. Come in. You must be looking for Tamra."

"That's right," he said eagerly. Stepping into the house, he recognized the aroma of a heavy smoker. But it was tidy and quaint. "Is she here?" he asked.

"No," she said, as if it should have been obvious.

"Do you *know* where she is?" he asked, hating the desperation in his voice that clearly expressed the dread in his heart. If he couldn't find her, what would he do? Could he wait and wonder for weeks, maybe months, until she decided to contact his parents again?

"Not exactly," she said. "The truth is, I've been out of town for weeks. I got back a few hours ago. Then I had to get some groceries so I wouldn't starve, and so I just walked in the door again five minutes ago." She grinned and added, "Your timing's good." Jess sighed, at least grateful for *that* blessing. If he hadn't been able to even talk with Rhea, what would he have done?

"So, what *do* you know?" he asked.

"Well," she said, "I have several messages on my machine; apparently she's been in town, looking for me. But the last message said she was leaving the country."

Jess felt his heart sink and his head spin. He was barely aware of Rhea saying, "Are you okay? Maybe you should sit down." He felt her hand on his arm, guiding him to a chair. *Leaving the country?* he echoed silently. "No," he muttered aloud.

"I didn't erase those messages, if you'd like to hear them."

"I would, thank you," he said, glad that he didn't have to move when he realized the phone was sitting on a little table nearby. He watched her turn up the volume and push the button.

His heart quickened as he heard Tamra's recorded voice say, *"Hi, it's your favorite niece. I'm in town and would love to see you."* The next message gave the name and number of a nearby motel which Jess quickly wrote down when Rhea shoved a pencil toward him. He doubted she would still be there, but he had to follow every lead. Another message from Tamra said, *"Hi, it's me again. I talked to Mrs. Phillips. She told me where you are. If you get back, call me."* She again gave the number of the same motel.

"There's one more," Rhea said. "I didn't erase them yet because it's so nice to hear her voice."

"You can say that again," Jess agreed.

"It's so nice to hear her voice," Rhea said, then they both laughed. He decided he really liked this woman, even after she lit up a cigarette.

"May I?" Jess asked, pointing at the phone.

"Of course," she said and he quickly dialed the motel number he'd jotted down. "Do you still have a Tamra Banks staying there?" he asked after they'd answered.

He heard computer keys clicking, then he was told, "No, I'm sorry. She's checked out."

"Can you tell me *when* she checked out?" he asked.

"I'm sorry," she said. "I'm not allowed to give out that information."

Jess groaned. "Okay, thank you," he said and hung up.

Rhea pushed the button on the machine to hear the final message. "It's me again," Tamra's voice said. *"It's hard to explain to a machine, but I'm going to the States. I need to see my mother. I'll be in touch."*

Jess sighed and rubbed a hand over his face, as if that might allow him to think more clearly. "How old is that last message?" he asked.

"I don't know," she said. "It's one of the last few on the machine, but it doesn't record the date and time."

Jess felt suddenly devoid of any strength. But he only had to wonder for a moment what he needed to do. Rhea interrupted his thoughts by saying, "You really love her, don't you?"

He turned to look at her and had to smile. "I really do, but I'm afraid I've been a bit of a jerk. No, to be completely honest, I've been a *very big* jerk."

She took a long drag on her cigarette and asked, "So, what are you going to do about it?"

It was easy to say, "I'm going to beg you to give me your sister's address, and I'm getting on the next plane to the States."

Rhea smiled. "That's the spirit. I'll be right back."

Jess stood up and wandered around the room, absorbing the personality of this woman that was the only real family Tamra had. His heart quickened to see three different snapshots of Tamra in little frames, sitting beside a lamp. *Oh, how he loved her!*

"Here," Rhea said, coming back into the room. She handed him a little piece of paper with two addresses and phone numbers in Minneapolis. "One is her apartment, the other is the bar she owns."

"Thank you," Jess said and she handed him a little angel, made from lace, that looked like it should hang on a Christmas tree. "What is this?" he asked.

"I came across it on my vacation, and it reminded me of Tamra. She was such an angel to me, especially after I lost my husband. When you find her, give her that, and give her my love."

"I will, thank you," he said and pressed a kiss to her cheek. "And thank you for being her family when she needed one."

"She's one of the greatest things that's ever happened to me," Rhea said.

"Then we have something in common," Jess said.

Rhea smiled and handed him the phone just before she sat down and started thumbing through the phone book. "I know a great travel agent," she said. "With any luck, you can get a flight out today."

Jess uttered a silent prayer that such a thing could be possible. Every hour he was away from Tamra increased his fear that he wouldn't find her for weeks. What if she went to her mother's and quickly left to go elsewhere? He could easily imagine following her trail for months, like some kind of third-rate private investigator.

Rhea told him a number and he punched it into the phone. When a kind voice answered, he said, "I need a flight to L.A. as soon as possible. Are you able to tell me when the next one going out is? I don't care which airline. I just need to get there."

"I can probably do that," the woman replied. "Just give me a few minutes."

Jess felt his nerves tightening while he waited. What if he couldn't get a flight until tomorrow? He'd go insane! *Oh, please Lord,* he prayed in his mind. *I know I've been blessed more in the last few days than I have ever deserved, but I need to find her. Please help me get on a flight—soon.*

"Okay," that voice on the phone said, "there is a flight leaving in about three hours. I can get you a seat, but if you're not close to the airport, you'll never get through security before it takes off."

Jess silently calculated the time it had taken him to get here from the airport earlier today, and he'd have to check in the car he'd rented. He had only one carry-on bag. It would be cutting it close, but he had to try. "Okay, do it," he said and gave her his credit card number. "And hey," he said, "I'm giving you my mailing address, so you can send me some information. I'm going to need to book a really great honeymoon."

Rhea laughed. Jess got off the phone and hugged her quickly. "Thank you, Aunt Rhea. With any luck, we'll be back to visit before long."

"I'll be looking forward to it," she said and hurried him out the door so he could make his flight.

Jess felt a heart-pounding nervousness as he drove back toward the airport. Several traffic slow-ups frustrated him to distraction. But he couldn't help noticing how less prone he felt to get angry and upset. He was truly a different man. He felt the changes so thoroughly that he now realized fully what Alma had meant when he'd talked about being born again.

At the airport, Jess glanced at his watch about every thirty seconds while he turned in the car he'd rented only a few hours earlier. He had no trouble getting his ticket, and he blessed the age of the computer. Then he waited in what felt like a ridiculously slow line to get through security, and he cursed the age of terrorism that made such precautions necessary. When he finally got through, he had ten minutes until the plane took off, and he had a long way to go to get to the correct gate. He ran as fast as he could manage and still dodge the people he encountered. He arrived breathless and exhausted just as he heard the last call for boarding.

"Oh, thank you, Lord," he muttered under his breath and handed his boarding pass to the flight attendant.

Jess heard the door of the plane being closed behind him as he started down the aisle. He was glad to see that the flight wasn't terribly crowded, which allowed him a choice of seats. He was stuffing his bag into an overhead compartment when his eye caught a flash of red hair, twisted and pulled up in a large hair clip. His heart quickened as it reminded him so keenly of Tamra. Then he did a double take and his pulse pounded in his ears. He turned his back and froze as he closed the compartment and leaned his hands there to steady himself. Two rows back, across the aisle and next to the window, sat Tamra Sue Banks. He sank into his seat on the aisle, grateful she hadn't seen him. He hadn't counted on seeing her so soon. What would he say? But she was *here!* He heard himself laugh aloud then had to suppress it when the woman sitting one seat over tossed him a dubious glance. He couldn't believe it. It was a *miracle!* Now, he had some idea of how Moses felt when the Red Sea parted before his eyes. How could he doubt to any degree that God was mindful of him and his need to be reunited with this incredible woman He had sent into his life? She had saved his life. She had saved his soul. And now they were practically within arm's reach. All he had to do was figure out how to let her know he was here without scaring her to death, and then he just had to convince her that he couldn't live another day without knowing that she would be his—forever.

* * *

Tamra was grateful to be one of the first on the plane, and even more grateful to have a window seat. As she sank into the chair, an emotional exhaustion overcame her. She was acutely aware that the numbness she'd felt blanketing her through the past several days was wearing off. She'd felt the comfort and guidance of the Spirit, but that didn't make her miss Jess any less. And while she'd spent days trying not to think about him, if only to keep herself from facing the emotions provoked by his absence, she suddenly felt too worn down to suppress her deepest feelings any longer.

A man in his early thirties, dressed casually, took the aisle seat, leaving the seat between them empty. He greeted her with some small talk and asked her some questions. She told him she was returning to the States to make a fresh start. He told her he was going to L.A. for business and to visit an old friend while he was in the area. His accent told her he was Australian. She could never hear a man talk like that again without thinking of Jess. But then, she was always thinking of Jess. Where was he? Was he all right? Or had he gone over the edge again and done something foolish?

Tamra closed her eyes and turned toward the window, grateful that she could pretend to be enjoying the view and keep her face turned that direction. The conglomeration of hurt and frustration and sorrow refused to be denied any longer. She simply didn't have the strength to hold them back. She prayed that the empty seat next to her would remain that way. She was in no mood to have anyone close enough to realize that she was crying. Her silent tears gradually eased her into a relaxation she'd not been able to feel since her last encounter with Jess—perhaps before that. Just knowing that she was leaving Australia—and Jess—behind, she was able to momentarily let go of fruitless thoughts and relax. She was vaguely aware of the plane taking off, and was grateful to note that the seat next to her had remained empty.

Tamra awoke later with no idea how much time had passed. She figured it couldn't have been too long, since there was no evidence that a meal had been served. And it was still daylight. Her peripheral vision told her the businessman was still in his seat, although he was turned the other way, visiting with a woman across the aisle. Again his voice reminded her of Jess and she fought against the pain burning in her chest. She thought of the advice she had repeatedly given Jess, to allow the Atonement to take the pain of his grief away. If only to avoid hypocrisy, she closed her eyes and prayed for that very thing in relation to her own pain. After several minutes, a subtle peace filtered into her conscious mind, and her prayer turned to gratitude. She knew that somehow she was going to get through this. But oh! How she missed him! And once again she turned her eyes to the view out the window and allowed the silent tears to fall.

* * *

Jess finished his conversation with the woman across the aisle, vaguely aware that Tamra had come awake. He turned carefully toward her, not wanting to scare her to death. His heart threatened to break when he saw her turned toward the window, discreetly wiping a steady stream of tears from her face. Had he caused her so much pain? Yes, he concluded firmly, he certainly had. And now he could only pray that she would be willing to give him a second chance.

Searching for the words to begin, Jess glanced around the cabin of the plane. His eye caught the gentleman who had eagerly agreed to trade seats with him, given a brief explanation while Tamra was sleeping. He was struck again with the miracle manifested by the very fact that he was sitting here now. It had all come together too well for him to believe there hadn't been divine intervention—one more piece of evidence that God loved him and was truly with him. He uttered a quick prayer of gratitude and a plea for guidance, then he turned back toward Tamra, who was still crying, apparently oblivious to her surroundings. He carefully cleared his throat and purposely lowered his voice to disguise it.

Tamra managed to get some control over her tears just as she realized the man sitting two seats over was talking to her. "I'm sorry," she said, keeping her face toward the window with the hope that he wouldn't realize she'd been crying. "Were you talking to me?"

"Yes, actually. I was just wondering if you're all right."

Tamra had to ward off embarrassment and choke back a new threat of emotion. Just hearing him acknowledge that there was a problem seemed to make it more acute. "I will be," she said. "Thank you."

Following a long pause, he said, "So, whoever it is you're running from must really be a jerk, eh?"

Tamra was surprised by his perception, but simply said, "No, not really. He just . . . had a broken heart that I couldn't mend."

"Not for lack of trying, I'm sure." Tamra marveled at how his voice reminded her of Jess, albeit being deeper. Was it simply the accent?

"No," Tamra said sadly, "not for lack of trying."

"So," the man said, "do you think if he—by some miracle—was able to mend his broken heart, and he went to great lengths to track you down . . . And if he were humble and full of regret and willing to grovel, do you think you might consider giving him another chance?"

Tamra squeezed her eyes shut, amazed at how a complete stranger had just put words to her innermost hopes—fruitless hopes, she reminded herself. Still, she had to admit, "It is my deepest wish."

"Well then, Ms. Banks, this is your lucky day. Your wish is about to be granted."

It took several seconds for his words to penetrate her clouded brain. She gasped and turned toward him, prepared to question him on how he might know her name. Her breath caught in her throat and her heart raced. She felt her mouth fall open and her grip tightened over the armrests at her sides. Were her eyes deceiving her? Her ears certainly had. Was she losing her mind, or was Jess Hamilton really sitting there where another man had been sitting before she'd fallen asleep? She attempted to say his name, as if it might verify that this man was not just a coincidental look-alike for the man she loved. But her voice was silenced by her inability to breathe. The emotion that she had managed to curb into silent tears, suddenly threatened to explode.

Jess absorbed the shock on Tamra's face, hoping she would be happy to see him and not angry for his unconventional approach. He saw her press both hands over her chest just as she started gasping for breath. Huge tears rose in her eyes and quickly spilled. She pressed one hand over her mouth as if to hold back a bursting dam. He heard the muffled sob and saw her shoulders tremble, and for a moment he feared she was going to go into cardiac arrest.

"Hey," he said, moving to the empty seat between them, "it's okay. Everything's going to be okay." He put his arms around her and felt her nod her head against his shoulder, as if in agreement. Feeling her take hold of him and press her face to his chest, his relief and gratitude became too much to hold back. He pressed his lips into her hair, if only to muffle his own emotion. Together they cried for several minutes while he hoped they were managing to remain discreet in such close quarters. When he could feel her calming down, he took her face into his hands and looked into her eyes. "I love you, Tamra," he said and his vision of her blurred behind a fresh rise of tears. He blinked them onto his cheeks and whispered, "I can never find the words to apologize sufficiently for the grief I have put you through. But I swear to you I am a changed man, and I only ask that you give me the chance to prove that."

Tamra had to convince herself that she wasn't dreaming. He was really here, really holding her, really saying what she wanted to hear. She could only pray that the sparkle in his eyes was deep and genuine, that this was not just a desperate ploy to get her back. *Please,* she prayed inwardly, *help me to have discernment, to know his heart.*

As if in immediate response to her prayer, Jess deepened his gaze and murmured with passion, "Oh, you were right, Tamra, you were right. I was so lost in pride and fear, so caught up in my own pain. After all the stupid things I did in my youth, I think I had just come to believe that everything that had happened was somehow a result of my own unworthiness. But I read those journals, and oh . . . what an incredible man. I had no comprehension what I had come from. And when I saw how he had changed . . . that it was *possible* to change . . . and to find happiness and peace after such anguish, I just felt . . . so grateful . . . so incredibly grateful. And so in awe. I prayed and I prayed. I didn't eat for two days. And then it happened. It took a while, given my thick skull. But it happened, Tamra." She saw his chin quiver and new tears glistened in his eyes. "The pain relented." He spoke the words in a hushed whisper, as if the experience was too sacred to speak of any other way. "The contrast was so . . . startling. I'd forgotten how it felt to be so free . . . so at peace. But then, maybe I'd never felt such joy in quite that way before. And I knew . . . I *knew* . . . it had been their time to go." The tears leaked down his face. "Their work was finished here. They had a mission on the other side. But I needed to stay. I had a legacy to carry on. I can't explain how I knew. I just *knew!* In an instant, my entire perspective changed. I felt loved, and secure, and strong, and so very, very blessed. And I couldn't find you fast enough."

Tamra heard herself laugh, but it quickly turned to tears again and she wrapped her arms around him. "Oh, Jess. Jess!" she murmured close to his ear. "I love you. I love you so much." She felt his embrace tighten and sensed his emotion as he buried his face against her throat. She eased back and took his face into her hands, wiping his tears with her thumbs. "You're really here," she laughed. "You're real, and . . . you're different."

He smiled, as if he liked the idea. "Different how?" he asked.

"Your eyes . . . they were always . . . dark somehow. But now . . . there's a light shining there." She laughed again. "It's incredible."

"Yes, it is," he said. "And it never would have happened if you hadn't given me a reason to try . . . and the pieces I needed to put it all together. You saved me, Tamra. Not just when you kept me from taking my life, but you gave me the means and the motivation to save my soul." He smiled and added, "Do you remember when you told me that you felt your mission was not very successful, that you hadn't had the opportunity to lead anyone to Christ? Well, you have succeeded with me. You led me to Him, Tamra my love. And for that I owe you my deepest admiration and gratitude."

Again Tamra was overwhelmed with tears and put her head to his shoulder. "Oh, I love you," he whispered. "I don't know how I thought I could ever live without you."

"I don't either," she said lightly and heard him laugh softly. She realized then that she'd never really heard him laugh so genuinely before. She'd heard an occasional chuckle or brief bout of laughter, but it had usually been bitter at worst and stilted at best. His laughter now was an authentic representation of the joy he felt that could not be disguised.

"Please tell me that you'll forgive me," he said.

"Of course," she insisted. "It's all in the past."

He eased her from his shoulder to look into her eyes. "Please tell me that nothing has changed . . . that you still feel the same way you did when we last talked."

"Nothing's changed, Jess . . . except you. As far as I can see, everything is perfect."

"Well," he chuckled, "not quite. I've got a bit of unfinished business."

While Tamra was waiting for him to explain he stood up in the aisle and said, "Ladies and gentleman. Could I have your attention, please."

"What are you doing?" Tamra whispered loudly.

He chuckled and motioned for her to be quiet. She put a hand over her eyes and sank low in her seat. She had a feeling he intended to embarrass her. Was there a side to Jess Hamilton she had yet to discover? She laughed softly at the thought, then recalled the glimpses she had seen of his humor and flamboyance. Wearing a tuxedo to a casual party. Lip-syncing rock music. Dancing like Fred Astaire and John Travolta rolled into one. And she loved him. As long as he remained true to the conviction she had just seen in his eyes, she was ready to take on just about anything.

"My name is Jess, and this beautiful American woman is Tamra. Say hello to Tamra."

"Hello, Tamra," several voices said in unison. Tamra shook her head in disbelief.

"Say hello, Tamra," he said and nudged her shoulder. She lifted a hand over the seat and waved. "No," Jess chuckled, "come out here and say hello."

He took her arm and urged her to stand beside him in the aisle. She knew her eyes had to be red and swollen from all the crying she'd done, but she just gave Jess a comical glare and said, "Hello."

"Now," he said loudly enough for everyone to hear—even the flight attendants had stopped working and were watching with interest, "since I have finally managed to stop being a jerk, and this woman has agreed to forgive me for being a jerk, I simply can't go another minute without taking care of something very important. So I ask that you all give me a moment of silence, so I can have the proper atmosphere."

Tamra heard a few chuckles and whispers, and then nothing could be heard beyond the low hum of the jet engines. She sensed where this might be leading, but she still caught her breath when he took both her hands into his and went down on one knee. His humor became immediately replaced with genuine adoration and sincerity.

"Tamra Banks," he said with a subtle quiver in his voice, "will you marry me?"

"Jess Hamilton," she said following a conscious effort to swallow her emotion, "it would be an honor to be your wife."

The humor returned to his voice as he asked, "Does that mean yes?"

"Yes!" she said and laughed. "It means yes!"

Cheers and applause errupted from the cabin as Jess rose to his feet, taking her into his arms. While he was holding her, a voice from the back hollered, "Kiss her!" Several voices echoed encouragement. Jess grinned at Tamra before he kissed her and cheers went up again.

"Thank you, thank you," Jess said, raising a hand to quiet the crowd while he kept his other arm around Tamra. "You would all be welcome to come to the wedding, except that we're Mormons. And we're getting married in the Mormon temple in Sydney, and you have to be a

Mormon to be there. But we're getting married there because if we do, we can be together forever. And when you're going to marry a woman as wonderful as this," he smiled toward Tamra, "how could anything less than forever be good enough? If you want to come to the reception, it's at the Byrnehouse-Davies and Hamilton Station in south Queensland, and there will be lots of food. If you want to know the date, you'll have to leave me a card. Thank you for your support and cooperation. You've been a great audience." He motioned Tamra toward her seat as he received another round of applause. "Oh, and . . . " the crowd quieted again, "if you want to know about that together forever stuff, we've got a long flight, and you know where to find us."

He sat down and Tamra whispered, "What was that all about?"

He grinned and said, "Once a missionary, always a missionary. Airplanes are always great for that kind of stuff."

"Of course," she said, then added with a smirk, "and now that we're out of the public eye, I've got some unfinished business."

"Really?" he said just before she pushed her hand around the back of his neck and pressed her lips to his.

Before their kiss ended, they heard over the intercom, "This is your captain speaking. We're sailing smoothly over the Pacific Ocean with fair weather, and I understand congratulations are in order. Have a great life, Jess and Tamra."

They both laughed and Jess said to her, "Oh, I intend to."

He kissed Tamra again, then he pulled a credit card out of his wallet and slid it through the phone in front of him to release it. "What are you doing?" she asked.

"I'm calling my parents. We've got a wedding to plan."

Tamra laughed and kissed him quickly while he was waiting for the call to connect.

Jess heard his mother answer the phone and he couldn't hold back a chuckle before he said, "Hello."

"Jess, is that you?"

"It is," he said.

"Where are you?"

He mimicked the captain by saying, "I'm sailing smoothly over the Pacific Ocean with fair weather."

"You're on a boat?"

"No," he laughed, "a plane . . . headed for L.A.. And then I assume I'm going to Minneapolis."

"You sound happy."

"Oh, I am," he said.

"Did you find her?"

"I did," he said and laughed again. "In fact, she's right here, and she's got something to tell you, and . . . oh, you'd better put Dad on the other phone." He heard her laugh and call Michael's name before he handed the phone to Tamra.

"Hello," she said and heard Michael and Emily both say "hello" in response.

"So, what do you have to tell us?" Emily asked expectantly.

"You can't guess?" Tamra said.

"Oh, we probably could," Michael said. "But we want you to tell us."

"Well, I went to sleep on this plane sitting next to some guy I'd never seen before, and I woke up sitting next to your son." She heard them chuckle before she went on. "After he'd groveled and begged forgiveness he made me stand up in the aisle for everyone to see. Then he got down on one knee and asked me to marry him."

Emily let out a squeal of delight. Michael laughed and said, "That's my boy." Then he added, "So what was your answer?"

"The answer is that you people need to be calling the Sydney Temple and making an appointment for us."

"You want us to set the date?" Emily asked.

"I've got nothing to work around once I see my mother and we can get back. How about you, Jess?" she asked him. "You got anything to work around?"

"Not a thing," he said.

"I heard that," Emily said. "But we can't plan a wedding if we don't know what you want, or—"

Tamra said to Jess, "Your mother said she can't plan a wedding if she doesn't know what you want."

He grinned and said, "Just tell them to do whatever they did when the others got married. That will be good enough for me, if it's good enough for you."

"It's good enough for me," Tamra said, then into the phone, "Jess said to tell you to—"

"We heard," Michael said. "I know what *he* wants, my dear. But what do you want?"

"I want to marry your son," she said. "Beyond that, it really doesn't matter. You know I have no family to speak of that would be involved. And you know what they say—beggars can't be choosers."

"I'm the beggar," Jess said loudly enough for his parents to hear and they both laughed.

"He sounds happy," Emily said.

"Yes, I believe he is," Tamra said, looking into Jess's eyes, "but no happier than I am."

"We're pretty happy too," Michael said with a poignancy in his voice that reminded Tamra of the anguish they had all endured. But now they all shared an equal joy—a joy beyond description.

They talked for a few more minutes, then hung up the phone and both sighed at the same time, then they laughed together. "How can life become so wonderful so quickly?" she asked.

"I don't know," Jess said, "but I think that's what they call a miracle."

"Yes, I think it is," she said, touching his face.

A flight attendant leaned toward them, holding two mini bottles of champagne. "The captain sends his congratulations, and some complimentary champagne."

"How nice," Jess said, smiling toward her. "Tell him thank you very much. But you know what? We don't drink."

"Oh, I'm sorry," she said, seeming a bit confused.

Jess smiled again and quickly added, "But we would love some gingerale. And please, tell the captain thank you."

"I will," she said and hurried away, returning a minute later with two plastic glasses of gingerale on ice.

"Well, it *looks* like champagne," Tamra said, holding it up.

"But it's much better," he said. "There's no hangover." He touched his glass to hers and added, "To forever."

"Forever," she repeated. They both took a sip then shared a quick kiss.

She laughed and he asked, "What's so funny?"

"I was just thinking that I feel like I'm flying."

Jess looked around himself comically, as if to verify that they were, indeed, sitting on a plane. "Could that be," he asked, "because you *are* flying?"

"No, silly," she laughed softly. "Remember in your grandmother's journal, after your grandfather had taken her for a ride in his plane, and then she was falling in love with him and deliriously happy and she said she felt like she was flying."

"Ah, yes," he said, "I think I recall that story. So what you're saying is . . . you're flying, and you're *flying.*"

"That's right," she said.

"Well, I'm flying too, in that case." He smiled and kissed her again.

"Oh, I forgot something," he said, reaching into his jacket pocket. "Rhea sent this." He pulled out the little angel and repeated what she had said.

"That is so sweet," she said, admiring the gift.

"And it's absolutely true, you know," he said, touching her face. "You *are* an angel, Tamra. *My* angel."

After they had finished breakfast, Jess said, "I can't help thinking about my last flight from L.A. to Sydney. I think of how completely depressed I was, and all that happened in the weeks after, and I . . . " His voice broke and he looked into Tamra's eyes. "I can't believe how happy I am now. I can't believe that I could be so thoroughly blessed."

Tamra drew in the growing evidence of the changes in him and said, "The feeling is mutual, Jess."

Jess took a deep breath and ventured to bring up something that had been hovering in his mind. "There's something I want to propose to you," he said, putting his arm around her and looking into her eyes. "It's been on my mind a great deal, but . . . I feel a little hesitant to bring it up. I wanted to let the idea settle a little more before I discussed it with you. I wanted to be sure that it felt *really* right. But now I just know that I need to tell you how I feel, and deep down I already *know* it's right. Does that make any sense?"

"Absolutely," she said.

"It's difficult to explain, but . . . there's something my brother has let me know that he wants me to do."

Tamra felt her heart swell to see Jess talk about his brother with a distinct light in his eyes, and no sign of pain. His voice quavered slightly as he continued, "I can't say for certain that he's been close or anything, but I know beyond any doubt what he wants me to do." He looked deeply into her eyes and said, "He wants me to raise Evelyn like my own."

Tamra caught her breath. She'd been so preoccupied with the feeling surrounding them that she hadn't even contemplated where this might be headed. While it took her a moment to gather her words, Jess went on. "Obviously, I can't do that alone. So, I need to know if that's something you might have a problem with or—"

"Oh, Jess," she interrupted, squeezing his hand tightly, "beyond being your wife and having your children, nothing could make me happier. It just feels right." She felt tears rise in her eyes. "I must confess that it's something I've thought about. I've felt drawn to Evelyn right from the start." He smiled and she pushed her arms around his neck. "Oh, Jess," she murmured close to his ear, "do you ever just feel like you've stumbled onto your destiny?" She drew back and looked into his eyes. "It's like dropping a piece of thread from the sky and having it fall directly through the eye of a needle, with a perfect fit. It's too incredible to even consider being coincidence, and you just have to *know* that this was the way God intended for it to be all along."

Tamra saw moisture appear in his eyes and felt his hand tighten over hers as she went on. "And here we are, from opposite ends of the world and opposite ends of the spectrum in every respect. And now we will be a family, working and growing together in a life that was meant to be ours, where even the tragedies bring pieces into the puzzle that fit perfectly."

Jess sighed and touched her face. "I love you, Tamra," he said, and she knew beyond any doubt that she felt exactly the same way.

They talked quietly of all that had brought them together, and the conversation turned to his ancestors, while Tamra felt a secret thrill at marrying into this family she had felt so deeply connected to. Their conversation continued through the meal that was served, and until the cabin was darkened for the night. He told her all he had experienced to bring about these marvelous changes in his life. They drifted to sleep holding hands, and Tamra could only think how grateful she was to know that she could spend the rest of her life with Jess Hamilton's hand in hers.

"Thank you, Jess," she said.

"For what?"

"For having the strength . . . and the humility . . . to realize that your pain had become my pain, and my life would never be right without you."

Jess pressed a hand to the side of her face and into her hair. "Thank *you* . . . for loving me in spite of myself, and for being strong enough to not put up with it. You know, from what I read in Jess Davies' journal, I think you might be very much like my great-great-grandmother."

"Really?" she said. "I can think of no greater compliment."

Jess just smiled and kissed her, and it was easy for Tamra to imagine Alexandra Byrnehouse-Davies on the other side of the veil, heaving a contented sigh of relief. And Tamra knew just how she felt.

About the Author

Anita Stansfield has been writing for more than twenty years, and her best-selling novels have captivated and moved hundreds of thousands of readers with their deeply romantic stories and focus on important contemporary issues. Her interest in creating romantic fiction began in high school, and her work has appeared in national publications. *Gables of Legacy: The Guardian* is her twentieth novel to be published by Covenant.

Anita lives with her husband, Vince, and their five children and two cats in Alpine, Utah.